WORDS of CONVICTION

Center Point
Large Print

Also by Linda J. White and available from
Center Point Large Print:

Seeds of Evidence

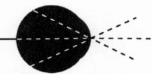

WORDS of CONVICTION

LINDA J. WHITE

CENTER POINT LARGE PRINT
THORNDIKE, MAINE

This Center Point Large Print edition is published
in the year 2015 by arrangement with Abingdon Press.

The text of this Large Print edition is unabridged.
In other aspects, this book may vary
from the original edition.
Printed in the United States of America
on permanent paper.
Set in 16-point Times New Roman type.

ISBN: 978-1-62899-587-9

Library of Congress Cataloging-in-Publication Data

White, Linda J., 1949–
Words of conviction / Linda J. White. —
Center Point Large Print edition.
pages cm
Summary: "When a senator's five-year-old daughter is abducted, the
FBI brings in Special Agent MacKenzie Graham to analyze the
kidnapper's vengeful written threats. Working alongside Iraq war
veteran John Crowfeather, she scours the Internet for clues. Time is of
the essence in any kidnapping investigation—but little Zoe has
diabetes"— Provided by publisher.
ISBN 978-1-62899-587-9 (library binding : alk. paper)
1. Kidnapping—Fiction. 2. Children—Crimes against—Fiction.
3. Government investigators—Fiction. 4. Large type books. I. Title.
PS3623.H5786W67 2015
813'.6—dc23
2015007341

For Sharon,
who knows words and loves the Word

Acknowledgments

"Friends," wrote Thoreau, "are kind to each other's dreams." I have had good friends, godly friends who have nurtured and nourished and prayed for my writing dreams, including this book. For them I will be eternally grateful.

Sharon Smith, PhD, my sister-in-Christ, a retired FBI agent and real-life forensic psycholinguist, has walked this journey with me now for many years. Every authentic bit of language analysis in this book is hers; any mistakes are mine. Sharon has shared with me her knowledge of threats, deception, analysis, psychopathy, and all manner of other law-enforcement subjects. More than that, she has shared with me her life. I'm so happy to have this brilliant, beautiful, and generous woman as my friend!

My prayer group—Sharon, Sue, Kathleen, Terri, and Terry—have worn out their knees on my behalf. What would I do without their support? My family, too, has lifted my weary spirits on many an occasion: my husband, Larry; son, Matt; daughters, Becky and Sarah; my sons-in-law, Chris and Michael; my sisters, Karen and Jackie; and my mom—you all have my gratitude.

I know all too well the way my brain works. I think globally, and miss the details, painting broad landscapes with words but leaving stones and pebbles in place that would make readers stumble. How grateful I am to have sharp-eyed people coming behind me! Retired FBI Agent Dru Wells pointed out many of those stumbling stones, as did my friends Kate Jordan and Hilary Kanter. Abingdon Press editors, including Ramona Richards and Teri Wilhelms, smoothed out the final product. Books & Such agent Janet Grant always offers wise counsel. Thank you all so much!

Finally, my Virginia license plate, RYTN4HM, says it all: I write to glorify Jesus Christ. He is the Way, the Truth, and the Life, and my greatest joy. When I write (paraphrasing Eric Liddell), I feel His pleasure! Thank you, Lord, for your unsearchable riches and unfathomable grace.

1

Mackenzie Graham leaned toward the flickering candle, her fork poised above the broiled Chilean sea bass arranged artfully before her on a square black plate. Her instincts told her that her companion was about to take the bait.

Across the table, Senator Bruce Grable cut lustily into his steak. He looked James Bond handsome, his dark hair perfectly edged in silver at his temples, his blue eyes set wide, his jaw strong. Silk palms and ficus trees separated the white-shrouded tables, giving the illusion of privacy in the trendy new Washington restaurant. "So tell me," Kenzie said looking intently into Grable's bright blue eyes, "what made you decide to get into politics?"

"I wanted to help people," he said, stabbing a piece of steak and thrusting it into his mouth.

"That's the way I see my job, too, Senator—helping people connect." Kenzie smiled demurely. She tossed her head and as she did, her blonde hair brushed her bare shoulders. She saw his eyes follow the movement. The senator was on his third marriage but he clearly hadn't stopped looking. "Your daughter must be about to start school."

He smiled. "Zoe? Yes. She starts kindergarten

in the fall." Grable had been quick to pull out pictures of the little blonde five-year-old when they first sat down.

"You're sending her to private school."

"Of course." Grable took a sip of his wine.

"And you told me your older children are in college," Kenzie shook her head, "I don't know how you do it on just a senator's salary!"

"I know. The taxpayers think what we make is a lot, but they don't know the expenses we have!"

Kenzie smiled. "That's why we'd like to help."

Grable swallowed. His eyes flickered and she knew he was once again considering her offer.

"When would it be delivered?" he asked.

She reached down, pulled a bulging *GQ* magazine out of her tote bag, and handed it to him, watching his face carefully. "Twenty-five percent. I can supply the rest as soon as the first contract is signed."

The senator kept the magazine low, nearly under the table, while he deftly slipped out the envelope hidden inside. Looking down, he peeked at the contents, then tucked it into the breast pocket of his suit coat. It looked like he'd done it before, many, many times. "And all you need is some help with the Department of Defense?"

She nodded. "An inside track on those contracts."

"I can do that," he said, lifting his glass.

"Great!" Kenzie raised her glass to meet his.

The couple at the next table stood up, stepped past the palms, and approached them.

"Senator Grable?" the man said. Tall, with salt-and-pepper hair, the man's sharp gray suit contrasted nicely with his white shirt.

Grable turned to look at him.

"Special Agent James Anderson, FBI," the man said, opening a leather credentials case and showing it to the senator. "You're under arrest, sir."

"What?" Grable pushed his chair back and stood up, his face red, his voice angry.

"Selling influence, sir. That's illegal."

"Special Agent Toni Carroll," Anderson's partner said, flashing her own creds. "Turn around, and give me your hands. Do you have any weapons?" She looked small next to Grable, but her voice had an unmistakable tone of authority.

"Weapons? Are you . . ."

"You have the right to remain silent."

Grable looked at Kenzie in disbelief. "Who are you?" the senator demanded, spit flying in Kenzie's direction.

"Special Agent Mackenzie Graham," she said briskly. "Oh, and don't worry about the tab, Senator—the director will pick it up." She threw her black shawl over her shoulders, reached down for her purse, and headed for the door. "Thanks, Paul," she said to the maître d' as she walked past him. "Jim will settle up with you."

● ● ●

"Great job, Kenzie," Jim said a few minutes later, standing next to her car in the parking garage. "You got everything we needed." He smiled.

The night air felt cool, a welcome relief from the hot August day. Kenzie placed the recording device she'd been wearing in an evidence bag labeled with the case number. She signed and dated the bag, noting the time, and handed it to the older agent, who signed the bag as well, establishing the legal chain of custody that would prove crucial in a trial.

"You're not going to come celebrate with us?" he asked.

Kenzie shook her head. "I've got to get home to Jack. And I've got to stop by the office and pick up some work."

Jim's gray eyebrows narrowed. "The boss giving you a hard time?"

"He still thinks psycholinguistics is voodoo science and because I'm short on street experience, he's convinced I'm not tough enough to be an agent." Kenzie sighed. "I think it's his personal mission to break me. So he's finding loose threads in my old cases and doubling my work." She frowned. "What am I supposed to do? The Bureau needed me at the Academy, temporarily anyway. I can't help it if that makes him short one agent at the field office."

Jim shook his head. "You do great work, Kenzie. Don't let him bug you."

Kenzie thanked him. She started to put the key in the lock of her dark red rental car, then froze. A spider was crawling across the door handle.

Jim's cell phone rang. "Hold on," he said, touching her arm. She wrenched her eyes off the spider and turned toward him. "Anderson. Yes. What? When?" Cradling the phone with his shoulder, he pulled a pen and a small notebook out of his pocket and began jotting notes. "OK, OK . . . right. She's right here. I'll tell her. Fifteen minutes, if not sooner." He clicked the phone off and looked at Kenzie, his brow furrowed.

"What is it?" she asked.

"D.C. police have responded to a possible kidnapping, 3217 27th Street NW."

"Senator Grable's house?" A jolt of adrenaline ran through Kenzie.

"His five-year-old daughter is missing."

"Zoe? This happened tonight?" Kenzie's heart raced.

Jim nodded. "While we were in the restaurant. The Bureau's been called out. That was the case agent, Scott Hansbrough. You know him?"

She could barely breathe. "He's why I'm with the Bureau."

"He wants you there."

"Got it!" She turned back to the car and jerked the door open.

13

2

The Grables' home, a typical Georgetown center-hall red-brick Colonial, sat on a narrow street on the edge of Rock Creek Park. Kenzie, still in her high heels and little black dress, scrambled to keep up with Special Agent Scott Hansbrough. He was tall and athletic, and it seemed like she had to take two strides for every one of his. The heels didn't help.

Kenzie could smell boxwoods near the house. There would be azaleas in the yard, too, she knew, and at least one tulip magnolia. It wasn't hard to imagine the standard Washington plantings.

One ambulance, lights flashing, stood out front next to a single police car. They were keeping things quiet, Kenzie realized. Causing a big stir might make a kidnapper do something rash.

"Kenzie," Scott said, stopping suddenly and turning toward her. His sheer size would stop anyone in their tracks. Kenzie looked up at him. He wore his brown hair short, like a Marine. His left cheek bore a thin scar from a long-ago suspect's knife. Dressed in a navy blue suit, white shirt, and red tie, he looked sharp.

Scott lowered his voice, "I want you with me when I interview Grable's wife. Watch her. See if you can pick up any deception, any hint that she might be involved." The lights of the ambulance reflected in his eyes and highlighted the intensity in his face.

"Right," she said. In a kidnapping case, law enforcement officers had to rule out those closest to the victim as suspects first. Kenzie searched her mind for what she knew about the senator's wife.

Scott turned and trotted up the front steps two at a time, knocked at the front door, and flashed his creds at the police officer who opened it. The cop glanced back at Kenzie, instantly reminding her how out of place she looked in her little black dress and high heels.

"She's with me," Scott said firmly. The cop nodded and stepped back to let them in.

Kenzie had always admired the way Scott could walk into a room and take charge. People instantly respected him. She figured it had to be some male pheromone. "It doesn't come so easily to me," she'd told Jack one day when they were jogging. "I've got to work at it."

"Special Agent Hansbrough, FBI," Scott said, announcing his presence to the distraught woman in the living room. "Parlor" they would probably call it, Kenzie thought. Mrs. Grable had grown up in Atlanta and despite her home's colonial style, she had decorated the inside with the melon colors of her childhood: Pale green, cantaloupe, and a touch of watermelon red here and there. It looked gorgeous.

"Where is he? Where is my husband?" Mrs. Grable demanded, rushing toward Scott. A thin, wispy blonde, she barely looked old enough to have a five-year-old daughter.

"Calm down, Mrs. Grable," Scott said. "He's at the FBI office. We'll get him over here as soon as we can."

Elizabeth Grable—her husband called her Beth—wore a pale pink suit, Armani, Kenzie guessed, with a white silk blouse and gold. Lots of gold.

"Why aren't you doing something? Why aren't you looking for her?" Mrs. Grable screamed, looking around. Her eyes fell on Kenzie and narrowed. "Who are you? What are you doing here?"

"Special Agent Mackenzie Graham," she replied. Mrs. Grable stared at her as if she didn't believe her. Kenzie blamed the little black dress.

"Mrs. Grable, is there somewhere we can go to talk?" Scott said, taking charge. "I'd like to hear what happened."

The sunroom off the kitchen worked perfectly. Plush cushions covered in a gorgeous green leafy design with yellow accents softened the white wicker furniture. A few throw rugs lay on the tile floor, while potted tropical plants added a natural feel. Beth Grable sat perched on the edge of the love seat, twisting a tissue in her hand.

Kenzie waited with her while Scott talked to the Metropolitan PD officer who had responded to the 911 call.

After a few moments, Scott appeared, sat down, and immediately Mrs. Grable launched into her story. "It was my mah-jongg night, you see, and Bruce said he had a dinner date with some . . . some aide and said he would be late."

Chalk up one lie for the senator. Kenzie made a mental note.

"Our nanny was here, so I didn't see the harm in going."

"You play frequently?" Scott asked.

"Every week."

"Always on the same night?" Scott leaned toward her, notebook in hand, his broad shoulders stretching the limits of his navy blue suit, his dark brown eyes focused on Mrs. Grable's face.

"Oh, yes, Tuesday night at seven o'clock."

"What time did you leave tonight?"

"Why, six-forty, I believe. Yes, that would be right. I was running five minutes late."

Scott was establishing the window of opportunity for the kidnapping, Kenzie knew.

"How many of you play?" he asked.

"How many players? Eight. We have two alternates."

"How does the evening go?"

"What difference does that make?" Mrs. Grable exploded.

Scott waited for her to calm down. "It matters. Trust me."

She rolled her eyes, her cheeks wet with tears. Then she brushed her hair back from her face. "We play for two and a half hours, with a half-hour break in the middle. The hostess provides refreshments. We rotate bringing prizes."

"So you left around what time?" Scott asked.

"Ten o'clock. We always leave at ten." Mrs. Grable twisted the tissue in her hands. "I drove home, and when I pulled up, I knew something was wrong."

"Why?"

"Zoe's bedroom light—why would it be on if she were sleeping?" Mrs. Grable got up and began pacing. "I felt angry at first. I thought maybe she was manipulating the nanny again, staying up past her bedtime. I parked in the garage and let myself in through the kitchen door. I put my purse down and headed for the stairs. And then I saw . . . I saw . . ." tears welled again in her eyes and streamed over her cheeks. "I saw her, the nanny, lying at the bottom of the stairs, lying there . . . with this thing on her head."

Kenzie noticed Beth didn't use the nanny's name. That registered as interesting. Nor did she accurately describe the "thing" on her head. Paramedics said they'd found the woman unconscious, with her head in a brown pillowcase containing a rag soaked with chloroform.

"What did you do?" Scott asked softly.

Beth sat down and shook her head slowly. "I ran up the stairs, screaming for Zoe. I felt terrified. And when I got to her room, I found . . . found . . ."

"Yes?"

". . . she was gone! Gone!" The anguish welled up in Mrs. Grable again, and she convulsed in sobs, dropping the mangled tissue on the floor.

Kenzie saw a tissue box across the room, got up, retrieved it, and handed it to her.

"You have to find her. You have to find her!" Beth wailed, pulling multiple tissues out of the box.

Scott and Kenzie exchanged glances. The woman's turmoil seemed real. But then, Susan Smith had shed crocodile tears over her two "kidnapped" little boys. All along, she knew they lay at the bottom of a lake. She had drowned them.

"We're going to do everything we can, Mrs. Grable," Scott said. "Let me ask you a few more questions."

Kenzie sat quietly while Scott continued to interview the senator's wife. Had they been having any problems with anyone lately? Was there anyone to whom they owed money? Had they had any workers in the house recently? What about former spouses? Ex-lovers? Current lovers? Who might have known her schedule?

How long had the nanny worked for them? Did she have any boyfriends?

Mrs. Grable answered through her tears, trembling.

"Agent Hansbrough?" An FBI technician appeared at the doorway and gestured toward Scott. Kenzie guessed Scott had called out a response team.

"Yes, one second." Scott turned back to Mrs. Grable. "I'll be right back."

Kenzie tried to comfort Mrs. Grable. "All the resources of the FBI are being activated to help find Zoe, Mrs. Grable," she said, but the woman simply responded with more sobs.

Scott returned. "Mrs. Grable, we've got your phone tapped, but there's a voice mail message. I need you to come listen to it."

The woman jumped up, nearly knocking the glass top off the wicker coffee table. "Could it be . . . ?"

"We'll know in a second."

But it was only a message from the pediatrician's office asking the Grables to call. "Zoe hasn't been well," Mrs. Grable explained to Scott. "I thought she had the flu but it wasn't clearing up. So I took her in for some tests yesterday."

Scott nodded. "We have agents canvassing your neighbors to see if they noticed anything tonight. We'll be monitoring all your phone calls, including your cell. And your e-mails. I'll set up a command center . . ."

"Just do it," she interrupted. "Do whatever you need!" She threw up her hands. "You've got to help me!"

"It could be a long night," Scott said. Quietly, other agents had been coming into the house. Through the kitchen window, Kenzie could see the Mobile Command Post, a huge RV-type vehicle taking a position in the alley behind the house. It would eventually serve as their headquarters, but for now, Scott said they'd meet in the house to strategize.

After handing Mrs. Grable off to a female agent, Scott and Kenzie moved into the dining room. "What's my role here?" Kenzie asked. Scott worked on a violent crime squad at the Washington Field Office. The Bureau had temporarily assigned Kenzie to the FBI Academy, teaching interviewing techniques and consulting in her specialty, forensic psycholinguistics. Anderson's public corruption squad had borrowed her back to sting Senator Grable.

"I told Shuler I wanted you assigned to the case," Scott replied. Tom Shuler was the assistant director in charge of the Washington office.

"And my classes?"

"He's calling the AD for the Academy."

Kenzie grimaced.

"Hey, your boss thinks you lack street experience, isn't that what you told me? This is your chance. If we don't find the kid in the next few days, the chances of ever finding her are slim."

Poor Zoe. Kenzie had seen enough pictures of her to feel sympathy. She took a deep breath. "This isn't my field. What do we know about kidnappings? Statistically?"

"If we're talking a child predator, in nearly 100 percent of the cases, the kid is dead in twenty-four hours. But if the kidnapper is doing this for money, we have a chance. He'll make his demands in twelve to twenty-four hours. He'll let the senator and his wife sweat for a bit first." Scott ran his hand through his hair. "Evaluating any messages we get will be crucial. And our responses must be carefully worded. I don't want to mess this up. There's too much at stake. I need someone good with words, Kenzie. I need you."

She took a deep breath. "OK. Let me go home, see Jack, and grab some clothes."

"You don't have a ready bag in the car?" he said, frowning.

"I don't get calls like this!" She glanced at her watch. Just after 11:00 p.m. "Three hours. I'll be back in three hours."

"Make it two."

3

The Academy lay forty miles south of Washington, straight down Interstate 95, not far from Kenzie's townhouse. She knew that Jack would probably have been better off in a place with a big backyard, but realistically, she had no time to mow grass.

Guilt dogged her as she cut through the night. She should have prepared for an emergency with work clothes and a toothbrush in the trunk. She'd gotten complacent, working at the Academy. Scott wouldn't say anything because he was Scott.

She'd known him for eight years, had met him when she was an assistant professor of linguistics and he was working on a threat case and needed her expertise. Impressed with her knowledge, Scott had recruited her for the Bureau. Kenzie was intrigued by the application of her specialty, linguistics, to law enforcement, and her visit to the FBI Academy cemented her decision. Eighteen months later, PhD in hand, Kenzie found herself a new agent in training. That was just three years ago.

Jack was waiting for her when she came through the garage door into the kitchen, a silly grin on his face, his stub of a tail wagging furiously. "Jack, I

am so sorry! Did Corey take you for a run?"
Kenzie patted the black and white springer
spaniel. "I know he did. But you're ready for
more, aren't you? And guess what? I have bad
news. I have to go back. It's a little girl, Jack, a
little five-year-old. I have to help her."

She threw her keys down on the kitchen
countertop and kicked off her high heels. "I've
got to change, Jack."

He followed her with not one, but two tennis
balls in his mouth. As she pulled off her dress,
her slip, and her stockings, Jack dropped the
balls at her feet and waited expectantly. "I don't
have time to play right now. I promise, when this
is over . . ."

But he kept following her around. She went
into her closet where she grabbed a clean pair of
khaki pants and a golf shirt with an "FBI
Academy—Behavioral Science Unit" patch.
Then she moved back out into her bedroom,
where she put them on. She threaded a holster
onto her belt, and filled it with her Bureau-issued
Glock. It felt heavy. She wasn't used to wearing
it every day. Not at the Academy.

"Of course, I feel guilty, Jack, but then, this is
my job! I'll make it up to you. I swear I will."
Grabbing a duffle bag, she threw in two more
pairs of pants, three shirts, underwear, more
socks, her travel kit, a brush, some elastics to
hold her hair back, and a toothbrush. "What am I

missing?" she said out loud. Her navy blazer. She retrieved it from the closet.

Jack barked at her, a solitary, sharp bark. "OK, OK." Kenzie kicked the balls out into the hallway, and then down the stairs. Jack went bounding after them and Kenzie followed him, her duffle bag in her hand. She grabbed her personally owned weapon, a small pistol, and put it in her bag.

There were four new messages on the answering machine in the kitchen. All four were from her mother. Clarice Graham lived in northwest D.C. in the house where Kenzie had grown up. At sixty-six, she was still beautiful, still trim, and still the most difficult person in Kenzie's life. Her messages demanded that Kenzie call her, tonight. It was a matter of utmost urgency. The last one, recorded at ten fifty-five, sharply accused Kenzie of ignoring her again. "Oh, good grief," Kenzie muttered. Being an only child definitely had disadvantages.

Jack barked again, his one sharp, insistent bark. Kenzie looked at him. He'd laid the two tennis balls, side by side, right in front of her, begging her to play.

"OK!" Kenzie said. "Five minutes. That's all. Then I have to go."

At 1:20 a.m., she arrived back at the Grables' house in Georgetown. She parked in the back, near the Mobile Command Center, and showed credentials to the agent at the back gate. Driving down the alley, she'd seen an agent walking the neighborhood. He belonged, no doubt, to the Special Operations Group, called out to scan the streets around the Grables' house.

The cooler night air, a perfect seventy degrees, felt refreshing. Overhead, the stars shimmered in the velvet sky. Kenzie grabbed her briefcase and made her way into the house.

"I'm back," she said. Scott stood over the dining room table, making notes. His deep brown eyes, set in a broad face, creased at the edges with tension.

"The senator should be here shortly," he said.

"No calls?"

"Nothing, not even . . ."

An agent appearing at the dining room door interrupted him. "Heads up!" he said, and motioned for them to follow.

"Showtime," Scott said quietly.

They walked to the front hall, and seconds later, Senator Bruce Grable, along with a man in an expensive suit who Kenzie figured must be his lawyer, and two additional FBI agents strode through the front door.

"Where's my wife?" the senator demanded, fixing his cold gaze on Scott.

"In the family room, sir," Scott said. He motioned with his head to Kenzie and they

26

followed the senator to the rear of the house.

"Bruce, do something!" Beth cried out and she half rose from the couch. He took her in his arms, then sat down next to her.

"It'll be all right; we'll find her," he said, but a catch in his voice told a very different story. He held his wife for a moment, their grief framed by the large picture of Zoe hanging behind the couch on the pale green wall; then he stood up and squared off with Scott. "Who are you?"

"FBI Special Agent Scott Hansbrough. I'm the case agent."

The senator looked past him, straight at Kenzie. "You! What do you think you're doing?"

"She's an expert in psycholinguistics," Scott said calmly. "She'll be invaluable if we get any communication from the kidnappers. I've asked her to join the case."

"Yeah, well, I don't like people who deceive me." He turned to the well-dressed man who'd come in with him. "Get her out of here!"

The man, the presumed lawyer, took a deep breath. "The director told me he specifically allowed it," he said. "She's supposedly an expert."

"You get that son of a . . . get him on the phone. Now!"

It only takes being a senator, Kenzie thought, to gain immediate access to the FBI's top dog. She could picture Director Joseph D. Lundquist now, patiently listening as he got an earful from Grable, who paced while he yelled into the cell phone his lawyer had handed him. Calming the senator down seemed to take forever. Eventually, the diplomatic talents of the director must have won out. The senator snapped the phone off and strode back toward the two agents. "Just what are you doing to find my daughter? Or is your job just to harass me?"

Scott took a big breath. "We have agents working hard on this already, Senator, canvassing the neighborhood, getting security tapes from local businesses, going over possible suspects, and reviewing similar cases. We have a tap on your phones and we're monitoring e-mail. Now we need information from you."

The senator tightened his lips into a straight line. "How long is it going to take you to find Zoe?"

"There's no way to know that," Scott replied.

"That's not an answer!" Grable stood with his hands on his hips, his jaw thrust forward.

"I need to ask you some questions, sir. Could we go into your office?"

The senator's home office, a one-story wing, stood off to the right side of the house, balancing the sunroom on the opposite side. A huge walnut desk dominated the room. The walls were a medium brown. "Mocha latte" is what Kenzie figured the designers would call it. Flanking the front window, framed by thick brown and cream curtains, were two brown leather chairs and a love seat covered in a dark green, brown, and cream plaid fabric. Very masculine. Very rich.

The senator walked right past the couch and chairs and stood behind his desk. He motioned for Kenzie and Scott to sit down. The lawyer pulled up another chair. "Now, what do you want?" Grable asked as he sagged into his high-back, leather desk chair.

Scott shifted in his seat, but did not respond to the senator's gruff prompt. Kenzie sensed he was asserting control, letting the silence grow between them until he was ready to initiate. She looked at the two of them, the senator with his polished good looks, and Scott, a brown-haired, thick-necked former football player. In a stand-off, Kenzie would put money on Scott.

On the wall behind the senator hung pictures of him with two presidents, with the prime ministers of Israel and Great Britain, with the secretary of defense, and with his little girl. Zoe was about two years old and wore pink corduroy Oshkosh overalls. Grable was throwing her in the air, and Zoe appeared to be squealing with delight. A diploma from the University of Illinois, his home state, hung next to the pictures. That explained the broad *A* Kenzie had heard in his speech.

Scott turned to the man on the senator's left. "First, who are you?"

"J. Barton Thompson. Senator Grable's lawyer. And I want to point out he doesn't have to answer anything."

"No, of course not," Scott interrupted, "if he doesn't care about finding his daughter." He returned his gaze to Grable. "Senator, we're covering all the bases as we search for Zoe. It's possible it was a random act, but my hunch is, and it's just a hunch, the kidnapper is someone who knows you or your wife, someone with a grudge. Someone who wants to strike directly at your heart."

Well put, Kenzie thought.

The senator glared at Scott. But as the agent's words sank in, Kenzie saw Grable swallow hard, his expression softening. "So who are we looking at? Political enemies? The gardener? The guy I cussed out last week at the parking garage?"

"All of the above," Scott said. "Let's start with people who might be angry with you."

Grable picked up a paper clip, straightened it, and threw it on his desk. "That could be a long list." He began by naming political enemies, two activists in the opposite party, a man he'd soundly defeated to win and keep his Senate seat, another senator who'd felt double-crossed when Grable changed his vote on a bill, a couple of people jealous of his position on the Senate

Armed Services Committee and the way he wielded power, some people on the White House staff. "But these are all professional politicians. They're not the kind to steal a little girl," he said.

"What exactly is that kind, Senator?" Scott asked. "Because we've seen them all."

Grable sighed with exasperation. "All right," he said, leaning forward, "that's all I can think of right now."

"OK. Now, Senator, who do you owe money to?"

Grable went over the list, ticking them off on his fingers—the mortgage company, an auto loan, an investment broker, a bank . . . no, two banks. He kept hunching his shoulders, the tension playing out in his body. "What else?"

"Senator, how's your marriage?"

The man visibly stiffened. He straightened up in his chair. "What are you insinuating?"

"I'm not insinuating anything. I just asked a simple question." Scott's eyes were fixed on Grable's face.

Grable blustered and fumed. He stood up and turned his back on Scott and Kenzie. When he finally turned around, his face looked red. "My marriage is like every other Washington marriage I know. Difficult. Struggling. Infuriating at times. But do I think my wife had anything to do with Zoe's disappearance? No. No way."

"That isn't what I asked, Senator."

Grable tightened his jaw. "What exactly are you getting at?"

"Any affairs going on?"

"No!"

"Has there been talk of divorce? Separation?"

"No, of course not." Grable sat back down in his chair. "We have our problems but look, I do the best I can as a husband, a father. And Beth, she . . . she tries, too. I've been there, done that when it comes to divorce. I don't intend to do it again."

"You're pretty close to Zoe."

"So what? So that's illegal now? Being close to your daughter?"

Scott switched gears, asking questions about the people who had access to the house, the neighbors, any workmen who'd been around lately. They'd recently had the house reroofed and repainted. They had a lawn-care company and they'd used a caterer for a party recently. The senator added that Scott would have to get the names of the contractors from his wife.

"Would any of the people who know you have any reason to believe you or your wife had a part in Zoe's disappearance?" Scott asked.

"Absolutely not!" the senator said, fuming.

"It's a standard question, sir. One more thing. You've accepted some money . . ."

"Don't respond to that!" Thompson said firmly.

He looked at Scott. "He will not answer any questions along those lines."

Scott refocused on the senator. "What I wanted to know, Senator, is have there been any potentially illegal transactions that might have put you in the company of unscrupulous people, people who now believe they can recoup some of their, uh, investments? Or people who may feel they didn't get their money's worth?"

"Don't say a word!" Thompson said to the senator. He sat on the edge of his seat. "Senator, I strongly advise you not to engage in this line of questioning."

"Although it could be the most productive," Scott said. "As you yourself pointed out, Senator, most of the people you've named would not be considered prime suspects. Anyone who's engaged in criminal activity, on the other hand . . ."

"Bruce, don't do it!"

Senator Grable took a deep breath, looked up at the ceiling, and closed his eyes. Kenzie could see the veins in his neck popping out. When he opened his eyes he focused on the fancy penholder on his desk, refusing eye contact with Scott. "I can't go there, Hansbrough. On the advice of my counsel."

Scott waited to see what would come next. After a full minute, he gathered his notebook and said, "All right, Senator. Would you be willing to take a polygraph? On the other issues?"

"Of course!"

Scott nodded. "We'll keep you advised." He and Kenzie stood up to leave. "One more thing, sir. If we could have a list of your associates at the Senate, in all of your offices, in fact, including contact information. Volunteers as well."

"I'll have my secretary get it to you as soon as I can reach her."

"Thank you, Senator. It's worth waking her up." Scott and Kenzie turned toward the door.

"Hansbrough!"

They looked back at the senator, who rose from behind his desk and walked toward them.

"I want you to know I don't like you—or her—one bit." Grable jabbed the air with his forefinger. "But I expect you to find Zoe. You find my little girl!"

"That's my job, sir. I intend to do it."

"I'll tell you one more thing. You fail at this and I will crush you. Your career will be over. What's more, I'll do everything I can to make sure your director gets nothing he wants on the Hill. Ever."

Scott nodded. "I understand."

"Do it, Hansbrough. Find Zoe!"

4

"No pressure," Scott said to Kenzie in a low voice after they'd left the senator's office. He shook his head. "What did you think?"

"I don't think he had anything to do with Zoe's disappearance."

Scott nodded.

"But his marriage is in trouble."

He looked at her.

"Did you hear his answer when you said, 'How's your marriage?' He hesitated, then responded with a question. 'What are you insinuating?' he said. That's not an answer. That's deception. He's hiding something."

Scott raised his eyebrows.

"And what about the others who might have bribed him?" Kenzie asked. "He wouldn't answer that line of questioning, obviously, but I think the area's a good place to look."

"I agree. Let's give him a little time. He may open up later. In the meantime, I'll get somebody on the ones we know about already." Scott set his jaw. "Come on. Let's rally the troops."

There were half a dozen FBI agents in the house, leaders of the teams currently staged around D.C., waiting for orders. Scott called them into the dining room. Kenzie checked her watch. Two-fifty a.m. Scott had set up his files and computer in the middle position of the large table, with his back to a huge buffet. Typically, he liked to have a view of the entrances and exits of whatever room he worked in, Kenzie knew. It was the fallout of many years of being on the street.

Kenzie chose a position standing next to the wall near him. She watched the agents arrange themselves in the room. She didn't know most of them, but she recognized Jocelyn, a dark-haired, olive-skinned agent in her mid-thirties; Alicia Sheerling, a member of Scott's squad; and an African-American agent named Jesse. The last person to walk in the room was a slender, ruddy-faced man with high cheekbones, black hair, and piercing black eyes. He walked in like he'd be comfortable anywhere. Another Scott. He looked in her direction. Their eyes met briefly.

"All right," Scott said, clearing his throat. "Let me update you. The last time Mrs. Grable saw Zoe was at 6:30 p.m., when she said goodbye on the way to her mah-jongg game. She reported her missing at 10:30 p.m., so we're a little over four hours now. Ninety percent of these situations are resolved in twenty-four hours. Most of these crimes are perpetrated by sexual predators. Kidnapping for ransom is very, very rare.

"Should we get a communication, the tracking van is ready to roll, as is a chopper. The door-to-door in this neighborhood has revealed nothing so far, which doesn't surprise me . . . there is so much traffic up and down this street, a strange car wouldn't be noticed.

"We've set up a website on the secure net with this password: jeh127lf. That's j. edgar hoover 127 louis freeh. Got it? When you get on that site, you will need to set up your own access code. There you will find the database we are using to organize the information we collect. Please upload your data as often as you can. Also, I want to be in direct telephone contact with each of you at least once every three hours. This child's life could depend on us connecting the dots sooner rather than later."

The sound of shuffling filled the room. Everyone seemed anxious to get on with it. Scott continued, "Jocelyn, you go to the hospital and stick with the nanny. There's a cop there already. I understand the nanny's still unconscious. The minute she wakes up, the minute the doctors will let you have access to her—find out everything you can.

"Alicia, you check out the senator's staff. He's getting a list for us now. Find out where each of them was last evening. Verify it. And for the ones back home in Illinois, contact the Chicago office and get them on it. When you're finished with that, here's a list of people the senator considers political enemies." The agent nodded.

"All right, Jesse, check on the mah-jongg players. Verify Mrs. Grable's presence. Check out her demeanor. The time she arrived and the time she departed. If she got any phone calls or text messages. Cover all the bases."

Scott continued passing out assignments: Family and friends, financial contacts, sexual offenders known to be in the area, similar crimes committed elsewhere in the country, and finally the senator's social contacts.

The dark-haired, dark-eyed man was last. "Crow," Scott said.

Kenzie looked up.

"Crow, I want you and your people to get background on the nanny and her relatives . . . everything. And the contractors who have worked on the house recently. Here's a list."

"Got it."

"All right. That's a start. Have at it."

"Crow?" Kenzie asked when everyone else had gone.

"John Crowfeather. Everyone calls him Crow."

"Is he an American Indian?"

Scott nodded. "Full-blooded Navajo. His grandfather was one of the World War II Code Talkers. You should get to know him. He's interesting. And he's single."

"Maybe I'll wait until we find Zoe," Kenzie responded dryly. She thought she'd broken Scott of his habit of trying to set her up. She changed the subject. "All right, victimology: I'd like to see Zoe's room."

"Go up the stairs, take a left, and come back toward the front of the house. You can't miss it. It's pink."

Kenzie stood just inside the doorway of Zoe's room, ignoring the black fingerprint powder that marred the pale pink of the walls and the white paint on the trim, looking instead at the décor and feel of the room. How long had it been since she'd been in a little girl's room? Zoe's furniture was white, trimmed in gold, and the curtains were white dotted Swiss—very old-fashioned and feminine, and charming, actually. In one corner lay a pile of stuffed animals. Next to it stood a tiny table and two bears having a tea party.

Kenzie took a deep breath. She had come to get a sense of Zoe's personality, to study the victim to get a clue about the psychology of the perpetrator. But instead of discovering Zoe Grable, she had unexpectedly come face-to-face with herself.

Was it the pink-and-white striped polished cotton bedspread? The stuffed animals? The shelf chock-full of books? Or the small cradle with its bald-headed baby doll?

All of that, plus the light scent of fresh linens and the tiny sock on the floor, instantly transported her back to age five. As the only child of her father's second marriage she had spent many hours alone in her own pink room, playing with dolls and stuffed dogs, creating her own companions, acting out the melodrama she so often heard coming up through the heating grates when both of her parents were home.

She had adored her father. Blond-haired and blue-eyed, a successful entrepreneur, her dad lit up her world when he came home. In contrast, her mother seemed to be perpetually angry, angry with Kenzie's dad and jealous of his relationship with their little girl. Still, every day, late in the afternoon, Kenzie kept her ears perked for the sound of her dad's car, for the tune he so often whistled or his voice calling out, "Where's my baby girl?"

She was twelve the last time she heard it.

Fingering a stuffed brown dog in Zoe's room, Kenzie thrust away the memories. No time for that now. She had to stay in the present. She had work to do.

She moved toward the window. It was locked tightly, and the sill was unmarred. It appeared whoever took Zoe simply came in through the door and probably left the same way. Had they taken anything from the room? Using a pen she carefully slid a dresser drawer open enough to peek inside. She had no way of knowing for sure, but it looked to her about half-empty, like some clothes were missing. If so, that was a good sign.

The kidnapper intended to keep Zoe alive long enough to need them.

"Kenzie!" Scott's voice boomed up the stairwell.

"Here!" she said, emerging from Zoe's room.

"I need you."

Kenzie moved down the stairs and entered the dining room where they'd set up a temporary command center. "What's up?"

"We got an audio file of the 911 call."

She stood behind the table, and Scott clicked on the file he'd loaded into his computer. Kenzie held her breath as the slightly distorted audio played.

Operator: 911. Do you need police, fire, or ambulance?

Caller: Oh God! Help me! She's gone, she's gone!

Operator: What is your address, ma'am?

Caller: It's my house! 3217 27th Street NW.

Operator: OK, calm down. Now, who is gone?

Caller: My baby! I came home and she's . . . she's not here!

Operator: Could I have your name?

Caller: This is Elizabeth Grable. Senator Grable's wife.

Operator: How old is the child, ma'am?

Caller: Five! She's only five!

Operator: And what's her name?

Caller: Zoe. Zoe Grable.

Operator: I'm dispatching the police. They'll be there shortly. Did you check outside? Maybe she just went into the yard.

Caller: She's gone, I'm telling you, she's gone! He's going to kill me . . . oh God! My husband will kill me!

Operator: Is your husband at home?

Caller: Oh, no . . . oh, no . . .

Operator: Ma'am? Is your husband with you?

Caller: No.

Operator: I can hear sirens. Go to the front door and let the police in.

Caller: Officer! Officer!

Scott looked at Kenzie as the digital recording stopped. "What do you think?"

"Let me listen to it with headphones on," she said, and she pulled some good headphones out of her briefcase and plugged them in. She sat down and listened again, taking notes, concentrating on the words Beth used. Then she took off the headphones and placed them next to the laptop. "Honestly, she sounds sincere. But what's the most obvious thing?"

"Besides her hysteria?" Scott replied.

"She never mentions the nanny. It's like she doesn't exist."

"Why would that be?"

Kenzie shrugged. "Maybe she wishes she didn't exist. Maybe Beth considers her totally unimportant. Maybe she's jealous of her. Also, she keeps saying 'Help ME!' not 'help us' or 'we need your help.' And she refers to 'my house' and 'my baby.' Those are fairly narcissistic statements."

"She says her husband will kill her."

"In context, I think she means figuratively. But still, it indicates conflict."

Scott rubbed his jaw.

"She repeats herself a lot during the call," Kenzie said, looking at her notes. "She says, 'she's gone, she's gone!' and then 'Zoe. Zoe Grable.' "

"What's that mean?"

"It could be deception, or just nervousness."

Scott sagged back in his chair. "So, she's neither on nor off the hook."

"That's right. We can't rule her out as a suspect; but I'm not hearing anything that makes me really suspicious." Kenzie tapped her pen on the table. "You have the statement of the first responder? Let's see what he said about her."

Scott pulled out the report from the first policeman on the scene. "Let's see: The officer says she was upset, crying. She kept grabbing his arm and begging him to find Zoe. He entered the house and found the nanny, and was surprised Mrs. Grable hadn't mentioned her. He called for an ambulance. He asked Mrs. Grable what had happened to her and she responded, 'I don't know!' The officer became suspicious and decided to stay with Mrs. Grable rather than search the premises. He radioed for back-up . . ." Scott shook his head. "Her reaction is pretty squirrelly."

"I'll say. But that's how a narcissist would react," Kenzie said, thinking of her own mother. "Like it had happened to her and not her child."

"I'd like to take a look at Mrs. Grable's calendar. See who she's been meeting with. How she spends her time," Scott said.

Kenzie paced away, tapping her lip with her finger. "In contrast, Senator Grable has been direct in his statements. When we asked him to name possible suspects, he did it. When we asked him who he thought could have done this, he didn't hesitate and had good reasons for the people he named. People who are being deceptive usually say things like 'Anybody could have done this!' It's to their advantage to keep the suspect pool wide."

"Interesting."

"When we asked him if he would take a polygraph, he readily agreed. When he talks about his daughter," Kenzie took in a deep breath, "it's clear to me he loves her."

Scott nodded. "That's my feeling, too. I'm not as comfortable with the wife."

"Nor am I. Nobody likes to think of a mother hurting her own little girl, but it happens."

"It could be her, or it could be a random

abduction, like Elizabeth Smart or Polly Klaas."

"In Elizabeth's case, the suspect had been in the home, doing odd jobs months before," Kenzie said.

"In a high percentage of cases of abduction for sexual reasons there's been some contact with the victim before, brief though it may be. Some visual contact, anyway," Scott added. "That's why I asked Crow to check out all these workmen. We could be talking about a serious pedophile. Someone bold enough or crazy enough to enter a home, rather than just take a kid off the street. If that's the case, we won't hear from him." Scott rubbed his hands together as he thought. "OK, so we could have an abductor who wants to get rid of the girl for some reason, an abductor who wants to possess the girl, an abductor . . ."

". . . who wants to hurt the senator." Kenzie stretched her neck and shoulders, tight from hours of tension. "If I wanted to get at him, Zoe would be my target." She bit her lower lip, a bad habit from childhood. "Wait! Did I tell you? I think there were clothes missing from Zoe's dresser. Did anyone else notice that? We should ask Mrs. Grable to confirm. If so, then it's more likely we're talking about a calculated kidnapping, for ransom or revenge."

"Good point. Let's hope that's it. Because there's a better chance they'll play if it's the case."

"How'd the UNSUB get in?" she asked, using Bureau parlance for "unknown subject." "There's no sign of forced entry. The door doesn't even look scarred. The nanny lay on the steps. Was she hit from behind? Did she know the abductor?"

"Or was she in on it?" Scott said.

"She had a pillowcase over her head and had been chloroformed. I can't think of too many people who would do that voluntarily."

Scott blew out a breath. "Yeah, they would. If there was enough money involved."

Kenzie reddened at the evidence of her inexperience. "So, she could have known the guy. She could be in on it, or he could have tricked her into thinking he had a legitimate reason to be here."

Scott's cell phone rang. He reached for it and took the call.

"That was Jesse," he said moments later. "All of the mah-jongg players confirm Mrs. Grable's presence from start to finish tonight. And aside from her usual complaints about her husband and Zoe, she seemed in a normal mood. In fact, she won, and left there elated."

"But could she have been elated because her plan to get rid of her daughter finally came to fruition?" Kenzie mused.

"There's no telling. We've seen it all."

5

"Good grief, how long does it take to get a kid to sleep?" the man complained as Sandy walked into the living room. He'd sat there alone with his memories long enough. This house, which he'd inherited from his mother, hadn't exactly been a happy home.

"She's scared, Grayson." The redhead plopped down on the couch next to him and put her head on his shoulder. "And I don't blame her. You're sure this is the only way to get that money he owes you?"

"You bet I am. You got to strike him hard, right where it hurts. That's the only way to get him to cooperate." He stroked Sandy's hair. When he'd met her a month ago he knew right away she was the perfect person to help him carry out his plan. He needed someone just like her—a woman desperate for attention and not too bright, but attractive enough for him to be with. He'd sat through boring chick flicks to learn how to touch a woman, how to talk to her, how to be a man around her. He'd watched couples in bars and cafés. He'd eavesdropped on their conversations. And he'd mined the Internet for more intimate information. He'd done his homework and could play the game.

"I dunno about this, Gray, I mean, she's just a kid." Sandy yawned.

"And we're not going to hurt her. I wouldn't do that." Zoe's not my target, he thought. Who was she? A bratty kid. Nothing. But Grable, now, he was something else, a star. A powerful man, made powerful by the unacknowledged and unappreciated efforts of one Grayson Chambers. And payback time had arrived.

"But Gray, she knows you! She can identify you."

He sighed with exasperation. "How many times do I have to explain it to you? By the time Grable finds her, we'll be long gone. Safe in Jamaica. No extradition. Sitting pretty there for the rest of our lives—white beaches, palm trees, turquoise water, everything you've dreamed of. And I'm going to give it to you, baby. Yes, I am, because you deserve it." He kissed her on the mouth. He was so tired of listening to her!

She nestled down, her head on his shoulder. "Can we go to bed now?"

"In a few minutes. I have some work to do first."

"Oh, Gray!" she protested, but obediently she flipped on the TV and within minutes got engrossed in a television show, one of those Washington political dramas he hated so much. They weren't realistic at all. Not at all! The thought briefly crossed his mind that maybe he should go to Hollywood and tell them how the Hill really worked. Be a consultant. He could make a big difference for them.

While she watched the TV, he extricated himself, pulled out his laptop, and started scrolling through some files he'd downloaded. Amazing what was available nowadays on the Internet. Just amazing. When he came across one of these sites for the first time, he'd been curious. Now, he found his curiosity almost unquenchable. So interesting, what people did.

A quiet tension gripped the Grables' house. Kenzie looked at her watch. Three-fifteen a.m. They were five hours into it and still no word from the kidnapper. She and Scott had talked possible scenarios, analyzed information, and outlined strategies until they could no longer think. The senator alternated between hovering over them, pacing, and disappearing for long periods. His wife, sedated, slept upstairs.

Outside in the Mobile Command Unit, agents were monitoring all of the calls going to the Grables' house and cell phones. Inside, agents subtly kept tabs on the Grables themselves. The investigation seemed so slow. They were waiting for the kidnapper to make a call, waiting for other agents to come up with more leads, waiting . . . waiting.

Scott had left to go outside, into the backyard.

Kenzie decided to join him. She stepped out onto the brick patio. He sat on an iron bench, his elbows on his knees, his head bowed. Instantly, she knew he was praying. She stopped in her tracks. She still didn't know what to do with his overt faith. It seemed so . . . inappropriate.

Scott must have heard her. He turned his head toward her and the light caught in his eyes. He sat up. "Hey."

"Sorry. I didn't mean to interrupt."

He shrugged. "God knows where this little girl is. I just thought I'd ask him." He picked up his Bible and read, "He reveals deep and hidden things; he knows what is in the darkness, and light dwells with him."

Really? Kenzie wanted to say. But she didn't respond. She looked up. The night air seemed unusually clear for August, the stars sparkling like glitter. She remembered making a picture on construction paper, writing "To Daddy" on it in glue, and sprinkling glitter over it. She remembered shaking the excess into the trash, and her mother's rage over the little bit that she spilled.

She sat down next to Scott. He smelled like lime aftershave. The smell brought back memories of sitting next to her dad in the pew of her childhood church. She remembered his dark suit and the feel of it when she leaned her head against his shoulder while the service went on.

She remembered how he'd slip her a mint from his pocket. She remembered praying fruitlessly for God to save him as he lay on the floor, dying from a heart attack.

"It's kind of quiet," she said, pulling herself back to the present.

"That's good. I want a low profile."

Kenzie took a deep breath. She wanted to ask him if he really thought God knew and cared about Zoe. If he really thought God would guide him in their search for her. But she didn't. She looked over at him. He looked tired. "Why don't you go get some sleep?"

He shook his head. "No." He set his thick, brown leather Bible on the bench. Once, Kenzie had tried to tell him not to be so obvious about his religion; it could work against him. She felt sure it had. But he had just laughed. Scott was Scott.

Kenzie heard a noise. The back door opened. John Crowfeather walked out of the house. He wore his straight black hair short on the sides, slightly longer on top; a shock of it hung over his forehead. He had on khaki cargo pants, a black golf shirt, and boots that were a cross between athletic shoes and hiking boots. A fishing vest covered his gun. Like Scott, his arms were ropey with muscles, but he looked slimmer than Scott, more like a middleweight wrestler or a lacrosse player than a football jock.

Crow pulled a patio chair out, flipped it around backwards, and sat down, propping his arms on the back of the chair. "Just checking in, boss," he said to Scott.

"We're counting on you to bust this wide open."

"You're in trouble, Kemosabe."

Scott smiled. "Crow, you know Kenzie?" he asked, nodding toward her.

Crow looked at her. His eyes were so dark. "No."

"Mackenzie Graham," she said, holding out her hand. "I work at the Academy."

"John Crowfeather. I help fulfill the minority quota at the Washington Field Office." He smiled and shook her hand. Then he pulled a small notebook out of his vest and began thumbing through it. "I'm not coming up with anything, Scott. The plumber's OK, roofers accounted for, gardener, electrician . . . everything looks legit. I'm headed to the office to start pulling files on the nanny and her family, but I had a couple of questions for the senator and his wife first. That's why I stopped by." He put the notebook back in his pocket.

Scott nodded. "All right. Mrs. Grable is sedated. Not sure how much you'll get from her. But the senator is around."

"What's the nanny's status?"

"Not doing well. Last I heard, she had some

52

kind of reaction to the stuff on that rag—chloroform or whatever it was. She may not make it."

Crow shook his head and stood up. "I'd sure like to talk to her. You have anything else for me?"

"No. We're quiet here."

"All right. I'll be in touch. Watch for the smoke signals." Crow winked at Kenzie.

Kenzie watched him reenter the house. "Is he from Arizona?"

"Yes, near Flagstaff. Raised on the Reservation, came to us through the Marine Corps."

"He seems nice."

"A great guy. My kids love him. I'm serious. You should get to know him." He poked her with his elbow.

She rolled her eyes.

Sunrise the next morning revealed the layout of the senator's backyard. As Kenzie had guessed, it contained an attractive garden with boxwoods, a small pond, and curved beds of perennials on either side of a flagstone walkway. The one nod to the child of the house was an outrageously bright climbing gym with an expensive foam base. The senator clearly didn't want his little girl hurt.

Her own father was like that—protective of her. But he also wanted her to be physically bold. He took her kayaking and climbing, taught her to throw a ball like a boy. Like her, he loved language, and while they hiked or ran he'd make up word puzzles or tell her about some new word he'd just learned. On dark winter nights, they'd play Scrabble, and she was just getting to the point where she could beat him once in a while, when he died, suddenly, unexpectedly, tragically.

Even now, when she thought about it, she felt a sinking sense of despair. What a shock it had been. Her parents had been arguing; her father had come out to the family room where she stood reaching for a book. He looked pale and shaken. She thought it was just the tension but then suddenly he doubled over, falling onto the Oriental carpet. She'd screamed for her mother, even tried doing CPR, but by the time the paramedics got there, her dad was gone, and she was alone, alone with the mother who'd never wanted her to begin with and in whose eyes she would never be good enough.

Oh, God. The thought of it still sent chills through her.

In response to her father's untimely death, Kenzie had accelerated her studies. Anxious to escape her home life, she graduated from high school at sixteen and from college at nineteen. By age twenty-three she was one of the youngest PhDs Georgetown University had ever produced.

Scott called her the "girl genius." She thought of herself as an escaped prisoner.

A motion caught her eye and interrupted her thoughts. Kenzie refocused on the screen of the door she'd been looking out of. A small black spider had caught a moth and was spinning a web around and around the moth's body. The moth, already paralyzed, was about to be hopelessly bound. Kenzie shivered and walked away.

Scott left to organize the teams working in the neighborhood. When he returned at 7:15 a.m., Kenzie was knee-deep in the database, analyzing the reports and making notes. "What's up?" Scott asked as he walked into the dining room.

"The Grables woke up. They're in his office. I'm looking for patterns and not seeing any yet. How'd you do?"

"I've got teams moving up and down the street, and over onto Wisconsin Avenue. They're getting security tapes from the businesses. There will be a lot to go through. I brought you breakfast." He put a bag down on the table in front of her.

She looked inside. "Greek yogurt, fresh fruit, and a granola bar. Good job! Thanks, Scott."

Kenzie's Bureau cell phone rang. She answered it and moved out from behind the computer so Scott could sit down. "OK, OK," she said. "Thanks, Marg."

Scott raised his eyebrows as Kenzie clicked her phone off. She grimaced. "I'll be right back."

Kenzie walked into the kitchen. She dialed her mother's number from her personal cell phone, wondering what "emergency" she had. Looking down the hallway, she saw Scott walk across the foyer. The next time he tried to talk to her about the sovereignty of God, she would ask him why God would let her father die and let her oh-so-difficult mother live. What kind of God would work that way?

"Hey, Mom, what's up?" she asked. Just after seven in the morning was too early for a conflict, right? Kenzie pressed the phone to her ear. "Yes, well, I'm on a case. Sorry. I didn't get your messages until midnight. What's the problem?" Talking with her mother felt like falling into the churning cauldron at the base of a waterfall. Kenzie had to fight to keep her head above water. "Yes. Yes. I know that. Look, Mom, Dad gave Aunt Cici the stock years ago—I mean, eighteen, nineteen years ago. What's the big deal? . . . No, no . . . he did it as a gift. He cared for her. She was his sister and he knew . . . Mom, listen, no, I won't do that."

In the middle of the battle, Kenzie heard the house phone ring. Scott emerged in the hallway and motioned to her. "C'mon, c'mon," he said.

"Mom, I've got to go. Now. Sorry. Look, I'll

talk to you about this later . . . Mom! I'll call you later." Kenzie snapped the phone off. "I'm going to pay for that," she muttered to herself. She raced to the office.

The senator, dressed in a blue-and-white nylon track suit, stood hovering over the clamoring instrument next to his wife. Beth had on Ralph Lauren jeans and a pink T-shirt. Both of them were gesturing anxiously, talking at the same time.

Scott held up his hands. "Wait . . . wait . . ."

Kenzie dashed in and grabbed a set of earphones. Both she and Scott would monitor the incoming call so they could coach the Grables if the kidnappers were on the line. In the van outside, agents would have recorders going.

On the fourth ring, Scott nodded. "Take it."

Grable picked up the phone. Everyone else fell silent. "Hello?" he said.

"Beth Grable, please," a woman's voice said.

"Just a minute." The senator swallowed hard and handed the phone to his wife. Scott silently counted down five seconds with his fingers. Then he pointed to her.

"This is Mrs. Grable." Beth's voice cracked.

"Mrs. Grable, this is Dr. Pinckney's office," the voice continued.

The pediatrician. An innocent call. Scott and Kenzie looked at each other and pulled off their headsets. They turned to leave.

"What? What does that mean?" Beth's question sounded almost like a wail.

Both agents turned around.

"She can't go to the hospital! You don't understand . . ." Beth dropped the phone. Her eyes fluttered back and she began falling. Scott moved quickly, grabbing her before she hit the floor. Kenzie helped him ease her down.

The senator snatched up the phone. "This is Bruce Grable, Zoe's father. What's going on?"

His voice became background noise as Kenzie and Scott worked to bring Mrs. Grable out of her faint. Another agent brought a glass of water and a cloth. "Ambulance?" he said.

"No, she's coming around," Kenzie replied, dabbing Mrs. Grable's forehead with the cloth. "Let's get her feet up."

"Is she all right?" Grable asked, hanging up the phone.

"She just passed out," Scott said. "What did the doctor say?" He stood up and faced the senator.

Grable's face looked drained. "Zoe has diabetes."

"What?"

"Type 1, insulin-dependent diabetes." The senator put his hand to his brow. "That's why the doctor's office called yesterday. He wanted her admitted to the hospital. Her blood sugar level was over five hundred. Do you know what this means? She could die!" Blood reddened his cheeks. He grabbed Scott's shirt. "For God's sake, man. You have to find her! Now!" Alarmed, Kenzie stood up, ready to intervene. "You have to find her!" the senator cried, shaking Scott.

Scott remained calm. "Take it easy, Senator." He reached up and removed the senator's hands.

"Bruce!" Mrs. Grable said, reaching for her husband. "Oh, Bruce!"

Grable went over to his wife. He knelt down next to her, grasping her hands in his. "I will not let her die. I swear. I will find her."

"Senator," Scott said, "I'd like to talk to that doctor, but I'll need your permission. Zoe's life could depend on it."

The senator took a deep breath. "I'll give you the number."

6

Fifteen minutes later, Scott stood in the sunroom with Kenzie. The sun streamed in, dancing off the yellows and greens of the fabric on the wicker furniture. Scott's face looked drawn. "We have a problem, don't we?" she said.

He nodded. "That out-of-control blood sugar is dangerous. The doctor said she needs to be in a hospital now." He rubbed his hand through his hair. "Nobody knew she had it! They just thought she had to go to the bathroom a lot. And maybe had the flu. But nobody suspected . . . nobody knew she had a disease that could kill her." Scott looked up and Kenzie could see the concern in his eyes.

Kenzie paced away. "So what's going to happen to her?"

"The biggest danger is something called 'diabetic ketoacidosis.' Sugar builds up in the blood, there's no insulin to break it down, ketones are released—the whole body gets messed up. She could go into a coma within hours and die."

"The symptoms?"

"Long term—increased thirst and urination. If ketoacidosis occurs, she'll have vomiting, drowsiness, abdominal pain, maybe difficulty breathing. Which sounds too much like those 'flu' symptoms Mrs. Grable took her in for." Scott shook his head. "I've got to get word out to our people: When we find her, she goes straight to the hospital. Will you help me with this?"

"Maybe whoever took her will recognize she's sick." As soon as she said it, Kenzie recognized her optimism as false. She felt grateful Scott didn't respond.

"I believe Crow is certified as an EMT. I want him to consult with the doc, and he'll definitely be on the first team in, whenever we get any idea of where she is. Remind me to call him," Scott said, rubbing his head. "By the way, what was the emergency with your mom?"

"With her, everything's an emergency." Kenzie rolled her eyes. "I'm sorry I let her intrude. It won't happen again." She sighed with frustration. "So where are we, Scott?"

He looked at the list of assignments he'd made on his computer. "I've got two teams checking security and traffic cameras in the area, one team doing another door-to-door in the neighborhood. I've got someone checking probation and parole to find out who the bad guys in the neighborhood are, including sex offenders. Crow is looking at the nanny's background." He took a deep breath. "And I've got someone checking for similar crimes all over the U.S."

Kenzie nodded pensively. "I'd like to work on

Beth Grable a little more. Jesse called the mah-jongg players, right? I'd like to visit them."

"What if the kidnapper calls when you're gone?"

"Have someone call me and patch it through to my Bureau cell phone. I'll be able to listen and then consult with you on my personal phone."

Scott nodded. "OK. Go for it. Just get the word out first about Zoe's diabetes. And I'll call Crow."

John Crowfeather knew just enough Spanish to get by, although he had to admit, the Salvadorans in D.C. had different accents than the Mexicans he was used to and he had a little trouble understanding them.

From what he'd learned so far, Nina Carmelita Valdez was an illegal alien who'd come to D.C. from El Salvador eight years ago. She'd worked for the senator for just a year; prior to that, she'd been a nanny for an undersecretary of state. A change in administration had sent him packing, and Senator Grable had been quick to pick her up.

Of course, it hadn't occurred to either of her employers that Nina Carmelita Valdez was in the U.S. illegally and therefore shouldn't have been working for them at all. Who knows? Maybe they used that little piece of information to control her. Crow wouldn't have put it past them.

But although she was in the country illegally, Nina had no criminal record, and Crow found nothing to raise suspicions about her. The fact that she'd been found with a pillowcase over her head containing a rag soaked in chloroform made him suspect she was innocent.

But what about her associates? Her boyfriend? Her other relatives? The people she might talk to in her neighborhood?

As he drove into Nina's Columbia Heights neighborhood, Crow's thoughts drifted back over the last twelve hours, to the call-out for the kidnapping, the assignments from Scott, the middle-of-the-night discussion in the senator's backyard. And as he pulled into a parking space, he wondered about the agent working with Scott. A forensic psycholinguist. What was that? An academic, he knew that much. Not his type. Not his type at all. Still, she looked pretty, he thought.

He turned off the motor and sat for a minute, watching the people on the street. He liked to get a feel for the neighborhood before he entered it, observing it the way he'd watched the mule deer he hunted on the Reservation for a long time before he took his shot. They were beautiful, and he hated having to kill them, but his grandfather had taught him well: Kill only what you need for food and use every part of the animal you can.

By all rights, he shouldn't have come to Columbia Heights alone, although his brown skin and black hair allowed him to get away with more than a white agent could. He wanted to be alone. Something was bothering him. He had some thinking to do. A partner would have interfered with that.

His eyes shifted to his hand, still on the steering wheel, and to the five-inch scar on his left arm. He touched it. A wild-eyed mustang, a bay mare he'd drawn to ride at an Indian rodeo, had pitched him into a poorly maintained corral fence. The fence had splintered under his weight, and a piece of wood had cut a gash in his arm, sending torrents of blood streaming down toward his hand.

Though just sixteen at the time, he could still remember his fascination as doctors in the Shiprock hospital emergency room cleaned and sutured that wound. The smell of the antiseptic, the neat black stitches, the sights and sounds of the ER stirred something within him that day. Most people look away when they're being stitched, but not John Crowfeather. He watched the doctor's every move.

Afterward, he finished his business with the mare. He went back to the rodeo grounds the next night when no one else was around and rode that mare, rode her bareback with just a rope halter to hang onto, rode her until she stood exhausted with her head down, nostrils streaming, her eyes no longer wild. The owner was none too happy when Wild Rose trotted placidly out of the gate the next day, calm as a pony. He couldn't figure it out. Crow heard he had sold her not long after that. He felt glad. He'd suspected the man had been abusing her anyway.

Crow gathered his notebook, put it in his pocket, and made sure he had a pen. He wore his gun on his side and his cell phone on his belt. When he'd taken the job at the Washington Field Office, his plan was to get as far away from the environment of the Rez as he could. Home was the high desert, far above sea level, in the windswept, canyon-scored, red-rock beauty of the American Southwest. Here, he lived in a city built on a swamp, buffeted by heat and humidity, his vision blocked by canyons of buildings or the towering trees of the Eastern hardwood forest, surrounded, not by Navajos, white cowboys, and Mexicans, but by a parade of faces in every different color imaginable. Here he could get lost in the sea of ethnicity, drifting with no expectations, no past, and no future. Which is just what he wanted.

Crow took a deep breath, opened his door, and stepped out into the world of Nina Carmelita Valdez.

Mah-jongg, Kenzie had discovered, had become popular with well-to-do white women, at least in ethnically diverse Washington. A social game, based solely on luck, it was good for the kind of chitchat some women loved. Kenzie had no time for it. At least bridge, which her mother had played every single week for as long as she could remember, required more thinking. But the social principle remained the same.

Beth Grable hung out with an elite group, the wives of Washington power brokers who lived in tony upper-Northwest D.C. They spent their days planning dinner parties and upscale charity fundraisers and driving their children around to the myriad of lessons considered must-dos in Washington society. Ballet. Piano. Tennis. Art. Soccer. There were also concerts at the Kennedy Center to attend, plays at Arena Stage, and openings at the art galleries dotting the city. Kenzie knew well the carousel of expected activities. She'd never had the desire to jump onto it.

Kenzie adjusted her navy blue blazer, handy for covering her gun, as she got out of the car at the first house, conscious that her cargo pants and boots would be considered quite out of style in the homes that she planned to visit. There were seven mah-jongg players, besides Beth. One of them lived in a stone house on Reno Road, another in an elegant row house off Wisconsin Avenue; two others were in blocky, porched, brick homes off Connecticut Avenue near the Washington Zoo. Kenzie mapped out a logical route and visited them one by one. By the time she interviewed her third player, she'd been exposed to enough designer fragrance to last a lifetime.

Washington heat and humidity, typical for August, defined the days. Traffic, especially around the zoo, seemed heavy. At one point, Kenzie wondered if she was wasting time covering the same ground that Jesse had the night before. But she knew sometimes a second interview would reveal something new. When Kenzie returned to her Bureau car after the sixth house, a fine glaze of sweat lay on her neck. One more to go.

Laura Barstow lived off of Wisconsin Avenue in a tall, narrow row house within sight of the Washington Cathedral. Growing up, Kenzie had had a friend who lived in a similar house nearby. In fact, she could envision the layout of the Barstows' home before she even stepped through the door.

"Mrs. Barstow?" Kenzie asked as a perfectly coiffed woman in her late thirties answered the doorbell. A silver toy poodle with a high-pitched bark danced around her feet.

"Yes?" The woman looked at her quizzically. She had bleached blonde hair pulled up in a French twist, gold earrings, and perfectly aligned white teeth.

"I'm Special Agent Mackenzie Graham, FBI. I wonder if I could talk to you for a moment." She showed the woman her creds.

Mrs. Barstow's mouth twitched slightly, but she recovered her poise and stepped aside. The poodle skittered around her feet. "Come in."

The interior layout looked exactly as Kenzie had envisioned it: small foyer, a stairway, then, to the right, the living room, dining room, and kitchen stretched out like train cars. In the kitchen would be a door leading to stairs going down to the basement, and a door to the outside.

Mrs. Barstow led the way to a pair of love seats covered in bright yellow-and-blue polished cotton facing each other in front of the fireplace. Between them stood an antique cobbler's bench that served as a coffee table, its rough wood contrasting beautifully with the smooth fabric of the love seats. A white area rug softened the light oak hardwood floors. White trim set off the sky blue walls. The room looked like a study in contrasts and the effect was striking. Kenzie thought of her own home: Every wall was painted antique white. The only paintings she had were cheap reproductions from the Smithsonian museum store. Her artifacts tended to be a couple of shattered skeets and an old copy of *Dog World* magazine.

"Sit down," Mrs. Barstow said, arranging herself on one of the love seats. The poodle jumped up and stood on her mistress's lap, her little black eyes focused intently on Kenzie.

As Kenzie sat down she could hear the muffled

sounds of gunfire—a video game being played downstairs. Mrs. Barstow, dressed in black Capris and a turquoise shell, stroked the little dog, which seemed wound up like a spring. "How can I help you?" the woman asked.

"I understand you were with Elizabeth Grable last night."

"That's correct. It was our mah-jongg night. But you already know that."

Kenzie shifted in her seat. Every time she moved, the dog barked. She wanted to soften things up, reduce the tension in the room. "Cute dog."

"She's a pain. My daughter wanted her. I didn't. Now I'm the only one Stella wants anything to do with." Mrs. Barstow sighed.

Kenzie smiled. "Well, she's adorable."

"Not if you have to clean up her messes."

As if on cue, the little poodle jumped off Mrs. Barstow's lap and ran toward the kitchen. Kenzie shifted the topic of conversation. "I don't know very much about mah-jongg. It must be fascinating, to keep you all interested week after week. Is it like bridge?"

"Much more fun." Mrs. Barstow seemed to relax as she began explaining the rules of the game. "We all take turns hosting. Whoever is the host gets to set the rules."

"They're not standard?"

"You can vary them. Beth likes to gamble, so

69

when we're at her house . . ." Mrs. Barstow stopped. She seemed suddenly aware that she might have revealed something negative. "Oh, I mean, the gambling isn't high stakes. It's just for fun. We set a limit."

"A limit?"

"No more than two hundred dollars. That way, nobody loses any serious money. There's no buy-in or anything."

Kenzie nodded and smiled sympathetically, trying to keep the woman talking. In her mind, though, two hundred dollars seemed like serious money.

"Anyway, we play and sometimes when we're done, Beth will read our fortunes."

"Read your fortunes?"

"Yes, with, you know, the mah-jongg tiles. She's really into it."

"OK. So how did Mrs. Grable seem last night?"

"Beth? Oh, Beth is always the most fun. I mean she is stuck, as we all are, in the Washington social scene. Everything so proper. Reporters everywhere. Constituents looking over your shoulder like you're their servants. It's hard. But Beth fights it. She won't give in to that pressure." Mrs. Barstow shook her head. "And you know, ever since Beau Talmadge reentered the scene, she's been high on life."

"Beau Talmadge?"

Mrs. Barstow colored. "You don't know about Beau Talmadge? I thought . . . oh my goodness." She covered her mouth with her hand.

Kenzie waited. Then she took a stab. "Is he the one from Georgia?"

Relief flooded the woman's face. "Yes. The college beau. No pun intended. He moved up here and suddenly Beth came to life. Not that they're having an affair," Mrs. Barstow explained quickly, "but you know, they're friends, and he has the time to do things Bruce isn't interested in."

"Like . . . ?"

"Like going places. Having fun. The kind of thing every woman needs."

Not quite every woman, Kenzie thought. She was getting tired of the foo-foo. "And where does Mr. Talmadge live?"

"Somewhere on the Hill. I don't know. He works for one of those think tanks. Or a lobby group. Sounds boring, but honestly, he is the most fun!" She hesitated. "And he is not the reason Beth went to see an attorney."

Kenzie forced herself to look nonchalant. "Yes, I guessed that," she said, thumbing through her notebook, pretending this was not new information.

"It was just to see what her rights were, you know? Every woman should know that."

Kenzie nodded. "In case of divorce."

"Of course."

The conversation turned to Zoe, and specifically Beth's feelings toward her little girl, which Mrs. Barstow characterized mostly as "concern" and "annoyance." Kenzie probed a little more. Just what kind of mother was Beth? From what Mrs. Barstow said, the answer seemed "maybe not the best." But would she kill her kid?

Fifteen minutes later, it became clear that Kenzie had milked the woman for all the information she could get. She thanked her and left, with the poodle nipping at her heels.

Driving back to the Grables' house, Kenzie called Scott. "I've got three things for you," she said. "A name, a lead, and information."

"Shoot."

"The name is Beau Talmadge. College boyfriend. Recently moved to the D.C. area. He and Beth have been seeing each other, just as friends, or so they say. He works for a think tank or a lobby group and lives on Capitol Hill."

"Terrific."

"The lead is this: Beth Grable has been to see a divorce attorney."

"Whoa."

She gave him the details.

"Thanks, Kenz. I'll get somebody on that."

"If somebody can find out where Talmadge lives, I'd like to follow up."

"Will do."

"One more thing: Mrs. Grable likes to gamble."

"Really."

"Yep. That may be a source of debt. I'll see you in fifteen minutes." Kenzie hung up, satisfied with her efforts. She had new, promising information and she'd come precipitously close to her mother's house on Woodley Road but had managed to avoid contact. Not bad for a morning's work.

He had spent his life in politics, working on the Hill, herding legislators like a border collie. He'd learned to anticipate their moves, outthink them, nip at their heels when he had to. He'd spent all of his energy trying to get the herd going in the right direction. It exhausted him, but he loved it. Loved it, until he woke up one morning and realized he, Grayson Chambers, was forty-five years old, unmarried, unattached, unappreciated, and unsung. An unsung hero, that's how he thought of himself.

Who had been responsible for the cable legislation that had opened up the market and earned investors millions? He had. Who had been responsible for highway funds being channeled into Illinois road projects? He had. Who had been responsible for the defense authorizations and homeland security bills that benefited the "clients" of his boss? He had.

And what did he have to show for it? Nothing. Not a thing.

He had begun to resent the long hours. The isolation. The lack of appreciation. When the senator hired a girl straight out of Northwestern, when he'd started grooming her to be equal to Grayson, it tipped the scale.

No one should have to take that. Not after what he'd seen. Not considering what he knew. And so he had left. But somehow the next job hadn't worked out. Not at all. Life was really not fair. Now he had to get even. This plan had been a year in the making. It had to be perfect. He believed it was imperative no one suspect him.

In the back, the little girl cried softly. Sandy comforted her. Why couldn't she get her to shut up? He had no idea kids were such a pain.

But this wouldn't take long. The senator would cave quickly. He knew his man.

As she walked up to the Grables' house, Kenzie nodded to the two D.C. police officers standing outside. She pushed open the front door and spotted Beth in the back, talking on her cell phone. She turned left, walked through the parlor and into the dining room. Scott had his phone to his ear, too. She waited for a moment but it was clear he would not get off soon. "I'm going to talk to Beth," Kenzie mouthed, and Scott nodded.

She walked back to the kitchen, where the senator's wife paced up and down.

When she saw Kenzie, Beth clicked the phone off, her eyes sparking with anger. "Well, did you have fun grilling my friends? I mean, what's that all about?"

"It's routine, Mrs. Grable."

"Well, it's an intrusion, an intrusion into my personal life."

"We're trying to find your daughter."

"Did you look at Bruce's friends, too? Now Bruce, he's got some winners on his list, let me tell you."

Kenzie interrupted her. "Mrs. Grable, can we talk? In the sunroom?"

Beth stared at her for a moment. "Come on," and she led the way.

Perfectly made up, dressed in a flowery summer dress and pearls, Beth Grable looked more like a woman about to go shopping at Filene's than a mother whose daughter was missing. Clearly, Beth focused on looking good. Kenzie tucked a strand of her own hair behind her ear.

She asked Beth again about the evening Zoe disappeared, the time she left, her instructions to the nanny, how long she was gone, about any uncomfortable encounters with strangers.

Beth answered her questions directly but seemed irritated at being interviewed again. She fidgeted with her pearls, picked a thread off her dress, and snapped at Kenzie periodically. "I mean, it's enough you all are here, in my home, but now you're interrogating my friends? Listening to my calls? I have no privacy!"

You have a missing daughter, Kenzie thought. *What else matters more?* Then she popped the big question. "Tell me about Beau Talmadge."

She thought Beth Grable would explode. "You have no right . . . !"

"It's for Zoe, Mrs. Grable."

"He's a friend, that's all. Just a friend." The tendons in Mrs. Grable's neck popped out.

"I'm sure of that. But I'd like to talk to him. Could you give me his phone number?"

Beth fumed. Suddenly, Scott appeared at the door of the sunroom, his face intense, and motioned to Kenzie. "Excuse me, Mrs. Grable," Kenzie said. "I'll be right back."

7

"What's up?" she asked Scott, following him back into the dining room.

He kept his voice low. "Crow found something." He glanced past Kenzie to make sure no one remained in earshot. "The nanny is an illegal alien. Her sister, who lives over on Columbia Road, is here on a green card. But the sister's boyfriend is a sex offender. Someone saw him yesterday with a little blonde girl."

She looked up at Scott. "So what are we doing?"

"Crow is in the process of finding out where the guy is." As if on cue, Scott's cell phone rang. As he took the call, Senator Grable, red-faced, entered the dining room.

"Miss Graham," he said pointing his finger at her, "I need to talk to you."

Scott turned away, struggling to hear his phone.

"Senator, let's go into your office," Kenzie said. She followed him, her neck already tense. Once there, she closed the door. "What's the problem?"

"My wife says you're harassing her and I want it to stop."

"What do you mean by 'harassing'? I've asked her a few questions, Senator, that's all." Kenzie's face felt hot.

"You're badgering her. Interrogating her friends. And I'm telling you, she had nothing to do with Zoe's disappearance. You cut it out!" Grable's blue eyes sparked with anger. "She's off limits!"

"No one's off limits in a federal investigation, sir." Kenzie's heart pounded. She crossed her arms. "You know your wife pretty well, Senator?" Kenzie asked.

"Of course!"

"Do you know she's been to see an attorney? A divorce attorney?"

Shock flashed onto his face. The senator's eyes searched hers, trying to detect any chance of a bluff. When Kenzie stood her ground, he suddenly turned, walked to his desk, and sagged into his chair.

Kenzie walked toward him. "I'm sorry, Senator."

Suddenly, he looked old and sad. He put his hand to his mouth, and stared at the penholder on his desk. He sighed. "I guess I'm not totally surprised."

Kenzie rested her hands on his desk and leaned toward him. "I'm going to check out everything I can to find Zoe," she said softly, "even if it embarrasses or offends some people. Zoe's worth it, don't you think?"

A glint of tears appeared in his eyes. He waved his hand. "Do anything you need to do. I just want . . ." he stopped, catching a sob in his throat.

"Kenzie!" Scott called out.

"Excuse me," she said to the senator. "I need to go." And she quickly left the office.

"You want to come with us? Or stay here?" Scott asked, after telling her what Crow had found.

"I want to go."

"Vest up, then," Scott said quietly, strapping his gun to his leg.

"Are you going to tell them?" she asked.

"Yes."

Seconds later, Scott stood in Grable's office, facing the couple who stood stiffly side by side, like intimate strangers. Scott wore khaki cargo tactical pants and a navy blue shirt covered by a blue tactical vest with bold white letters proclaiming "FBI." A broad black strap secured his gun holster to his leg. "We're getting a search warrant now," he said. "The man lives off Kalorama Road, in the third floor apartment in a Victorian row house. There's a back stair leading up to his place, so he has the perfect opportunity to go in and out with no one noticing. He parks in a small garage behind the row house, goes in through the alley, and up the stairs."

"And how exactly does he know Nina?"

"He is the boyfriend of her sister."

"And a sex offender." The senator spit the words out.

"And he's been seen with a little blonde girl."

"I told you to fire her!" his wife snapped. "Why didn't you listen to me? You never listen to me."

The senator rubbed his hand through his hair.

Scott actually felt sorry for him. "I'll call you when we know something," the agent said. "We need to roll."

"Ride with me," Scott said, motioning Kenzie toward his Bucar, his Bureau car. It wouldn't be a long trip—barring one of D.C.'s traffic jams they'd be on Kalorama in fifteen minutes.

Kenzie climbed in and buckled her seatbelt. The ballistic vest felt uncomfortable. So would being dead. She adjusted it and turned the air conditioning vent toward her face. Stress gripped her. "Fill me in, Scott," she said as he turned onto Wisconsin Avenue. "How are we doing this?"

"We've got three teams. There's just one door into his apartment, and one access from the outside of the building, off the back alley. We'll have one team out front, one in the alley, and one will go up the stairs." He braked as traffic stopped. "You can stay with me if you want. But if you do, I want you behind me."

"OK."

"OK, then it's you, me, Crow and three others. We'll go in with the ram, and . . ."

"We know he's home?"

"He's there."

The two were silent for a moment as Scott swiftly negotiated the narrow streets of Northwest D.C. Kenzie's stomach knotted. This would be the second raid she'd been on in her entire career. Just the second one, confirming her boss's assessment. She had very little street experience.

The other time, she'd been assigned to one of the rear teams. Now Scott said he'd let her get up close and personal. How would she feel? Could she handle it? The aggression, the danger, the noise, the fear?

Kenzie looked over at Scott. His brown eyes stayed focused straight ahead. "Look, if you're going to pray, keep your eyes open, OK?" She plastered on a goofy smile to signal she was kidding.

He ignored her attempt at humor. "Every time we go out I pray. Every time. Are you worried?"

"Me? No, not at all." She turned toward her window, swallowing her deception.

Scott took a right turn. His cell phone rang. As he spoke into it, his frown intensified. "How bad? Did she cry? Which hospital?" Tension filled his voice. Kenzie watched him carefully. "Thank you. Tell her I love her and I'll come see her as soon as I can."

"What's up?" Kenzie asked.

"My wife called to tell me my daughter, Cara,

fell out of a tree. Lisa thinks her arm is broken."

"Do you need to go to them?"

"Lisa will have to handle it," he said, his jaw flexing with tension, his hand forming a fist on the steering wheel. "It's not the first time."

Kenzie looked out of the window. Lisa was an attractive brunette, a former nurse who now stayed home with their two kids. They seemed to be doing all right, but Kenzie knew being an agent worked hardships on families. The divorce rate among law enforcement officers was very high. The stresses of the job and the inability to leave it at the end of the day combined with the worry and loneliness of the spouse left at home made marriage difficult.

"Cara's very active." Scott turned a corner.

"Maybe she'll want to be an agent."

He shot her a look. "That's exactly what she says. She lines up her stuffed animals on the couch, and jumps out from behind the chair yelling, 'FBI, FBI! Drop your gun!' Then she blows them away." Scott raised his eyebrows. "Apparently, her subjects always resist arrest."

Kenzie laughed.

"It drives her mother crazy."

The two dozen agents who would be involved in the raid had gathered in a hotel parking lot near the target location. After listening to Scott's plan, they moved quickly to their cars. Surprise and overwhelming force were their main weapons, safety their main concern.

Crow questioned Kenzie's involvement. "She's a linguist," he said to Scott when the two of them were by themselves. "What's she going to do, talk the guy to death?"

Scott cut him off. "She can handle herself, plus she's fluent in Spanish. She's coming. Deal with it."

From across the parking lot, Kenzie saw them talking, saw Crow glance in her direction, frowning. What was he saying? She tossed her head and tightened her vest straps. She had no intention of letting on just how nervous she felt.

An ugly shade of yellowish beige covered the stucco surface of the row house. Trash littered the front yard, enclosed by a falling-down iron fence.

The group in the rear of the house, with Scott carrying the battering ram, moved in first. The front team would attract more attention, and so it waited to approach the house until the back crew was in place. When they got the signal, they positioned themselves so they had control over the front door and the suspect's apartment front window.

"All right," Scott said in a low voice, and he and his squad moved up the back stairs. Kenzie stood right behind him. Her hair was damp with sweat, her body alive with adrenaline. The rustling of their raid jackets and the thumping of their feet seemed amplified in the narrow stairwell. The stifling heat made it difficult to breathe.

The subject's apartment door had three locks on it, no peephole. According to plan, Crow knocked loudly on the door. "Mr. Lopez? Open up, FBI!" He repeated it in Spanish.

They counted twenty seconds. On signal, two agents heaved the heavy ram once, twice, and the door shattered. Scott and Crow, guns drawn, shouting "FBI! FBI!" stepped in.

Emilio Ernesto Lopez jumped to his feet.

"Get on the floor, get on the floor!" Scott shouted.

Instead, Lopez tried to run.

Where's he going? Kenzie's mind raced along with her feet as she followed Scott and Crow after the man, into the kitchen. She saw Lopez grab something off of the counter. "Gun!" she screamed.

Lopez was halfway out of the window before Scott had his hands on him. Then Kenzie heard a muffled boom, the sound of gunfire. "Scott!" she yelled, raising her gun. She had no clear shot.

"I'm OK," Scott said, hauling the man back into the kitchen and cuffing him as he dragged him to the floor.

Crow stood next to him, his gun trained on the suspect, bleeding from a massive wound to the gut. "Call an ambulance!"

Kenzie realized he had directed that command at her. Hands shaking, she holstered her gun and made the call.

"Where's the girl? Where's the girl, Lopez?" Scott yelled at the man.

"*Donde está la chica*?" Crow repeated. But Emilio Ernesto Lopez's life was draining out onto the floor in a spreading pool of blood.

Kenzie's head spun. She couldn't take her eyes off the body before her. "Did you shoot him?" she asked Scott.

He shook his head. "He shot himself. Clear the rest of the apartment."

Kenzie snapped out of her daze and, with other agents, paced through the rest of the rooms. "Clear! Clear!" they announced, declaring each room empty.

But what about the girl? Where was she?

They entered a bedroom last. A double bed mattress lay on the floor. Magazines and DVDs lay nearby. The bedcovers were askew. An old, cheap TV on a stand and a DVD player stood at one end of the room, across from a large chest-on-chest.

The other agents left after peering under the mattress and into the closet. But something held Kenzie there. Something felt wrong. But what? A drip of sweat ran down her back. She stared at the chest-on-chest. It looked like it covered a door. Why would anyone cover a door?

Kenzie felt Crow's eyes on her. Heart drumming, she said, "Help me move this."

It took both of them to do it. Then Kenzie carefully opened the door. Behind it was a second closet, empty—except for a pile of clothes on the floor. Kenzie reached up for a string and pulled on the light. Her eyes widened. From under the clothes, a little foot protruded. She froze. "Oh, no!"

Crow pulled her back, moved past her, and squatted down. He reached out and touched the foot, then he stood up and shouted, "Scott!"

Zoe? Dead? Kenzie fought to keep from showing her emotions. She stared at the pile of clothes and the little foot. Then her eye caught some movement. A spider scurried across the pile that covered the body. Stomach acid rose in Kenzie's throat.

"Are you OK?" Crow asked.

She choked it back. "Fine."

Scott brought in an evidence tech team. When they uncovered the little girl's body, her blonde hair was spread over the dirty floor like a sunburst. Kenzie gritted her teeth.

Crow stood next to her. "You don't look good," he said quietly.

"Just hot." She turned away and as she did, she had to catch her balance. Crow steadied her and she felt herself flush with embarrassment.

"Here," Crow said, handing her a stick of gum. "It helps."

Her face burning, she took it.

The medical examiner, a crusty old man with white hair, showed up an hour later. He approached Scott. "Approximate age five. White, female. Dead about two hours. She has bruises on her neck. Strangled, possibly. I suggest you get the Grables down to the morgue."

Two agents would bring the Grables downtown. Scott told Crow and Kenzie to stay behind and supervise the rest of the crime scene investigation, but Kenzie insisted on coming with him to the morgue. "Somebody needs to be there for Mrs. Grable," she said. He shrugged and agreed.

The bright summer day seemed an incongruity with what Kenzie had just seen as Scott negotiated the narrow streets on their way to North Capitol Street NE. The muscles in his jaw worked overtime. The suspect killed himself. A child was dead. And he'd just called his wife and found that Cara had a compound fracture of her left arm and would soon be in surgery.

Not a good day, thought Kenzie. She aimed the car air conditioner so it blew full force on her face. She felt glad she hadn't passed out. It had been close. She blamed it on the bulletproof vest.

Scott turned right only to find himself blocked

by a double-parked delivery truck. He glanced over at her. "Are you feeling all right?"

"Fine," she replied in her most professional voice, and she felt a tremor pass through her. She turned to stare out of her window, visions of Emilio Ernesto Lopez and a little dead child playing over and over in her head. Then there were flashbacks, surges of emotional memory, intrusive thoughts. And questions, lots of questions. Why'd the little girl die? Was she dead before her killer threw her in the closet? What did he do to her before that? And where, pray tell, was God? Watching?

8

The D.C. morgue sat near Union Station on North Capitol Street. The senator stood waiting for them in the lobby. His wife elected to stay at home, sedated, he said. Kenzie felt glad. Grable had changed into a suit and, except for his haggard face, he looked ready to meet the press. Had they been notified, Kenzie wondered?

"How does this go?" he asked Scott, his voice trembling slightly.

The agent took a deep breath. "Dr. Marcus will call us in. They'll have the body on a table, covered, and pull back just enough for you to see her face." He hesitated. "The body was not, uh, mutilated in any way. Preliminary indications are that she was strangled."

The senator winced. Then he nodded. Kenzie had to admire his courage.

The door opened and Dr. Marcus stuck his head out. He motioned with his hand. "Come on," he said, gruffly.

Scott led the procession, followed by the senator, then Kenzie. The other agents would wait in the lobby. The smell of the morgue got to Kenzie immediately; the chemicals made her head spin.

She'd been in a morgue before, but this felt different, much more intense. At the end of the room, a woman in a lab coat worked on the body of a young black man. Closer to the door, in a fiberglass tray on a stainless steel table, lay a smaller body, covered with a white sheet.

They walked toward it. The senator stopped abruptly. "It's not her!" he said.

Kenzie's heart thumped. She looked at him.

"Look!" Grable pointed. The child's tiny hand lay exposed. He looked at Kenzie. "She always wears nail polish. Can't go without it. Pink. It's got to be pink. Pink nail polish. It's not Zoe!"

Poor guy, Kenzie thought.

"Senator," Scott said gently, "let's take a closer look." He touched the senator's arm.

"The victim's face may look swollen," the medical examiner warned. He lifted the sheet off the child's face.

Grable shook his head violently. "It's not her." He took two steps back and turned away. "It's not Zoe."

Kenzie looked at Scott. How could there be two missing white five-year-old girls in D.C. on the same day? Scott raised his eyebrows, then moved his head almost imperceptibly toward the senator. Kenzie nodded. She moved toward Grable and touched his arm. "Senator, let's be sure. Will you look again?"

"It's not her! I'm telling you, it's not her!"

"Please, Senator, just one more time, just to be sure."

Grable hesitated, then relented. He moved toward the autopsy table, and looked again at the face of the child. "No, no. No." He turned to Kenzie, his face resolute. "This is not my child." His eyes narrowed. "I told you about the mole she has, didn't I?" The senator pointed to a place just in front of his right ear. "She calls it her kissing spot. I kiss her goodnight there, every night I'm home. This is not my child. You look for yourself. You'll see."

"Doctor?" Kenzie asked.

On cue, the medical examiner moved the child's hair aside and looked at her right ear. He shrugged. "No mole."

Tears welled up in the senator's eyes. He pulled a handkerchief from his back pocket and wiped them, then blew his nose.

Scott nodded. "Thank you, sir," he said to the doctor, and he put his hand on the senator's shoulder.

Grable shrugged him off.

Kenzie and Scott drove back to the Grables' house. The glare from the summer day glinted off of windshields and shimmered up from the asphalt road. Kenzie had a headache, one she figured she had earned.

She rested her head back on the seat, images

91

from the day playing over and over again in her mind. The heat of the stairwell in Lopez's house had been oppressive, the tension like nothing she'd ever felt. Her body felt tight, as if encased in a pressure suit. Now, she felt drained, washed out, as if she'd just run twenty miles.

"I would have thought Grable would be happy," she said to Scott, pulling herself out of her thoughts.

Scott shrugged. "He is. But he's also an angry father."

She bit her lip.

"You did well, Kenzie. Are you OK?"

"Sure." She turned toward him. "The child in the closet—why did Lopez think he could just hide her body, like a pair of outworn jeans, in a pile of clothes? What was he thinking?"

"About himself. And the problem is, we can't rule him out in our case," Scott said, shifting his weight in his seat. "He killed one little girl. He could have killed Zoe."

"Two in twenty-four hours?"

"Who knows?" Scott sighed. "I've asked Marcy Lake to follow that line." An experienced agent, Marcy had a background in child sexual abuse. Kenzie had consulted with her on another case. "She'll track Lopez's movements over the last forty-eight hours, see if we can put him near the Grables," Scott said. "If I had to guess, I'd say Lopez had nothing to do with Zoe's disappearance. He got in a jam. He got this little girl in his apartment, and things got out of hand. He killed her accidentally."

"You think?"

Scott nodded.

Ahead of them a bread delivery truck had double-parked. Scott checked his rearview mirror and waited until he could get around it. "How do you deal with this?" Kenzie asked him as he pulled around the truck.

"What?"

"You're a father. How can you stand to see what people do to children?" The minute the sentence left her mouth, Kenzie realized more smoldered in her head than even she would admit.

Scott hesitated. He looked thoughtful, like he was carefully considering his response. "If some scumbag hurt Cara I could easily kill him," he finally admitted. "If I were Grable right now I'd probably be on the streets with a gun, ready to shake down anybody I figured could even be remotely involved. And if I found the guy . . . he'd wish he were dead. I'd tear him apart with my bare hands and enjoy doing it."

Kenzie looked at Scott. He looked dead serious.

"Nobody messes with my family. But this," he said, gesturing, "this is my job. I have to compartmentalize. I have to stay logical, shove my feelings behind a wall, and be sure I stay within the law. It's like a chess game, or a military maneuver. There's too much riding on it for me to let my emotions have any play." Scott glanced at her. "What lets me do so is this: My anger is nothing compared to what these scumbags are going to get from God. You know that Scripture, 'If anyone causes one of these little ones to stumble, it would be better if a millstone were hung around his neck . . .' It's what I think about. God is not going to let this go unpunished. And God's anger . . ." Scott shook his head, "is nothing I'd want to face."

"But why didn't he just stop it?" Kenzie said, her words tart on her tongue.

Scott looked at her carefully. "I don't know. But I do know this: He knows and understands pain. He hates evil. Why he doesn't act sometimes, I don't know. I can give you the philosopher's answer, but on days like today, it rings kind of hollow. All I know is he promises one day his justice will come. It'll all be made right. Even for that dead little girl."

Kenzie had nothing to say to that. It didn't make sense to her: Why promise things would be right in the sweet by-and-by? Why not now? How much trauma did this little girl have to endure?

Scott continued driving and Kenzie laid her head back on the headrest. Fatigue had given way to exhaustion and soon sleepiness tinged the edges of her vision. "You know what I want more than anything?" she said.

"What?"

"A shower and some strawberry sorbet."

Scott laughed. He started telling her a story about his family, about the last time they'd gone somewhere together. Something about getting gelato at an Italian ice place near their house. His baritone voice sounded soothing and soon it grew distant, his words muddled, their edges rounded and fuzzy. The next thing Kenzie knew, he was shaking her awake. "C'mon, Kenzie," he said, "we're here."

The Grables were in the family room. The senator had his arm around Beth, and for an instant, Kenzie wondered if maybe this trauma would bring them together. Maybe it would make their marriage better.

Then Beth Grable opened her mouth. "You all scared me to death," she said, glaring at the two agents, "believing it was my child. Bruce, with all your alleged power, I'd think you could demand some better investigators."

The senator's eyes met Kenzie's. She saw his frustration. He removed his arm from around his wife.

Scott said, "We are continuing to view Lopez as a possible suspect. But I'm glad for you the little girl was not Zoe."

The senator wiped his hand across his brow. "All right, Hansbrough. Where do we go from here? So far, what you're doing doesn't seem to be working. You got any other game plan?"

Kenzie saw the muscles in Scott's jaw twitch. Grable was trying to regain some control in front of his wife, but it didn't play well with her partner. "Senator," Scott said, "right now my eleven-year-old daughter is in surgery, having a compound fracture in her right arm set. I can assure you, I'd much rather be there with her, and with my wife, than standing in this room." Scott put his hands on his hips. "I'm here, Senator, because at least I know where my daughter is. You don't, and I'm doing everything I can to change that. I wouldn't be here if I thought we were spinning our wheels."

Grable exhaled and Kenzie could see he knew he'd overstepped. A loud knock on the front door interrupted the conversation. An agent stuck his head in. "Scott? There's a delivery for the senator."

Scott looked at Kenzie then back at the Grables. "Are either of you expecting a package?"

"No," they said in unison.

The two agents headed for the front door with the Grables right behind them. Behind the agent stood a deliveryman in a brown uniform holding a box in his hands. Grable rushed to take it.

"Senator! Don't touch that!" Scott yelled, grabbing Grable's arm and controlling his forward progress. Still holding the senator, Scott faced him. "We have to check it. It could be anything."

Chagrined, Grable nodded.

Scott let go of him and jerked his Bureau radio off of his belt. "Dispatch a bomb squad to 3217 27th Street Northwest," he said.

"What? What now?" Beth Grable wailed. She tried to move past Kenzie.

"Hold on, Mrs. Grable," Kenzie said, restraining her. "Let us take care of this."

"Put the box down gently on the front walk out there, away from the house," Scott told the deliveryman. He flashed his creds. "I'd like to see the shipping orders on that, please." He moved the man down the sidewalk, toward his truck. "Stay back," he yelled to the Grables.

While Scott was dealing with the deliveryman, Kenzie looked at the package. It was addressed to Senator Grable. The return address was from out of state. "You know anybody in Chambersburg, Pennsylvania?" she called out.

The senator shook his head.

Thirty minutes later a robot from the bomb squad was handling the package, first X-raying it, then using sensors to check for explosives. Finally, when the squad leader seemed satisfied that no explosive or chemical devices were apparent, he asked Scott if he wanted them to destroy it or open it up.

Kenzie knew the safest thing would be to let

them destroy it. But what if evidence lay inside? Or a note?

"Open it, if you can do so without undue risk," Scott said, wiping a drop of sweat off his face with his sleeve. The afternoon sun seemed white hot.

"All right. You go inside and move away from the windows," the bomb squad leader said.

"I'd like to watch," Scott said.

"No, sir. We'll tell you what we find."

The discomfort of a ballistic vest is nothing compared to the heat generated by a bomb suit. Bomb techs call it "the stupid suit." Once in it, their vision, hearing, and physical agility became so limited they would feel stupid and clumsy.

"All right?" the squad leader asked the tech who had suited up.

He nodded his helmeted head.

The leader had given Scott and Kenzie the frequency of their communications channel and would give them a play-by-play as the bomb squad opened the box. The police had closed off the street and warned the neighbors, and now a man in a hundred-pound suit was about to discover what the mysterious package contained.

"The box is twelve by twelve by fifteen," the tech said into his microphone. "No outer wrapper. We collected several latent finger-prints from the exterior. Probably belong to the delivery company's employees, but we'll see." Sweat beaded on Kenzie's forehead as she stood next to Scott in the Grables' foyer, listening on the radio.

"The box is sealed with clear package sealing tape. I'll save it so we can send it to the lab. OK," the voice continued, "I'm opening the flaps. There's no packing, no peanuts or newspaper or anything inside, just . . . just . . ."

Kenzie's heart stopped. Just what?

". . . just about eight inches worth of blonde hair. A whole head of hair."

Kenzie followed Scott as he jogged down the front walk.

"No, no!" Beth started screaming as she emerged from the house and saw the hair. The senator took her arm, but she pulled away.

"What do you think?" Scott asked the senator, who stared at the hair in the bomb tech's hands.

"Yeah. It could be hers. Could definitely be hers." Grable's voice cracked.

"Scott," Kenzie said, "let's see if we can get a rush DNA scan." She turned to the distraught parents. "The evidence team already took Zoe's hairbrush. I'd like to collect some strands of hair from the two of you as backup." She ushered them back inside.

Scott had the tech put the hair in an evidence bag, labeled with date and time, and sign it. He collected the tape and the box itself, and the fingerprints taken off the box. He'd have another agent run all of the evidence down to the lab at Quantico.

Kenzie came back outside to where Scott stood. "So he may have cut off her hair," she said quietly. "We'll have to change the BOLO."

"And we'll have to tell our people he may be trying to pass her off as a boy."

Kenzie shook her head. "This is so sadistic."

9

"Just tell her no!" Grayson barked. "She can't have pink nail polish!" Every word seemed emphasized, like the bang . . . bang . . . bang of a pistol repeating.

The little girl wailed louder, burying her head in the blanket she clutched.

"But Grayson, she gets so upset when I try to take it off!"

Sandy looked like she wanted to start wailing, too. That's all he needed, two hysterical females. "For crying out loud. Give it to me." He grabbed the cotton and the nail polish remover from Sandy's hand, sat down on the couch, and tried to pull Zoe's hand away from the blanket. "Come on, honey, this won't hurt," he tried crooning but it soon became apparent Zoe wasn't going to cooperate. Gray cursed. He resolutely unscrewed the cap of the nail polish remover bottle, doused a cotton ball, and set the bottle on the coffee table.

"Come here!" he said, and he grabbed the little five-year-old's hand.

Zoe screamed. She fought. She tried to bite him.

"Give me your hand!" Gray commanded.

The little girl screamed louder. Sandy put her hands over her ears.

"Give it to me!" Gray tried prying Zoe's fingers off the blanket. "Let go! Let go!"

The screams increased. Zoe twisted around and tried to kick him. Frustrated, Gray threw down the cotton ball, picked Zoe up by her upper arms, and held her up in the air. He shook her, and said, "Shut up! You shut up, do you hear me?"

And Zoe threw up all over him.

Grayson flew into a rage. He threw Zoe back down on the couch and turned away, wiping his eyes with his arm, but he knocked over the nail polish remover as he did and the smelly liquid spread all over the coffee table and spilled onto the floor. "You take care of this!" he screamed to Sandy. "Clean it up!" And he ran back to the shower.

Sandy stood motionless for a moment. Zoe lay on the couch, sobbing and hiccuping. Sandy found some towels and began gently cleaning the little girl's face. "It's all right, baby. It'll be all right," she said. She stroked Zoe's newly shorn head. The poor little thing. Why did Grayson have to be so rough with her? How would he like it if someone cut his hair off? "We'll work it out."

The nail polish remover had stripped the finish off a large swath of the dark pine coffee table. Serves him right, Sandy thought, as she began sopping it up. Zoe lay curled up on the couch, sucking her thumb. After returning from the kitchen where she'd rinsed her rag for the third time, Sandy noticed the little girl had fallen off to sleep. Her hands were relaxed and visible. And Sandy thought for a moment of putting some of the remaining nail polish remover on a cotton ball and taking the polish off the little girl's hands now, while she was unlikely to wake up. But no. She stopped herself. Zoe had fought for those pink nails. She'd won. She deserved the little bit of her own personality she had left.

Gray would just have to deal with it.

Kenzie reentered the Grables' house. Her shirt had plastered itself to her back and her hair felt damp and stringy around her face. She got a big glass of water from the kitchen, downed it, and moved into the dining room.

She could hear Scott talking to the Grables in the senator's study. He'd already dispatched an agent to take the evidence to the lab. This late in the afternoon, it would be a two-hour drive at least.

Kenzie would resume where she'd left off earlier in the afternoon: checking out Mrs. Grable's friend Beau Talmadge. She stood in the dining room, searching Scott's database for information.

Fifteen minutes later, Senator Grable walked in, his face weary. "What a day," he said, blowing out a breath.

"Yes, sir."

He had changed back into his nylon athletic suit and in an instant, looking at him, Kenzie could almost see his history: High school football star, college fraternity president, successful politician, and now a man who'd seen his world fall apart in the space of less than twenty-four hours. For all of his past achievements and even his huge mistakes, now he was just a dad who missed his little girl, a husband plagued by his own inadequacy in the face of a family crisis.

"Look, I'm sorry if I got a little testy." The senator sat down heavily in a chair. He rubbed his hands together and tented them in front of his face "Why the hair?" His words were sparse, like he could hardly stand to articulate his question. He looked at Kenzie, his eyes pleading. "He's a pervert, isn't he?"

She sat back and studied his face, the face of a frustrated, terrified father. "I think the kidnapper is trying to scare you. I think he's trying to disguise Zoe. And I think we're going to find out what he wants from you very soon."

Grable raised his eyebrows.

"Look at it this way." Kenzie leaned forward. "It's true: We can't rule out the idea that this is a sexual crime. But if this were that, if some predator had grabbed Zoe for that reason, why would he bother tweaking you? He'd have what he wants, and he wouldn't risk being ID'd

104

through the package. This guy doesn't want Zoe—he wants YOU. Zoe's just a way to get to you." She sounded convincing, even to herself.

A spark of hope flickered in Grable's eye.

"Think about it: If a sexual predator wants a kid he can grab one off the street, from a store, at a playground, anywhere kids go. Why would somebody case out a house—go to all the trouble of planning an abduction? It's too risky! He could have been surprised by someone else in the house; he could have failed to knock Nina out completely, a gazillion things could have gone wrong." Kenzie could see the impact of her words in his demeanor. "No, Senator. This is all about you. Someone's trying to get at you. That's why I'm so interested in the people who've had dealings with you."

Grable sighed and looked beyond Kenzie, to a picture on the wall behind her. In her mind, she could see it: A Georgia O'Keefe–style oil painting of magnolia blossoms. She watched his face. His eyes flickered back to her. "Is he really the best?"

Kenzie leaned forward. "Scott? He's very aggressive, and very smart. A terrific leader. And he has a heart. He has kids of his own. He empathizes with you."

Grable grimaced. "With a crook?"

Kenzie had to resist the impulse to reach out and take his hand. "With a father."

He leaned forward, his elbows on his knees, staring at the floor. After a time, he spoke. "She spends an awful lot of money," he said softly.

Kenzie stayed quiet.

"Designer clothes, trips, the gambling . . ."

"Gambling?"

"Oh, yes. Atlantic City, Vegas, Foxwoods Casino . . . she does them all. And when she can't go anywhere else, she heads for Maryland Live!"

"So there's debt."

"A lot of debt." He looked up and gestured with both hands. "This house, it just sucks money. But you know," he looked at Kenzie, "I love her. I don't want another divorce."

"But you don't know what to do."

He shrugged. "She doesn't see it as a problem. So she won't get help."

Kenzie leaned toward him. "You know, Senator, it might help us find Zoe if we knew the names of the people with whom you've had financial dealings."

"I've had to borrow and borrow, just to keep up."

"That must be very frustrating."

"But what can I do? What can I do? If I divorce her, she'll get Zoe. That happened with my older kids. I missed their childhoods. Missed the soccer games, missed the proms, missed all the day-to-day stuff. I don't want to miss that again." He sighed. "So I have to, you know, get along."

"Including covering the debt."

He snorted. "Trying to, anyway."

"How'd you meet her?"

"Beth's father was a big-deal lawyer from Atlanta. Met him on business several times. One time we were all on a golf trip, a whole bunch of us, and then she showed up, saying, 'Daddy, who are these fine gentlemen undercutting your game?' That old-fashioned Southern charm. I just never knew," he hesitated, "I never knew behind it lay a thoroughly modern woman, independent, strong-willed, and bent on spending me into the grave."

"Her father was rich?"

"Very rich. Only he lived rich, and when he died, he didn't leave much. Beth's mother . . . she's pretty destitute, by their standards, anyway." Suddenly the senator sat up straight. "Look, Miss Graham . . ."

"Kenzie's fine."

"Kenzie, you must be tired. We have a bedroom, a guest room, on the third floor. It has a full bath . . . shower, everything. Sometimes . . . sometimes, my staff would stay up there if we were working late here. Feel free to use it."

"That's very kind of you, Senator."

"The door to it is next to Zoe's room."

"Thank you."

The senator stood up and began to walk slowly out of the room.

"Senator!" She stopped him. He turned to look at her. "Don't give up. My best guess is we'll be hearing from the kidnapper very soon."

He simply nodded.

The news that the nanny, Nina Carmelita Valdez, had died shocked even Scott and Kenzie. "Apparently, she had a reaction to the chemical the UNSUB used, or maybe it was the stress. In any event, her heart failed and she died an hour ago," Scott said, repeating the message he'd gotten from Jocelyn at the hospital.

"So now, we have kidnapping and felony murder charges," Kenzie replied. She focused on the beautiful Oriental carpet as she thought. "This kidnapper is getting in deeper."

Scott sighed heavily. "It isn't going to make it easier to find him, that's for sure. He has less and less to lose." He picked up his attaché case. "Kenz, I need you to handle things here. I'll be back as soon as I can."

"You're going to see Cara?" Kenzie asked.

He grimaced. "No. I've got a command performance downtown. I've asked Crow to come and relieve you so you can get some rest."

"All right," she replied.

"I'll be on my cell."

After handing off the Emilio Lopez case—which had become a homicide-suicide—to D.C. police,

John Crowfeather left the Kalorama section of the city. He'd gotten Scott's permission to take an hour-long break, long enough to accomplish the one thing he needed most: a shower.

Crow lived in Foggy Bottom, near George Washington University. He rented an English basement in a brick townhouse owned by an elderly woman whose husband had been an assistant secretary of state in the Bush administration. The arrangement worked for both of them—the widow liked having a man around, and the house stood not far from Rock Creek Park, where Crow could run and bike and escape the intensity of the city whenever he wanted to.

The widow had stopped driving many years before and so allowed Crow to use the single, tiny garage for his Bureau car. A door from the garage opened directly into his main living area—a large living/dining room with a small kitchen off to one side. A single bedroom and bathroom completed the arrangement.

Friends at the Bureau told Crow he was an idiot for not buying into the robust Washington housing market and taking the mortgage tax write-off, but Crow liked his living arrangement, liked the impermanence of it, and he felt somehow by helping the landlady he was making up for his inability to do it for his own grandfather.

Today, he wished he had time for a run. The

woods of Rock Creek Park beckoned him. He surely could use the tension relief. He ran six to eight miles most days of the week, allowing the forest to envelop him on the seldom-used trail he'd discovered. Frequently, he'd find the tracks of deer, or a tuft of animal hair caught on a bramble, or he'd see a snake slithering off into the undergrowth.

Although the desert southwest flowed through his veins, Crow loved the hardwood forest of the East. On the Reservation, since he'd come back from Iraq, he felt exposed as he ran, vulnerable, out in the open with barely a piñon tree for cover. In the big, empty country, he could travel a hundred and fifty miles in his car and people would still know him by the Navajo name he'd been given when he was still a boy: "One who runs."

Here, in the East, people surrounded him, but few knew his name, fewer still would stop him to talk, none knew his story. He was just another brown-skinned man in a multihued city. He could run and only the birds and squirrels and other critters living there would notice.

But today, he had no time for a run. Crow pulled off his clothes, turned on the shower, and stepped in as steam began to fill the room. He felt sorry for the little girl whose body they found, and for her parents. He knew she was dead before he even touched her—he could tell by the color of her skin. What had she suffered before she died?

The woman, Kenzie, was green. She'd come close to passing out at Lopez's house, though she'd tried to hide it. It's not easy, handling the adrenaline of a raid and then the smell of death. She looked great, attractive, as Scott had said: A natural beauty with blonde hair, trim and fit. Smart. Crow had felt protective of her.

He shook his head to dislodge his thoughts. He didn't want to think about her, didn't want to think about any woman. Women were not in his plan right now. And that's the way he wanted it.

Kenzie, staring at the computer, looked up when Crow, smelling of soap and shampoo, showed up. The dark-haired, dark-eyed agent seemed to appear out of nowhere. "Scott asked me to come and relieve you," he said. "He said to tell you to go take a few hours off. Get some sleep, if you can. And he asked me to bring you this." He held out a plastic grocery bag.

Kenzie took the bag. Inside sat a carton of whole fruit strawberry sorbet. She smiled. "Thank you! Want some?" she asked, holding it up.

Crow hesitated. "Sure." He dropped down into a chair with the grace of a big cat.

She went out into the kitchen, found a couple of bowls and spoons, and dished out the sorbet.

The senator had invited them to use what they needed. Kenzie returned to the dining room, handed Crow a bowl, and sat down again, studying the agent as she took tiny bites.

The bone structure of his face was well-defined, with high cheekbones and a strong jawline, proportioned brow and slightly arched nose. With little trouble, Kenzie could picture him in buckskins. On a horse. Was that racist, she wondered?

"Tell me what's going on," he asked, nodding toward the open laptop.

"I'm going through the reports people have posted, correlating data while I look for information on a lead I gave Scott. I'm looking for patterns—key phrases that could be clues."

"You're a linguist."

"Yes," she replied, "A forensic psycholinguist."

"Which means . . ."

"I analyze language for its psychological basis in criminal cases. For example, I may do a statement analysis to detect deception, or I may do threat assessments, or analyze notes to determine authorship. There's a lot to it."

"Sounds boring," he said.

She fought to keep from being offended. "There are all kinds of things you can learn from language."

"But it keeps you cooped up in an office all day."

She had to give him that.

Crow's eyes shifted slightly. "Scott speaks very highly of you."

She blushed. "Scott's a good friend." Kenzie took another bite of the sorbet. "You're from Arizona?"

He nodded. "Near Flagstaff. The high desert."

"I'll bet it's beautiful. Do you speak Navajo?"

Crow nodded. "Sure. I grew up on it."

"You pretty much have to from what I understand." She knew very little about American Indians—their problems, their culture, their religion, their art, their language. She grew up in D.C.—she didn't even see how the name "Redskins" could be offensive. Still, she'd learned a little about the Navajo language in her linguistics courses. Kenzie toyed with her sorbet. "The different dialects, the syntax, and the tonal qualities—Navajo is a very difficult language. Very verb intensive." She looked up at him. "How would you say, 'We need to catch this guy?' "

His eyes narrowed slightly. "I don't perform."

Kenzie blinked and blushed at his rebuff. An awkward silence followed. She tried a different tack. "Scott said your grandfather was one of the Code Talkers in World War II."

"That's right."

"Did he speak much about his experiences?"

Crow leaned back. "People who've actually been in war don't talk much about it," he said.

"A lot of what I know, I had to pry out of him."

Kenzie hoped he'd continue. She felt wary of pushing him. His dark brown, almost black eyes flickered. "My grandfather was a friend of Philip Johnston, a white guy who grew up on the Reservation, the son of missionaries. Philip spoke our language. One day he came to Grandfather and asked him to help him sell his idea of using Navajos to encrypt messages in the Pacific theater. So he did. He became a Marine. He fought his way across the Pacific islands and saw a lot of action. He was on Iwo Jima, working all night as the Marines captured the island."

Kenzie nodded. "Some people say it turned the tide of the whole Pacific campaign. The Japanese never broke the Navajo code."

"That's right."

"Amazing."

Crow shifted in his seat. "My grandfather says it was the work of God."

Curious, she cocked her head.

He shrugged. "I don't know that I get that."

"Is that part of the Navajo religion? Attributing things like that to God?"

Crow shook his head. "The Navajo people are divided. Some believe the American Indian way, some are Christians, some people try to mix the two. Grandfather is a Christian." He laughed softly. "A really strong, ninety-year-old Christian."

The sorbet felt cool and sweet, so refreshing on

her throat. "I thought a lot of American Indians had Christianity pushed on them and they resented it," Kenzie said.

"My grandfather never excused the wrong methods some white men used, but he told me the truth is the truth. It is also wrong to hold a grudge. The way of forgiveness, said my grandfather, is the only way to peace." Crow shook his head. "As I said, he's very strong in his faith. I thought I would escape it, you know? Moving East? No more God talk. But no, here's Scott. He sounds just like my grandfather. He says God is chasing me."

"Is he catching you?" she said, smiling.

"I've learned to move fast," he joked.

The clinking of their spoons on the ceramic bowls filled the gaps in their conversation. "Scott's faith seems to work for him," Kenzie said.

Crow stopped moving. "I don't think that's it."

Kenzie looked at him, surprised.

He stood up. "I've thought about this a lot," Crow said. "If what Scott and my grandfather say about God is true, then it isn't just true for them and it isn't a matter of it 'working' for them. It's a matter of reality."

Kenzie's heart beat faster. "What do you mean?"

Crow closed his eyes, his face tilted toward the ceiling. "My grandparents raised me." His voice tightened and he looked at her. "They lived their faith every day, from praying for rain to praying for me to stop getting into fights, from saying grace to thanking God for the beautiful sunset, from giving when they had nothing to give, to loving people who treated them wrong. For them, worshiping God was like breathing. If the sheep were healthy, they thanked him. If a baby was born, they thanked him. And even when my parents were killed in a car accident because my father was driving drunk, even then, my grandparents chose to believe nothing was by chance, everything was God's will, and they trusted him like . . . like I trust my right arm." Crow held up his clenched fist and looked directly at Kenzie. "Scott's the same way. Even when things go wrong, even when his faith doesn't 'work,' he trusts God." Crow's eyes were bright. "Scott and my grandfather, they live in a different reality. They soar above the world I know."

Kenzie felt a tremor within her. "Those are some deep thoughts."

"Out in the desert, at night, you have time for deep thoughts. The skies demand it."

Kenzie stood up, crossed her arms, and began to pace. "I went to church as a little girl, until my father died. And I believe, you know, the basics: God, Jesus, all that. But Scott . . . he goes one step beyond, maybe ten steps beyond." Kenzie tossed her head and looked at him, capturing Crow's eyes. "Like bringing God into this"—she gestured toward the table where the computers were set up. "He's convinced God's in control, but that child we found today," an involuntary tremor shook her voice, "where was God when she was being killed? Where was God . . . in that closet?" Her stomach felt tight.

Crow silently watched her as she spoke. His eyes followed her with an intensity that sent a shiver down her spine. When she finished talking, he said, "There's a lot I don't understand —much that is a mystery. But you have to be all in or all out. You can't follow him halfway. Either God is who Scott says he is—sovereign, all powerful, all loving—or he's no god at all."

"And which is it, in your opinion?"

Crow turned away, looking up toward the ceiling again as if the answer were there, then he dropped his head. "My grandfather wanted me to be strong. He used to make me wrestle whatever was around: Sheep, dogs, horses, trees . . . anything to build muscles and endurance. Today, I think I am wrestling God."

"Why?"

Crow hesitated. He met her gaze and for a moment, she thought he would speak. Then he shook his head slightly. "That's a story for another time." His eyes were burning. He took a deep breath and shoved his hands in his pockets.

"Did Scott get motel rooms? Why don't you take a break? I can handle this."

She told him about the senator's offer. The room on the third floor.

"Fine. I'll be here. You go rest. I'll come get you if anything happens," Crow said.

She started to protest. There were so many more questions she wanted to ask him. What did he do in Iraq? Why did he decide to become an agent? His words had stirred something in her, and left her longing for more. But clearly he was finished. "All right, thanks," she said, swallowing her disappointment.

The sound of his voice and the cadence of his speech echoed in Kenzie's head as she climbed the stairs. Automatically, she began sorting out the slight accent she'd detected, the sound of his *A*s and *E*s, the almost singsong quality of his language. And his thinking! Very deep.

The senator and his wife were in their bedroom. As she walked up the stairs, Kenzie heard arguing.

Kenzie looked into Zoe's room. The late afternoon sun set the pink ablaze, like a tropical sunrise in the world of a little girl. My Little Pony. Barbie. Baby dolls. Dress up. Books.

Zoe loved her books, from the looks of her room. There were books on shelves, books near her bed, books mixed up in the covers. Who read to her? The senator? Mrs. Grable? Or did all of her listening take place in the accented world of her nanny?

Kenzie picked up a copy of *Go, Dog, Go*. It had been lying on the floor, perhaps the last book someone had read to Zoe.

She put it down again, returned to the hall, and found the door to the attic bedroom. Three steps led to a landing, then a turn in the stairs. Eight more steps and she found herself on the third floor.

It should have been hot, this nest in the upper reaches of the home, but Kenzie found it remarkably comfortable. Wallpapered in a neat American eagle design, the room held a twin bed made of cherry, a matching dresser, and a small desk and chair. Dark blue paint matching the wallpaper covered one wall. The desk held a lamp, paper, pencils, and a stapler. The room's two dormer windows looked down on the front street. Next to the bed was a door that led to a small but adequate bathroom, equipped with fresh towels and soap.

A shower would make her feel so much more human, a shower, and then a nap. She turned on the spigot, but even the sound of the rushing water could not get Crow's words out of her head.

10

Scott inserted his Bureau ID into the card reader and entered the parking garage. His boss had said he'd meet him in the director's outer office. Outer office. Street agents were lucky to get a battered old desk in a bullpen. The director had an inner office and an outer office!

It's OK, though, Scott thought. Anyway, I'd go crazy sitting behind a desk all day.

All the way over, he'd been thinking about Cara. Praying for her. He hated not being able to be with her now. But Cara was a trooper. She felt proud of him, she said, proud of his job. And all he had to do to stay motivated to find the Grables' daughter was to think of his own in the same situation—kidnapped, helpless, at the mercy of an abductor.

Just the thought of it made him angry.

Methodically, Scott worked his way past security into the building. Since 9/11, you needed an act of Congress to get into Bureau headquarters, even if you were an agent. He took the elevator to the director's floor, stepped out, and checked his watch. Fifteen minutes. He had fifteen minutes to download any new information on the Grable case website through the secure net connection. The director's secretary could help him out.

Entering into yet another secure area, the hallway where the Bureau's top executives had their offices, he greeted her. "Hey, Miss Sampson!" he said.

Bea Sampson had been with the Bureau over forty years and was legendary for her devotion. She hadn't taken a sick day in anyone's memory. At age seventy, retirement wasn't anywhere on the horizon as far as she was concerned.

"Well, young man. You're here to see the director?" Miss Sampson was thin, gray-haired, and crisp. Just what you would expect.

"Yes, ma'am. At his request. Special Agent Scott Hansbrough from the Washington Field Office."

"Oh, yes. The Grable case. I do hope you find that little girl."

"Yes, ma'am. I do, too." Scott smiled at her. "Is there a place I could hook into the secure net?"

"Absolutely. Right here." She pointed toward a credenza running along the wall behind her desk.

"Thank you."

Swiftly, Scott booted up his laptop, accessed the website he'd set up, and quickly reviewed the data entered by agents involved in the investigation. He took a few notes on a small pad and shut down the computer just as his boss entered the anteroom.

"Miss Sampson, you look absolutely wonder-ful," Tom Shuler's booming voice proclaimed.

"Tom! My goodness, how long has it been?"

Scott rolled his eyes. Shuler was a player, even with seventy-year-olds.

A loud buzz from Miss Sampson's phone interrupted the two. "Yes, sir?"

"Send Shuler in when he gets here."

"He's here now, sir. Along with Special Agent Hansbrough. I'll send them both in." Miss Sampson winked at Scott as she said that. The director's voice continued to bark over the speakerphone. "Yes, sir. Yes, sir." She hung up. "Gentlemen?" she said and she ushered them in.

Joseph D. Lundquist was not a J. Edgar Hoover kind of director. He liked to delegate. He liked interaction with his deputies, thinking outside the box, and letting street agents do their job. "They know more than I do," he would say, and it instantly bred loyalty in his troops. Joe Lundquist understands. That was the word all over the Bureau.

He didn't have as much rapport with Congress. One senator in particular, Chuck Schwartz of Wisconsin, rode him pretty hard, especially at budget time. And Scott knew that Schwartz played tennis regularly with Grable.

"Sit down, gentlemen," the director said,

nodding toward two leather chairs facing his substantial desk. Behind him, a large window looked out on the Capitol building, resplendent in the late afternoon sun. He saw Scott staring at the view, glanced over his shoulder, and said, "It's beautiful, huh? That's what I thought, too, when I first moved in here. Now I feel like there's a vulture just over my shoulder, staring at me all day. If I don't keep moving, I'm dead." He smiled and shook his head.

Scott and his boss, Tom Shuler, both laughed.

"All right. Update me on the Grable case," Lundquist said.

Scott's boss nodded toward him. "Yes, sir." Scott checked his watch. "We're at approximately twenty hours, sir. Mrs. Grable reported Zoe missing around twenty-two thirty yesterday. The nanny died before we were able to question her. We've done a full evidence sweep of the Grables' house and collected a few prints, including a partial palm print we've not been able to iden-tify."

The director sat with his elbows resting on the arms of his chair, his hands forming an A-frame in front of his face. His gray eyes were piercing, his gray hair conveyed the impression of wisdom, and he focused on Scott as if the agent were the only person in the world.

"As you know, sir, we've been in a dry spell, and the grass and garden were hardened. So we don't have footprints. No tire marks either. We've collected tapes from surveillance cameras in the area, sir, and we have agents reviewing them now."

"What about this other child?"

Scott told him about the tip on the man in Kalorama, about the entry, the suicide, and the body in the closet. He felt himself getting emotional now, as he talked about it, and he wondered why. Was it the little girl they'd found in Lopez's apartment, Zoe, or his own daughter Cara who played on his heart? Maybe all three. He gripped his hand into a fist, forcing himself to focus.

"So, it wasn't Zoe. Which was both bad and good news."

"Yes, sir. D.C. police have taken over that investigation."

The director nodded.

Then Scott told him about the hair in the package delivered to the senator's house. He saw Lundquist stiffen, saw the corners of his eyes grow tight and his mouth become a straight line. "So he's a sadist," the director said.

"He at least wants to goad the senator," Shuler chimed in. "It's what this seems to be about. Getting at Senator Grable."

The director took a deep breath. He swung his chair around halfway, and stared at the Capitol, at the statue called "Freedom" on the top, at the

124

flag hanging still and limp in the late afternoon. He turned back to the two agents. "Mrs. Grable called me."

Scott raised his eyebrows.

"She wants our agents out of the house and the command center out of the alley."

A rush of anger swept through Scott.

"How do you feel about that?" The director looked at Scott.

"Sir," Scott said, fighting to keep the tension out of his voice, "if we hadn't been there when that package came, it would have been mishandled. Had it been a bomb, the senator would be dead."

"I know." The director was a patient man.

"Having immediate access to the senator and his wife will help us respond right away when the next development occurs." Scott paused. "And sir, we have not yet ruled out Mrs. Grable as a suspect."

"Tell me about that."

So he did, summarizing her statements, her attitude, her odd behaviors. The director listened carefully, asked a few pertinent questions, and then thought for a moment. "OK, Agent Hansbrough. I hear what you're saying. But see what you can do to lower our profile."

"Yes, sir." What else could he say? Scott immediately started thinking about the implications of moving their operation and lost track of the conversation. Until he heard his name. "Yes?" he said, regaining focus.

"I was just suggesting we could use some help with the Lab," Shuler repeated.

"Oh, yes, sir. The DNA scans, fingerprint identification, hairs and fibers—we could certainly use some grease on the skids there, sir."

"You've got it," the director said, and he buzzed Miss Sampson. "Get me Fuller on the phone, please." Seconds later, his call connected with the director of the FBI lab, now located down at Quantico. "Fred, let me give you a case number." He motioned with his fingers and Scott hurriedly scrawled it on a piece of paper. "You get anything with this number on it, you pull out the stops. Top priority, understand? All right. Thanks." He hung up the phone. "Hansbrough, you keep going. We want this child back."

"Yes, sir."

The director stood up and began moving toward the door. On cue, Scott and Shuler followed. As he opened the door, the director clapped Scott on the back. "How long have you been up, son?"

Scott checked his watch. "Going on thirty-three hours, sir."

"You get some sleep, you hear? Six months from now, I don't want to have to be answering Senator Schwartz's questions about why my case agent was making such poor decisions."

"Yes, sir."

• • •

Grayson and Sandy sat on the couch. She watched TV while he worked on his laptop. Gray had made her help him remove the coffee table. Looking at its damaged finish irritated him. But he couldn't get away from the large white splotch on the carpet. Like the blood on Lady Macbeth's hands, it remained.

"You need to do a better job handling her," Grayson said, looking up from his work. "She's a five-year-old for crying out loud. How hard can it be?" He sighed with exasperation. "Look, I'm doing everything I can to make this come together. But you're not helping!"

"Well, Gray, honey, you've jerked her out of her house, cut off her hair . . . no wonder she's upset! Plus, she just seems a little sick to me, like she's got the flu or something." Sandy was filing her nails with an emery board. "How long is it going to take you to do this? I mean, what are you waiting for?"

"I'm working on it! I'm telling you, you don't know the half of what's going into this. Making sure we get the money without the cops finding us . . ."

"And finding a place to let Zoe go that won't lead to us, right? Are you working that out?"

"Sure, sure." Better soften up, he thought. He reached over and stroked Sandy's neck, just below her ear. "I've got to figure it out, too. Just be patient, baby. And for crying out loud, take care of the kid."

The show on the TV ended and loud commercials took over. Sandy hit the mute button on the remote. "I want to go shopping," she said suddenly.

"No."

"Why not?"

"Because I'm not babysitting."

"But I'll take her with me. Isn't that why we cut her hair? So she'd be disguised? I mean, Gray, nobody's going to look twice at us."

"We'll see."

Sandy moved over and began stroking his arm. Then she touched his chest. "Gray, honey, you promised." She kissed him on the lips. "Come on, baby. Let me go out. I'm bored. Besides, she needs some more clothes. Everything you grabbed from her room is pink."

"All right, all right!" he said, returning her kisses. At least she was good for something. "Tomorrow," he said, snapping shut his laptop. "Tomorrow I'll take you to a mall. IF you get that nail polish off. Who ever heard of a boy wearing pink nail polish?" He rose to his feet and picked up his car keys.

Her eyes widened. "Where are you going now?"

"I've got something I've got to do." And with that, he left.

11

Kenzie slept for three hours straight. When she woke up, the attic bedroom had grown shadowy with the declining light of dusk. She startled, remembered where she was, and jumped to her feet. She threw her clothes on and raced downstairs.

Crow looked up as she entered the dining room, his dark eyes capturing her immediately. The deep yellow shirt he wore set off his dark hair and red-brown skin. "Sorry I slept so long. What's up?" she asked.

"I sent an agent up to Chambersburg. The package came from a shipping store. False return address. False phone number. The kid paid cash."

"What kid?"

"The kid who shipped the package. Black kid, about fourteen. The clerk actually ID'd him. She had seen him hanging around the arcade in a shopping center. So we found him. Some dude paid him a hundred bucks to send that package. A hundred bucks! Big money to the kid."

"Can he identify that person?"

"Never saw him. Guy came up to him while he was playing a video game and said, 'Don't turn around.' Then he offered him the deal. Go to the elementary school where there's a package in the culvert. Mail it, and return the receipt to the same place. Then come back and pick up the money."

"What did he sound like?"

"Middle-aged white guy. Nothing more specific."

"No accent? Speech impediment? Exactly what words did he use?"

"Not everybody's a linguist, Kenzie."

She blushed. "How about the child that we found?" she asked, changing topics.

Crow shrugged. "I don't think we know anything about the child."

"The DNA results on the hair?"

"That'll be a while." He hesitated. "Scott called."

Kenzie raised her eyebrows.

"He's on his way back. Mrs. Grable got to the director. She wants us out of the house."

"Are you kidding?" Kenzie responded. "Why?"

"We're intruding on her privacy."

"Good grief."

"What's going on?" Senator Grable walked into the room. Crow told him about the Chambersburg connection and Mrs. Grable's request. "That's ridiculous. I want you here. I want to know what's going on!" he said, his eyes snapping with anger, and he turned on his heel and walked out.

Kenzie raised her eyebrows. "I don't want to be in on that conversation!" she said.

They spent the next hour alternating between the house and the Mobile Command Center. They fielded phone calls from agents, asked more questions of Senator Grable, and correlated the information that came in, sometimes in dribbles, sometimes in a flood.

Kenzie and Crow were working side by side in the Grables' dining room, taking bites of dinner in between surges of activity when they got an urgent radio message from an agent behind the house. "We've got an intruder, a runner," he gasped. "Back alley."

The two agents sprang to their feet. Kenzie touched her side, feeling for her gun.

"What's happening?" Senator Grable asked, as they raced toward the back door. His eyes were wide.

"Someone is in the back. You stay inside, in the hallway, away from the windows until we check it out," Crow commanded. He radioed for another agent to come into the house.

Kenzie followed Crow out the back door. The heat and humidity smacked her like a hot, wet towel, and she sucked in a breath of the thick air. She could smell the ozone. Thunder rumbled in the west. A storm was on the way. They raced down the garden walk toward the back gate.

"What do you have?" Crow asked the agent in the alley behind the Grables' house.

"Kid was creeping around here. We saw him, ordered him to halt, and he took off."

"Which way?"

"Down there." The agent pointed.

Crow took off. Kenzie chose a different direction, jogging to the right, around the back fence of the Grables' property.

Five minutes later, Crow and a second agent returned, a teenager in tow, everyone puffing from exertion. The teenager wore jeans, torn at the knee, and a black T-shirt with a picture of Bob Marley on the front. His hands cuffed behind him, his head hung low. His dark blond hair hung down in dreadlocks. He was fourteen, maybe fifteen—a rich white kid. Crow and the other agent began to interrogate him.

"What were you doing back here?" Crow asked. "Why didn't you stop? Where do you live? What's your name, kid?" Their questions peppered the young man, who shook with fear.

Crow had the kid lean over the hood of a Bureau car as he searched him. Something told him the kid was just a teen snooping around, but he wanted to scare him a little. Someone else called the teenager's mother. Crow pulled a pocketknife, a movie stub, and a couple of pills out of the kid's pockets and put them on the hood. What were the pills? Crow looked more closely. Prozac. Why did he have them? Why were so many kids depressed these days? Rich city kids, who'd never known hunger or how cold it could get in a hogan in January.

The thunder rumbled louder and rain began

splashing down, making tiny explosions in the dust of the Bucar. One more pocket: As Crow pulled out a hundred-dollar bill, Scott arrived.

"What's going on?" Scott said. "Grable said you were . . ."

Crow stared at the bill in his hand. A C-note? He blinked, then looked at Scott. "This young man was hanging out here in the alley. When our agent told him to stop, he ran."

Scott nodded. "You have his identification?" The other agent handed Scott the kid's wallet, which contained a picture ID from a fancy D.C. private school, a library card, a racy magazine picture, and three dollars.

"He says he was just curious about all the activity," the agent said.

"Stay still!" Crow yelled as the kid turned to speak and defend himself.

"Let's put him in the back of the car," Scott suggested.

Crow took the kid by the arm and guided him into the back seat, and shut the car door.

Scott glanced around. "Where's Kenzie?"

Alarm flashed through Crow. Kenzie? "I don't know. In the house maybe? She was here when I ran after this kid."

"She isn't in the house," Scott said.

"She went that way," the other agent said, motioning with his hand. "Over there. Quite a while ago."

"You watch him," Crow said, gesturing toward the kid in the car. Then he started moving toward the direction the other agent had indicated. Scott followed him. Where was Kenzie? Rain began to fall harder. They jogged along the stockade fence at the rear of the Grables' house to the corner and made a hard right turn. There, the property abutted an undeveloped area of Rock Creek Park. Just beyond the fence, a steep slope studded with thick woods dropped away toward Rock Creek Parkway.

Crow stopped, trying to see into the dark, unlit area. All of his senses were on alert. Where was Kenzie? Why hadn't she come back? He wiped the rain out of his face with his arm.

On the Reservation, they called this the male rain—the hard-driving kind of a rain sending torrents pelting down, stinging bare skin and soaking clothes; this kind of rain would send a wall of water crashing down the washes with a force able to sweep a man away. It was the dangerous kind of rain. Crow moved forward as the male rain pelted his shirt, his shoulders. Lightning flashed.

Suddenly, the hair on the back of Crow's neck stood up and fear arrowed up his spine. He knew she was there, knew she was nearby, before he ever saw her.

His heart began drumming. He heard a high-pitched ringing in his ears. He saw a lightning-lit hardwood forest; he saw a bright, sunlit desert field. He slipped on the wet grass, imagined sliding sand beneath his feet, saw a drifting cloud, and, in his mind's eye, saw smoke lifting from a hot tent in Iraq. He saw a body, lying on the ground. He saw Julie, he saw Kenzie . . . and his heart nearly broke.

"There!" Scott shouted.

Crow ran to her, slipping on the grass, the thunder roaring in his ears. He dropped to the ground next to her prone body, felt for a pulse, a breath. Behind him, Scott yelled for agents to search the area, calling for an ambulance, summoning a K-9 unit. And Crow's head began to feel like it would burst.

Kenzie moaned softly. The back of her head felt sticky and a trickle of blood streaked her face. Crow found a strong pulse. He flicked on a small light and looked for more wounds—a gunshot, a knife wound. His hands were shaking. He called her name. Thunder rumbled again.

"Is she all right?" Scott asked.

"Lip is cut. Head's bleeding—blunt trauma wound. I need some ice." Crow bent over her, shook the rain out of his eyes, and tried to rouse her. "Kenzie? Come on, wake up." He felt like the ground underneath him was moving, like sand slipping into a hole. "Kenzie!"

"I want people down in those woods!" Scott shouted. "Grab anybody that's moving."

"Hansbrough!" The senator's voice sounded frantic.

Crow and Scott looked up. Grable ran toward them. He had something in his hand. Scott put his flashlight beam on it.

He held a doll, her eyes poked out, her neck half-severed, her clothes splattered with a red liquid. "Where'd you find that?" Scott asked, grabbing his arm.

"Just over the fence," Grable said, nodding toward his backyard. "What does it mean? Oh, God . . ." his voice trailed off in a stream of panic.

Scott took the doll. Around her neck hung a zippered plastic bag on a string, with a piece of paper inside.

Lightning split the sky and the heavens opened up as more and more rain fell. Male rain.

Scott turned to Crow. Rain plastered down his hair, streaked his face, and dripped off his nose. "You go with Kenzie," he said. "I've got to handle this."

"What about the kid?"

"I'll have someone take him downtown and talk to him and his parents. We'll get what we can from them."

12

The note seemed straightforward:

Senator Grable:

You want your kid back? Do just as I say. You will never find me, so don't bother calling the cops. You do not know who I am. But I've studied you, you and your family. You think Zoe's your only vulnerable spot? I know about your other kids, too. How does Jillian like William & Mary? And James? Is he still having a little alcohol problem? You can't hide from me, Senator.

I've been watching you. For years, you've been using people. You've sold out your constituents. Betrayed your office. Because you're greedy.

Now, it's payback time.

I want two million dollars.

Then I will tell you where to find Zoe. Then and only then.

You ever watch TV? The show called *High Stakes*.

No, I'm sure you're too busy collecting payoffs. Monitor the Internet message board. Starting now.

Don't think you can find me. You can't imagine the lengths to which I will go to get what I want. I will not hesitate to kill Zoe.

I'm the dealer now, Senator. I'm calling the shots. I'm in control.

You will follow my instructions. Or you'll never see Zoe again.

Scott's stomach felt tight as he bent over the note, reading each word. The senator stood just over his shoulder, dripping rainwater on the kitchen floor. The agent looked up. Their eyes met, and Scott could see the fear filling Zoe's father's eyes.

"What's *High Stakes*?" Grable asked, his voice tight.

"It's one of those 'the country's under a terror attack' shows, I think. I'll have someone check it."

"Two million? Where does he think I can get that kind of money?" Grable asked, fear adding a tremor to his voice.

"He was brazen to deliver this to the house," Scott mused, "and smart to catch Kenzie off guard like that."

"Bruce? What's going on?" Beth Grable demanded, walking into the kitchen. She wore a long pink terrycloth robe and had her blonde hair pulled back in a ponytail. One strand hung in front of her face.

The senator swallowed and glanced toward the doll, lying on the island.

Then Beth began screaming. "That's hers! That's Zoe's! Oh, God! Where is she? What did he do to her?" She moved toward the doll.

Scott grabbed Mrs. Grable's wrist to keep her from snatching it.

Her eyes blazed into him. "You let me go! Let me go!" She spit the words at him.

"Mrs. Grable! Don't touch that! It's evidence."

"You let me see . . ."

Scott forced her away from the island. "You may not touch the doll or the note." She twisted against his grip. "Calm down, or I'll have to take you out of this room."

"Bruce! Did you hear him threaten me? Did you hear him?" Beth tried to pull away from Scott. "You are so out of here!" she hissed.

"Beth! Shut up! For once, just shut up!" the senator roared.

She looked at him, stunned. Her jaw jutted out. Her eyes bore into her husband's, then she turned to Scott. "You let go of me," she hissed again.

Scott's heart raced. Slowly he released Mrs. Grable's wrist. The woman pulled her arm to herself and rubbed the place where he'd held her with her other hand. Then she tossed her head and started to leave. "You'll hear from my lawyer."

"Beth!" her husband yelled.

She stopped and turned around, her face a mask of fury.

"This man is trying to help us. Furthermore, I know you called the director, and I want you to know they are not leaving," he said. "They can do their job better if they're here. If you're uncomfortable, you can go to a friend's house. Or home, to Atlanta. But they're staying."

Her eyes widened. Then she cursed, turned, and walked away. "OK, Bruce. I'm leaving!"

Scott looked at Grable. "Will she be OK?"

Grable sighed. "We have Zoe to worry about."

Scott walked back over to the note, adrenaline still pumping. "Anything about this strike you?"

"Nothing."

"The amount: two million? That's not significant?"

The senator shook his head. When he looked at Scott, he had tears in his eyes. "Where am I going to get that much money?" he asked softly.

Scott took digital pictures of the note and copied the words exactly into a document file. He then placed it and the doll in evidence bags and summoned another agent to drive them down to the FBI lab. He wished he had Kenzie to analyze the language.

Outside, other agents marked off the backyard and the area outside the fence for a grid search. They would cover every inch. Who knew? If

140

Kenzie's attacker had dropped something, if he had left some tiny piece of evidence there, it could be just what they needed to identify him.

"How did he get close to her? That's what I want to know," Scott said, standing at the edge of the search area. The rain had stopped and water dripped from the trees, but thunder still rumbled in the east, and lightning flashed periodically in the dark clouds.

"There's a road down there," the senator said, pointing toward Rock Creek Parkway. "He could have parked down there and come up the hill. He could have hidden in these bushes and surprised her."

Scott crossed his arms and rubbed his chin. "How many people would know which house is yours from that angle? Or where to park down there?" He gestured toward the parkway.

The senator shrugged. Despair etched his worn face.

"Look," Scott said, "this guy knows you, he knows your house, he had a pretty good idea he could avoid the cops. He delivered that doll to scare you. Now don't let him throw you." He called to another agent. "Jesse! I want motion sensor lights and cameras installed all along this fence. Pronto."

"Yes, sir," Jesse responded.

Scott said, "Let's go inside, Senator. I'm going to have someone pick up your gardener. And I want to interview your neighbors again. See if anyone heard or saw anything. We are not going to let this man win."

Special Agent Alicia Sheerling sat focused on the computer when Scott and the senator walked into the dining room and sat down. For a moment, the clicking of the keys was the only sound in the room. Grable rested his elbows on his knees, his head sagging as if weighted down with sorrow. He played with a small piece of paper, rolling it between his fingers, focusing on it as if it were the key to finding Zoe. Then he sighed, sat back, looked at Scott, and said, "How'd your daughter do, with the surgery and all?"

Scott looked at him, surprised at the odd question. He studied the senator's face. Was it the lateness of the hour, or the fatigue, or the trauma they'd all just experienced? Why had Grable asked about Cara?

Scott told Grable about his conversation with his wife. Cara had come through the surgery fine. He showed the senator the picture on his cell phone his wife had sent: Cara, in the hospital, a bright pink cast on her left arm.

"I don't usually tell my family about the cases I'm working on," Scott said, "but I felt bad I couldn't be with Cara. So I told her about Zoe. And do you know what she said, Senator?"

Alicia looked up.

Grable shook his head.

"She said 'Dad, they need you to find that little girl. I'll be all right. And Dad, I'll be praying for Zoe.' "

The tears in Senator Grable's eyes matched Scott's. "You love your daughter."

"You bet."

He sighed deeply, and then, in a low voice Grable began speaking about Zoe, about his utter frustration he couldn't protect her, about his hopes for her, and the games they played together, and the terror now gripping him, his fear that he would never see Zoe again.

"Senator," Scott said, focusing on Grable's face, "we don't know how all this is going to work out, but we've got the best team in the FBI on this case." He hesitated. "Sir, I believe God knows where she is. I'm asking him to help us. I trust him to." He was pushing the line, but he didn't care. This man needed hope. And it's what Scott was offering.

He waited for a response. None came. So he went on. "We need to know everything we can so we can pursue every possibility," Scott said. Then, very gently, he began probing about other possible avenues of investigation . . . including the dealings the senator had negotiated under the table.

And the man spoke. He opened up. For Scott, it

felt like being in a confessional. The weight of the information fell on his shoulders like a vestment. He listened quietly. Out of the corner of his eye he could see Alicia taking notes like mad, her eyes wide. The senator leaned forward, his arms resting on his legs, and stared at the floor. And in the end, when he had outlined all of his illegal deals over the last four years, the senator dropped his head even further, and Scott saw a tear drip onto his shoe.

Scott touched his shoulder. "You did the right thing, Senator. You've given us a lot of help."

The senator nodded, then got up and walked slowly out of the room.

And Scott looked at Alicia, who stared at him in utter amazement.

"Incredible," she said.

When Crow got back to the Grables' house around midnight he felt prickly, unnerved. His jaw felt taut as a bowstring, and his head ached. Out of *hohzo*, balance, his grandfather would say.

"How's Kenzie?" Scott asked, standing up.

"She has a possible concussion." He fought to keep his voice neutral, business-like. "They're keeping her to do a CT and the machine's backed up." Crow rubbed the back of his neck, trying to diffuse the tension gripping him, wishing the churning inside would stop.

"You left her alone?"

"I got the D.C. police to supply a guard. And I had the office call her next of kin. Her mother should be there by now." Truth was, he couldn't stay there, couldn't stand to be in that hospital.

"Her mother?"

"Something wrong with that?" Crow realized immediately he sounded defensive.

Scott eyed him narrowly. Then he said, "They have problems, that's all. You had no way of knowing." His head tilted. "What are you so uptight about?"

Crow shoved his hands in his pockets and looked away. Why did he feel so stressed? "She shouldn't have been working this case."

"Why?"

"She's green! You know it and I know it. She should never have gone off alone like that, without backup. She's an academic, fine for the classroom, but out here . . ."

"That's not fair."

"Anybody her age with a PhD can't have a lot of street smarts. She's spent her life with books!"

"So somebody hit her from behind. It could happen to anybody." Scott waved his hand dismissively. "What did she say? Did she see him?"

Crow paced away. "She doesn't remember a thing." He looked back at Scott. "Where has she worked, anyway?"

"Her first office was New York, then she got

transferred to WFO. Quantico pulled her to fill in there. They needed her to cover the classes of another agent."

"So she's never really been tested as a street agent, right? Day after day, month after month." Crow had his hands on his hips.

Scott tightened his jaw. "Even you started somewhere, Crow."

Crow scowled. "I had been well tested before I ever walked into the Bureau. She's a hazard, Scott, to herself and everyone else."

When Scott walked into the kitchen a few minutes later, Crow found himself staring out of the window, into the dark backyard, memories pulsing and exploding in his soul in a macabre display. He didn't want them, he didn't need them, and yet they were there, rising up from the deep well inside, undesired, untamed, unnerving.

He sensed Scott behind him and forced himself back into the present. "I'm sorry," he said, turning around.

"It's all right. You need a break?"

Crow grimaced. "I need to get back to work. What's with the doll?"

Scott told him about the doll and the note, and about the new information Grable had given him.

"Remarkable," Crow said, shaking his head.

"I have Alicia and Jesse and their teams

following those leads." Scott stood up and paced, shoving his hands in his pockets. He stopped and looked at Crow. "Can you refocus? Because I need some help thinking this out."

Crow took a deep breath and nodded. He crossed his arms as if guarding himself against further intrusive thoughts. He had worked with a lot of women. He would not let this one get under his skin. "Go on," he said to Scott.

"So let's play this out," Scott continued. "Let's say I'm the UNSUB. I want to harass Grable. And I want money. I decide to kidnap his kid. So I come to his house when I know he's out, ring the bell . . ." Scott said, role-playing.

"Wait, how do you know Grable's not home?" Crow asked, forcing himself to play along.

"His car's gone. Or, I know his schedule. Mrs. Grable is at her weekly mah-jongg game. I know that." Scott rubbed the back of his neck. "I ring the bell and talk my way into the house. How? What do I tell the nanny to make her let me in and let me go upstairs?"

Crow shook his head. "She opens the door, you throw the pillowcase with the chloroform rag over her head. She's out, and you are in."

"No, she lay at the bottom of the stairs, remember? That's a good ten feet from the front door."

"So you talk your way in that far . . ."

Scott continued. "Yes. I get in. I grab Zoe and

then, when I want to deliver the ransom note, instead of calling or e-mailing or sending it through the mail . . ."

". . . or a delivery service, like you did the hair . . ."

". . . yeah, instead of that, I bring it here myself. Why?"

Crow's brow furrowed. "You can't stand to be away from the scene. You've got to know what's going on," he said, gesturing. A thin sheen of sweat lay on his neck. "Are you scaring Grable? Is your plan working?"

"I'm so arrogant, I'm sure I won't get caught." Scott rubbed his chin. "I know about the fence and the way the property adjoins the park. I come up through the woods, intending to throw the doll over the fence. But I see Kenzie instead and I can't resist—I hit her with something. Knock her out. It makes me really powerful."

"Now you've delivered the note." Crow nodded thoughtfully. "And you've assaulted a Fed. It's going to either make you a little nervous—or a little more arrogant." He paced away. Who was this jerk? "Any other similar crimes recently?"

Scott shook his head. "There's nothing in the database."

Suddenly, Crow's eyes grew bright. "The hundred-dollar bill! Scott, the kid had a hundred-dollar bill. I looked at it and with all the stuff with Kenzie, it didn't register until just now!" He felt a rush of emotion.

"What are you saying?"

"Maybe the kidnapper paid that kid to distract the agents in the back, just like he paid the kid in Chambersburg to ship the package. They both had hundred-dollar bills!"

Scott jerked his phone off his belt. "We need to talk to that kid again."

The dreams crept in like a stain, seeping into her mind, dark with pain. Why did her head hurt so much? And her mouth? She heard herself groan, a lonely, sad sound. She struggled to open her eyes.

She saw bright lights. Where was she? In a hospital? She smelled antiseptic. Yes, a hospital. She turned her head. Her mother sat on a chair across from her. Clarice Graham, staring at her with her mouth in a prim, straight line. Kenzie groaned again. She drifted back to sleep and then the dreams came again, bright and focused this time, horrifying in their detail.

She was a little girl, just five years old. She was painting a picture in her room, her pink room, which she was not supposed to be doing. Suddenly, her mother pushed open her door. Startled, Kenzie jumped and bright red paint spilled all over the white carpet.

Her mother's face twisted with rage. She

grabbed Kenzie and shook her, screaming at her, spit flying into her face. "You are so clumsy!" her mother screamed, while Kenzie, terrified, tried to breathe. Her mother, so beautiful. So frightening.

Kenzie heard herself groan.

"Are you awake?" her mother demanded.

She retreated again, into the dreams. *Her mother grabbed her arm, opened the bedroom closet, and threw her in. Then she slammed the door. Kenzie screamed. Her father had killed a spider in the closet just the day before. It was pitch black in there, and soon her skin was crawling. She had to get out! She begged, crying loudly, but the sound of a heavy piece of furniture—her dresser she would discover later—being pushed in front of the door told her it was no use. Eventually she lay down on the floor with her cheek on the carpet and her nose near the crack under the door.*

It was late afternoon—just before her father was due home—before the door opened.

"Mama?"

"What? What is it you want?"

Her mother's sharp response snapped Kenzie back to reality. She tried to sit up. The pain in her head made her drop back down immediately, and tears formed in her eyes. She put her hand on her forehead. "What happened?"

"You were mugged, that's what happened, so

150

you're in the hospital," Clarice Graham said, remaining seated, her purse on her lap. "Someone clunked you on the head. And they called me and I had to come over here."

Kenzie turned her head. Was she joking? No, of course not. "Who called you?"

"One of your people." She waved her hand dismissively.

"Oh," Kenzie said. Oh, wow, her head hurt. She tried to think. She remembered being outside, but where? The backyard at the Grables'. The Grables! Zoe! Who hit her? The UNSUB? She tried again to sit up. "I have to leave."

"You can't leave. They're waiting to do a CT scan. Plus, you have no clothes."

"What?" Kenzie sagged back on the pillow.

"They took them. For evidence or something. What they think they'll find on an old shirt and khaki pants is beyond me. But they took them and unless you want to go out on the street in that backless hospital gown, you're stuck."

Oh, good grief. Kenzie turned her head away. A wave of helplessness swept over her. Scott. Where was he? Her mouth felt funny. She touched her lip again.

"You look terrible. Here, want to see?" Her mother thrust a pocket mirror in front of Kenzie's face.

Wow. Kenzie looked at herself in the mirror

that her mother held. She had a bruise on her cheek, and her lip—yuck!

"See? What did I tell you? You're a mess!"

Kenzie sagged back onto the pillow. What now? She needed clothes. She needed to get out of there. She needed to find Zoe. "Could you see if there's a bag with my name on it somewhere in here? A personal effects bag?"

Sighing, her mother put the mirror back in her purse. Her hair lay perfectly in place and she wore large pearl earrings that matched her beige suit and cream blouse. Why she got so dressed up to come to a hospital at midnight seemed beyond understanding. She began rummaging around and eventually pulled a plastic bag out from under the bed. "Is this it?"

"Yes. Probably. Look inside. What's in there?"

Her mother peered in. "Just these." She pulled out Kenzie's key ring and her creds.

Kenzie took a deep breath. "Can you drive to my house and pick up some clothes for me?"

Her mother frowned. "All that way? Tonight?"

Who else could she call? Kenzie's mind began working.

"Well, yes, I guess I could," her mother continued. "At least I'd be able to see your home. How long has it been since you've invited me down there?"

Though dazed, Kenzie still had to fight to keep her temper. "We usually get together at your house, Mom, so you don't have to make the drive." Why did every interaction become a fight?

"I suppose I could do it."

"Great. Just don't forget—Jack is there." She touched her mouth again. Talking felt so awkward!

"You left Jack alone?" Clarice shook her head. "It's a wonder the SPCA doesn't come after you."

For a minute, she considered just telling her mother to go to Walmart and buy her some sweats. But no, she needed her tactical pants. She needed her shirts. She wanted her underwear. "I have someone taking care of him. He's fine. Let me tell you exactly what to get."

Her mother shook her head. "You dress like a man, Mackenzie," she said, sighing hopelessly. "That's not how I raised you."

13

After Clarice finally left, Kenzie lay staring at the wall, her head pounding, counting her mother's narcissistic statements. The barrage of criticisms, the "I" statements never stopped. Every time she was with her mom, Kenzie fought feeling little and insecure and inadequate. Like a five-year-old. Would she ever get over that?

"Feeling better, honey?" a nurse asked, her white teeth gleaming against her cocoa skin.

"Sure," Kenzie said, trying to smile back. "I'm ready to get out of here."

The nurse laughed. "Not so fast, sugar. We've got to take pictures of your head. And CT is backed up tonight. I don't know why they get so behind."

Kenzie glanced at her watch.

"Somebody hit you upside the head. Now you got a concussion, maybe, and bruises all over you. What happened to you anyway, hon?"

"Somebody jumped me." The less said the better. "What's your name?"

"Yolanda. I'm your nurse. And you need to just wind down and let me keep an eye on you, hon. Shift into a lower gear. We got to make sure your brain is OK."

154

"Some people wonder about that anyway," Kenzie muttered.

"You get some rest. I'll be waking you every two hours, long as I'm on duty," she said, "so you get some sleep while you can." She turned to leave, then stopped, and looked back at Kenzie. "You're a cop, right?" she asked.

Kenzie frowned. "Why do you ask?"

"Because you got a guard right over there." She gestured toward the door of Kenzie's room. "A big, nice-looking D.C. cop. So, you've got to be a cop or a bad guy. I'm guessing, little as you are, you're a cop."

Kenzie touched her mouth. "Yeah. I'm a cop."

Every time Yolanda woke her up, Kenzie looked over expecting to see her mother sitting in that salmon-colored vinyl visitor's chair, looking pinch-faced and annoyed. But she wasn't there, not at two in the morning, or at four, or at six when Kenzie finally got her CT, or even at eight in the morning when the doctor decided to release her. By then, the sun was up, streaming in the door of the ER with all its August brightness and energy, rejuvenated by the storm last night. Kenzie began to wonder if something had happened to her mom.

But no. Clarice walked in at eight-thirty as Kenzie was explaining once again to a nurse's aide that she needed to wait for her ride.

"Well, you're awake," her mother pronounced.

Kenzie swallowed. "Mom! You were gone for a long time. I was afraid something had happened."

"Of course not. I went to bed, that's all. I slept for a while. You didn't expect me to stay up all night, did you?"

What could she say to that? "Did you get the clothes I needed?"

"Oh, yes. And some other things."

Kenzie's heart clutched at the mental image of her mother rummaging through her drawers. Clarice handed her a bag and she looked inside. Tactical pants, shirts, underwear . . . "Mom, what's this?" Kenzie asked, holding up a ruffled dress she hadn't worn in a decade, if ever.

"I thought you'd look so cute in it. You know, if you would dress better, maybe you'd have a chance of attracting a man. You're not getting any younger, Mackenzie."

The pounding in her head did a pretty good job of drowning out the rest of the speech, a speech that Kenzie had heard many, many times. Reflexively, she began getting dressed.

Why hadn't she "settled down"? At first, immersed in her studies, she didn't take the time to date. Then came the concentration and work of becoming an agent. After that, well, it seemed like all the good guys had married, all the ones she met, anyway.

Maybe she was just too picky. Maybe she

hadn't tried hard enough. Maybe she did dress like a boy.

". . . and Mackenzie, honestly, your hair . . ."

Gingerly, Kenzie felt her head. Her hair was a tangled mess. She winced as she felt the spot where she'd been hit. She closed her eyes, but she could not completely block out her mother's words.

". . . so I thought, what you need is a little make-up and a decent haircut." She glanced at her watch. "As soon as Mario opens his shop, I'll call and . . ."

"Mom, no. Stop." Kenzie opened her eyes and held up her hand. "I don't want anyone messing with me right now."

"Mackenzie, don't be stubborn."

"Mom! My head hurts. I can barely keep my eyes open. This isn't a good time for a make-over."

Her mother's lips grew pinched. "Honestly. You've always been so hardheaded."

Kenzie took a deep breath and said, "Look, Mom, I really appreciate you getting those clothes for me and driving all that way, late at night. It was wonderful of you. And I take it you didn't have any trouble with Jack."

"Jack? Oh, no. He's fine. But Mackenzie, you know, you really shouldn't leave him alone like that all the time. He seemed so happy to see me! And I thought, 'This poor neglected dog. Here by himself all day.' And who knows how long you'll be involved in whatever you're doing. That's why I brought him with me."

"You what?" Kenzie's eyes widened and she sat straight up, forgetting the pain.

"I brought him with me."

"Where is he now? Where is Jack now?" Kenzie's heart pounded.

"Why, in the car. You wouldn't expect me to bring a dog into the hospital, would you? Where else would he be?"

Kenzie looked at her watch. Almost nine o'clock. What was the temperature yesterday at nine? "Mom, it's August. It's already getting hot outside. You can't leave a dog in the car."

"He'll be fine. I cracked the windows."

"Mom! Go! Now! You go and get Jack out of that car!"

"Why are you making such a fuss?"

"Because all it takes is fifteen minutes in a hot car and a dog's brain is fried! For crying out loud, Mom. It's not even legal!"

"Legal. For heaven's sakes."

"Mom! Go!"

Kenzie finished jerking on her clothes, called for the nurse, signed the release papers, half-listened to Yolanda's instructions, and tried to stay patient while a volunteer wheeled her to the exit. The D.C. cop who'd been guarding her followed along.

158

Reaching the front door, she jumped up and said "thanks" to the volunteer. "My mother's taking me home," she said to the cop. "She's parked out here somewhere." Her head pounded, her side hurt, and her heart lay in her throat. If her mother had killed Jack, it would be the last straw. The last straw.

But when she spotted Clarice's red Cadillac, she saw Jack sitting in the front passenger seat, erect, alert, and panting happily. And Kenzie's heart made a U-turn from fear back to anger. "Honestly, Mother," she said, jerking open the back door, and feeling a blast of cold air, "I don't know what you were thinking."

Jack turned around and looked at her, his tail wagging madly. Then Clarice reached over with those perfectly manicured, red nail-polished hands and petted Jack behind his ear. He turned his head and licked Clarice's hand, and then, though Kenzie could hardly believe it, her mother leaned toward the dog and let Jack kiss her chin.

Her dog. Kissed her mother. Like she was his best friend.

Suddenly, Kenzie couldn't bear to be in that car. She glanced over her shoulder. The cop was still within shouting distance. She took a step back. "You go on, Mom. Take him home with you. I need to go to the office. I'll call you later." And she grabbed her bag, shut the door against her mother's objections, and turned away.

"Can't your IT people trace these messages?" the senator asked, motioning toward Scott's computer. The screen displayed a fan page for the TV show, *High Stakes*.

"We've already got them working on it. But there are hundreds of people posting messages, and so far I'm not seeing anything that's a red flag," Alicia Sheerling said. The slim, brunette agent stayed focused on the screen, her fingers dancing nimbly over the keyboard.

"This is the kind of thing Kenzie could really help us with," Scott said, taking a deep breath. His eyes shifted toward the door as Crow walked in. He had a laptop in his hand. "What did you get on the kid? Anything?"

Crow put the computer down, took off his black leather jacket, hung it over the back of a chair, then sat down. He could feel the fatigue settling in, like the weariness of a long walk over the trackless expanse of the desert, with few landmarks to measure your progress. "I had the boy's parents bring him down to the police station. They were cooperative: His dad's an exec with the power company and his mom works for a nonprofit on the Hill. The boy, Mark, got scared —I made sure of that."

Scott smiled.

"After I pressed him, he finally came clean. He snuck out of the house around ten o'clock and was skateboarding by himself about three blocks from here in a church parking lot. I saw it: It's surrounded by a tall brick wall on one side, and the landscaping is mature—there are plenty of places to hide. As Mark focused on his board, a man grabbed him from behind and stuck something metal in his neck."

"A gun?"

"I'm guessing." Crow continued, "The guy told him what he wanted him to do—see if he could get the cops to chase him—and stuck a hundred bucks in his jeans."

"Did the kid get a look at him?"

Crow shook his head. "No. Mark said the guy threatened him and said he'd be watching and if he told his parents or the cops he'd kill him." He shifted his weight. He'd dealt with enough bullies in his day to feel for the kid. "Mark's all right—but he's shaking in his boots right now. His parents let me take his laptop," Crow said, nod-ding toward the computer, "just to verify nothing hinky's going on."

"What do you mean?" the senator asked. "What are you looking for?"

"Porn. Pictures of your daughter. That kind of thing. For a kid Mark's age to kidnap a real live child would be a pretty big step. There'd be a lot of evidence he'd been traveling down that road for a while. I don't think that's the case here."

"You know," Scott said, "his story matches what the kid in Chambersburg told us, the one who shipped the package. Except for the gun, it's the same MO. I think Mark is telling the truth. The kidnapper used him as a diversion." His eyes shifted and widened. "Kenzie!"

Crow swiftly turned around. His heart raced when he saw her.

Kenzie touched her lip self-consciously and moved into the room, avoiding looking at anyone but Scott. "Where's the note? I heard you have a note."

"What are you doing here? How do you feel?" Scott asked. "Are you supposed to be working?"

"I feel all right. I can work," Kenzie said firmly. That was deceptive speech, she thought—a lie. The doctor hadn't given her permission to return to the job, but this is when they needed her! "Jesse stopped by the hospital early this morning and said you had a note. I'm here to analyze it." Out of the corner of her eye, she could see Crow looking at her closely. She couldn't read the expression on his face.

"How's your head?" Senator Grable asked.

"It's fine, really." She turned to Scott, pain zinging up her neck as she did. She'd refused to get the prescription for painkillers filled—she certainly didn't need to feel drowsy right now. Ibuprofen would have to do. "Where's the note?"

Scott hesitated, then said, "I'll put the text on a jump drive for you."

Kenzie nodded, her head throbbing. "I'll need my gun back."

"I have it," Scott said. "Lucky for you, whoever hit you must not have seen it in the dark."

Lucky indeed. Losing a gun, even when it wasn't your fault, was a huge deal for an agent. The forms alone could take days to complete.

"How about my cell phone?"

"Your Bureau phone is over there, on charge," Crow said, pointing to the edge of the room. He seemed to be sizing her up, and a sudden tremor went through Kenzie.

Crow motioned to her. "Come out in the kitchen with me," he said to Kenzie. His voice sounded cool. "Let me get you a cup of coffee while Scott is putting the note on the jump drive. And I'll bring you up to speed with what we have."

14

Kenzie followed Crow into the kitchen, thankful that updating her on the case was what he had in mind. "So what's new?" she asked, as he pulled a mug out of the cabinet and began to pour her coffee.

He turned and handed it to her. "What's wrong with you?"

She looked at his dark eyes, his intense face, and she stiffened. It was like looking at an approaching storm. "What are you talking about?"

He exhaled in exasperation. "Don't mess with me. You're hurting."

Kenzie's eyes narrowed. Her neck tightened.

"I see you wince when you move. You blanch. Your face turns white."

"I am white," she snapped.

"Don't be funny. Something's wrong."

Her lips were pressed together. "My head hurts. I think that's normal, under the circumstances." A wall of resentment rose within her. "Are you going to update me? Because if this is just an interrogation, I'll opt out, thanks."

Crow turned and opened a cabinet, pulled out a glass, filled it with water, and downed it. "What is your diagnosis?"

"Why should I tell you?"

"Because I'm a paramedic, that's why. I was an EMT on the Rez and a medic in Iraq. Because on this job we have to know when an agent is endangering herself or the rest of us by being foolish. You read words, I read injuries. And I can tell you're hurting. Why are you being so stubborn?" His eyes were flashing like lightning.

I'm stubborn, Kenzie thought. Just like Mom said. She swallowed. But maybe she was being stubborn. She cupped the warm mug in her hand and sipped the black brew. "They said I had a possible concussion. Not a bad one. And I got four stitches." She touched the back of her head.

"So you were supposed to go home and rest."

"I've got to work this case, Crow." Kenzie's throat was tight. "I need to find Zoe."

"We all do."

"Scott needs me to analyze that note," she said.

Crow grimaced. "You have no business being here." He paced. "How'd this assailant get to you?"

"I never saw him! I walked around the fence . . ."

"Did you do a turkey peek? Did you look before you turned?"

"He must have been hiding in the bushes. He hit me from behind!"

Crow shook his head. "You went off without a battle buddy. You should never do that!"

"What?" Kenzie said, bristling. "You went one way, I went another. What's wrong with that? Don't . . ." Kenzie stopped mid-sentence as Scott walked in the room. She blushed deeply as he looked from one to the other, sensing the conflict.

"That file's ready," he said.

"Thanks," Kenzie responded, and she shot an angry look at Crow as she left the room.

In her work, she could lose herself.

In her work, she could forget her mother, her anger at Crow, her fear, her sense of violation, her embarrassment, even her pain.

In her work, using words to put together the puzzle of a criminal mind, she could gain some control over the swirling circumstances of her life.

Kenzie stared intently at her laptop screen. She sat at the desk in the third-floor guest bedroom, her head still pounding, her ears still ringing with Crow's indictment. Why had he been so angry? Why did he care? What was the big deal?

She'd come upstairs to be alone, so she could concentrate. She had to shake her thoughts off, and focus.

She transferred the verbiage of the kidnapper's note to another file so she could pull it apart, phrase by phrase, word by word, phoneme by phoneme. But after one quick read-through, she already had a question. She called downstairs to Scott, who quickly responded. "What's *High Stakes*?" she asked as he came into the room.

Wearily he sat down on the bed. "It's one of those tense, we're-all-about-to-die TV shows. Very violent. Very popular. The protagonist is a Jack Bauer knock-off—his name is Connor something . . . Connor Stearman. He's out to save the world. His techie girl genius is Joie Gorulski. They work for a secretive government entity called CISU, the Central Intelligence Security Unit. They battle foreign and domestic terrorism and the worst threat of all—Congress."

"Congress—that's interesting."

Scott snorted softly. "None of us has ever watched it. Who has time?"

"Did you check online for the old shows?"

"No, but that's a great idea. I'll get somebody on that."

Scott started to leave. "Are you OK?"

"Of course!" she said, and returned to the note. She began cataloging what she noticed:

The narcissistic phrases: "I've studied you." "I know about your other children." "I've been watching you . . ." "I'm the dealer now." "I'm calling the shots." "I'm in control."

The lack of emotional language. The writer was most likely a man.

The command tone. "You will follow my instructions."

The arrogance. ". . . you can't imagine the lengths to which I will go . . ."

The excruciatingly proper use of English. ". . . the lengths to which I will go . . ."

The threat itself.

From the time she was little, her father had told her words were important. Words meant something. Words were a window into the mind. All the years she'd studied psychology and linguistics, all the criminal cases she'd worked, all the discussions she'd had with her mentors, had formed a primordial soup of information in her subconscious mind; out of it began to emerge an image of Zoe's kidnapper.

Kenzie pored over every line. She took notes on the structure, the syntax, the word choice. She read it out loud, listening to the cadence, the rhythm of the sentences.

Was he working alone? Was he an amateur? How old was he? His educational level? Was he even a "he"? How about his mental state? His familiarity with the senator? Questions, questions.

Normally, a complete analysis would take her days, if not weeks. But she had no time for minute detail work now. Zoe's life hung in the balance.

She heard a knock on the door. Crow had a Ziploc bag of ice for her. "Put this on your lip," he said, and left again.

Kenzie looked at the bag of ice. A peace

offering, she wondered? Maybe he was concerned about her. But then, why did he seem so gruff?

She had no answers, so she returned to her work. Once Kenzie had made all of her observations, she entered the language of the note into a computer program to compare it with other known threats and their outcomes. It was a program she had developed, based on data collected in excruciating detail for her doctoral dissertation. And in the case of Zoe's kidnapper, the program said the correlation between words and action seemed high. This guy meant business. He would do what he said.

In three hours, she had a preliminary analysis.

"With a head injury, who knows what she's thinking or how she'll react," Crow said in a low voice. He and Scott were standing in the Grables' kitchen. "I sure would hate to have to depend on her in a shooting situation!"

"I need her expertise!" Scott responded.

Crow had just opened his mouth when Scott held up his hand. "I don't want to talk about this anymore."

And then, Kenzie walked in. "I'm ready with a preliminary profile," she announced. She dabbed her mouth with a tissue. The cut seeped blood.

Scott glanced at Crow. He took a deep breath. "Let's go in the dining room."

• • •

Kenzie preceded the men. She felt awkward, like they were staring at her back. What had they been discussing? When she got to the dining room, the senator was standing off to the side, looking weary.

"Senator Grable, could you excuse us for a few minutes?" Scott said. The senator's wife had not yet been cleared. No sense revealing too much to him yet.

"Sure," Grable responded. "I'll be in my office."

The three agents watched as he walked out, then listened for the sound of his office door shutting.

"Where's Beth?" Kenzie asked.

"She left last night. Probably with a friend." Scott glanced at his watch. "I'll call her in a little while."

Kenzie straightened her back. She dabbed her mouth and glanced at Crow again before she looked down at her notes. He leaned up against the wall, his arms crossed over his chest. She felt a tremor run through her, perhaps prompted by confusion. She cleared her throat and began: "Our UNSUB is a native English speaker, an educated, middle-aged man. He knows the senator well. He's familiar with the house, with the family. He takes a lot of pride in his ability with words . . . he's most likely college-educated, could be a communicator, a speaker or writer. His attention to detail is notable. I believe he's between the ages of thirty-five and fifty. The man has a lot of anger toward those whom he perceives have mistreated him. And he has some psychopathic or at least narcissistic tendencies."

"Meaning?"

"A marked lack of empathy, a coldness, self-centeredness . . ."

"A psychopath?" Scott asked.

"I would say he may have psychopathic tendencies. There's a range, you know. Some who score pretty high on the scale aren't even criminals. They could be cutthroat businessmen or women. They may be charming, bright, attractive—but they have in common an inability to empathize and a singleness of purpose: Whatever they're into, they're in it for themselves. This guy may have been that type of corporate psychopath and now something has triggered an escalation: He's crossed the line. He may not be married. Not involved with any women long-term. He's too self-focused and angry. He's absolutely dedicated to his work. But he feels morally superior, almost invincible. Puffed up, like a balloon. I think this is his last attempt to wrest from life what he's sure he deserves and has never gotten. Money. Respect. Power. Those are his goals." She lowered the notes in her hand. She looked directly at the two men, keeping her expression calm.

"The note said, 'I'm the dealer now.' I'm wondering if this emerged from the mind of a person who regularly played a game involving a dealer."

"Like mah-jongg?" Crow suggested.

"Other clues indicate the note writer is a man," Kenzie said.

"But could he have had a woman mah-jongg player standing at his side? Beth Grable, maybe?" Crow asked.

"I don't know."

"What about violence?" Scott asked. "How likely is he to hurt Zoe?"

Kenzie shifted in her chair. "By nature, he is not a violent person. He probably has no criminal record. But according to the measures we use, the correlation between the threat and the UNSUB acting on it is high."

Scott nodded. "He did assault the nanny . . . and you."

"Assaulting me seems more opportunistic. I was at the wrong place at the wrong time." The pain in her head throbbed. She avoided looking at Crow. "And we can't rule out the idea he paid some low-level criminal to deliver the note," she said.

Crow interrupted. "No, he did it himself. We know that."

Kenzie wondered how exactly he knew that. What piece of information had she missed? "Then that's consistent with his narcissism. I don't know about the nanny. I'm going to keep working through the note. In the meantime," Kenzie said, "I'd like to get access to the senator's office on the Hill. I'd like to read some of the paperwork his staff has written, and some of his correspondence. I'd like to get a sense of the words his associates are using."

"Because the kidnapper could be someone he's worked with, either directly in his office or from somewhere on the Hill, or one of his other contacts," Scott added. "I'm sure he'll cooperate." Scott looked at Kenzie. "That's great. Good work. What about the show's fan page? What do you recommend we do about that?"

"Assign someone to monitor it twenty-four/ seven. I'll give them a list of words and phrases to watch for. I would rotate personnel every three or four hours. Those message boards can be deadly boring."

"We're on it, Kenz."

"I'll get the senator on board," Crow said, and he turned and left the room.

"You feeling OK?" Scott asked Kenzie.

No, Kenzie thought. *My head hurts, I'm exhausted, and my dog is with my mother, of all people, and I can't figure out why John Crowfeather is so angry.* "Fine," she said out loud.

"Because if you need to take a break, it's OK. We can handle things."

"No. Did you get the information on Beau Talmadge?"

"Jocelyn got his home address. She's on that."

She reminded him about the reference to "dealer" in the note. "Give me the information," she said. "I'll get in touch with her and if she hasn't interviewed him, I will, before I head up to the Hill."

Scott frowned. "Are you sure you're OK to do that?"

"I want to."

"Go with Crow."

"Why?" she snapped, surprised at her own irritation.

"Because I want you to."

That was not a direct answer, she thought.

15

"Come on, honey." Sandy unbuckled Zoe's seat belt.

"Two hours, understand?" Grayson said, turning around in the driver's seat of the silver Ford.

"OK, Gray. That'll be four-thirty. I'll see you right here."

"And be careful, OK? I don't want this whole thing unraveling because you screwed up."

She shut the door and took Zoe's hand. "We are going to have fun!" She gave the little girl's hand a squeeze. Just before they entered the mall, she leaned down and said, "Now remember our pretending game. I'm going to call you Joey. That's almost like Zoe. And we're going to pretend you're a boy. If you're really, really good, I'll buy you some candy when we're done."

Zoe looked up at her. "I want my daddy."

That's all she'd been saying for the last four hours. "Maybe he's in the mall. Let's go see, OK?"

Somehow, Sandy had talked Zoe into wearing a Boston Red Sox baseball cap, blue jeans, and a red shirt. She actually looked like a little boy. But traces of the nail polish, the pink nail polish, were still there, on the edges of two fingers. All Sandy could do was hope no one would notice. Especially Grayson.

Fortunately, she'd deftly covered the two offending fingers when he'd checked Zoe's hands. He'd missed that little bit of polish. Good thing, too, because Sandy didn't know what she would do if he had forbidden her this one little excursion. Tensions in the house were high, and she could hardly stand being cooped up anymore. If he wasn't yelling at her, he was screaming at Zoe.

But Grayson had said the senator had already begun responding to his demands, and they'd have the money soon. Zoe would be home, and they'd be gone and the stress would be over. She couldn't wait.

Crowds of back-to-school shoppers and bargain hunters filled the mall. Sandy hoped to snag a good deal on a bathing suit, maybe even some tropical slacks and shirts. Jamaica would be warm all year 'round. She'd already given away all of her sweaters and winter coats. When her sister asked why, she had smiled coyly and hinted there'd be a big surprise soon. As much as Sandy had wanted to let her in on the secret, she couldn't. Carol had been married for twenty years —she had no idea what it felt like to be a lonely, divorced woman in a dead-end job. No future, no hope. Nothing. Until Grayson came along.

Sandy headed for a big department store anchoring one end of the mall. As relaxing as she'd imagined this shopping trip to be, it turned out to be anything but. Zoe kept wanting to look at pretty little dresses and bows for her hair. When Sandy tried to shop for herself, the little girl swung on the clothes racks in the misses department and sang a song she'd made up about her daddy. She screamed "No!" when Sandy suggested buying some boys' shirts and seemed to have to go to the bathroom every fifteen minutes. The kicker came when Sandy, engrossed in looking for a blouse to match a really cute pair of capris, looked up and saw Zoe talking to a uniformed security guard.

Her heart jumped into her throat and she quickly retrieved the little girl, apologizing to the officer. "My husband and I are going through a divorce," she hastily explained, "and Joey misses his daddy so much."

"My name's not Joey!" the little girl yelled, but the security guard just laughed knowingly and Sandy scooped her up and left the store.

She tried letting Zoe ride the airplane in the kids' play area of the mall. She bought her candy. Tried bribing her with a DVD. But Zoe would not be bought off. She was not a boy. She wanted her daddy. And everyone was going to hear about it.

In the end, Sandy had to settle for grabbing two pairs of jeans and a couple of T-shirts for Zoe in a children's specialty shop. Nothing for herself.

And when Grayson picked her up, she practically threw Zoe in the Ford, and slammed the door shut.

"Have fun?" Grayson asked, seeing her expression.

"This better be over soon," Sandy muttered.

Beau Talmadge lived on Capitol Hill in an old Victorian row house three blocks from the Capitol, on the gentrified edge of one of Washington's most crime-plagued areas. His gorgeous old house had a tiny yard portioned off by an iron fence and granite front steps. Kenzie pulled her Bucar to the curb out front.

Scott had said to wait for Crow. But she had called him and he couldn't get there before four o'clock, half an hour from now. She wanted to get on with it.

Kenzie's head hurt. Her last interactions with Crow had left her gun-shy. In fact, she'd been obsessing about his behavior all afternoon, and she'd already decided to confront him. Why had he been giving her such a hard time?

She gently touched her injured lower lip with her tongue as she walked up the front steps. It felt four times its usual size. She punched the doorbell. A dog began barking. A big dog. The door swung open and a man about her age grinned at her, and grabbed the collar of the Rottweiler lunging across the threshold. "Best burglar alarm ever," the man said.

"Are you Beau Talmadge?" Kenzie asked.

"I am."

"Special Agent Mackenzie Graham, FBI. Mind if I come in?"

He laughed. "I don't, but Jackson might."

"Jackson?"

"My Rottie," he said, nodding toward the dog. "Named after one of Auburn's most famous football players, Bo Jackson." He grinned sheepishly. "I couldn't call him Bo."

"No, of course not," Kenzie agreed. Despite her trained neutrality, she instantly liked the man.

"C'mon, Jackson," Beau said, giving the dog's collar a good shake. He stepped back from the door opening and Kenzie stepped through. The dog growled. "Let me put him up," Beau said, closing the door, and he disappeared upstairs with the Rottie in tow.

Kenzie looked around. The tall, narrow house had a beautiful staircase ascending to the second floor. The foyer was small but handy, with pegs for jackets and a small mat for boots. The living room with a fireplace was off to the right. Over the mantle was a large oil painting of a brick building with a clock tower. She moved closer to it so she could see it better.

"Samford Hall, Auburn University," Beau's voice boomed behind her. "Best five years of my life."

She turned to look at him. "Most people do college in four."

He grinned. "Now that's foolish. Pretty women, all you can drink, and a poker party every night. Couldn't get enough of it."

Kenzie noted his boyish good looks, brown hair, blue eyes, and easy grin. Every part of Beau Talmadge screamed "frat boy." And not in a bad way.

"Sit down, sit down," he said, gesturing toward a brown couch. "Can I get you something to drink?"

"No, I'm fine."

Talmadge plopped into an upholstered chair. "What can I do you for?"

"Mr. Talmadge, I'm sure you've heard that Beth Grable's daughter, Zoe, is missing."

Beau straightened up and put both feet on the floor. He leaned forward. "Yes, and I'm so sorry, really I am," he said.

"I understand you've been seeing Mrs. Grable."

He blushed. "We're old friends from Auburn. She had pledged a sorority, I lived in a frat house. We had a lot of fun together, Beth and I, although to be honest, I don't remember much of it." He grinned. "When I moved to D.C., her momma told me to look her up. I did, and yes, we've done a few things together."

"What sort of things, Mr. Talmadge?"

He gestured with his hands. "No sex. Honest.

No affair going on, I swear. But Beth, she likes the ponies. Actually, she likes gambling of any kind, and her old man's a bit stiff. So I've taken her a couple of times, to Charles Town, or Dover Downs. Once to Atlantic City. And the new Maryland casinos. But no hanky-panky, I swear." His eyes were fixed intently on Kenzie, as if he were trying to read her response to him.

Kenzie nodded. "How often do you see her?"

"She calls me maybe once a week, and we've gone out maybe half a dozen times in the three months I've been here." He suddenly changed the subject. "What happened to your lip, anyway? Looks like you've been in a fight."

Kenzie ignored the question. "Mr. Talmadge, where do you work?"

"Jefferson & Maddox. A PR firm. Has a nice ring to it, doesn't it? Don't know if you're getting old school Virginia or redneck Georgia." He grinned again, and Kenzie thought, yes, he's probably really good at public relations.

"And what do you do for them?"

"Lobby the Hill for clients, write press releases, do radio and TV interviews, you name it. If it involves people, I'm there. Throw in drinks and I'm there all night."

"Did you ever meet Zoe?" Kenzie watched him carefully.

"No," he said. His demeanor changed and his voice softened. "Beth didn't want me coming to the house. Guess she wanted to keep our relationship, uh, private."

Out of the senator's line of sight, Kenzie thought. She nodded in affirmation. Beau rested his arms on his knees and played with a tiny piece of paper he'd found on the carpet. He looked like he was trying to decide whether or not to say something, and Kenzie let him have all the time he needed.

He finally looked up at her. "Beth gets easily bored. She's always been that way. In college she played the sorority party girl role. It's hard for me to imagine her married, much less a mother. But I wasn't breaking up their marriage, you know? That wasn't my intention. And I had nothing, absolutely nothing, to do with Zoe's disappearance."

"Where were you that night?"

"What night?"

"Tuesday night, between six p.m. and midnight."

Beau leaned back and put his finger on his chin. He stared at the ceiling, trying to recall. Then he reached into his back pocket and pulled out a smartphone. He scrolled through the menus and looked up at Kenzie. "I had a dinner date that cancelled on me at the last minute. So I stayed here, with Jackson, all that evening."

"Alone?"

"Yes, alone, with my dog." He sighed. "Is the testimony of a Rottweiler permissible in court?"

Kenzie smiled. " 'Fraid not."

Suddenly the front door opened and a male voice called out, "Hey, Lucy, I'm home!"

Both Kenzie and Beau stood up as a good-looking young man dressed in black pants and a pink shirt walked in. "Oh, I'm sorry. I didn't know it was girls' night in," he said in a singsong voice. He put a package down on the floor. "Where's my little Jackson?" he crooned.

Beau looked at Kenzie. "As I said, I am really not interested in Mrs. Grable, except as a friend."

She smiled and handed him her business card. "Call me if you find out anything you think I should know."

Crow came jogging up the sidewalk as Kenzie walked out to her car. "I'm done," she said, heading him off.

"What?"

She saw his look of astonishment, but before he could say anything else, her cell phone rang.

"We're live on the five o'clock news shows," Scott said over the phone. "Can you come back here and help us frame what Senator Grable says?"

"Sure!" she responded. "You got him to agree to it?"

"Reluctantly. Tell Crow to come, too."

"We're leaving now. Be there in twenty minutes."

Crow opened his mouth as she clicked the cell phone off, but again she blocked him. "Scott needs us in Georgetown, ASAP."

No quick route through Washington existed at four o'clock in the afternoon, but Kenzie took her best shot, taking Pennsylvania Avenue straight through to Georgetown. She worked on a game plan in her head, and forced herself to ignore Crow's angry face in her rearview mirror as he steered his car behind hers. If she'd waited for him before interviewing Talmadge, she wouldn't have been able to make it to the Grables' in time for the press conference. Correctly framing the media interview could make or break this case. And the way they constructed it would be predicated on the correct profile of the UNSUB. So she had to be there.

She turned her racing mind to him, the kidnapper. Presumably a "him." If he proved a true, out-and-out psychopath, appeals to his humanity would have no effect. Missing the ability to empathize, concerned only for himself, he would not respond to pleas from a grief-stricken father. It would have to be something else. She rolled over the facts of the case in her head, mentally matching them to the picture of the perpetrator created there, imagining different scenarios. And as she turned the corner onto M Street, the right tactic came into sharp focus.

16

Crews had already set up cameras in front of the senator's house when Kenzie arrived. She pulled around back, parked her Bureau car in the alley, and started walking toward the house. Then she heard Crow's voice.

"Kenzie!" He caught up to her and touched her arm.

"Scott's waiting for me!" she said, quickening her pace.

Crow kept up with her. "Why didn't you wait? I thought we were interviewing Talmadge together."

With each footfall, her head pounded. "You were late. I wanted to get it done," and as she jerked open the back door, she heard him mutter something under his breath—in Navajo.

"Let's go in the senator's office," Scott suggested.

The senator, dressed in a dark blue suit and white shirt, had already had his on-camera makeup done and was tying his tie. He looked nervously at Kenzie, searching her eyes as if to seek reassurance that this plan would really work, and as a result of this personal appeal, his daughter would be in his arms again, laughing and tugging at his tie.

"Senator," Scott said, "we want to be sure to do this right. We may only have one shot at it." Kenzie sat down next to him. "This is where Kenzie can really help us, so let's listen to her plan."

"All right."

Kenzie looked at Scott. "Is Mrs. Grable going to appear with you?"

Scott shook his head. "She isn't back."

"And she ran out without her cell phone," the senator added, "so we haven't been able to find her."

Kenzie shot Scott a look. Not knowing Beth's whereabouts was a mistake. His eyes told her he understood that. Turning to the senator, she began. "Senator, I believe the kidnapper knows you. And I believe he has psychopathic tendencies. Practically speaking, that means appeals to his conscience won't work. We have to frame everything in terms of his self-interest. It's important that you not appear to be weak—it would only strengthen him. You have to think of this as a business deal. Here's what you want, here's what I'm offering, that sort of thing."

The senator swallowed hard. He blinked and looked away, as if the reality of the situation unnerved him.

Kenzie shifted in her chair, drawing his eyes back to her. "We don't want to reveal too much information," she said, continuing. "It could preclude a positive identification of the kidnapper later. For instance, we're not going to release details about the note. Understand?"

He nodded.

"Here's what I want you to do: Emphasize Zoe's illness. Not for sympathy's sake, but because if she dies, his plan is thwarted. No kid, no ransom." Kenzie saw Grable flinch at the word *dies,* but then he tightened his jaw and kept listening. "It must be in the kidnapper's self-interest to get on with this, to communicate with us again, to make the deal happen. You understand?"

"Sure."

Kenzie looked at Scott. "Nothing on the fan page yet, right?"

"Right."

"OK. We've got to push this guy. So here's what you're going to say." She outlined the points the senator needed to make and she saw him make some notes on a three-by-five card, a good sign. He was used to the press, used to public speaking, used to getting his message across, used to managing his image.

"Are we allowing a Q&A?" he asked.

"A couple of questions, that's all," Scott responded.

"What if the reporters go a different direction?" the senator asked.

"You control the interview," Kenzie said.

"Divert back to your topics. You can do this. You're good at it. I've seen you, Senator."

His mouth twitched. "This is different. This is my kid."

"I have confidence in you." Kenzie looked deeply into his eyes.

And he blinked hard and nodded. "OK."

Scott made some other clarifications, then Kenzie checked her watch. "It's 4:50. You're going to have maybe two minutes on air. Let's role-play for a minute."

And so, assuming the part of reporter, she and the senator went over and over his part until a knock on the door announced his moment had come.

The horde of reporters outside included the national press, Kenzie noted, peeking out from an upstairs bedroom window. Scott, reminding her that the UNSUB knew her identity and had attacked her, had told her to remain inside, and although she chafed at that restriction, she knew it was wise. Behind her a television aired the final commercials leading up to the five o'clock news. She had a DVR set to record.

Already the station had promoted the live press conference from the senator's house. Of the top field reporters clustered on the senator's front lawn, Kenzie recognized most of them. A gaggle of microphones extended from their hands and behind them stood cameramen with their equipment trained on the front porch, ready for the signal to start. Along the edge of the crowd stood Crow, dressed casually, his gun covered by a chambray denim shirt. When she saw him, she felt a tingle run up her spine. He looked good standing there in the sun, his coppery skin and dark hair setting him apart from the crowd. Anybody would be attracted to him, she thought. Anybody.

The television stations' remote trucks jammed the street, their transmission antennae stretching into the sky like giraffes, their heads pointed all different directions.

Although she couldn't see them, Kenzie could tell when the senator and Scott emerged from the house as every eye turned toward the front porch. Faintly through the closed window she could hear a producer counting down, "Three, two, one . . . GO!"

Scott took charge of the multi-station event. She wondered if they'd get his name spelled right on the supers. He looked so good, so professional, so FBI-like talking to them. "Sometime between 6:30 p.m. and 10:30 p.m. on Tuesday," Scott said, "an abduction took place at this address. An unknown subject took a five-year-old child, Zoe Grable, daughter of Senator Bruce Grable and his wife Elizabeth, from her bedroom."

Kenzie listened to the television, but turned to watch the street below carefully. The kidnapper could even be in the crowd. They couldn't rule that out. Anyone brazen enough to enter the senator's property to leave a note could do just about anything. That's why Crow stood down there. That's why, even now, he scanned the crowd, his eyes obscured behind dark sunglasses, his face a mask.

Scott finished speaking. Without looking at the television, she could envision what he was doing—stepping aside and letting the senator have center stage. "Stay strong," she said quietly, coaching the senator in absentia. "Don't appear vulnerable."

His voice emerged from the television behind her. "As Agent Hansbrough said, two days ago, our daughter disappeared from our home." His voice wavered. Kenzie gritted her teeth. He continued, stronger. "Whoever took her may not realize she is very ill. The day she was abducted, tests revealed she has diabetes, insulin-dependent, Type I diabetes. Unless she receives medical attention immediately, she will die. They could charge the abductor, then, with a far more serious crime than simple kidnapping. Zoe requires special care, care most strangers would not know how to give. We are waiting for further instructions and are prepared to cooperate for the sake of my daughter."

He held up a portrait. "Zoe is a beautiful little girl. Like all little girls, she likes ponies, dolls, and pink. Pink anything. But her appearance could have changed. Here is the police artist's sketch of what she would look like as a boy. I know someone has seen her. I just need your help in getting her back. That's all."

Good job, Kenzie thought. Good job. He'd played it just right.

"Senator! Senator!" numerous reporters called out as he stepped away from the microphones.

But Scott took control. "A twenty-five thousand dollar reward has been posted for information leading to the recovery of Zoe. We have set up a direct telephone line for tips: 1-800-FINDZOE. The National Center for Missing and Exploited Children will also take calls related to this case." He gave their phone number. "Thank you."

As he stepped back, reporters called out questions. "Senator, is it true you were under investigation for bribery when this occurred?" the Channel 4 newswoman yelled.

"No comment," the senator responded.

"Has there been contact with the kidnapper? A note or anything?"

"We've been in contact; we await further instructions."

"Senator, does an ethics violation have anything to do with this crime? Did you bring this on yourself?"

Kenzie groaned.

"I would never put my daughter at risk. She's an innocent child. What we should be concentrating on is getting her back. Someone out there has seen her. I'd appreciate your help."

Scott intervened. "That's all the questions for now. Thank you."

As if choreographed, the reporters below turned toward their own cameras to make a final comment. Within seconds, crew members were wrapping up wires, putting away microphones, and reinstalling cameras in their cases. The show was over.

Kenzie flipped off the television and went downstairs.

"How'd I do?" the senator asked her.

"Perfect," she said. "Want to look at it?" She held up the disk. "Where's Scott?"

Before he could answer, there was a knock on the front door and an attractive, blonde woman stuck her head in. "Senator? How 'bout an interview? You owe me, remember?"

Kenzie froze. Reporter Peggy Tripp had breached security.

Grayson Chambers stood in the living room of his dead mother's house, sipping a cup of coffee, and watching the television. The five o'clock news hour was approaching and he felt curious. Would Zoe's disappearance be made public?

If so, he'd have to be even more careful. Already a neighbor in the seedy little community in which his mother had lived had recognized him and asked about the child and the woman who were with him. "She's my girlfriend," he'd said, smiling, "and that's her kid."

He hated the fact someone had recognized him. Why did his mother have to be so social? She wasn't really, not by any stretch of the imagination, but you don't live somewhere for twenty years without getting to know the people around you. Unfortunately, that now worked against him.

Inheriting her little gem of a house didn't exactly thrill him. The one-story, two-bedroom frame rambler sat beside a large pond. Although neat and trim, the house would be a pain for him to sell. The privately maintained roads in the community were deteriorating, filled with potholes and ruts. Apparently, his mother had no concern about how easily the house could be sold. It was just perfect for her, she'd said when she'd bought it, with room for flowers and a grassy lawn for her little dog. Always thinking of herself. When she'd died suddenly of a heart attack a year ago, the first thing he'd done was take the little mutt to the pound. Good grief. He got stuck with the house; he refused to be saddled with her yappy Chihuahua.

Out of the corner of his eye, he could see Zoe sitting on a chair in the kitchen, swinging her legs and eating jelly beans from a bag. Great. As long as she stayed occupied. The lead up to the news was beginning, with lots of yada-yada and swooshing graphics. Pressing a button on the remote, Grayson turned up the volume. His heart quickened as he heard the promo for the lead story.

Better not let her see or hear her father, he thought. He reduced the volume and stepped closer to the TV, blocking the line of sight from the kitchen. His pulse pounding in his ears, he focused on the television.

Some suit did the introduction. Had to be an FBI agent. Grayson had seen plenty of them around Washington. Fit, trim, wearing good suits and Italian leather shoes. He hated their sharp confidence. Even the women had it. He smiled to himself. But I got at least one of them, he thought. I took one FBI female down.

"As Agent Hansbrough said, two days ago, our daughter disappeared from our home."

The senator stood before the crowd of reporters. Grayson scanned that familiar face, the boyish good looks, the black, neatly trimmed hair, those brilliant blue eyes. Could it be fatigue edging their corners? Worry? Fear, maybe?

Yeah, you should be scared, Grayson thought. *I got your little girl. I got the only thing you really care about in this world.*

You sure didn't care about me, Grayson

continued. *Didn't matter how I saved you over and over on the Hill. You didn't care how I covered for you when I knew people were slipping you thousands and thousands of dollars. The thought didn't even cross your mind to give old Grayson a little pat on the back or credit for all your brilliant legislative moves, much less a cut of the cash. No. You let me do the job, while you took the glory.*

"The day she was abducted," the senator continued, "tests revealed she has diabetes, insulin-dependent, Type I diabetes."

What? Grayson's attention snapped into focus.

"Unless she receives medical attention immediately, she will die. They could charge the abductor, then, with a far more serious crime than simple kidnapping. "

Holy . . . Grayson broke out into a sweat. He wiped his hands on his trousers. Diabetes? His mother's heart attack had come from diabetes. What did she take for it? Medications? Insulin shots? He'd never paid much attention. Maybe if he looked around he'd find some leftover meds.

"We are waiting for further instructions and are prepared to cooperate for the sake of my daughter."

Just his luck! He finally pulls off his plan and gets a sick kid. If she died, things would get complicated. Mess him up completely. He'd have to dispose of the body, yet maintain the ruse long enough to get the ransom money. How would he do that? And Sandy—good grief, Sandy would freak. Irritated, he watched the rest of the press briefing and snapped off the television. When he turned toward the kitchen, he saw Zoe with a mouthful of jelly beans. Sugar! He strode toward her, grabbed the bag from her hands, and yelled at Sandy. "Stop feeding her all this candy!" he roared. "You're going to make her sick!"

Peggy Tripp's blonde hair and bright smile had helped gain her entry to many a home and office around town. A political reporter for a local news station, she specialized in gotcha journalism. She claimed as one of her recent trophies the head of a Virginia senator defeated in his last election after a misstatement in a Peggy Tripp interview.

"Peggy!" Senator Grable said, giving her a hug. He looked relieved that the TV news conference had finished, but Kenzie, seeing the reporter's forwardness, worried that he would drop his guard. "Senator," she said, but the man wasn't looking in her direction at all. Kenzie moved to intervene. "Excuse me, Ms. Tripp, the senator . . ."

"It's all right, it's all right," Grable said, taking the reporter by the arm and bringing her further into the house. Clearly, he knew her. Clearly, they had a history.

Kenzie rolled her eyes. Where was Scott? She looked toward the kitchen. Nowhere in sight. She grabbed the senator's arm. "Senator. Sir." She waited until his eyes had turned to her. "I don't think . . ."

"Bruce, you owe me. You said that yourself," the reporter said sweetly, folding herself toward him, diverting his attention. "Besides, it could help."

"I don't suppose it could hurt."

Oh yes, it could hurt! Kenzie screamed inside. *It could ruin everything!* "Senator, wait . . ." but the senator began moving toward his office, the reporter on his arm, and the best Kenzie could do was follow them in.

17

"He's not a prisoner. We can't keep him from talking," Scott said twenty minutes later.

She still fumed with anger. "How does he expect us to resolve this if he's going off like a loose cannon? Bruce Grable is an idiot."

"Kenzie, relax," Scott replied. "It's not the end of the world. Did you sit in on the interview? Monitor what he said?"

"Yes, and a couple of times I stopped him, but," she hesitated. That reporter had reminded her of her mother: blonde, beautiful, and manipulative. She hated the way Peggy Tripp had taken control. Hated it. Kenzie shook her head. "It was so wrong."

"It's all right. It's going to be all right." He ran his hand over his head. "We've got more important things to worry about. Are you feeling all right?"

"I told you, yes!" she snapped.

"Why didn't you wait for Crow?"

"What?"

"Why didn't you wait for Crow before you interviewed Talmadge, like I asked you to?"

Kenzie stiffened. "If I had, I wouldn't have been here on time."

"I told you to wait."

"And I said Grable shouldn't give individual interviews! Things don't always work out, do they, Scott? So don't worry about it!"

Scott's eyes narrowed. The skin above his mouth mottled, his anger ignited. "Team play beats brilliant individual play anytime," he snapped.

Beyond him, Kenzie saw Crow watching them. "What is that supposed to mean?" she said, and turned and stalked out to the kitchen.

She felt tired. Incredibly tired. And her head hurt and she hated thinking of what she'd just said to Scott, and she hated thinking of her dog alone with her mother, and she hated thinking of Zoe with the kidnapper, and she wanted to rewind the tape and successfully keep Bruce Grable from giving Peggy Tripp a personal interview. How could she have failed at that? She pounded her fist into the side of her leg. She was an agent, for crying out loud. She had been taught to control the situation!

And she hadn't. She'd let the blonde charm her way right into Grable's office. And Grable had let his human side come out, just what she, Kenzie, had warned him against. If the kidnapper were truly a psychopath he would feel empowered. He'd gotten to the senator—just what he wanted to do.

She had let Peggy Tripp get to Grable, she'd let her mom take her dog, she'd let some guy clunk her on the head . . . what an idiot! Maybe Crow was right. Maybe she shouldn't be on this case.

Outside the kitchen window, the evening light had begun to fade. Another day for Zoe. Another night away from home. Another scary, terrifying . . .

"Hey," Scott said.

She turned around. He filled the doorway, looming over her like Judgment Day.

She folded her arms across her middle. "I'm sorry," she said quietly.

"It's all right. We're all tense. And you drive yourself pretty hard."

She started to protest but immediately recognized it as useless. She did drive herself hard. Very hard. She looked at Scott. "I shouldn't have yelled at you. I felt angry with myself for letting Senator Grable talk to that reporter."

Scott leaned against the kitchen island, his brown eyes soft, his expression calm. "You couldn't have prevented it. I couldn't have, either."

She frowned.

"If she hadn't gotten in the house, she would have called him. I'll bet you anything she's got his home number, his office number, his cell phone number. She was going to get that interview. I know her. She's very aggressive. And we can advise the senator regarding what's wise, but we can't keep him from talking to her."

Kenzie turned away.

"It's not going to be perfect."

Mentally, she filled in the part he left out: *God is in control.* His mantra. But she hadn't asked for a sermon, and she didn't want one.

Scott cleared his throat. "We need to make sure we're working as a team. And unless you have good reason not to, when I tell you to do something a particular way, I want you to do it that way."

She turned toward him and lifted her chin. "Ever since I got back from the hospital, Crow has been pressing me, like I'm to blame for getting hit." She tossed her head. "I'm not going to put up with that."

Scott stood up and stuck his hands in his pockets. "He's got an issue . . ."

"With what? Women in the Bureau? I would have thought by now . . ."

Scott waved his hand. "No, no. It's not about women nor is it about you, per se. It's something else. I'll talk to him. Now look, Kenz, we're all tired. You were assaulted last night. I need you to be in top shape if we get something from this guy. So get some rest, OK?"

She took a deep breath. Her head pounded. Her whole body felt weak, wrung out, like a dishrag. "All right."

He started to leave, then turned around. "Kenzie, you're on this case for a reason, and it isn't just linguistics. God's doing something. Just relax. Lean into it. Let him take you where he wants you to be."

She bristled. "Just call me, OK? If our subject shows up on the board?"

Kenzie trudged upstairs, her conversation with Scott playing over and over in her head. What did he mean, it wasn't about her, per se? What did that mean? Why couldn't he tell her? She fell asleep, despite all the thoughts rolling around in her head. And although she intended to remain angry with Crow, the last image in her mind was him standing in the crowd, the sun glinting off his black hair, his burnished skin glowing like hot metal.

"Kenzie." A hand on her shoulder pulled her out of a dream. "Kenzie."

She opened her eyes.

"Scott told me to wake you up," Crow said gently. "We think we have something."

She sat up quickly. A sharp pain rewarded her. She put her hand to her head.

"Easy . . . easy," he said. "Take your time." His voice sounded soft, gentle.

Kenzie tried to stand up, losing her balance in midair. Crow steadied her, catching her arm, and as he did, their eyes met. He looked away quickly. "Come down when you can," he said, suddenly letting go of her and disappearing through the door.

• • •

When she arrived downstairs, Alicia Sheerling sat at the dining room table, peering at a computer hooked up to the Internet. Scott stood beside her. Crow was present, too, off to the side, his arms folded across his chest. He didn't look up as she entered the room.

"Here," Alicia said, moving out of the way. "Look at this."

The computer screen displayed a page from a message board about the show *High Stakes*. It read: *Joie doesn't wear much pink anymore. She's always frowning. Why is she so unhappy? Somebody better do something—if he's able.*

Joie—Zoe

Able—Grable

No pink—she's dressed like a boy.

Kenzie looked up at Alicia. "Good job."

"What do you think?" Scott asked.

"Could be our guy." She pointed out the word plays. "So remind me: Who is Joie in the TV show?"

"She's the computer geek," Alicia responded.

"OK, where's Senator Grable?" Kenzie asked. "I'd like to know if the screen name means anything to him."

"I'll get him," Crow said.

"I scanned back on the board," Alicia said. "Jackson423 just started posting about two weeks ago."

"What's he been saying?"

"It's the usual fan-page garbage. Talking about plots, torture techniques . . . honestly, it all looks normal, until this. It just didn't read right, you know? It's what caught my attention. Who says 'if he is able' on a message board? And why would he suddenly, after all this macho stuff, why would he suddenly point out Joie's mood?"

Kenzie nodded. "You're right, Alicia. It stands out. Scott? I'm going to respond to this guy."

"Do whatever you think best," he replied.

Her fingers flying over the keyboard, Kenzie created two screen names. She'd use "Big Dog" as if she were Senator Grable, and "Brandigurl" as a cover, a flirtatious, shallow female persona through which she would try to draw this guy out. Jackson423, what was the significance of that screen name?

Senator Grable entered the room. "What's going on?"

"Do you know anyone named 'Jackson'?" she responded, glancing at him.

"No," Grable responded.

"The name 'Jackson423' doesn't mean anything to you?" But as the name rolled off her tongue, she suddenly made a connection.

"Absolutely nothing," the senator said.

Her heart pumped hard. She looked up. Scott had just clicked off his phone. "Excuse me for a minute. Watch the screen, will you, Alicia? I'll be back in just a second." She caught Scott's eye and he followed her out to the kitchen.

"What's up?" he asked, quietly. Crow must have sensed something because he followed right behind Scott.

"That guy I went to see today? Beau Talmadge? I just remembered something." She pressed her fingers to her temples. "He has a dog named Jackson."

Scott's face tightened. "A dog."

"A Rottweiler."

"But you didn't see anything there."

Kenzie thought she saw a grimace of disapproval on Crow's face. "Nothing raised my suspicions!" she said to Scott. "Talmadge said he'd been a college friend of Mrs. Grable's and since moving to D.C. he'd taken her a few places, gambling venues like Charles Town. Atlantic City once. But they were just friends. Honestly, Scott, I think the guy's gay. And he seems like . . . like an overgrown frat boy."

"You didn't see any evidence of a kid being in the house?"

"No, of course not."

Scott nodded. "Still, it's a lead." He turned around. "Crow, get on that, will you?"

A stiff conversation followed in which Kenzie explained to Crow what she had seen, heard, and observed in her visit to Talmadge. Then he left, his dark hair and black leather jacket disappearing into the night.

It was a pain, having to drive all over to use the Internet. But his mother's house didn't have an Internet connection. The old lady was too cheap. She didn't even have cable! The major networks were all she watched, that plus *Wheel of Fortune*. Getting Internet service now would attract too much attention, especially for the short period of time he'd be there. Plus, it made his activity too traceable. Moving around gave him advantages.

Dealing with the house once he made it to Jamaica would also be annoying. He'd just about decided to torch the place and have them send the insurance check to him. An old house like that ought to have plenty of wiring problems he could take advantage of. Of course, he had to avoid raising anyone's suspicion.

Suspicion. He didn't want any of that now. But he was smart. He could avoid it. That's what made him drive around looking for places with free wireless. Not even the FBI would be able to track him down.

Grayson pulled into a parking place at the twenty-four-hour coffee shop and glanced at his watch. Nine forty-five. Three hours after he'd posted his bait on the message board. Hopefully the senator had responded.

How would he know it was Grable and not

some geeky agent? That question kept working at him. He had to deal directly with Grable. He wanted to feel the senator tug on his line, nibble at the bait. Then he wanted to get him on the hook, reel him in, and gut the old boy while he lay on the dock. It was the whole purpose of this deal . . . plus the money. He thought of the money as his 401k.

But determining the senator was responding to his posts without revealing so much inside information he himself would be identified, that was the trick.

And oh, he had plenty of inside information. Like the twenty thousand dollars the senator "earned" from connecting Gros Bros. with the U.S. Army. Or the cool forty thousand from paving the way for SynUS, or the golf trips to Scotland, the cruise in the Caribbean, the Vail vacations . . . all perks of the job, all under the table, all "paid for" by using the senator's influence in a big way.

Then came his family: Beth, who never met a casino she didn't like. Grable's son from his first marriage, who collected DUIs like some kids collect baseball cards. The senator surely did throw his weight around keeping his kid out of jail. And then Jillian, the senator's older daughter, and the little matter of her abortion.

And all the time, he, Grayson Chambers, legislative aide, stood at Grable's side, fixing things, cleaning up things, smoothing over problems, fronting for him. Being the brains and the charm for Senator Bruce Grable. And for what? To be ignored, usurped, and abandoned? Replaced by some younger version of himself, one with long blonde hair and ovaries?

No. Never. He wouldn't stand for it. It wasn't fair. He deserved better.

Grayson jerked his laptop out of the car and slammed the door shut. He'd parked at the back of the building, out of line of sight of the counter. He didn't want anybody associating him with his car, in case he needed to use this place again. He wanted to be strangely unmemorable. Which is why he had on jeans, a T-shirt, and an old cap. Nothing special in this part of the woods, no sir. Nothing special at all. He'd even glued a fake ponytail into the cap to further his disguise. Would the coffee shop have security cameras trained on the cash register? If so, he wouldn't look anything like the preppy legislative assistant Grable saw every day.

He walked into the busy coffee shop. The young girl at the counter was a pretty brunette and normally Grayson would have come on to her. But tonight, he needed to keep a low profile. He kept his personality as flat as possible, his voice dull. "Tall Kenya," he said.

"Room for cream?"

That annoyed him. If he'd wanted room for

cream he would have asked for it. "Nah," he responded, taking two one-dollar bills out of his pocket. He wouldn't tip her, no sir. No money would go in that jar.

Coffee in hand, he moved to an empty table in the far corner, where the gas fireplace in the center of the room would block her view. Then he opened up his laptop, accessed the wireless network to connect with the Internet, and went to work on *High Stakes*. Who'd have thought that stupid show would come in so handy?

18

Kenzie walked back into the dining room. Had she missed something with Talmadge? Would it come back to haunt her? She felt guilty. She'd been immature, not waiting for Crow at Talmadge's. She'd been irritated with him and she failed to simply confront him directly. *I'll have to do better,* she told herself. *I've got to do better.*

She had to force herself to shift her focus back to the mission at hand: Capturing Jackson423's attention.

In the dining room, Alicia looked intently at the computer while Senator Grable paced.

"What's going on?" Kenzie asked.

"There are five members of this board online," Alicia responded. "Nobody's responding to Jackson directly yet. You want to take it?"

"Please."

Kenzie sat down as Alicia moved out of the way. "All right, let's see here. I'm going to be Big Dog and Brandigurl."

"And all you need is a split personality," Alicia quipped.

"What are you going to do?" Senator Grable asked, looking over her shoulder.

Kenzie's fingers flew. "I'm going to finish these

profiles. If this is our subject he has narcissistic tendencies, and he's going to want to talk to you directly, Senator. He might ask a question only you would know, which would be good, because it might give us a clue to his identity. So before I post a message under the Big Dog screen name, I'm going to try to draw 'Jackson423' out with the female persona." Kenzie began typing.

*Hey, r u a fan of Joie? She's my fav. Totally. She saves Connor's b**t every episode. Brandigurl.*

"What time did Jackson post his message?" Kenzie said out loud.

"Two hours ago," Alicia responded. "Six forty-seven."

"After the news conference," Kenzie mused.

"Do you think that's what motivated him?" Grable asked.

"Maybe."

But was it even the suspect? With no instant response to "Brandigurl's" comment, Kenzie had another idea. "Alicia, call somebody at WFO, would you, and get them to search for other posts by somebody named Jackson423. Usually, these Internet people will post all over and they get to know each other. In fact," she said, using the cursor to click onto another screen, "I'm going to make sure Brandigurl seems legit."

"How's it going?" Scott asked, walking into the room.

Kenzie glanced up at him. "Can we get someone to start watching old episodes of *High Stakes*? In case we have questions?"

"Sure."

Sandy felt a rush of relief when Grayson said he was leaving and would be back in three or four hours. Make it four, she wanted to say. The only time she could relax was when he was gone.

As soon as his car had left the driveway, she put Zoe to bed. The little girl seemed so tired, and Sandy had no problem getting her settled. She'd purchased some books and a few toys, and after one reading of *Are You My Mother?*, the little one drifted off, holding tight to the little stuffed puppy Sandy had given her.

She wondered if the little girl had a dog at home. Or if her mother read to her. Gray said Zoe had a nanny. Sandy couldn't even imagine that. Why have a kid if you didn't want to take care of it?

How odd. Here she was, hovering over a child . . . and not her own. After two abortions in her late teens and early twenties, she'd found she couldn't have children. She knew she'd go to her grave missing being a mother. Wasn't much point in keeping her alcoholic husband after that, so Sandy had struck out on her own. Had a lot of mishaps. Missteps. Some success. And now this.

Surely things would get better once they were in Jamaica.

Sandy gently stroked the tear away from the corner of the sleeping girl's eye. "Don't worry, baby," she whispered. "I'll take care of you."

Quietly leaving the room, Sandy went to the kitchen and cleaned up the dishes. Then she plopped down on the couch and reached for the TV remote. She felt something in the couch cushions, so she reached between them and pulled out a piece of paper. A receipt. An Internet receipt for an airline reservation. One Gray had made. And Sandy's face grew hot as she comprehended what it said.

Kenzie spent fifteen minutes trying to get "Jackson423" to talk to "Brandigurl." Her coffee grew cold in front of her. Her stomach growled. He wouldn't take the bait. Time to push it a little. She took a deep breath.

Joie's the most valuable part of the whole team, she typed under Big Dog's screen name. *If they're smart, CISU will do anything they can to keep her going. Even if it takes big bucks.*

She sat back, satisfied at the slight tone of desperation, the direct negotiation offer . . .

"This is so slow!" the senator said right behind her. "Isn't there some more direct tactic?"

"The kidnapper is trying to make it hard for us. He'll make a move soon," Kenzie replied.

Grable muttered something she couldn't hear.

To keep the Internet conversation going, Kenzie

posted a message from Brandigurl inviting Big Dog into a chat room. Then she began interaction between Big Dog and Brandigurl, flipping back and forth between the two personalities in her mind as she typed. With the female screen name, she imagined herself chewing gum and talking on the cell phone while typing; she made the man more mature, stiffer. Not used to chatting. He was a senator, for Pete's sake. How much time did he spend on the Internet?

She had to put in a little angst. A little desperation. A little anger. A little fear. All while talking about a TV show she had never watched. Meanwhile, Senator Grable hovered behind her, peppering her with questions.

Twenty minutes into it, she had her reward.

I wonder if CISU understands how much Joie is worth? Jackson wrote in the chat room.

Kenzie's heart thumped. She took a deep breath. "Where's Scott?" she called out.

"Is that it? Is that the kidnapper?" the senator asked.

"Very possibly. Let's see if we can keep him talking."

Which name should she use? Which identity? Kenzie's hands paused. She closed her eyes momentarily. Then she made her decision, and posted another line under the Big Dog screen name: *At least $2 million.*

The key amount taken from the note.

Jackson423 took off, proposing a plot line for the show, something these amateurs often did, involving Joie being kidnapped and held for ransom. Kenzie watched, breathless, as he outlined his ideas on the screen. Behind her, she could hear the senator's shallow breathing. She focused like a tightrope walker, narrowing her eyes, careful of each step, as if life and death depended on it. Which it did.

She responded: *Hey, that's cool!* wrote Brandigurl. *'Cuz Connor would be in deep if that happened. I mean, like, he needs Joie. All men need a woman to do their grunt work for them.* Kenzie continued, typing bubblegum phrases, leading into a little flirting, trying to work this guy, get some more words from him.

Big Dog, on the other hand, responded quite differently. *An interesting idea. But exactly how would Connor get her back?*

"I'm going to find Scott," Senator Grable said.

Kenzie took a deep breath. Her eyes remained fixed on her keyboard, her mind raced.

Finally, Jackson423 responded to her last posting. *The abductors would require an EFT to a Cayman Islands bank. $2 million.*

Kenzie took a deep breath. "OK. He's affirming our response from a few minutes ago."

Scott came into the room and stood behind Kenzie and she scrolled the words on her computer screen up so he could read the exchanges. "Good. Good!" he said. "Good job, Kenz!"

"What are we doing with this?" the senator asked. "Can we trace him? Can we find this guy?"

"We have enough to justify a warrant to take to the Internet service provider," Scott said. "I'll get on that."

Kenzie's head really began pounding. She typed, *But how would Connor know Joie was really alive? He would not pay all that money unless he knew he would get her back safely.*

The response came quickly. *Likewise, the mastermind behind Joie's disappearance would want to insure he was dealing with the big guns at CISU, not some lackey in law enforcement.*

How would he affirm that? Big Dog wrote.

Personal information. There's one thing about Joie's father the kidnappers should know, Jackson typed.

"There you go! He's checking you out, Senator!" Kenzie exclaimed.

"What should we say?" His voice sounded anxious.

A thousand things began running through Kenzie's mind. She began sorting them out, rolling over options, thinking intuitively. She turned to the senator. "The kidnapper knows you well. I think we have to play to what he expressed in his note: You've used people, this is somehow justified because of it."

The senator nodded.

"Again, we want to keep him talking, so let's affirm him."

"Go for it."

Her hands trembled again as she placed them on the keyboard. *I remember Joie's father from an old show,* Big Dog responded. *He'd made some big mistakes. Hurt some innocent people. Took money he shouldn't have. But Joie means the world to him.*

She sighed audibly as she finished. Breathlessly, they waited for a response. Five minutes. Ten. Where was the UNSUB? Scott's cell phone rang. In the background, Kenzie could hear him talking softly. "We've got an agent looking at the show online," Scott said. "The warrants are on the way." Kenzie nodded in response.

Finally, twelve minutes later, Jackson typed another message. "Got it, Scott!" Kenzie called.

Yes, if CISU went so far as to confirm that, it's clear they're serious about . . .

The post stopped, right in the middle of a word. How odd! Kenzie waited and waited for him to begin again, to continue the message. She kept staring at the words on the screen. Why did he stop mid-thought? That seemed so weird!

"What happened?" Alicia had moved right behind Kenzie.

"He just stopped."

"How could he? Why would he?"

"He got interrupted? I don't know."

Kenzie tried messaging him back. But after ten minutes, they had no response. Like a balloon deflating, the intensity went out of the room. Kenzie moved around the Internet, looking to see if Jackson423 had shifted somewhere else. She reaccessed the Web site. Maybe it was stuck. But nothing worked. Communication had just shut off.

Her head pounded and her neck felt stiff. Frustrated, she stood up.

Grayson shut the lid of his laptop with a loud click, disgust churning in his stomach. The network had gone down before he could resume posting! And he had Grable sweating, too, yes he did. He felt sure of it. He could sense it. How frustrating! He cursed loudly, then remembered his location. When he looked up, half a dozen people nearby stared at him.

Great. He smiled sheepishly. "Wireless is down. Must be lightning in the area." Then he tucked his computer under his arm, hunched up his shoulders and headed for his car. Well, Grable would just have to wait for the rest of the instructions, he thought. He'd just have to wait.

He muttered to himself as the first drops of rain began splatting on his windshield. All his work, and he had to stop when he was so close. How unfair! He backed out of his space, turned, and headed for the exit of the parking lot. He had a solid hour's drive back to his mother's. That kid had better be asleep, he thought. He sure didn't have the patience to deal with a brat.

Thirty minutes went by. Kenzie began pacing the floor.

"Why don't I go get dinner?" Alicia said.

"Fine. Anything . . ." Kenzie stopped herself. "No, wait. There's a Peruvian chicken place on Wisconsin, about five blocks up. Could you get something from there?"

"Sure! I'll get enough for everybody."

Scott and the senator had gone off somewhere to talk. Kenzie glanced at her watch. After nine p.m. Her cell phone rang. "Agent Graham," she answered.

"Mackenzie?" a male voice said.

She could hear loud music in the background. "Yes." She tried placing the voice.

"It's Beau Talmadge."

She pulled out a pad of paper and a pen, her senses suddenly on high alert. "What can I do for you?"

"Call off the goon squad, will you? You're making my friends nervous."

Kenzie pressed her right ear shut hoping to hear him better. "What are you talking about?"

"There are two white guys in suits sitting half a block down the street. Actually, one of them looks like an Indian. The Lone Ranger and Tonto. Tonto's driving. They've been there for an hour. Everybody knows they're Feds and it's ruining my party." He laughed.

"Your party . . ."

"Yeah. Even Beth is freakin' out."

"Beth Grable? She's there?" Kenzie turned around as she said it. She looked up. Senator Grable stood right behind her, a mixture of shock and anger on his face. She caught his eye, then quickly looked away.

"She *was* here. She said her husband kicked her out."

"That isn't what happened."

"Whatever. Just call off the dogs, OK?" Talmadge said.

"Don't know if I can," Kenzie said, but Talmadge had hung up.

"Who was that?" the senator demanded.

Kenzie hesitated, considering the ramifications of answering him. "Beau Talmadge."

The senator swore again.

"I am 99 percent sure he's just a friend," Kenzie added.

He didn't respond.

"Look. Stay focused. The important thing is getting Zoe back."

He frowned. Then he heaved a big sigh and said, "Yes. You're right. I'll deal with Beth later."

Kenzie looked at him and thought, *I need to talk to his wife again.*

"Nothing new on the message board?" Grable asked.

"No."

"Have you eaten?" Kenzie asked.

He shook his head.

"Alicia's coming back with food."

The corner of Grable's mouth twisted. "I just don't feel like it," he said, and he brushed past Scott, who walked toward them.

"Talmadge called," she told Scott. He raised his eyebrows. She told him about their short conversation. "Beth was there earlier."

"Did you let Crow know?"

She shook her head. "I just found out."

"What do you make of it?" he asked.

"It's odd, to say the least."

"Could she be that cold?"

Kenzie shrugged. "Sure."

"Her daughter's missing, and she's at a party? I've known shallow women, but c'mon!" Scott grimaced. "Call Crow and tell him. Let's get somebody else calling her other friends. We need to find her."

He had driven all the way back to his mother's house, but when he got to the driveway, Grayson could not turn in. No way could he sleep with his plan hanging in the balance. The soft blue glow of the television told him Sandy was still up. He just didn't feel like dealing with her or the little brat. Impulsively he drove on, bypassing the house. He pulled off to the side one street over so he could think.

The thunderstorm that had interrupted his Internet work had blown by. He'd been making good progress before that. With just a little more time, he thought he'd be able to get the deal in place.

Grayson retrieved a little black notebook from his laptop case. He couldn't find the paper copy of his airline reservation. Where had he put it? Luckily, he had a backup.

He looked at his notation and closed the book, satisfied. Now, he just needed to finish this business.

Where could he find another wireless location? By changing origination points, he figured he could keep the FBI guessing long enough to work his plan. He didn't want to give them too much time. It would increase the odds they'd find him. No, he wanted to keep Grable moving in the right direction. Most of all, he wanted his money.

Grayson flipped through his book. What would be open late, say, after midnight? He smiled. "Yes."

He could feel fatigue beginning to overcome him. No matter. He pulled a small can of energy drink out of his glove box and downed it. He'd be good, now, for five hours or more.

19

Another half hour went by with no communication from Jackson423. Kenzie had been left hanging, and she didn't know what to make of that.

More frustration: She had called Crow, told him about Talmadge's phone call. Crow responded that he would see if he could find Beth and call her, so she could interview the woman. But he hadn't. Not yet, anyway.

Her injury was getting to her as well. She felt like her head would explode, but she didn't want to take a break, didn't want to be missing in action when the kidnapper started posting again.

Crow. She'd liked him at first, and she thought he'd liked her, too. At least they were friendly. But after their initial camaraderie he'd become angry, aggressive. When he came to wake her up when the subject began posting, he seemed gentle. Then he seemed aloof. What was going on inside him to make him feel so unsettled? How could she read him?

Worse, how could she read herself? She felt like someone was twisting her hot and cold taps on and off, on and off.

While they waited, Alicia talked incessantly about the men she'd been dating and all their faults. And in the back of her mind, Kenzie kept thinking she'd soon hear Crow walking through the front door, after turning over surveillance of Talmadge to a squad under his command.

She felt attracted to him, no question, even though at the moment, she didn't want to be. Something about him, his confidence, his physicality, his looks, she found intriguing.

Her mother would have a fit. Blonde, green-eyed Kenzie involved with a black-haired, black-eyed Navajo.

That made her smile.

She did her best thinking outside, away from the constraints of interior space. "Alicia, I'll be out back. Come get me if he starts posting again."

Kenzie pushed open the door to the Grables' backyard, and took a deep breath. She thought back to the night she'd been assaulted, thought of the dangers lurking outside in the dark and dismissed them quickly. She refused to be caught off-guard again. Whoever assaulted her would not find her an easy mark a second time. She'd be smarter this time.

She grimaced. Even to her, it sounded like bravado. Truthfully, she needed to get away from the computer, away from Alicia . . . to see the sky, to feel the air, to be enveloped by the darkness . . . to have silence so she could sort out her feelings before she saw Crow again.

The night air felt soft and warm after the chill of the air-conditioning inside. Kenzie breathed it in. Washington humidity often seemed daunting, leaving her hair limp and her skin sticky with sweat. But Washington was home and she was used to it. She embraced the weather like a homemade quilt.

Off in the distance, she heard a noise, like a dog barking, a yip-yip-yip, followed by a howl. The moon, full this night, had risen above the trees. The Perseid meteor showers would be peaking soon, sending arrows of light racing across the black sky, Heaven's fireworks in a splendid display. She'd see little of it tonight, though, because of the city lights.

When the Perseid meteor showers put on their annual show, her father would take her to Sky Meadow State Park in the Virginia mountains. They'd take blankets and lie on their backs for hours, counting the shooting stars and telling stories and drinking the hot chocolate they'd packed in a Thermos. Her father understood her need to be outdoors, understood, encouraged, and shared it. Maybe he, too, was escaping from her mother's domain.

Her mind turned to Crow, to his dark looks, his confidence, his demeanor, and then she tried tracking it back to when and why, perhaps, it had changed. She thought about him growing up without parents, about being an only child, like her, and about how he ended up all the way back here, in the East, so far away from everyone. And then she began to wonder: Why had he joined the FBI? Why not the Navajo police, which would allow him to live on the Reservation? Why did he seem so thoughtful, so deep, and yet so volatile?

Kenzie saw a meteor blaze across the sky. She found the Big Dipper, the North Star, and the Little Dipper. She gazed at the vast wonder of the universe and felt something stir inside. "Oh, God," she whispered, "what does it all mean?"

Then she heard the sound of a car door shutting in the alley. She stood up quickly and backed up to the porch, her hand on her gun, her senses on high alert. Who was coming? The gate at the rear of the Grables' garden opened and shut, then one of the automatic lights Scott had ordered installed flicked on.

Crow. He walked down the path toward the house, his gait confident, assertive, athletic. She watched him for a minute, watched the light play on his black leather jacket, saw the shadows on his face, the set of his shoulders. She felt those hot-and-cold, confused feelings rise up once again. And then, to keep him from being alarmed, she stepped forward and said, "Hi."

Crow stopped. The floodlight temporarily blinded him and he shaded his eyes. "Kenzie?"

"What's up?" She kept her voice neutral.

He looked around. "You out here by yourself?"

She bristled. "My bodyguard quit."

He blew out a breath, aware, perhaps, of the foolishness of his statement. They were close now, close enough for Kenzie to see the light in his eyes, to hear the creak of his jacket, to feel the rush of emotion he engendered in her. Close enough for her to begin testing the waters.

"How did things go at Talmadge's?" she asked.

"I took a look inside. It's clean."

"You got a warrant?"

"No, I got permission."

"How'd you do that?"

"I used my best Indian technique: I walked up, rang the doorbell, and asked." He smiled at her.

She almost smiled back. Almost.

"Humor is a Navajo principle," he said, shoving his hands in the pockets of his jacket.

"I didn't know that," she admitted. He looked good, there in the light. Confident and strong. And he seemed friendly again. Why?

"Talmadge was very cooperative. Inside, I saw a bunch of inebriated white people."

"Beth?"

"No Beth. She'd left, Talmadge said."

"He didn't mind you coming in?"

"I think he was happy to have us take a look."

"You must have charmed him."

"I acted straight with him. Told him what we wanted. Treated him with respect. He responded to that."

She pursed her lips and nodded. "I thought you guys just staked people over anthills."

Crow laughed softly. "You're thinking of the Apaches. Besides, how easy is it to find an ant-hill on Capitol Hill in the dark? So, I used one of those interviewing techniques you folks teach at the Academy instead."

Was that a bone, thrown to her for the purposes of reconciliation? A flutter ran through her. "Good choice."

Her father had always taught her to address problems straight on. To confront. Clear the air. It's the way men do it, he told her. She took a deep breath and set her jaw. Then, looking straight into Crow's eyes, she voiced her complaint: "The next time you have a problem with me, I wish you'd come to me." Her voice sounded tight, even to her, and she realized she felt nervous. "Scott said you expressed concerns about my fitness. I don't like it when people talk behind my back, or when they try to undercut me." She waited, like a cat with her back arched, for his response.

He cleared his throat and glanced down. "In Navajo culture, we have a principle of community I don't find common in the white man. If one person starts to go off track, or if he runs ahead of the rest of the clan or starts becoming a lone wolf, the elders bring him back to restore the balance. I think it must have helped my people survive, out there in the desert."

Kenzie's mouth tightened into a straight line. Her heart beat hard. Were Crow's words an explanation or an apology? "You think I was running off?"

"You were not protecting yourself."

She studied him carefully, observing the tilt of his head, the skin around his eyes, the thrust of his chin. She thought about the way she felt when he walked in a room, the interest she had in the way he moved, and in his thinking, about the chill that ran down her spine when his hand accidentally brushed hers. How long it had been—how very, very long it had been—since she had allowed any of those kinds of feelings to gain traction in her conscious mind.

"I'm sorry if I offended you," he said. "I admit, I've been tense. And I acted more aggressive than I should have. I just . . ." he stopped.

"What?"

He shook his head, looked away, and refused to answer.

Behind Crow, she saw a light streak across the dark sky. Another meteor. She took a deep breath. Time to take a risk; time to act on the ideas she'd been developing in her head. On her theories. "What was her name?" she said.

"Who?"

"The woman you lost in Iraq."

Crow reacted viscerally, his whole body jumping, his hands jerking out of his pockets as if preparing for a fight. "What did Scott tell you?" he demanded.

"Nothing!" Kenzie said. "Nothing about her. Just that I shouldn't take your anger personally." She rubbed her arms. The tension had produced goosebumps on her flesh. "We were fine, you and I, until someone assaulted me. Then suddenly, I was your enemy. I felt so confused. I couldn't understand why you'd changed so suddenly. I've had time now, time to think it out."

"I don't know what you're talking about!" he said, throwing up his hands.

She looked straight at him. In the past, her instincts had not let her down. "Yes, you do. When I came back from the hospital, you were telling me how wrong I'd been to go off by myself. You were quizzing me, but you used expressions like 'turkey peek' and 'battle buddy.' You said I shouldn't have gone off without a battle buddy. It's not an FBI term . . . it's military jargon. Specifically, from Iraq." She paused and took a deep breath. "And so, the thought occurred to me that somehow, my getting hurt brought back some strong feelings for you. What else would explain your shift in mood? And I'm guessing, just guessing, you lost someone you loved, a woman, in the war."

"Who are you?" Crow said, incredulous. He

turned away from her, his shoulders hunched. Then he sat down on the bench, dropped his head in his hands. The moonlight reflected off his hair, and Kenzie had to stop herself from stroking his head. Her heart was drumming, her mind flashing ahead to his possible responses. Had she offended him? Ignited his anger? Would he open up? Her stomach tightened.

When he finally began speaking, he kept his voice soft, so soft she could barely hear him. "This time of year on the Reservation, a thunderstorm miles away can send a wall of water racing down an arroyo. I walked down one, looking for a lamb, and suddenly I got hit by one of those flash floods. Before I knew it, I was fighting for my life." He reached down, plucked some grass out of a crack in the paving stones, and began throwing it, blade by blade, back onto the patio. "When I saw you lying injured on the ground, I felt just like that. All these emotions came rushing at me. I didn't expect it. They came out of nowhere."

Kenzie sat down on the bench next to him. Her shoulder touched his, very lightly. He didn't move away. Overhead, a sky full of stars bore a silent witness to this moment. Her heart beat so hard she wondered if he could hear it. "I know what it is to lose someone you love," she said. "My father dropped dead right in front of me. Just like that, the person I loved most in life was gone." She waited for his response, but he remained quiet. She continued, "I know it's not exactly the same, but I know something of what you've gone through. So now I'm asking you: Who was she? The woman you lost?"

She felt like she could almost see the stars bending low to listen. Sitting still, waiting for this man to speak, the pregnant silence engulfed them, the universe surrounded them. She'd learned to be patient over the years, patient with her mother, patient with the subjects of her studies, patient with her life, and she rested on that patience now, like a woman rocking, rocking, waiting for a baby to be born.

His hand shook. "Her name was Julie Tyree," Crow said finally in a barely audible voice. "Born to the Bitter Water clan, the Tódích'íi'nii, born for the Corn Pollen People, the Taadiin Dine'é." It sounded like he was singing the words. He stopped and shook his head, and for a minute, Kenzie wondered if he would continue.

"We grew up together. She was beautiful. She had long, dark hair that she wore in a braid and a broad, open face. She was smart—very smart, and her eyelashes," he hesitated, "her eyelashes were as long as a doe's.

"In high school we fell in love. Soon, we were like this." He held up two fingers side-by-side. "At night, under the stars, out there in the desert, we began dreaming of the future. One day we

232

would go to college. I'd become a physician's assistant; Julie, a nurse. We'd get married, and then we'd come back to the Rez and help our people. And we'd have children, lots of little Navajo children. Julie said God gave us those dreams.

"Our families didn't have any money, but we both got ROTC scholarships at Arizona State. She studied nursing; I majored in bio. I wanted to get married when we graduated, but Julie's mother got sick—breast cancer—and she wanted to wait until her mom got through the chemo.

"That first year, both of us got sent to Iraq, Julie with the Army in southern Iraq, me with the Marines in Anbar Province. Julie was one month from the end of her deployment—one month from going home—when I got word," he stopped and cleared his throat, "I got word that she'd been killed."

Kenzie felt a shudder run through his body. Her heart twisted. "John, I'm so sorry. What happened?"

Moments ticked by. He swallowed, hard. "They were operating on a wounded soldier when a rocket-propelled grenade hit the tent. She had no chance. She never saw it coming."

"That's horrible. You must have been in shock."

"I didn't sleep or eat for three days. I kept working, kept going through the motions, but honestly, I felt paralyzed emotionally. Trapped, like a bug in a spider's web, you know? I kept seeing her, imagining the explosion, imagining her body flying apart . . . and I couldn't get to her, I couldn't protect her, I couldn't save her. Some guy in my unit tried talking to me about it, but I told him to go away. The last thing I wanted to hear was how God loves us."

He stood up, rubbed his hands down the sides of his pants, and looked up into the night sky. "Because we weren't married, I couldn't get leave to return to the States for Julie's funeral. All I had were some pictures—her casket, covered with an American flag, and the military honor guard—and what Grandfather had told me in an e-mail someone helped him send."

Crow's eyes were shining. "I lost my taste for medicine after that. I wondered what had happened to the God who gave us those dreams. The Reservation seemed empty. Someone I knew from Flagstaff began talking to me about the FBI. And here I am. Here I am, working with a white, East Coast city girl, and . . ."

What was he saying? Kenzie's breathing was shallow.

". . . suddenly I'm attracted to her. And then, she gets attacked, and I realize how vulnerable she is, and how I can't protect her, either."

Kenzie heard the yip-yip-yip and the howl she'd heard before.

Crow laughed softly, incongruously. He rubbed

his hand over his face. "You know what that is?" he said.

"A dog?"

He shook his head. "No. That's a coyote. There's a bunch of them now, living in Rock Creek Park. I leave the desert, but they follow me." He looked at her, a slight smile on his face. "I think that coyote's laughing at me. I think he's saying, you tried to run away from life, and from loss, and you came all the way to the East to avoid it, but you can't outrun your heart. You can't do it."

Kenzie shivered at his words. She got up from the bench and began pacing. "I felt devastated when my dad died." She turned quickly and looked at Crow. "I know it's not the same, not exactly, but it was still horrible. My mother scores very high on the narcissism scale. When my dad died, all the joy went out of my life. Even that young, I learned quickly to submerge myself in work."

Crow blew out a breath and smiled softly. "Scott calls you the girl genius. He says you got your PhD before most of us learn to feed ourselves."

"When I first met Scott, he used to try to fix me up with single agents. When I turned him down for the fifth time, he said to me, 'Kenzie, *perfect* died when you were twelve. Are you going to spend your whole life as a nun?' Of course, I felt angry. I also didn't know what he meant." A crape myrtle bush grew at the end of the bench. She walked over to it, broke off a dead twig, and began snapping pieces off. "I've been thinking . . . and I wonder, now, if I've just been blocking my own happiness. Getting God back for taking my dad by refusing to love again." She let those words sink in before she turned and sat back down on the bench. "It sounds so immature."

Crow blew out a breath softly. "My grandfather says my work with the Bureau is just me living in my anger—I am called to be a healer, but I am resisting." Crow shook his head. "My grandfather is not someone whose words I take lightly."

Kenzie looked up. Was the sky always this dark? And the stars so white? Did the night air always seem so enveloping? She opened her mouth to speak again when she heard the back door squeak.

"Kenzie!" Scott cried. They both turned around. He looked from one to the other, obviously aware he had interrupted something.

"What?" Kenzie asked, rising to her feet.

"We need you. Jackson's back online."

She looked back at Crow, one more long, lingering time, and went inside.

20

Pretty clever of me, Grayson thought. He had cruised down Rock Creek Parkway and pulled into the area around George Washington University. College kids are always up. Surely, there'd be some coffee shop with free wireless open around the GW campus, he'd reasoned.

And there was. What's more, he fit right in, with his jeans and fake ponytail. All the way down to D.C., he'd rehearsed what he would write. But he felt anxious. Would Grable still be up? Would he be watching the board?

Someone would, he presumed, and that someone would get Grable. He had to count on it. The Feds were in it now, so he just had to assume they'd be there. No matter. He'd set up the deal. It would be up to Grable to complete it.

He had it all figured out. Once the money had been transferred to his new Cayman Islands account, he would drop Sandy and Zoe off at a park in Fairfax. He would tell Sandy to leave the little girl in the play area and then walk back out. He would pick her up on the other side. Only of course, he wouldn't. No way would he share his two million with that broad. What had she done to earn it?

Grayson sipped his macchiato. Two coeds were

talking about some guy, discussing his body. Women these days were just as coarse as men, he thought. They deserved whatever they got.

He booted up his laptop, smiling inwardly. He had signed on now from an entirely different location. Even if the Bureau traced his messages, they'd still never catch up to him.

Satisfied, he turned his attention to the *High Stakes* message board. He went back to his last message, read it and the responses, and then picked up the thread. The time on his computer read 11:37.

Kenzie raced into the dining room, her head still focused on her conversation with Crow. She looked over Alicia's shoulder at the computer.

Jackson had written, *Lost power for a while. Back now. I'm headed back to the chat room.*

Quickly, Alicia made the switch.

"Have there been thunderstorms? Find out where the power has been out," Kenzie said.

"Got it," Scott responded.

Jackson423's message sprawled across the board: *What I was saying was that if CISU confirmed the message through Joie's father, then they would know the mastermind of the plot was on the up and up. It shouldn't be any problem for them to collect $2 million. CISU seems to throw money around like crazy. But* *how would they deliver it? It would be wired to the Out Islands Bank in the Cayman Islands, to a numbered account. Maybe her name in code. Once the transaction was made, then Joie would be safe. She is, in fact, her father's life.*

"Look at that!" Alicia exclaimed. " 'Life'. That's 'Zoe' in Greek!"

"Good job," Kenzie responded.

"What's the rest of it mean?"

Kenzie focused. She didn't like to do a snap analysis. But she had to, because she had to respond. "The question is how would they deliver it? How would CISU deliver the ransom money?" she told Alicia. "The answer is, they would wire it to the Out Islands Bank in the Cayman Islands. And there's a key to the account number in the name."

"So, like a code," Alicia responded.

"That's right."

"Maybe just the simple number code . . . *A* is one, *B* is two, and so on."

Crow came in. Kenzie glanced at him, and he met her eyes. Her heart skipped a beat. She refocused on the computer screen.

"Look at this," Alicia said, pointing to the message. "Any idea how we could decode it?"

Crow reached for a notepad. "Let me try."

Kenzie took a deep breath. She had a decision to make. "Do you all think Big Dog should respond right away?"

239

"If we do, he'll know we're monitoring it," Alicia said.

"But he would anyway, right? I mean, it would only be logical."

"Do it," Crow said. "Only wait five minutes or so, so it's as if we had to go get Grable."

"All right," Kenzie said.

"How many numbers in a Cayman Islands bank account?" Crow asked.

Kenzie had no idea. And the banks, of course, would be closed.

"Hey, we had a fraud case involving an offshore bank," Alicia said. "I could check the case file."

"Downtown?"

"Out at Tysons." Alicia flipped open her phone. "I'll call my old partner. He's still at that office." She punched in a number and put the phone to her ear. "He's going to love me calling him this late." After a short conversation, she said, "He's going to check the case file and call me back."

"Good." Kenzie stared at her computer. "It's been seven minutes. I'm going to answer him."

"Go for it," Crow said.

She typed: *That's a good plot line. I'm sure CISU would respond to that. But just out of curiosity, how long would you expect it to take them to come up with $2 million?*

These things can't drag on, Jackson423 wrote. *That's one thing about* High Stakes. *The shows move right along. So I'd say, forty-eight hours. Forty-eight hours would be the limit.*

Starting the day the instructions were given?

Yes.

"Oh, gosh," she said, pushing back from the table. "This guy's playing hardball. Two days!"

"Considering Zoe's diabetes, it may be all we have anyway," Crow said.

"What do you have there?" she asked him.

"Here's the number if the guy is using the straight alpha-numeric system: twenty-six. That's for the 'Z.' then fifteen for the 'O,' five for the 'E,' and then seven, eighteen, one, two, twelve, five. Zoe Grable. That number sequence seems long, though, for an account number. I'll have to wait for the proper length. And maybe he's using Zoe's name backwards. Or just her last name."

"Why would he make it hard?"

"To tweak Grable. He's enjoying the game. I mean, what we'll have to do is call the bank and give them some possibilities and see if anything matches."

"But wait. These are anonymous accounts. How will we know we have the right one? That we didn't accidentally get another account?"

Crow nodded toward the computer. "Ask him."

She did, typing her question into the message board. Several minutes later, the response came.

The account would have a code word associated with it: Curtis.

Kenzie looked at Crow. "Curtis. Do you get that? Is it from the show?"

Crow shook his head. He looked at his watch. "I'll call the kid Scott has watching those shows."

Kenzie responded to Jackson423: *Smart.*

The minutes ticked by. Kenzie kept the chat up between her two characters, but Jackson423 remained quiet. She was acutely aware of Crow's presence, his breathing, the faint smell of his shampoo, the fact that he was watching her intently. Just a few hours ago, she'd been angry. So had he. Now, they'd moved to a different place. She could feel it.

Finally, Kenzie decided Jackson423 had finished for the night. Crow had given up a while ago. He lay on the floor, sound asleep.

Her neck and shoulders were tight and she rotated them to loosen them up and slouched down in the chair. Kenzie closed her eyes, and her mind began to drift. Suddenly, she found herself praying. Maybe it was the fatigue. Maybe it was the stress. Maybe it was just sheer emotion. But she prayed. *God, make this work. Please, make this work. Help us find Zoe. And God, please help me sort all this out. My relationship with Crow, my relationship with you . . . help me. I'm tired of fighting you. I want to let go of my anger. I want to love someone. Please help me.* She shivered and opened her eyes.

• • •

Kenzie was standing in the kitchen, sipping a cup of coffee and thinking, when Scott walked in.

"Did you get some sleep?" he asked.

Kenzie shook her head. She wanted to tell him about her conversation with Crow. Scott would help her. He would put it in perspective for her. But she knew she had to stay on task. Over Scott's shoulder, she saw the senator walking toward them.

"Senator, I'd like to get into your Capitol Hill office," she said.

"You can go now, if you want," he said. He was dressed in navy blue sweats and he looked worn and tired. He rubbed his hand through his hair. "I couldn't sleep. If you want, I'll give you the keys to my office, and the key to my filing cabinet, and the password to my computer, and you can go through anything you want."

Kenzie raised her eyebrows.

"Please. Anything to move this along."

"Scott?" Kenzie asked.

"It's two o'clock in the morning. Don't you need some rest?"

"I can't sleep."

"OK, then. Fine by me."

The senator handed her the keys. "I don't care," he said, "if I go to jail for the rest of my life. I want Zoe back. Anything you find, anything at all, is fair game."

"Your lawyer . . ."

"I don't care." He took a handkerchief out of his pocket and blew his nose. "Zoe is all that matters. Do whatever you need to do to find her."

"You want someone to go with you?" Scott asked. "I can wake up Crow."

"Let him sleep. I'll be fine."

The streets of Washington were still shiny wet from the storm that had passed through a couple of hours before. Kenzie eased her Bucar out of the senator's clogged neighborhood and found her way to M Street. At two-thirty in the morning, there were still a surprising number of vehicles on the road in Georgetown. But then, the bars had just let out.

She wanted some coffee, so she swung by an all-night coffee shop near George Washington University, parked, and went in. The place seemed deserted except for a couple of young women browsing a fashion magazine in the corner.

Kenzie ordered a tall Sumatra, room for cream, fixed it, and left. She shot down to Pennsylvania Avenue and raced past the White House, the Washington Monument, the Smithsonian museums, and FBI headquarters. While she drove, she tried to work out a game plan in her head. Her mind, however, kept skipping back to Crow.

The buildings she passed shimmered in the night, each beautiful in its own way. For most people, they were the perfect postcard images of the nation's capital; for Kenzie they represented home. She couldn't imagine living anywhere else. Not far away lay the street on which her father had had his office. Just a few blocks beyond that, her grandfather had owned a shop. Her great-grandfather had installed the windows at the top of the Washington Monument, another long-lost relative had done the gold-leaf work in the Supreme Court Building.

But now, the desert southwest seemed intriguing. Monument Valley, the Grand Canyon . . . maybe she'd like to go there sometime.

She swung the Bucar onto the road around the Capitol, rolled down her window and talked to a Capitol police officer, who inspected her creds and directed her to a special spot next to the Everett Dirksen Senate Office Building. She found it, parked, and went into the building.

Security was tight, as it had been since 9/11. She had to show credentials and then a Capitol police officer escorted her to the senator's office. Kenzie used Grable's keys to open the door, and then flipped on the lights. The officer dropped into a chair. Apparently, she had orders to stay.

Kenzie looked around. Grable's office contained lots of wood, plush carpets, brass lamps, and a "me wall" full of grip-and-grin photos. The secretary's desk looked neat and tidy, backed by bookcases full of papers and weighty tomes. Two offices for assistants were off to the left. Beyond the secretary's desk lay the inner office. Kenzie walked back to where the senator's desk sat and noted the photographs of Zoe on the credenza, the childish drawings pinned to the walls labeled "to Daddy," and the toys in a crate on the lowest shelf of his bookcase.

She unlocked the filing cabinet and began pulling out files at random. There were hundreds marked with the numbers of bills, like S.632 and H.R.4994. She skipped those, and instead went to memos to others on Capitol Hill: Letters to senators and congressmen and women requests for data, press releases, notes to colleagues, and memos to staff. Intrigued, Kenzie sat down on the floor, put her coffee next to her, and went through the correspondence page by page. Gradually a picture of the senator's work life began to form. He was a very busy man. A very powerful man. One who relied heavily on his staff. One whose advice was frequently sought by others.

How could he have engaged in criminal activity? She found it an amazing contradiction—the involved, effective senator and loving daddy, and the crook who had betrayed his office. Kenzie soon lost herself in the words of his work. She was vaguely aware the Capitol police officer had dozed off. She heard her snoring. Her mind, however, remained fixed on the papers in front of her.

By the time dawn began sending shafts of light through the windows, Kenzie's brain was full. She had jotted notes and made some copies. She'd found some angry memos, and some letters from constituents frustrated with the federal government, demanding Senator Grable's attention.

By six a.m., she was ready to go back.

Returning to the senator's house, Kenzie's cell phone rang. The female voice at the other end sounded vaguely familiar.

"Agent Graham?"

"Yes."

"This is Laura Barstow. You interviewed me about Beth, remember?"

Ah, yes, the blonde woman with the silver toy poodle.

"I'm calling you because . . . well, because I'm concerned about Beth."

Kenzie pulled over to the curb so she could listen better. "Why is that?"

"I saw her last night. We were at a party. And Ms. Graham, I have never seen her so low."

"Describe that."

"She's the life of the party, usually, but last night she just sat on the couch, dabbing her eyes with a handkerchief, and blowing her nose. Her eyes looked so red. And her hair . . . I have never seen her so disheveled. It bothered me, and all I could think of to do was call you."

"Did she threaten suicide or anything like that?"

"No, but I think that's next. Except I don't think she'll threaten to do it. She'll just do it. And we'll all be sorry we didn't see it coming."

When Kenzie walked into the Grables', the senator sat slouched in a chair with his eyes closed, and Alicia was nowhere to be seen. Scott had fallen asleep in front of the computer. Kenzie quietly walked over to it, reactivated the screen, and checked the message board. There were no new postings. Scott stirred. "Go back to sleep," she whispered. "Nothing's happening."

Grable heard her. He got up, and followed her out to the kitchen, where they found Crow making coffee. The Navajo worked quickly, precisely, as he measured the coffee, filled the carafe, and poured the water into the reservoir. He glanced up, saw Kenzie, and his eyes softened.

Bruce Grable spoke up. "Find anything?" he asked Kenzie.

"Some." She thought just a moment about telling him about Laura Barstow's phone call, but she decided not to. "I'd like to go back when the secretary is there."

"Louise?" Grable responded. "She'll be in at seven-thirty sharp. She always is."

"Has she worked for you for a long time?"

"Twenty years. She's wonderful. I don't know what I'd do without her."

"Your files are well kept."

"That's Louise."

"I found a lot of correspondence from angry constituents," Kenzie said.

"Yes, we get that all the time. Always threatening to do something if their VA checks aren't straightened out. Or their Social Security. Money. It all has to do with money."

"Do you report these to someone?" Crow asked, leaning back against the counter and crossing his arms. That's when Kenzie noticed the ragged, five-inch scar on his left forearm. She hadn't seen it before, and she wondered where he'd gotten it.

"No. We try to help them with their claims, but reporting all those threats would keep a lot of people employed full-time."

"Do I smell coffee?"

All three of them looked up to see a disheveled Scott standing in the doorway.

"Nothing like a good night's sleep," he said, yawning. "And believe me, it was nothing like a good night's sleep."

Even the senator smiled.

"What's happening?"

Kenzie told him about her visit to the senator's office, and what she'd found. "Senator, I did have some questions," she said, turning to Grable. "I found a lot of correspondence from Senator Morrison. He seemed angry."

Grable grimaced. "He's an old foe. We've grappled for years. He's about to lose his reelection, and he's ticked off."

"Do you consider him a threat?"

"Morrison? A personal threat? No, he's just blustering."

Kenzie nodded. "Back in some older files, I saw this name, 'Grayson Chambers.' Who's he?"

The senator's face brightened. "Grayson Chambers? My old legislative aide. Great guy! Wonderful! A whiz when it comes to politics. Hardworking. Resourceful. I called him the best butt-kicker on the Hill."

"But he's no longer working for you?"

"Left a while back. He's teaching at a college in California, small town, up the coast from LA. Santa Barbara maybe."

"You keep up with him?"

Grable look chagrined. "No. I should, but to be honest, I don't have much time. Haven't heard from him in a while. Christmas, maybe. Yes, I think we got a Christmas card from him."

Kenzie tried to absorb all he said. Grayson Chambers. Of all the memos she'd read, and all the briefing papers, his were the best written.

"Grayson was my right-hand man for fifteen or sixteen years. Great guy. Loyal as a hound dog. Smart as a whip. And ugly as a toad." He chuckled. "I always told him he'd scare the feathers off a hen." He looked over at the coffeepot on the counter. "Hey, coffee's done."

While Grable pulled mugs from the cabinet and Crow retrieved the cream from the refrigerator, Kenzie mulled over the senator's words. Ugly as a toad. Just what was wrong with Grayson Chambers?

Scott's cell phone rang. He listened, responded in monosyllables, and clicked it off. "The surveillance squad reports your wife just got pulled over by D.C. police. They're taking her in on suspicion of DUI."

The senator groaned. "Beth? What next?" He sighed with resignation. "I'll call my lawyer."

"Hold on. I want to talk to her," Kenzie said suddenly.

Scott looked at her parentally. "You've been out all night."

"This is my chance! I'm fine! I want to see her." She raised her eyebrows. "Crow can come and babysit if you're concerned." Out of the corner of her eye, she saw the Navajo smile.

21

Beth Grable looked pale and wan, sitting in the police station interview room under the fluorescent lights, her hands nervously twisting a tissue. Her red-rimmed eyes were sunken, the skin of her cheeks almost transparent, her lips dry.

"So what's going on, Mrs. Grable?" Kenzie asked. She and Crow had arrived at the station before the desk had officially booked Mrs. Grable, and they had been able to convince the cops that prosecuting her for a DUI at this time wasn't in anyone's best interest. But Kenzie would withhold that information. Let her think she was in trouble, for now.

"You know. Don't tell me you don't know." Beth sniffed and dabbed at her nose with the tissue.

Kenzie, who had been trying to analyze Beth Grable's behavior from the beginning, proceeded carefully. She wanted to get the facts, but more than that, she wanted Beth to open up, to reveal the motives behind her actions. "Mrs. Grable," Kenzie said, "is this your first DUI?"

Beth nodded. "And Bruce will kill me. It'll be all over the news tonight. 'Senator's tipsy wife parties while he grieves.' I can see it now."

"The press is very intrusive, isn't it?"

"It's horrible. You have no idea." Beth rolled her eyes and looked around.

"You want some coffee? Or tea?" Kenzie asked.

"I would kill for a cup of tea. Not literally, of course."

"Let me see what I can do."

Kenzie returned a few minutes later with a steaming mug in her hand. Thankfully, the cops had more than coffee available. "Mrs. Grable . . . Beth," she said, after the woman had taken her first sip, "I'm just curious: Why did you leave your home? Aren't you worried about your daughter?"

"Worried? About Zoe? Do you have children?" Beth snapped. "No, of course you don't. I can tell." She sat back and folded her arms. "Of course, I'm worried. Bruce kicked me out."

Kenzie frowned. "That's not what happened."

"Well, he didn't want me there, for sure." Beth looked up toward the ceiling and Kenzie saw tears in her eyes.

"Why are you crying?" she asked.

"Crying? I'm not crying." But as Beth refocused on Kenzie, tears dripped from the corners of her eyes. She wiped them away with the back of her hand. "You can't imagine what it's like."

"What?"

"When you're beautiful you're just an object,

that's all, a toy for men to play with. First, my father, then those college boys, now Bruce. I'm nothing but a toy."

Had she been abused? "Did your father abuse you?"

"No, of course not."

"What do you mean, a toy?"

Beth waved her hand toward her tear-streaked, fatigue-filled face. "They don't think of you as a person, you know? A person with needs and emotional depth, and thoughts, and opinions . . . you're just a trophy, a status symbol to affirm their own masculine power. I hate it. I really hate it."

Kenzie watched her carefully. "But you're not just a wife—you're a mother."

"I'm a brood mare," Beth responded. She shook her head slowly. "Oh, don't get me wrong. I felt thrilled when I got pregnant. But guess what? After we had Zoe, Bruce had eyes only for her. What's worse, he insisted we get a nanny. So suddenly, there I was, stuck on a shelf so to speak, like the trophy wife I am. Useless, except for the occasional public appearances demanded of a senator's wife." She snorted. "I don't think those include police mug shot sessions."

Kenzie tried not to smile. "Do you feel jealous of Zoe?"

"Jealous? Of course! But then, I also love her. Even with all the barriers Bruce tried to erect between us." Beth's eyes grew distant, misty with tears. "She reminds me of me—cute, feisty, a little spoiled. I remember when she was born, and I saw her hands for the first time. They were miniatures of mine! And as she grew, she quickly learned how to play us, Bruce and me, just like I played Daddy and Momma. Oh, she's so smart!" Again, she dabbed her eyes. "I felt hurt she loved Bruce more than me. So hurt. And as for him, it seemed to me he was purposely excluding me. They created this . . . this circle," she gestured with her hands, "that left me out.

"Thank God Beau moved up here. I can talk to Beau. He understands me. He knows how rejected I feel! And he told me some things . . . I was trying to figure out how to get back in the circle again when . . . when . . ." She broke down in sobs.

"So where do you think Zoe is now?" Kenzie asked quietly.

"How should I know? Oh, God! How should I know? Why did you even ask me that?" Beth demanded. "I love her and I would do anything to get her back. Anything."

Kenzie rubbed her finger gently over her still-swollen lip. Beth seemed believable, and in her own mind, she absolved her of guilt in Zoe's disappearance. The woman seemed immature, and not just a little narcissistic. But guilty of taking her child? No. Still, what might she know? She wondered what Crow, who was watching through one-way glass, had picked up. "Beth," Kenzie said, making her voice as nonthreatening as possible, "if you were me, who would you suspect?"

Beth's lips pressed together. She shook her head slightly. "Washington is a shark pool. And Bruce . . . Bruce has a lot of friends. He has enemies, too, but even his friends, the ones I've met . . . I don't really trust them."

"Tell me about that."

Beth tossed her head. "Well, the enemies' list is easy. You can classify them as political or people he wouldn't do favors for. Maybe a few he DID do favors for. Jealous people who envy his power. I can't give you those names, but I do know this: Bruce isn't honest with me about who he's seeing." Connecting with the look on Kenzie's face, she clarified her statement: "Oh, he's not having affairs. No little prostitute scandals in his life. He knows what I'd do to him—I'd divorce him and take Zoe with me. But he's got some-thing else going on. He gives me the 'don't worry your pretty little head about it' response." Beth sighed. "Anyway, you'll have to find out about it on your own. As to his friends . . . some of them seem pretty shady."

"Where have you met them?"

"Parties. At the office. And some of them at the house. That guest room on the third floor? Some of his staff has stayed there when they've been working late at the house."

"Right near Zoe's room?"

"Yes."

"Who has stayed there?"

Beth ticked off half a dozen people. "The most frequent was Grayson Chambers, that weasly little . . . oh, I can't stand him!"

"I thought the senator liked him!"

"Oh, Bruce does, for sure, because Grayson sucks up to him. But I hated him from the get-go."

"Why?"

"Well, first of all, you talk about jealous. . . . He acted so jealous of me! When we got married, Grayson Chambers just about spit all over me. He seemed so worried about me bending Bruce's ear, encouraging him to think differently than Grayson wanted him to! Like I cared about politics. I found it disgusting."

Kenzie recalled the writing she'd read that Chambers had done. He was clearly bright, clearly articulate, but why would he kidnap Zoe? "What reason would Grayson Chambers have to kidnap Zoe?" she said out loud.

"Oh, I don't think he did that," Beth said dismissively. "He doesn't have the courage. He's bright, but he's not much of a man."

"But would he have the motive? Might he have paid someone to do it?"

Beth shook her head. "Grayson Chambers is off in California somewhere. Working at some college. He didn't do it."

"So of all the people who have stayed in your guest room, can you think of anyone you'd suspect? Anyone who might have taken Zoe?"

Beth frowned. She tapped her finger on her lip and focused on a ring on the table, left by some cup or mug. When she looked back at Kenzie, she had tears in her eyes. "I just don't know!" And she began to cry.

Kenzie thought she looked like a slightly more grown-up Zoe, a little girl-woman, sad, lonely, and scared half out of her mind.

"And I don't know what to do!" Beth said, panic in her voice. "I . . . I don't even have Daddy to help me!"

"Beth, listen," Kenzie said. She reached out and touched the woman's hand, and, much to her surprise, Beth didn't pull away. "Listen to me." She waited until Beth made eye contact. "I think you should go home, to your husband."

"Why? He doesn't want me!" she responded plaintively.

"I think you'd be surprised. I think Senator Grable is pretty . . . upset. I think he needs you." Beth looked at Kenzie as if she didn't believe her. "He's a broken man, Beth. This is a time when you need each other. You need to go home. Would you let us take you?"

"I . . . I can't. I've been arrested."

Kenzie shifted in her chair. "Look. We've

258

talked to the police. We've asked them not to press charges."

Beth's eyes grew big. "No charges? Are you kidding?"

"If you want to go, I'll have someone take you home. I know your husband would be glad to see you."

More tears. Sobs. Then a nod. Beth got up. "Thank you!" she said, and unexpectedly, she gave Kenzie a hug.

Kenzie walked out to where Crow waited. His eyes communicated his approval. "Will you take her?" Kenzie asked. "I want to go back to Capitol Hill."

Washington seemed alive this Friday morning with traffic and pedestrians, tourists, and government workers. Kenzie edged her way toward the Hill, trying to go over in her mind what exactly she had picked up about the Grables, their marriage and their lives. When she arrived at the Dirksen Building, she showed her creds to an officer and he pointed out a parking space she could use.

Kenzie walked into the Senate office building, displaying her creds yet again, and yet another officer escorted her back to Grable's office. The place looked so different by day.

Louise greeted her. A sixty-something woman, she struck Kenzie as being old Washington, the kind who grew up in the city before the population explosion in the early '70s catapulted what had been a sleepy, semi-Southern town into a bustling, multicultural metropolis. Sure enough, as she spoke, Kenzie detected the slight remnants of the old D.C. accent. A slight Southern drawl. An even more slight hard *r*— rendering the city's name "Warshington."

"Did you grow up in D.C.?" Kenzie asked.

"Oh, yes," Louise responded. "In Northwest."

"Wilson High?"

"Of course."

"I lived over on Woodley Road," Kenzie said. "My mother insisted I go to a private school. Or I would have gone to Wilson."

"I got a good education there, despite what they say about D.C. schools," Louise said. "Tell me, do you have any news for me on my little Zoe? That poor little thing. I am just praying you all will find her soon. Poor Senator Grable."

"We're continually working on leads," Kenzie responded.

"Well, I know you're doing your best. Now, what can I show you?"

Kenzie gave her a list of the kinds of files she hoped to see, and Louise promptly produced them. She sat down on the leather couch in the senator's office and began reading and reading, and the more she read, the more curious she became about this guy, Grayson Chambers.

"Louise," she said finally, "tell me about Grayson Chambers."

The older woman smiled. "Nice young man. We worked together for quite some time. He seemed very bright and polite to me. One time, I went down to the garage to leave. It was late, maybe eight o'clock at night, and I had a flat tire. Grayson just happened to come along and he changed it for me. How I did appreciate that!"

"Quite a good aide, I take it."

"Oh yes, the senator depended on him. It seemed that Grayson knew just who to go to when they needed a vote for this or that. He knew how to wheel and deal, that young man." Louise laughed. "I call him 'young' though he was forty-something when he left. He had a reputation all over the Hill for being a sharp opponent . . . or an invaluable ally."

"He left two years ago, right?"

"That's right."

"Why did he leave?" Kenzie watched Louise's eyes carefully.

"I don't know, really," she said, frowning. "Things seemed to be going along just fine. Then one day, he said he'd gotten a job teaching at a college, and he was leaving. I was quite surprised."

Kenzie pondered that. "Did he get along with people well?"

"He was wonderful to me. And to the senator. Now April, there," Louise nodded toward one of the small sub-offices, "she didn't like him. But you know how people are."

Unfortunately, Kenzie thought, I do know how people are. And one of the characteristics of people with psychopathic tendencies is often that others experience them very differently. They know how to "play" people. They can be smooth and charming to some, and downright abusive to others, depending on how they perceive that person's usefulness.

"Senator Grable made a funny comment," Kenzie said lightly. "He said Chambers was 'ugly as a toad.' "

Louise clicked disapprovingly. "Now that's not nice. Men!" She shook her head. "Grayson looked, well, plain. Here, we probably have a picture of him." She walked over to the "me-wall," covered in grip-and-grin shots. Kenzie looked over her shoulder. In each picture, the senator was smiling and shaking hands, or holding some document. In many, in the background stood a much shorter man, partially obscured.

"Would you still have a staff photo of him, in the system somewhere?" Kenzie asked.

"I'm not sure. Let me look."

Louise returned to her computer and began going through files. "Oh, yes," she said, "here."

Kenzie looked. Her screen held a mug shot of a man with a small face punctuated with an overly large mouth and bulging eyes. Thick glasses sat perched on a snub of a nose. Shaggy brown hair hung over his ears. It looked like he'd forgotten to get a haircut. He had a serious look on his face, and yes, if you wanted to be mean, his face looked a little amphibian-like.

"Could you print that for me, please?" she asked Louise.

"Of course."

"And you mentioned April? I need to talk to her."

"Let me introduce you."

April Silcox worked as Senator Grable's correspondence aide. A plain-looking brunette in her twenties, she spent her days answering letters and e-mails from constituents. Kenzie guessed she'd been a poli-sci major in college and now was paying dues, hoping to make legislative aide in some office on the Hill. Washington seemed full of such talented young people, fresh-faced and full of enthusiasm.

She was sitting at her desk surrounded by papers when Kenzie followed Louise into the room. "April, honey, this is Special Agent Mackenzie Graham of the FBI. She's working on Zoe's disappearance. And Senator Grable has asked us to fully cooperate with her. She'd like to talk to you, OK?"

Louise moved aside and Kenzie reached across April's desk and shook the young woman's hand.

"I'll leave you two alone," Louise said, withdrawing.

"Have a seat," April said, gesturing toward a chair. "What can I do for you?"

Kenzie started as she always did, asking April's name, address, phone number, and basic background information. She was, as Kenzie had guessed, a political science major at Northwestern. Her father had pulled some strings to get her a job on the Hill. Now she lived in a cute little one-bedroom in Arlington, just across the Potomac River, and followed her dreams on Capitol Hill.

"Well, I hope you enjoy the area," Kenzie said. She asked her then about her job on the Hill, the people she worked with, the others she met in the cafeteria, the hallway, the copy room, the coffee shop. Finally, she got around to Grayson Chambers.

"Grayson? What a jerk," April said, rolling her eyes.

"Tell me. How is he a jerk?"

April leaned forward, resting her arms on her desk. She wore a dark blue business suit and a light blue silk shirt with a small coffee stain on the front. Her computer screen, which Kenzie could partially see, had flipped into standby and a screensaver bounced around.

"I have never been around such a manipulative person in my entire life," she said, almost spitting out the words. She leaned forward, her eyes intense. "You know, when I first got here, I heard how bright he was. How adept at politics. And I thought, *This is great—I can learn something from this guy.* The problem is what I learned is how to use people."

"How so?"

"I was nice to him, in a normal kind of way. Offered to get him coffee when I went downstairs, that sort of thing. But he acted so rude toward me, so demeaning. And I thought, what's up with this guy? I began watching him and I noticed he'd play up to people he thought would be useful to him. And I wasn't. I mean, I'm just a correspondence clerk. I've got no power. No prestige. No access. No useful information. I'm not even pretty. So he could be as rude to me as he wanted and he wouldn't lose anything."

"Sounds like a real charmer," Kenzie said. She'd been studying her she spoke. April seemed to be one of those young women who had plenty of brains and personality in a plain package—and therefore, sadly, most men overlooked her.

April sat back in her chair. "If you ask a lot of people around here, they'll say he's a great guy. A terrific person. It's weird. The people he wanted to be nice to, he would be, and the rest of us . . . eh!" She flipped her hand like she was brushing off a fly.

Kenzie touched the top of her pen to her lip,

which was still swollen, and still hurting. She wondered if Grayson Chambers could have been the one to assault her. "April, would you call him athletic?"

"Grayson? No. I mean he isn't overweight, and he's very short. But he's not built or anything. Never spent time in the gym as far as I know." She frowned. "But now that I think about it, he did take some kind of karate or self-defense classes. Yes, yes, I remember now. He talked about it."

So, he could get aggressive, under the right circumstances. "Any family that you know of?"

April shook her head. "Never married. Dated a few women on the Hill but all short-term. Nothing lasted with him." She laughed softly. "Initially, I thought maybe I'd give him a whirl, you know? See if we were compatible. That thought lasted about four hours." She picked up a pen and wrote something on a pad of paper, tore off the top sheet and handed it to Kenzie. "Here."

Kenzie looked down and saw a woman's name on the paper.

"She works down the hall," April explained. "She dated Grayson for a while. Maybe she could tell you more about him."

"Thanks," Kenzie said, tucking the note in her pocket. "One more thing, April. How did Grayson and the senator get along?"

"Oh, famously. They were best buds. Senator

Grable thought quite highly of him and Grayson did a great job shepherding his bills. I felt kind of surprised when he left. It was like, a year after Taylor came."

"Who?"

"Taylor Martin. Beautiful woman just out of graduate school. The senator took her on as an aide to Grayson but she worked more for the senator than she did Grayson."

"Where is she now? Can I talk to her?"

April shook her head. "Gone to law school. Pepperdine, out in California. I mean, I guess you could call her, but I don't know her number."

"All right, thanks, April. You've been a big help." Kenzie stood up to leave.

"Agent Graham? One more thing: You want a read on his ego? Check out the blogs."

"He blogs?"

"He's compulsive about expressing his opinions online. Thinks he knows politics, which he unfortunately does. Whatever he's up to now, I guarantee you he's still blogging, or at least commenting on posts."

Kenzie wrote all this down. "Does he have his own blog?"

"I'm not sure where it is. You could Google his name. When he worked here, he used the screen name 'KickerG.' No space, capital G. Look for it. You'll get some insights into this man, believe me. He's got an ego a mile wide."

22

Women. He could never figure them out. All those emotions. Sandy seemed stiff and distant this morning, like she felt ticked. Why? Because he was gone until the wee hours of the morning? So what? He was busy. And he'd have to leave again. Soon. Like right after he ate.

He shifted his thoughts to the game he was playing and smiled. In two days max, he'd see his money. And what if Grable didn't comply? No way. He'd have to. No way would that man let harm come to his precious little Zoe. Funny what people valued.

Grayson clicked on the television. Nearly nine a.m. He'd missed most of the morning news shows. Just one left, a recap of the local news. "Hey, Sandy!" he yelled. "Can you whip up some eggs?"

Focused on the television, he missed her muffled reply. A reporter was giving an exclusive on "the Grable kidnapping." Peggy the Tripp, that's what he'd called her when he worked on the Hill. Blonde, bright, and beautiful. "To be avoided at all costs" he'd written on many a request for an interview, 'cause for a politician, she was a human landmine. Grable usually ignored his advice, on that subject anyway. He must have a thing for her, Grayson figured.

He turned up the volume.

"Police say they have no firm leads on the whereabouts of little Zoe Grable and they're asking for the public's help in finding the five-year-old. If you have any information, you're encouraged to call the number on your screen. And so the wait continues for one very distraught U.S. senator. This is Peggy Tripp in Georgetown."

Grayson clicked the remote. *Yeah,* he thought, *I'll bet you are "distraught," Senator. And it's about time.* "Sandy!" he yelled, striding out to the kitchen.

Grayson never saw the little girl hiding behind the couch, never saw her peeping around the side and staring, wide-eyed, at the TV, never realized the cover story he'd thought he'd sold her—that her daddy needed him to take care of her for a little while—had just been irredeemably blown.

Now, Zoe Grable knew the truth.

When Kenzie got back to the Grables' house she went immediately to the dining room, empty except for Crow, who stood in the corner talking on his cell phone. Only after Kenzie had sat down at the computer and activated the screen did she hear enough to realize he was speaking Navajo.

His words flowed, one after another, like a

brook over smooth stones. So many long vowel sounds, so few fricatives or gutturals. He was singing more than speaking.

She cleared her throat so he would realize he wasn't alone. He turned around, saw her, and kept on talking. Ten minutes later, he clicked the phone off. "Did you get all that?" he said, smiling at her.

"It's a beautiful language," Kenzie said, looking away from the computer.

"There's no point in talking to my grandfather except in Navajo. He insists on it."

"Is he all right?"

"My grandfather? He's fine. I had some things I wanted to talk to him about, that's all. I've got to go. I'm headed over to the field office to see if I can get those offshore banks to cooperate with us."

She watched him go. Momentarily, she wondered what it would be like to have a mother she could call and just talk to, someone to whom she could say, "I've met this guy, Mom, and I can't wait for you to meet him."

Impulsively, Kenzie picked up the phone and dialed her mother's number. "Mom? How's Jack?" she said.

Why had she hoped it would be different? After her mother complained about him drooling water on the kitchen floor and chastised Kenzie for not taking him to the groomer more often, Clarice began a litany of criticisms of her neighbors, her friends, and, of course, Kenzie's Aunt Cici. Ten minutes later, Kenzie hung up. Her head was pounding. She looked up. Beth Grable stood in front of her, her purse in her hand.

"I just want to thank you," the senator's wife said.

Kenzie rose to her feet.

"You were right. He did want me. And . . . and I'm going now, to see a counselor. I do need some help."

Impulsively, Kenzie touched Beth's arm. "Anyone in your circumstance would. Good luck to you." The senator's wife responded with a hug.

Standing in a bullpen on the third floor of the Washington Field Office, where he was directing a team of three agents trying to identify the kidnapper's Cayman Islands bank, John Crowfeather kept thinking about Kenzie. He'd worked with many women, many of them beautiful. Agents. Support staff. Lawyers. He'd had plenty of opportunities, he realized, to get involved, but no one had really captured his attention until he met Kenzie. And why was he attracted to her?

He thought his grandfather would be upset with him, even mentioning a non-Navajo woman, but that didn't happen. Instead, his grandfather told him he'd been praying and asking for a sign his grandson would be all right. Three days ago, he said, he'd seen a white deer.

It was the day, Crow realized, he had met Kenzie.

Crow wasn't superstitious, nor was he a believer in such signs, but his grandfather, like most Navajos, believed there were no coincidences. "Everything has a cause," the old man would say, "and the first cause is God."

What would Scott say about that?

Kenzie looked pretty, beautiful, really, in an all-American girl sort of way—minimal makeup, hair casually pulled back in a low ponytail, her clothes simple and serviceable.

He liked that about her. But there was something else, too. It took him a while to put his finger on it.

Kenzie was smart. It took about two seconds to figure that out. But more than smart, she had a depth about her that most women Crow had met didn't. She actually reminded him of Julie. He could talk to her, and she understood him.

That, Crow thought, was about as rare as a white deer.

Ten minutes after Crow left, Kenzie was sitting in the senator's home office, waiting for Scott. The senator sat behind his desk. He picked up a pencil and rolled it between his fingers. "Thank you for convincing Beth to come home."

Kenzie smiled slightly and nodded. "Sure."

"We've talked all morning. I never realized . . . well, how she felt." Grable sat back. "I've got some things I have to change." The senator placed the pencil, point down, on his desk blotter, and then flipped it and pressed the eraser end, repeating the movement over and over in a display of nerves.

Kenzie felt sorry for him. "Anything else new?"

"The code word he gave for the bank account seemed odd: Curtis. Alicia came up with something: Curtis is the name of a CISU SWAT team member on *High Stakes*, a loyal, para-military figure. He lost control on a mission and was about to kill a terrorist who was actually working with them. Connor had to kill him, instead."

"Connor killed a friendly?"

"One of his best friends."

"Wow," Kenzie said. She tapped her lip with her finger. "So wait. If you are CISU . . ."

"Or Connor . . ."

". . . or Connor, and you killed your good, loyal friend . . . does this guy think he's Curtis?" Kenzie sat straight up. Just then Scott walked into the office.

Kenzie had to stay level, professional, to pitch her idea. "Scott, I have a theory."

The two men waited for her. She opened a

folder on her lap and handed each a picture of Grayson Chambers.

"What?" Senator Grable said. "No way . . ."

"Listen to me. As I read documents at the senator's office I noticed some of the writing seemed extraordinarily good. The syntax, word usage, logic . . . all pointed to a highly literate person. I found out that Grayson Chambers, the former legislative aide, was the writer."

"He'd never do something like this! He was a loyal employee, personally loyal, to me!" The senator's face looked red.

"Sort of a 'Curtis'? Like the one Connor had to kill? Listen." Kenzie looked at Scott. "Louise, the senator's secretary, gave Chambers high marks for politeness, effectiveness, and so on. But another coworker, April, had an entirely different view of him."

"So what? People get along with some people better than others!" Grable said.

"Yes, but it's typical for a corporate psychopath, a sub-criminal psychopath, to be very adept at using people, at playing up to those who are valuable to him and dismissing those who aren't. You, obviously, were a valuable source of power and prestige. Louise would be a great source of information and access. April, a correspondence intern, could be dismissed, ignored, and put down with abandon."

The senator stood to his feet. "But he loved

Zoe! Every time he came over here he would bring her toys."

"He came over a lot?" Scott asked.

"He slept right upstairs in the third-floor bedroom on many a night," the senator responded.

Kenzie's heart began beating hard. "So she would be used to him."

"Sure, but . . ."

"And he knew exactly where her room was."

"Yes."

"It wouldn't have been totally unusual for her to see him in that upstairs hallway. So he might be able to show up and talk her into some ruse, some story about why she had to go with him somewhere. And he certainly knew how much you loved her."

The senator looked flustered.

"Did Grayson Chambers know about the inside deals you'd arranged?" Scott asked.

Grable reddened. He hesitated before responding. "Well, yes, I guess he had to know."

"Did you cut him in on the money?"

The senator sat down heavily in his chair. He put his hand to his brow. "No. I guess I didn't."

Kenzie and Scott looked at each other. "Where is this guy now?"

Grable waved his hand. "Teaching. At some college in California."

"Louise didn't know exactly where he was either," Kenzie confirmed.

"Get on that," Scott said to Kenzie. "Let me know if you need help."

But before she could even move out of her seat, Scott's cell phone rang, and his immediate response to the caller, the way he stood up, pulling his notepad out of his pocket, the way he furiously started taking notes while cradling his phone between his shoulder and his ear, kept Kenzie transfixed. Something was up. Grable saw it too, and he rose to his feet with a mixture of fear and hope on his face.

Scott clicked off his cell phone. He looked straight at Kenzie. "Alexandria police have nabbed a suspect in a couple of cold cases they've been working. They think we ought to look at him."

"What?" Kenzie asked. She tried to regroup. "You go and I'll keep tracking Chambers," she said, the frustration clear in her voice.

"No. I need you. Come on."

Outside, Scott opened up. "This guy's DNA connects him to two abductions and murders several years ago, two children, taken from their homes."

"But, Scott . . ."

"He shaved their heads, Kenzie."

A feeling of dread washed over her, sucking whatever energy she had away.

"Crow's going to meet us there."

• • •

Kenzie insisted on taking her own Bureau car. Maneuvering through the traffic, she kept right behind Scott's SUV. Their blue lights were activated, but that seemed a big ho-hum to Washington drivers, whose lives were routinely interrupted by processions of high-level government officials and foreign diplomats, and few seemed to notice, much less move out of the way.

Finally, Scott shook off the congestion, whipped onto the Francis Scott Key Bridge, and crossed the Potomac. Once on the Virginia side, he entered the George Washington Memorial Parkway and headed south, past the Boundary Channel, Roaches Run Waterfowl Sanctuary, Reagan National Airport, and into the brick, colonial charm of downtown Alexandria. They pulled their Bucars up onto the sidewalk outside the police station and went inside.

The police chief, Ed Sikorsky, waited for them, along with Crow. He had changed into a black suit, a white shirt, and a blue and black striped tie and he looked sharp to Kenzie. His eyes met hers and she could tell from his look he felt tense.

Sikorsky, a fifty-something, graying, slim veteran, greeted Scott warmly. Kenzie wondered if there was anyone in the greater Washington law enforcement community who didn't know Scott. After introductions all around, he ushered them into a small conference room. Kenzie put her dark blue portfolio, embossed with the FBI seal, on the table and sat down. Crow sat down next to her.

Two Alexandria detectives came in, plopped thick files on the table, and, after introductions, began briefing the agents on the cases. "The first incident occurred April, 2003," the burly man named George Carter reported. "Six-year-old female, abducted from a single-family home located at 2669 Pickett Street. Perpetrator entered through an open window by cutting the screen. Used chloroform to drug her, according to a rag we found. Parents reported her missing the next morning. Somebody walking their dog in a nearby park found her body six months later.

"The second case is similar: A four-year-old girl taken from her bedroom in the Glebe Road area, August, 2005. Buried in a shallow grave in a park nearby. In both cases the victims had long blonde hair. When they were found, their heads had been shaved."

Kenzie's head spun. "But he never asked for ransom, right? There were no notes or calls?"

"No."

The other detective, as slim as Carter was stocky, took over. His name was George Miller. Together, the two detectives were known around the station as Team George. "The suspect is Lee Richard Waller," he said, "age forty-four. He's a construction worker, lives up near the airport.

One of those areas where the duplexes are being torn down and condos built. Lives alone. Has priors for drug possession, DUI, and one assault. Did short time here in the city jail for a bar fight. Fairfax ID'd him in a child porn sting. DNA registered a hit on these cases for us.

"We didn't have much on those murders," Miller said, continuing, "just a similar MO and the chloroform. But we found a little DNA on the second child, a single hair, and that gave us enough to start looking at Waller."

"We've been talking to him all night," Carter said.

"Has he lawyered up?" Crow asked.

"Not yet. Says he 'ain't got much use for them types.' "

Kenzie blinked. "Is that a quote?"

Carter looked at her blankly.

"Are you quoting him?" Kenzie repeated.

The cop nodded. "Yep, that's what he said."

Kenzie looked at Scott. It sure didn't fit the profile she'd come up with. "Did you ask anything about Zoe?"

"Left it for you all. We just noticed the similarities."

Scott nodded. "OK. I guess it's our turn."

"I want to do the interview," Kenzie asserted.

Crow looked sharply at her.

Scott paused, considering her request. Then he nodded. "OK. He's yours. Let's strategize."

23

Half an hour later, they were ready. They had read the files on the two old murders, asked more questions, and prepared an approach. Kenzie would lead off and when she hit a wall or got tired, Scott would come in. Scott cautioned her, "He's shackled and cuffed to the chain on his waist. But he's got nothing to lose, so watch it. Crow and I will be right outside."

"OK." Kenzie straightened her suit jacket, brushed a stray hair out of her eyes, and pushed open the door to the interview room.

Immediately the smell of stale tobacco and unwashed skin hit her. The odor seemed almost feral.

When the prisoner saw her, he grinned and began rhythmically clanging the waist chain his cuffs were secured to. "Well, lookee what they sent me!" he said in a rough, raspy voice. "Lookee, lookee." His graying hair looked scruffy and unkempt. He had a two- or three-day beard and he was missing an eye tooth on the right side. His creased skin held a large scar from his eyebrow down across his temple.

But it was his eyes that nearly did Kenzie in. They were blue, light ice blue, and when he fixed them on her, his gaze assaulted her. It felt like he was undressing her. Her skin crawled.

Resolutely, she sat down across from him and put a file folder on the table in front of her. The point of the interview was to find out if Lee Waller had abducted Zoe Grable. To do so, she needed him to open up.

If Waller was a psychopath, or had psychopathic tendencies, he would have no conscience. Appeals to a sense of fair play, or justice, or compassion for the survivors would go nowhere. He would also be quite narcissistic. Appeals to his ego, to his grandiose sense of self, might work. She had talked Scott into taking that approach.

"Mr. Waller," she said, staring right into those pale blue eyes, "you are amazing."

An expression of surprise passed momentarily over his face, then Waller started laughing the wheezy, phlegmy laugh of a man who'd spent over half his life smoking. "How'd you guess?"

"Five years we've been looking for the person who killed little Wendy Williams. Seven for Catherine Jones. We're usually pretty good at finding people . . . how'd you keep us from identifying you?"

"What do you do for the Bureau?" he asked.

"I'm an agent."

"I never did think much of women in that job."

"I study people like you. Not very many can do what you did."

"I guess not."

"Talk to me for a minute about Catherine Jones. Was she your first victim?" Under the table, Kenzie's knee shook. Waller looked at her as if he was inspecting her, or recalling that crime and thinking of her along with it. It gave her the creeps. "What about Catherine Jones, Mr. Waller?"

"Lemme see, which one was she?"

Kenzie reminded him of a couple of details and put a photo of the dead child in front of him. "How did you do that?" she asked him with intense interest.

Waller began talking about his crime, step-by-step recounting the details, the same way some people talk about their vacations. He seemed to relish the memories, and Kenzie knew he had gone over this many, many times in his own mind in the intervening years. Why he had chosen that girl; how he had gotten into the house; the tools he'd brought with him; and most disturbing, the pleasure he'd taken in killing her.

Then he started again, with Wendy Williams.

All the time Waller talked, Kenzie noticed his arms and shoulders moving. She couldn't see his hands, but she could tell the man was letting off tension by tugging at his cuffs. Sometimes she could hear the chain rattling as he moved.

So many of the details of both crimes fit Zoe's case: the chloroform, the entry into the house, the shaving of their heads. But why would Waller pick a house in Georgetown? Most of them were alarmed. Had he known only the nanny would be there with Zoe? And so many of the indicators in the Grable case pointed to someone trying to get at Grable. Did Waller have any reason to do that? Did he even know Grable? Had he worked on their house?

For the next hour, Kenzie asked questions. Waller denied taking Zoe, denied even being in Georgetown. "I ain't been down there in twenty, thirty years," he said.

Kenzie moved the interview a different direction, intending to come back to Zoe from a different angle. Waller explained some of his methodology to Kenzie, sending cold chills down her spine. "I like to shave their heads, you know? Makes 'em crazy. And then . . ." He laughed hoarsely and began rattling his chains again. Then, suddenly, his right arm flew back, and a look of startled surprise filled Waller's face.

Grinning, he held up his hand. He'd slipped the cuff.

Crow cursed. He moved toward the door of the interview room.

"Hold it!" Scott commanded, reaching out and grabbing Crow's arm. "Wait. Get the chief." Crow stared at him like he was crazy.

Adrenaline poured through Kenzie when she saw Waller's freed hand and the maniacal look on his face. He stared at Kenzie, and smiled, and his smile became a leer.

Kenzie looked into his eyes and realized how empty they looked, like a shark's eyes—devoid of expression, vacant. It was like looking straight into the Abyss. A loud buzzing began in her ears. Her throat tightened. Somehow, she knew from his expression exactly what he was thinking. The hair on the back of her neck stood up, and fear, cold as steel, gripped her.

Her mind raced. Could Waller sense fear?

Just then, the chief and two detectives walked into the interview room. "All right, Waller, let's stop playing games," the chief said.

"Are you all right?" Scott asked Kenzie as she emerged.

"Fine, except for my heart, which stopped beating a couple of minutes ago." She shook her head. "If I believed in demons, I'd say I was just in a room with one." Kenzie shivered involuntarily.

"I thought Crow would jump right through the window. He had to go outside to cool off." Scott ran his hand through his hair. "What did you think?"

"Waller's all over the map. Some of the methodology fits but none of the linguistics does. He's very bright, despite the way he talks, but Scott, he's weird."

The police chief appeared down the hall and

called Scott. Kenzie stood still, trying to recover. Crow suddenly appeared beside her. "What did you think?" she asked him.

He didn't answer her at first. She could see the tendons in his neck were as tight as bowstrings. He glanced around as if making sure they were alone. He took a deep breath. "There are witches among the Diné," he said quietly, "evil people with empty eyes. People who my grandfather would say have given themselves over. I've seen the same thing myself. This man," he said, nodding toward where Waller had been sitting, "is evil."

Kenzie shivered again.

Ten minutes later, Scott, Kenzie, Crow, and the chief met to discuss their progress. "Honestly," Kenzie said, "I don't think Waller is the man who took Zoe."

"What makes you say that?" the chief asked.

Kenzie explained her psycholinguistic analysis of the ransom note, and how the language and the profile it suggested didn't fit Waller. Midway through her explanation, she saw the chief's eyes glaze over—he wasn't buying it.

She turned to Scott. "I want to pursue the other lead." By that, she meant Grayson Chambers, but she didn't want to reveal his name.

Scott understood. "Have you called Alicia? Has there been any other Internet activity?"

Kenzie grimaced. "No. I checked with her a few minutes ago."

"So it all stopped right about the time the police picked up Waller."

She had to admit that it had.

"And he's pretty facile with computers. More facile than his occupation might suggest," Scott added.

"He's got three computers, loaded with porn, plus an iPod, wireless network, the whole bit," the chief said.

Crow had been standing with his back to the group, staring out of the window. He turned around. "I think you should let her go back," he said to Scott. "I'll stay with you. Let her go."

Scott looked at him curiously. "What are you thinking?"

"She knows what she's talking about. Waller's not the guy. Let her go. You and I can stay and break him down."

Kenzie studied Crow. He looked tense. Was he buying the profile she'd created or simply protecting her?

"I don't know how much more support we can give you," the chief said, looking at his watch. "Overtime is killing us."

"If we need another agent, we can bring one in," Crow retorted.

Scott's cell phone rang. He looked at the number and said, "Hold on." Standing up and moving to the edge of the room, he spoke quickly, quietly, and then clicked the phone off with authority. He looked straight at Kenzie. "Grable's complaining to the director. He doesn't believe the other lead is valid."

Kenzie sighed with exasperation. "It's ridiculous to allow him to affect the course of an investigation, even if he is a senator."

Scott frowned.

An officer opened the door of the room, came in, and spoke quietly to the chief, who then turned to the group and said, "Waller wants to show Kenzie something near his house."

"Waller wants a field trip," Crow said.

Scott took a deep breath. "He's not going to call the shots. Let's you and I go, Crow, and Kenzie, you go on back. Pursue whatever you want to pursue. Finding Zoe is more important than placating Grable. And if this turns out to be a dead end, we won't have invested all our resources here."

All the way back to Grable's house, Kenzie rolled over the evidence for her premise in her mind. Chambers had motive: To avenge what was in his mind poor treatment by the senator. He had means: He'd been in the third-floor bedroom, knew Zoe, and knew how to observe the goings-on in the house. And he had opportunity: Surely, he would know about Mrs. Grable's mah-jongg night.

But where was Grayson Chambers now? Kenzie had to answer that question. More specifically, where was he the night Zoe was abducted? But a deeper, unstated question knotted her stomach: Would her understanding of psycholinguistics and her application of it in this case be accurate? Or would her work just give the naysayers, from her boss on down, more evidence it was voodoo science?

Grable had said Chambers taught at some college in California. So, Kenzie started with Pepperdine University in Malibu, and worked her way up the coast to U.C.-Santa Barbara, checking faculty lists on websites and making phone calls. No one had heard of a Grayson Chambers. She thought perhaps he may have published an academic paper, so she searched for one but found nothing. She got other agents working on accessing California driver's license records and other public information—even newspaper archives. Then she went back and called colleges north of Santa Barbara and inland toward the San Joaquin Valley.

Still empty-handed, she called the senator's secretary. "Did he have his doctorate?" she asked Louise.

"I don't think so," she responded. "Just a masters. As far as I know." She chuckled. "I'm sure I would have heard about every step of his progress if he'd been working on a doctorate."

Masters only. If that were the case, he'd probably be teaching at a community college, Kenzie reasoned. So she began calling all she could find in California, starting with the area north of L.A. "There are an awful lot of community colleges in California," she muttered as call after call produced nothing. One hour went by, then two.

Frustrated, Kenzie turned another direction. She Googled KickerG, Chambers's online screen name. And she got two hundred thirty-seven hits.

"Awesome," she said.

"What did you find?" Alicia asked. They were in the Grables' dining room. Alicia was monitoring the *High Stakes* message board, while Kenzie searched for information on Chambers.

" 'KickerG' is the screen name Grayson Chambers used for political blogs," she explained, keeping her voice low. No sense running the risk of having Grable hear her suspicions about Chambers. He and his wife were upstairs, but Kenzie wasn't taking any chances. "I've got two hundred thirty-seven hits on that name on Google."

"All right!"

"I want to read through these as fast as I can," Kenzie said. "I want to see if I can find any correlations, any patterns." She wiped her hands on the tactical pants she'd changed back into.

"Will you back me up on this? Google KickerG, and make a file of everything he's posted."

"Will do."

"And then e-mail it to me and print it. Be sure you have URLs, times . . . everything we'd need to get back to each posting."

"Grayson, I have to go to the store! Look at this refrigerator! It's empty!" Sandy motioned toward the open door.

She stood toe-to-toe with him and he didn't like that. He didn't like being challenged, especially by a woman. This wasn't her plan. It wasn't her house. And it certainly wasn't her money soon to be sitting in an offshore bank.

Grayson hit the door so that it slammed shut. Eyes glaring, he snapped at her. "You will do as I say, or I swear . . ."

"But Gray, we need the food! Just let me go. I'll be real quick. Then you can have the car and go anywhere you want. C'mon," her voice softened. "Gray, honey. If you leave now, me and Zoe, we're gonna get hungry."

He backed down. He sure didn't want her doing something stupid, like ordering out for pizza. Over at the kitchen table, Zoe sat on a chair. She seemed to be studying them, her hand to her chin. Good grief. She looked like her old man.

Grayson turned back to Sandy. "All right. Go. You have one hour."

"I'll need money."

He swore and pulled two fifty-dollar bills out of his wallet and handed them to her. "Take her with you," he said, nodding toward Zoe.

Sandy remained very quiet.

"What?" he prompted.

"Last time? When we went to the mall? I had a hard time with her. She kept telling everybody her name: Zoe."

"What? What?" Rage poured through him. His blood pounded in his head and his anger felt like a white heat in his body. He pointed his finger in Sandy's face. "Can't you control her? What's the matter with you?" He stood very close to her, close enough to see the fear in her eyes and something in him liked that. "If you blow this, I'll . . . I'll . . ." And then he did something he'd never done in his whole life. His hand flung out, and he slapped her, slapped her hard across the face.

"Oh!" she said, reacting to the blow. When she looked back up at him, she had tears in her eyes. "I'm sorry. I'm sorry," she whimpered. A red handprint marked her cheek.

"You go," he hissed, "and get back here pronto. You understand? ASAP." He threw his car keys down on the floor. Sandy picked them up, and scurried out of the door.

An odd mixture of anger and satisfaction filled Grayson. He'd stayed in control of the situation.

He'd kept that woman in her place. He'd made his point. He turned and looked at Zoe. The little girl stared at him, those blue eyes, so like the senator's, fixed on his face.

And suddenly, he felt helpless again. He raced to the door and yelled out, "What does she like to do?" His question unanswered, he came back inside. "Hey, want to watch some TV?" he asked Zoe.

"No."

"Want to play with your toys?"

"No."

"Want to read a book?"

"No."

The kid was a brat. "What do you want to do?"

"See my daddy."

"You will. In a while."

"You stole-ed me," she said, "and I hate you."

He flew into a rage. "What are you talking about?"

"My daddy's gonna get you."

"He told me to take care of you!"

"No. You stole-ed me."

Grayson looked around for a distraction. He threw some paper at her. "Here. Draw." And he left the room.

When he peeked in a few minutes later, the little girl had her head down, focused on the paper, drawing. Great. Now he could do what he wanted.

He went out to the living room, booted up his laptop, and started working on blog entries. He couldn't access the Internet, but he could write offline and copy and paste it later. Most people on the Hill still weren't getting it. They just didn't understand politics! Amazing that the most powerful country in the world had such an incompetent legislature. They just weren't grasping the issues correctly. He had his arguments ready. He rubbed his hands together like a baseball player about to grip the bat. He still had game. And he would let people on the Hill know it.

Grayson got lost in his work. When he looked up fifteen or twenty minutes later, Zoe had left the kitchen and was tiptoeing through the living room. When she saw him, she shrank back against the wall. "I got to go to the bathroom," she said.

"Well, go on!" he responded. What was he, her nanny? She disappeared down the hall.

Much later, he realized he hadn't seen her come out. Much, much later he realized it probably wasn't a good idea to leave her alone. Much, much, much later he got up to find her.

24

Grayson glanced in the kitchen. Where had Zoe gone? Her chair stood empty, her crayons scattered on the table. "Zoe?" he called. He walked to the bathroom, in the small hallway leading from the living room to the two bedrooms, and looked in. No Zoe. He even checked behind the shower curtain. And her bedroom was empty, though her toys lay scattered on the floor, like she'd been in there playing.

Grayson's heart began really pounding now, and he cursed out loud. He went into the room where he and Sandy were sleeping. Nothing. But then a tiny voice caught his ear.

"My name is . . ."

He dove across the bed. Zoe crouched in the corner, his cell phone at her ear. He grabbed it from her hand, clicked it off, and threw it across the room. She screamed. He grabbed her arm and hauled her onto the bed. Zoe kicked and tried to bite him. Her voice pierced his ears! He hit her hard, harder than he should have, across the face. Then he pushed her down with both hands, bouncing her into the mattress. "Don't . . . you . . . ever . . ." he yelled, ". . . do that again!"

She writhed and tried to push him away.

Grayson hit her again. "Shut up. Shut up!" he yelled. Glancing around the room, he grabbed the sashes off the curtains, and flipping her over, he forced her hands behind her back and tied them. Then he tied her ankles together. And when the little girl screamed, he spanked her.

The 911 dispatcher rewound the recording of the last call. The childish voice said, *My name is Zo* . . . He glanced at his coworker. "We got another kid, playing with a phone."

His coworker frowned, and shook his head. "Call them back to confirm. Don't these kids have parents?"

Grayson had just gotten Zoe quiet when his cell phone rang. He picked it up, expecting it to be Sandy. But the caller ID said "Emergency Dispatch."

What did they want? "Hello?" Grayson said, moving quickly away from Zoe. He forced himself to sound relaxed. "Oh, no trouble, officer." He managed a chuckle. "My daughter. She just learned about 911 and . . . yes, sir. My name?" His heart raced. "Everett. Bob Everett. Yeah. Everything's fine here. We just need to teach her *when* to call."

Grayson hung up the phone and cursed. That kid! What if the dispatcher didn't buy his reassurance? How do they track cell phones?

How close could they get if they wanted to investigate further?

If he could get on the Internet, he could find out. But he couldn't. No Wi-fi! Hands shaking, he jerked the battery out of the phone. Walking quickly to the kitchen, he took a meat hammer out of a drawer and began pounding and pounding until the phone was a mess of plastic and metal and tiny pieces. Then, for good measure, he scooped it all into a zippered plastic bag, added a can of soup for weight, took it outside, and heaved it into the pond behind his mother's house. When he heard the splash as the bag hit the water, he felt instant regret. What if he hadn't destroyed the tracking part?

By the time Sandy got back half an hour later, Zoe lay asleep in her bed, clutching a stuffed animal, her thumb in her mouth. "How'd you do that?" she asked Grayson.

"You just have to know how to handle them," he said. Sandy would never know about the restraints, or how Zoe sobbed until she fell asleep and he was able to remove them.

Sandy hesitated, like she wanted to ask him more, but then changed her mind. "You want lunch before you go?"

"Nah. Got to run. I'll be back later," and he gave her a peck on the cheek like nothing had happened, grabbed his laptop, and left. "Watch your cell phone!" he yelled as he opened his car door. "Don't let her get to it."

First job: Get a replacement phone. One of those disposable ones.

"Here's the interesting thing," Kenzie said to Alicia, who was looking over Kenzie's shoulder. "KickerG's last posts on these political blogs roughly coincided with the times our suspect was posting on the *High Stakes* board."

"Could be coincidental."

"What are you doing?" The senator stood in the doorway, demanding an answer.

Kenzie looked at him. Grable looked tired, and she wondered if he'd slept at all over the last two days. Grief and anxiety had aged him almost overnight. The suave, handsome senator had disappeared. In his place was a graying older man, drowning in a sea of fear. Instantly, she decided to be up front. "Scott and Crow are in Alexandria, investigating that man the police arrested. I interviewed him, Senator, and I don't think he had anything to do with Zoe's disappearance."

"So what are you doing?"

She moved toward him. "I'm pursuing the Internet leads. More specifically, I'm still looking at Grayson Chambers." Kenzie brushed a stray lock of hair out of her eyes. "I know you're having a hard time imagining him as a kidnapper.

But you will not direct the course of this investigation." She looked straight at him, staring at him as a mosaic of emotions crossed Grable's face. Anger. Fear. Concern. Then finally, resignation. She softened her voice, "As soon as I can clear him, I'll get off that line of investigation. But until I know for sure he's innocent, I'm going to pursue it. Because I really want to find your daughter. And I know you do, too."

He cursed softly and walked out of the room.

Scott checked in half an hour later and she told him of her conversation with Grable. "Good job," he said. "He can't control this one."

Then she updated him on the KickerG blog entries, and on her continued inability to identify Grayson Chambers' location. He gave her a name of a friend in the L.A. office. "Try her," he said, and Kenzie scribbled down the name. She asked him about Waller and what they'd discovered on their field trip. She half-hoped he'd say it was a dead end and they were coming back. But he didn't. Instead, he detailed the secret room in Waller's house, and the macabre things they'd found, evidence of his sordid life. Scott sounded exhausted.

"But no sign of Zoe, right?" she said hopefully.

She heard a long pause.

"No. Not yet. We have evidence techs scouring the place."

Kenzie resumed her own search. She called L.A., and spoke to Scott's friend, turning her loose on the hunt for Grayson. Then she laid her head down on the table and shut her eyes. Just for a minute, she told herself, yawning.

Less than two hours later, her cell phone rang— it was her response from L.A. She looked at Alicia, adrenaline racing. "L.A. tagged him," Kenzie told her colleague. "When Chambers left Washington he went to teach at Bear Canyon College, north of Santa Barbara. He got fired after less than two semesters. Three female students, one of them a thirty-eight-year-old woman, accused him of harassment. They found enough evidence to terminate him."

"A precipitating circumstance?"

"That's what I'm thinking," Kenzie replied.

"Why didn't they tell you this? Hadn't you called that college?"

"When I called, I got a student working in Human Resources. She didn't bother looking back through their records. She only looked at those currently employed." Kenzie couldn't stay seated. She stood up, her heart thumping. "One of Scott's friends in the L.A. office knew the right person to talk to."

She dialed Scott and relayed the information

she'd received. He sounded encouraged, and when she hung up the phone, she realized the senator had come into the room.

"What's going on?" he asked.

"Chambers got fired from his teaching job."

Grable collapsed into a chair, and groaned.

"It must have been a terrible failure, after all of his success in Washington," Kenzie said.

Beth Grable appeared and Bruce explained the situation to her. Kenzie expected an explosion, an "I told you so!" moment, but instead, Beth sat down in a chair next to her husband, took his hand, and leaned her head on his shoulder.

"What else?" the senator asked, dispiritedly.

"Getting fired from a job can be a precipitating incident," Kenzie said, "enough, I think, to make him cross the line and do something crazy. It would certainly bruise his ego. It would be an affront to him. He'd be angry and resentful. His plan didn't work. His overblown self-image didn't make it in the real world. But he couldn't go back to the Hill. That would really be embarrassing. So now he has a problem."

She paced across the room as she spoke, touching her lip with her forefinger. "The more he thinks about it, the more he realizes how unfairly he's been treated. First by you, now by this college. And then he comes up with a plan to get back."

The senator sat slumped in his chair. He looked

pale. "How could I have misjudged him?" he muttered.

His wife filled in the blank. "You don't really see the people around you, Bruce," she said. Surprisingly, her voice bore no anger. "You see what you want to see, what fits your plan, but you don't see the real person."

Grable shook his head. "So where'd he go, when he left the college?"

"That's the sixty-four-thousand-dollar question."

"So what good does it do to know it could be him, if we don't know where he is?" Frustration edged his voice.

Kenzie rubbed her neck. "Since you employed Grayson, you must have some records on him, like a Social Security number."

"Call Louise. She'll have all the information we ever got on him."

Kenzie did a public records check and had the last four digits of Grayson's SSN. Louise provided the other five. Kenzie called those in to an agent at the office, and he began looking for anything they had on one Grayson Chambers.

"No arrest record, not even a speeding ticket," she told Scott when he arrived back at the Grables' two hours later.

"I'll go for a warrant for his bank records including credit card information and any ATM

301

cards he may have. We might be able to track him that way."

"Will the prosecutor rush that?" Grable asked.

"Absolutely."

"What about the Alexandria suspect?" Beth asked.

Scott hedged his answer. "We didn't see any traces of Zoe. He claims he hasn't been in Georgetown for twenty years. We still have agents going over his house and they may interview him again. We don't see the link at this time."

"But what about . . ." Senator Grable began to say. A look from Scott stopped him.

"We'll keep that line open. But for now, I'm going to go with what Kenzie's finding."

They stood in the senator's backyard, enveloped by heat and humidity, trying to get away from the tension inside. Kenzie's head still hurt. No wonder: It was five p.m. and she hadn't thought about eating since breakfast. "Where's Crow?" she asked Scott.

"He's back on, trying to identify the Cayman Islands account. He left Alexandria several hours ago and has a team of agents working from WFO."

"So you both are now thinking that Waller isn't our man?"

Scott shook his head. "I got to thinking, why

did I bring you on this case if I wasn't confident in your ability to psych this stuff out? I still don't understand why Waller's methodology matched this case."

Kenzie nodded. "But the language . . ."

"Completely different. Absolutely wrong," Scott said. "Now whether I can convince the director a suspect using 'ain't' is grounds for backing off of a lead I don't know."

Kenzie took a deep breath. "I'm going to get Alicia to help me run some of KickerG's blog entries through some language programs to compare them to our suspect's postings."

"Good."

Crow's team worked for hours trying to identify recently opened accounts in the Cayman Islands bank and attempting to find an account with an encrypted number that might relate somehow to the Grables. After finally convincing the bank officials to cooperate, he identified the account and had the IT staff setting up a false front for the Out Islands Bank website. The kidnapper would think he had accessed the real bank's website. In reality, he'd be looking at a phony site being run by FBI computer specialists and a phony two-million-dollar deposit.

"Like those phishing schemes," Kenzie said, when Scott explained it to her.

"That's right." Scott shifted his weight on his

feet. "Look, Kenz, Crow is coming back here. We have to work on a plan for when we find out where Grayson is."

"HRT?" Kenzie asked. The Hostage Rescue Team was based in Quantico, just a few minutes away by chopper. Specially trained for these situations, they remained the Bureau's go-to guys, especially for a high-profile kidnapping.

"They're on alert. But there's a situation in New York they might have to deploy for. So we've got to have a back-up."

"The SWAT team from WFO?" Kenzie guessed.

"Probably." Scott shoved his hands in his pockets. "It depends on where Chambers is." He shook his head. "It's complicated."

"Where is Grayson from, originally?"

Scott looked at her. "Good question. Why do you ask?"

"His Social Security number starts with two-one-two, which would be a Maryland number." She ran her finger over her lip. "My guess is he isn't in California—he'd run from there. He'll be drawn toward D.C. It's the place he knows best. But he might not be right in town because people would recognize him. I wonder if he'd come back to some place familiar."

"His old home?"

"Maybe."

Scott nodded.

Kenzie began to pace. "I think you should put

Crow back in touch with Zoe's doctor. They should plan out contingencies on what to do depending on what condition she's in when we find her. HRT has their own medic but just in case they are deployed elsewhere, it would be good for Crow to have a plan, since he's an EMT."

"That's a great idea," said Scott, and he immediately pulled out his cell phone and called Crow.

"Kenzie!" Alicia called from the dining room. "He's active again!"

Zoe wouldn't talk, and Sandy couldn't figure out why. The little girl seemed listless. All she would do was sit on the couch and watch TV. And she was sucking her thumb! Again!

Kids. Sandy hadn't realized they were so complex. She busied herself putting a nice pot roast in the oven before she sat down to watch Oprah. Zoe snuggled up to her, and Sandy stroked what was left of her hair. Pretty soon, the little girl fell asleep. Sandy turned her full attention to the TV.

And that's why she didn't hear the motorcycles pull up, didn't hear the footsteps on the porch, heard nothing at all, in fact, before her younger brother Billy and three of his thug friends came striding through the side door.

"Billy! What are you doing here?" Her brother had called her on her cell phone as she drove to the store. Billy hadn't seen her for a couple of weeks, and he said he wanted to check to make sure she was OK.

She knew it meant he needed money. Still, he was her brother, one of her few emotional connections, and foolishly, she'd begun crying and she'd told him about Gray hitting her. Even more foolishly, she'd mentioned the name of the store she was about to go into. By the time she'd finished shopping a half hour later, he was waiting for her in the parking lot. Billy could smell a handout a mile away.

And now, here he was, standing in the kitchen of the Tulip Circle house, bold as life.

"Why are you here?" she said. "You can't be here!"

"Well, I am."

"How did you find me?" Sandy asked, her heart drumming.

"That weren't hard, Sandy. After we seen you at the store, we followed you, then just waited for your friend to leave," Billy said. His boots were muddy and his jeans were covered with grease. "This the kid?" He leaned to where he could see Zoe, sitting wide-eyed on the couch.

"You can't come in here!"

"We just did," one of the thugs said, laughing.

Billy turned his attention back to his sister. Six feet tall and two hundred thirty pounds, he towered above her. He wore a day's growth of beard and his hands remained black with grease, perpetually dirty from working on motorcycles, which is what he did for a living. That and deal drugs. Meth. Coke. Pot. He delivered. She'd bailed him out of jail more times than she could remember. He'd bailed her out of several abusive relationships. "The guy we saw, is he the guy who hit you?" Billy asked.

"If he comes back and finds you . . ."

"You sure can pick 'em," he said.

She reddened.

"This is his kid?"

"I'm helping him by taking care of her."

"Her? She looks like a him."

"We had to cut her hair. She got it all tangled."

One of her brother's friends walked into the living room, squatted down in front of the couch, and said, "Hey, sweet thing. What's your name?"

Zoe kicked at him and he reacted and fell backward. The other guys laughed.

"Billy, you can't stay here. You have to go," Sandy pleaded.

"Anybody hit my sister, I'm not lettin' them get away with it. You understand?" He grinned at her. "And besides, we're hungry." He rubbed his hand over his greasy T-shirt.

Sandy's mind began racing. She'd just bought all this food but she couldn't give it to them! How would she explain it to Grayson? All that food being gone? "Look, I'll give you some money and you can go to McDonald's. Or Pizza Hut." She found her purse on the kitchen countertop and removed a twenty-dollar bill from her wallet. She added a ten and handed it to her brother. "Take it and go. Please. And don't come back. Honest, Billy, I need you to leave."

"Honest, Billy, I need you to leave." One of her brother's friends mimicked her in a falsetto voice and then laughed and jostled his buddy with his elbow. She had never seen two of the three before, but that wasn't unusual. Her brother picked up friends like other people picked up trash—whatever was lying around.

He had been the despair of their parents, but then, their parents hadn't been exactly prize picks themselves. Both were alcoholics, both had, early in her youth, left most of the mothering to Sandy. It was OK until Billy got into drugs and alcohol himself. Now, with two prison terms and a string of trouble behind him, her little brother remained a constant source of stress, stress she hoped to leave behind by going to Jamaica with Grayson. But had he bought her a ticket? "Billy!" she yelled. "I mean it!"

He laughed again. "I got one more favor to ask."

She crossed her arms. "What?"

"I need some more cash."

"I just gave you thirty bucks!"

He held up his hand. "I know, Sis, but I need just a little more."

Sandy cocked her head. "How much more?"

"Fifty."

"Fifty dollars?"

"Yeah."

"No. I'm not giving you . . ."

Billy sagged back against the counter and crossed his arms in front of himself. His face became sad, the sad, hurt little kid expression she'd been falling for over the course of thirty years. "Why do you need it?" she asked. She'd intended the question to be a mark of strength on her part, a demand for a rational reason for giving him the cash. But as soon as the words came out of her mouth, she recognized them for what they were: The first signal to Billy that eventually she'd give in.

"My kid needs some stuff for school. A backpack and stuff."

Sandy grimaced. Billy's son, Bobby, was an adorable little blond, the absolute spitting image of Billy at that age. And Bobby's mother, who Billy never even thought of marrying, was smart: You want to see the kid, you show me the money. The only way she or Billy got to be with the little guy was if Billy paid child support, and often whatever else Bobby's mother demanded.

How could Sandy keep her brother from seeing his son?

Sighing, she dug into her wallet again, and counted out fifty dollars, all that she'd just gotten at an ATM at the shopping center. "There. Now leave, and don't you dare come back."

Billy grinned at her. "C'mon guys," he said, and he pushed his friends toward the side door. "See ya, Sis," he said, winking. "Thanks for the dough."

As she stood at the side door and watched their motorcycles roar off, tears came to Sandy's eyes. What a pain, this brother of hers. But she loved him. Sighing, she turned and as she did, her eyes fell on the kitchen floor and the mud from their boots. Good grief. If Grayson ever knew Billy and his friends were here, he'd . . . he'd . . . well, she didn't want to think about what he'd do!

She grabbed a couple of paper towels and dropped to her knees. She had to get this cleaned up! She had to!

Only when she had finished and the kitchen floor looked spotless did she think of Zoe. Sandy went into the living room, expecting to see the little girl on the couch. But she wasn't there. Her heart thumped. She raced back to the bedroom, and sighed with relief when she saw Zoe lying in the bed, curled up, sucking her thumb. She appeared to be fast asleep.

"I have got to relax!" she said to herself, and she poured herself a drink and plopped down in front of the TV.

25

Kenzie sat down in front of the computer. Jackson423 had just posted a message, a feeler to see if he could get Grable online again.

"I've been doing what you said," Alicia told Kenzie. "I've been posting as Brandigurl on and off so she and Big Dog aren't yoked together."

"Good job." Kenzie sat with her fingers poised above the keyboard trying to figure out what to do.

"What's going on?" Senator Grable joined them.

"Round Three," Kenzie said. "Scott, can you get an estimate from the IT guys about when they'll have that false website constructed? So I know a time frame?"

"He gave us forty-eight hours," the senator prompted.

"I just need a confirmation." Out of the corner of her eye, Kenzie saw Scott on the phone then saw him finish his conversation.

"They're building it now, then they'll need time to test it. So twelve hours—that's their outside limit."

"OK, good," Kenzie responded. She leaned forward a little, ready to post. Her fingers twitched. Then she said, "No, no," pushed back and stood up quickly. "You go at him first, with Brandigurl," she said to Alicia.

"Me?"

"You've been Brandigurl all day. Keep it up for a few go-rounds."

Alicia's eyes searched Kenzie's face. Kenzie guessed her thoughts: Randomly posting messages was one thing. Interacting with the kidnapper seemed another.

"All right," Alicia said finally, and she sat down and began responding to Jackson423.

"Oh, my gosh," the senator said, standing behind her. He looked at Kenzie, his eyes wide. "That number, 423. It means something."

"What?"

He had his cell phone out, checking its calendar app. "April twenty-third, two years ago, I had a meeting with a big contractor."

"Who paid you," Kenzie suggested.

Grable nodded slightly. "Right in front of Grayson." He swallowed hard. "Oh, God! What have I done?" the senator cried out. He put his hand to his chest as if he were having a heart attack and closed his eyes.

"So Grayson knew about it."

Grable nodded, looking at her again, and whispered, "Yes."

"But you didn't include him on the deal."

"I never gave him anything. Nothing." His

voice cracked. "I bragged about how much I got. Bragged about it! To him!"

Scott and Kenzie exchanged glances, then Scott went over to the senator, sat down next to him and put his hand on his shoulder. "Taking money was wrong," he said, softly, "and not cutting him in on it may turn out to have been stupid. But nothing you did justifies what Chambers is doing now. Nothing."

When the senator looked up, tears were streaking his face. He took a handkerchief out of his pocket and wiped them away. "I never saw this coming. I thought . . . I thought he was so loyal to me, that he was just intense about politics, and that he wouldn't care about the money. He had no family to support, no expensive hobbies. I just thought . . . I just thought . . ."

"All right, let me take it," Kenzie said to Alicia, and the two women switched positions. "C'mon, Jackson423. Let's deal."

She was a new hire at the dispatch center, a young woman with a degree in psychology and an interest in law enforcement. She'd made it through the interviews, the background checks, the psychological tests, the mental quickness and multitasking exercises. And now she was on the job for the first day, a raw trainee. Her supervisor told her to listen to old recordings to hear how the dispatchers handled calls.

Jessica sat with her headphones on, intent on everything she heard. The ambulance calls, the police chatter, the fire department dispatches. Sure, she'd listened to scanners for a long time, but this was for real, this was what she'd soon be doing on her own.

One call puzzled her. A tiny little voice said just one thing, then she heard the voice of an adult male, who sounded angry—then the call cut off.

A shadow fell over her small desk. "Any questions?" her new supervisor asked.

She hesitated. She certainly didn't want to appear stupid. But she couldn't let go of the call. "Would you listen to this?" she asked, and she handed her headphones to Mr. Gravely.

He put them on his head, leaning forward because the wire was short. He listened to the recording twice. "What's your question?"

"How do you handle something like that? A fragment of a call?"

"Let's ask the dispatchers who took it."

Together Jessica and Mr. Gravely walked into the heart of the center, where nine dispatchers sat at their stations handling traffic from all over the county. A huge electronic map hung on one wall. Mr. Gravely led her to a station where a gray-haired man in a white shirt was dispatching an ambulance. He touched the man on the shoulder, and waited.

When he was finished with the call, the dispatcher turned around. "What can I do for you?"

"Jessica here has a question." He described the call. "I think you handled that. You want to explain what you did with it?"

Jim leaned back in his chair. "Sure. It was a kid, playing with a cell phone. We get that all the time."

"How did you know it wasn't a real emergency?" Jessica asked timidly.

"I called back. Talked to an adult. He told me it was his daughter who'd just learned about 911."

Jessica frowned.

Catching her skepticism, Jim laughed. "Hey, if we dispatched a unit for every call like that we got, we'd need twice as many officers, just to keep our head above water."

"I see," Jessica said, but she really didn't see, because in her heart, she thought that kid sounded like she needed help. Then again, maybe she had just watched too many episodes of *CSI*.

"All right?" Mr. Gravely asked.

"Fine," Jessica responded, and she went back to her desk.

But the little girl's voice gnawed at her. Bugged her. Chewed on her until her dinner break when she sat in the employee lunchroom, eating her special recipe chicken salad sandwich and her tortilla chips while staring at the TV suspended from the ceiling, watching the six o'clock news. "And now," the anchor said, "for an update on the abduction of Senator Bruce Grable's daughter, we turn to Peggy Tripp."

The blonde reporter, standing outside a brick, two-story home, began her story. "It's been three days now since little Zoe Grable disappeared . . ."

Jessica stopped chewing. She stood up. She began moving toward the TV.

"Ah, this is malarkey. Face it. The kid's dead," said another worker, laughing, and he pressed the remote and changed the channel.

"Wait, stop!" Jessica tried to say, but her mouth was full and by the time she had swallowed, the man had sat down again with his buddies and they were joking about something. No way was she going to approach that crowd.

Quickly she scooped up the remains of her dinner and threw it in the trash. Then she went back to her station, found the spot on the recording, and listened to it over and over and over until it echoed in her head.

"My name is Zo . . ." the little voice said. And Jessica's heart began pounding, hard. *Zo, as in Zoe?*

"The IT guys tracing these messages have tracked them back to three different locations," Scott said. He stood in the senator's dining room with an unfolded one-hundred-mile radius map in his hand. "Senator, do you mind?" he asked over his shoulder.

"No. Let me help," Grable responded, and the two of them taped the map to the wall.

"Look here, Kenzie," Scott said. "The first message came from Hagerstown, the second, from right here in Georgetown, and they're narrowing down this current location. It appears he's using Internet cafés with free wireless."

"So we don't know for sure where he is now?"

"No, but I've e-mailed his picture to field offices and they're coordinating with local police. Teams are headed to both known locations. We'll know within fifteen minutes."

"But if you get him, where does that leave Zoe?" Grable asked.

"One step at a time, Senator. One step at a time."

Joie is always intense, Jackson423 posted, *but when I think of her in this circumstance, I see her as helpless, crying, and scared. She's all alone and she's terrified.*

That son of a gun, thought Kenzie, he's tweaking Grable. *Yes, but she's so valuable to CISU,* she responded under the Big Dog screen name. *I don't think it would take them long to come up with the money. One more episode, that's all. Of course, then they'd have to come forward with the details about where CISU would find her.*

Jackson423 responded, *Oh, the mastermind*

of all this would have that all figured out. It would be someplace public, like a park. Foxstone Park for example.

"Oh, this is cute," Kenzie said out loud. "Scott, come look at this."

Scott came around to where he could read the computer screen. "Very clever," he said.

"What?" Senator Grable asked.

"He's naming the park that Robert Hanssen used as a drop for packages for the KGB. After all, he was the biggest embarrassment the Bureau has had. A thirty-year agent who'd been giving us up to the Russians for most of his career." Scott shook his head.

"So not only is this guy tweaking you, Senator, he's thumbing his nose at the Bureau. He's smarter than all of us!" Kenzie said, sarcastically. "And a tad narcissistic, don't you think?"

"Yeah, but he forgets the rest of the story. That's the same park where we arrested Hanssen," Scott recounted.

"Do we need to start watching it now?" the senator said.

"Let me think about that. Offhand, I'd say that would be premature, but let me consider it," Scott said.

Kenzie began typing again. "I'm going to resist the urge to call him on it." *How long would this guy wait after he confirmed the money transfer before dropping Joie off?* she typed.

The mastermind would want to ditch her real soon. Real, real soon. I'm thinking within four hours of confirming the transfer. But of course, he's not going to get real specific. The feds would be all over him. He'd have to have a plan . . . like shooting her from a distance if he got an idea the feds were double-crossing him. All he wants, after all, is the money. He doesn't care about anything else. Just the money, and not getting caught.

Kenzie changed persona. *Hey,* Brandigurl wrote, *r u thinkin of writin this cuz it sounds good. Like a reel story. Ha ha.*

He came right back at her. *The story's been written. I'm just waiting for the go-ahead to submit it.*

Big Dog responded. *Personally, I think you should set the ball in motion. It's all going to come together. I have absolute assurance of that.*

Awesome! Brandigurl wrote. *Lemme know when it comes on. I can say, I knew you when!*

Scott's cell phone rang. He picked it up and talked briefly, then hung up. "Nothing at any of the locations," he said. "The guy's clever. He's moving all over the area."

"If he's using Internet cafés, I doubt he'll use the same place twice," Kenzie added.

"I agree."

Kenzie heard the senator sigh.

319

"Excuse me, Mr. Gravely?" Jessica's stomach churned. Why was she being such an idiot on her first day, she wondered.

Her supervisor looked up. "What is it, Jess?"

She blushed. "I am so sorry to be such a pain. But that call I asked you about?"

He frowned and cocked his head. A silver-haired forty-something man, he'd been on the job for twenty years. Now, he was probably wondering why in the world HR had hired her.

But she took a deep breath and continued. "I was just in the lunchroom, and the news came on. And there's a little girl they're looking for? A senator's daughter named Zoe Grable."

"And . . ."

"And, the little girl on the call says 'my name is Zo—.' Then it cuts off. Could she be saying 'Zoe'? Could it be the kidnap victim, sir?"

Her boss stared at her, and for a minute, Jessica felt afraid that he would laugh out loud. But he didn't. He studied her face. He pursed his lips. His thoughts played across his face like a movie. And then he stood up. "I want to listen to that again."

"Nothing else, eh?" Scott said.

Kenzie sat behind the computer, tapping a pen against her hand. "Nope. Nothing for half an hour."

"Then he's probably done for now."

"Right. I assured him the money was coming. He told me he'd let Zoe go within four hours of the confirmation of deposit. Then nothing." She sighed. "And now," she looked at her watch, "it's 6:20 and I'm thinking that's all we're going to get."

"We made the top of the news at five and six," Scott said.

"Are we getting anything out of that?"

"Lots of leads from our tip line. Most of them are nonsense. But there's one," Scott looked over his shoulder, "there's one that sounds interesting."

"What's that?"

Scott looked around. The senator didn't appear to be in earshot, so Scott continued. "A clerk at a children's store at a mall in Frederick, Maryland, reported seeing a blonde woman with a little boy with her two days ago. The kid had remnants of pink nail polish on his fingers."

Kenzie's eyes widened. "Scott! Do you think . . ."

"I don't know."

Kenzie mulled that point. "Yes, but don't some little boys, especially the ones with older sisters, sometimes want nail polish?"

"I honestly don't know." His cell phone rang. He looked at the caller ID and answered it. "Hansbrough," he said.

Kenzie turned to the computer screen while he spoke, checking for other entries from KickerG on the political blogs. Sure enough, she found two. When she looked back at Scott, his face looked animated. "We could have something," he said.

"What?"

"A 911 dispatcher in Carroll County, up near Frederick, took a call from a little girl seven hours ago saying something like 'My name is Zoe.' They thought it was a kid playing with a cell phone, but somebody questioned it. A new hire, actually. They contacted the Baltimore FBI office and they're e-mailing an audio file to me."

Kenzie jumped to her feet. "Great! Take the computer, then."

"What's going on?" Senator Grable asked. Kenzie told him. The room remained absolutely silent except for the clicking of the keys on the keyboard as Scott typed. Kenzie saw him move the mouse and click it, and a media program came up. It seemed slow, very slow, and she thought her heart would pound right out of her chest while she waited.

Finally, the file began to play: "911 operator. Do you need fire, police, or ambulance?"

And then they heard the tiny little voice.

26

"That's Zoe!" Senator Grable cried out. He put his hands to his head and yelled. "That's her! That's Zoe!"

Kenzie grabbed his arm. "Are you sure?"

"Bruce! What's going on?" Beth Grable came running.

"Let me hear it again!"

"It could be a hoax," Scott cautioned, giving the senator headphones. He moved so Grable could sit down. Beth moved right behind him.

"It's Zoe, it's Zoe!" the senator cried, pulling off the headphones. "You've found her!"

"Let me hear it!" Beth cried, grabbing the headphones.

"What do we have on it?" Kenzie asked.

"It was a cell phone call, so the closest we can get to a land location is a particular tower. And who owns the phone number. We're tracking that now." Scott rubbed his hand through his hair. "I've got to call the boss."

It felt satisfying, really, seeing his plan work out, step by step by step. Another twelve hours or so, and the money would be transferred and he'd be out of here. It had worked like clockwork. He had orchestrated everything beautifully.

As he drove along, his thoughts returned to another subject—what to do about Sandy. And Zoe. Rather than risk running into surveillance in a park, he thought why not just leave them at the house? Just drive off and not come back? By the time Sandy had figured out he wasn't going to return, he'd be long gone. He shifted in his seat. He liked that idea better.

A good plan was flexible, after all. And his was a good plan.

But what about torching the house for the insurance money? Grayson frowned. What if they were asleep when he did it? They'd wake up, right? As soon as they smelled smoke? So the house would burn down, they'd get out, but he'd be MIA. Maybe presumed dead.

He liked that! Pulling into the driveway of his mother's home, Grayson shoved his car into park. He'd driven all the way to an Internet café in Annapolis this time, a good two hours. Had to keep the monkeys jumping. Then, after he'd transmitted his message to the senator, he'd blogged elsewhere for a while, read some e-mail, and watched a pretty Asian girl at a table across from him. Now, at nearly ten p.m., he felt tired. It looked like Sandy was in bed. He hoped so. He didn't want to put up with her yapping, and he had to figure out how to torch the house.

He opened his car door, grabbed his laptop case, and got out. The air felt thick with humidity.

He wondered, momentarily, if it would be humid in Jamaica. He hoped not.

Grayson walked to the side door, the gravel from the driveway crunching under his feet. Sandy had left the light on for him. He jiggled his keys, found the right one, and inserted it into the lock. As he pushed open the door, a blow to the back of his head exploded in a blinding light in his eyes. He fell forward, his laptop case clattering to the floor, and he heard the sound of his own voice screaming in surprise.

The first thing Grayson heard as he came to was Sandy's voice. "Billy! What are you doing?"

He opened his eyes. His head hurt and felt so heavy. And he had the weirdest thought: Is this what he made that agent feel like? That blonde that he hit?

He couldn't move his hands. As he struggled to see, the forms in the kitchen were blurry. The lights were so bright! But gradually his head cleared. He was sitting on a kitchen chair, his hands tied behind his back. Before him stood a big man with tattoos and a bandanna on his head. Laughing. At him!

"What do you want?" Grayson managed to say.

The man looked beyond Grayson. "Sis, you didn't tell me the kid is worth twenty-five grand."

"Billy, what are you talking about?" Sandy came into view, dressed in her nightgown and a robe, her hair disheveled.

"Who is he?" Grayson asked her, but she ignored him.

Sandy shoved the big guy with one hand. "What do you mean?"

"The kid that's with you. There's a reward out for her—twenty-five grand. We saw it after we left, on a TV at the bar."

"Billy, you can't do this!" Sandy's face looked red.

"Oh, yeah, we can. We turn the kid in, we get the reward. What's the deal, anyway? Why is she with you?"

Don't tell him, don't tell him, Grayson begged silently. But he felt disoriented and he couldn't get his words out quickly enough.

"All right, look," Sandy said, crossing her arms. "Grayson knows the kid's father. He owes Grayson money and it's the only way to get it out of him . . ."

"How much money?" Billy asked.

Grayson groaned.

"A lot more than twenty-five K," Sandy said, matter-of-factly.

"Yo, Bill."

One of his friends appeared from behind Grayson. He wondered how many were there. How many would he have to outsmart? And how could he think with his head hurting like this?

"Yo, Bill, man, is this like, a kidnapping?" the dude said.

Billy moved forward suddenly, grabbed the front of Grayson's shirt, and shook him. "You tell me, man, you tell me what's going on. Or by God . . ."

Grayson's heart pounded. His head spun. He pulled against the ropes tying him to the chair.

Sandy rushed forward and grabbed Billy's arm. "Stop it! Stop! For crying out loud, Billy, stop."

Her brother looked at her, his small eyes flashing. Then he relaxed and let go of Grayson. "Sandy. This is the guy who hit you, right? What do you care about him? Tell me what's going on. Be straight with me."

Sandy took a deep breath. *Shut up,* Grayson said, silently. *Shut up!*

But she didn't. "Grayson here used to work for a senator, Senator Grable. That's Zoe's father."

"Zoe's the kid?"

"Right. And the senator, he owed Grayson some money. A lot of money. But he wasn't going to pay, so Gray had to push his buttons."

"How much does he owe you?" Billy asked Grayson.

Grayson's mouth tightened into a line. No way would he let this guy in on this. No way.

"How much?" Billy roared.

Someone grabbed the back of Grayson's chair and began shaking it, hard, and terror streaked through him, a deep terror he hadn't known since . . . since high school. "Stop it!" he cried out. To his chagrin, it sounded almost like a scream.

"Billy, stop!" Sandy said. "You're scaring the poor guy to death." The thug behind Grayson stopped, throwing up his hands and laughing. Sandy turned to Billy. "He told me five-hundred thousand dollars. And when Grable paid him, we were going to go live in Jamaica." She looked at Grayson. "That's what he told me, anyway."

Billy gave a low whistle. "Did you hear that, boys? Five hundred grand." He rubbed his chin. "How close is he to giving you the money?"

Grayson's mind raced. How should he play this? How could he string them along? "I've got to keep contacting him. He's close, but I don't have it yet."

Billy looked at his friends. "So we got a choice. We turn the kid in and take the twenty-five G, or we let Mr. Toad here take us on a wild ride."

A fresh surge of anger swept through Grayson. He fought it. "I'll split it with you," he said quickly. "Two hundred fifty thousand dollars for me, the same for you." He felt sweat pooling under his arms.

Billy wiped his hands on his jeans. They were greasy hands, the kind of hands Grayson just abhorred. "Nah," Billy said. "There's four of us. So we'd want a hundred grand each." He laughed. "Heck, we could kill you and be heroes! And get twenty-five grand free and clear." He scratched the back of his head. "I dunno. Me and the boys got to talk this over." Billy pulled a huge pistol from the small of his back. He walked over to Grayson and shoved it into his neck, right under his jaw.

Grayson swallowed hard. The smell of the guy's breath made his head spin.

"You move one inch and I swear I'll splatter your brains all over this kitchen. You hear? You hear?" Billy pressed the gun harder into Grayson.

"OK," Grayson said, weakly. He trembled all over.

"You just sit still. I'll be watching you." And Billy and his three thugs left the room.

"Untie me!" Grayson demanded in a hoarse whisper. When Sandy didn't move right away, he swore at her. "Who is he?"

"My brother," Sandy said, stiffly. "And I'd suggest you don't mess with him." She moved closer to Grayson. "I found your receipt," she said in a soft, bitter voice. "I see you only bought one ticket to Jamaica. Just one. What kind of game are you playing with me? What am I, the babysitter?"

He thought fast. "I bought that a long time ago. Before we hooked up," he said. "I was going to buy you one once I got the money."

"Liar!" she said, spitting at him. "You are lying to me, Grayson Chambers, and I know it!" And she slapped him hard, across the mouth.

Rage filled him. He did not allow a woman to strike him. Ever.

"All right," Billy said, coming back into the kitchen. "We've made up our minds."

"Where's Crow?" Kenzie asked as she picked up her ballistic vest.

"He's picking up copies of Zoe's medical records. Her doctor agreed to meet him at his office. When he finishes there, he'll proceed to Carroll County."

"I want to go with you," Senator Grable said.

"No." Scott checked his extra magazines and shoved them into the cargo pocket of his tactical pants.

"I want to go."

"Absolutely not."

"Senator, we need you here," Kenzie said, "on the chance Jackson423 posts another message. I don't think he will, but if he does, we need you to help Alicia respond. You've watched what I've done." She tightened her belt.

"Why are you going? You're the linguist. You ought to man the computer."

"We may need her help if we have to negotiate," Scott said. "I promise you, though, you will be the first one we call when we have Zoe, and we'll rush you to her. I promise that."

Resigned, the senator nodded. He turned toward Alicia, who sat at the computer. "Well, it's you and me," he said and he sat down heavily.

The drive up to Carroll County would take about an hour and fifteen minutes. The Bureau's Hostage Rescue Team had been deployed to New York, so Scott had arranged to meet a SWAT team from the Baltimore office at an elementary school near the cell tower location. "I can work with Baltimore's SWAT team," he had told Kenzie. "I know several of them. They're good guys."

Kenzie looked over at him as they raced up I-270 North. His eyes were intense. "You're praying, aren't you?" she said.

He glanced her way. "Yeah."

She settled back in her seat, a slight smile on her face. "Well, I'm glad somebody is because . . ."

"Kenzie!"

His voice was sharp and it took her by surprise.

"You need to quit playing games with this."

"What are you talking about, Scott. I just . . ." she stopped short at his fierce look. His hands gripped the steering wheel.

"Anything could happen tonight. Anything! Any one of us could die."

A half-laugh emerged from her throat. "Don't be so dramatic."

"That's not drama, it's reality."

"Oh, Scott."

His voice dropped. "Anything could happen. And if it does, are you going to stand before

God and say, 'Well, I sorta believed in you but I didn't really want to commit because, you know, you might leave me like my father did.' "

Kenzie's face burned. "Wait. That's over the line!"

"No, it's right on the line," he said fiercely. "And you know it. I don't know what we're going to run into tonight. But life can end like that," he snapped his fingers. His voice softened. "I care about you, Kenzie. I'd like to know you'd be okay if . . . if it happened."

"I'll be fine, Scott . . ." She stared out of the window, aware that tears had formed in her eyes, fighting anger, fear, resentment . . . what else churned inside? Scott should just shut up, she thought.

But he wouldn't. "You're like the rich young ruler. You've given God everything but your treasure, your father. Let him go, Kenz. Let him go. Trust God, even through your pain. Let God be God, and I'm telling you, your life will change. You'll feel the difference. You'll know what love is."

Her throat tightened. *Love. Yes, what was love? What did it feel like?* Outside, the lights zipped by as Scott drove well above the posted speed limit. "I know . . ." she started to say, but truly, she didn't know. Not really. She shivered. She had so little control over anything. Yet it was so hard to let go, to let God . . .

Scott's cell phone rang. Kenzie closed her eyes, relieved at the interruption.

Scott's one-syllable answers didn't reveal the identity of his caller. Kenzie leaned her head against the cool glass window, as if it could calm her feverish thoughts.

Then Scott said, "Hang on," and turned to her. "Kenzie, take down an address."

She pulled her small notepad out of her pocket.

"It's 2647 Tulip Circle, Mount Airy, Maryland, 21771," he said, and she wrote that down. "All right. Fantastic, Crow. Hold tight. I'll call you back with further instructions." Scott hung up. "Crow's got the location!"

"Really? How he'd get it?"

"He went to the courthouse in the county where we located the cell phone tower and he got a magistrate to order a clerk to let him in to check public records. He and the clerk and a county deputy found what they were looking for: a recently settled estate. Chambers inherited a small house in a little community. Crow gave me that address."

"And does he know if they're there?"

"He drove to the neighborhood. It's very small and the roads are unpaved—twisty, windy little things with all kinds of potholes. He opted not to go in, because it's one of those places where every new car gets noticed. And the big, black SUV he's driving just screams 'law enforcement.'

So no, we don't know for sure if Chambers is there." Scott took the exit for Route 27, and then pulled onto the shoulder. "Switch with me, would you? I've got some calls to make." He threw the vehicle into park and unbuckled. Then he touched Kenzie's arm. "I'm sorry, Kenz. I didn't mean to offend you. But just know I care about you." He scribbled something on a piece of paper. "Here, stick this in your pocket."

She did, without looking at it.

The county sheriff, Sam Hughes, suggested they meet at Thelma G. Hardesty Elementary School. His own emergency response team, along with an FBI SWAT team from Baltimore headed by an agent named Jeff Kingston, and Scott, Kenzie, and Crow formed a huddle in the middle of the parking lot.

"Good work," Kenzie said to Crow in a low voice as they gathered. He had changed into tactical pants, a black shirt, and a vest.

"How do you feel?" he asked her. "How's your head? You don't need to be in on this, you know."

"Are you kidding?"

The sheriff had brought along copies of a subdivision map for the house where they believed Grayson to be.

"All right," said Scott. "Here's what I'd like to do. I'd like Sheriff Hughes, Jeff, and one other

SWAT team member, Kenzie, and Crow to accompany me to the house. You see this area here, where the mailboxes are," he said, pointing to a place on the map. "We'll leave our car parked there and walk in. Jeff, you and your guy walk this way," he made a motion, "and cover the back door. Sheriff, you take this side route. Crow, you and Kenzie stick together and take a position here." He pointed to a spot across from the house. "Unless we perceive a clear and present danger to our target, we are going to observe the house for fifteen minutes, maybe longer." Holding up his radio, he said, "Everybody come up on A-One.

"Sheriff, we'll need one of your deputies to go along with us and watch the cars," Scott continued. "Depending on what we see, the SWAT team will come in and take the house. Your deputies will maintain control of the ingress and egress. How does that sound?"

Everyone nodded approval.

"All right. We'll squeeze into two cars for the ride over. Vests on? Let's go."

27

The humid air left a thin film of sweat on Kenzie's neck as she moved toward the subject house. Fortunately, the lot across the street remained both empty and wooded. Except for the barking of a lone dog, Crow and Kenzie went undetected. He motioned her down on the ground. They lay still, under a moonlit sky, and just watched.

The house Chambers had inherited was a one-floor rambler with a small front porch and another on the side. The gravel driveway ended in a walkway up to the side door. The house showed a mild state of disrepair, with some loose shingles and a broken handrail on the front step. The driveway, overgrown with weeds, looked like it hadn't been used much, and the lawn needed mowing.

There were no lights on in the house, no movement, no sound. At midnight, that wasn't surprising. But there was also no vehicle visible.

Lying there on the ground, Crow next to her, Kenzie tried hard not to think about the lecture she'd gotten from Scott or the spiders that could be crawling around in the leaves and underbrush. Both, in her mind, seemed equally dangerous. She brushed her hair back from her face. "What do you think?" she whispered after ten minutes.

"I wonder if anyone's in there."

"Why are we watching it for such a long time?"

Crow leaned close to her so he could keep his voice a quiet whisper. "When I hunt, I take the high ground. And I watch. The more patient I am, the more likely it is I will succeed." He nodded toward the house. "That works for both deer and men."

Scott's voice came over their radios, into their ear buds. "Jeff, what do you think?"

"I'm not getting any infrared readings," the leader of the SWAT team reported.

"OK. Crow?"

"Nothing."

"OK. Stay steady."

Five minutes later, Kenzie saw Scott move down the street a little away from the house, sheltered by the woods. Then he crossed over the street and worked his way back up to the target location. He made a complete circle around the house, and then came back to his original position. "Nothing," he said, over the radio. "Crow, you have the warrant?"

"Yes."

"All right." Scott radioed the SWAT team, waiting a half-mile away. "Jeff, bring your team in. Be careful. I want to be able to take footprints if we can get them. Understood?"

"Yes, sir," Jeff's voice responded.

"I want to be first in," Scott said. "Pick whoever you want for the ram."

Off in the distance, a whippoorwill called, an eerie sound to Kenzie. She waited silently, her heart thumping, until she heard the sound of car engines. A wet leaf stuck to her hand as she scratched her nose. Crow lay next to her, his eyes focused on the house. She could feel his tension. She shared it.

Over across the way, behind the subject house, she could see a row of SUVs moving into position with just their parking lights on. They moved down the hill, and out of sight, and then came up on Tulip Drive. They pulled over, and eight black-clad men got out. Three moved through the yard and behind the house, two moved to each side, and three moved up to the front. Then Kenzie saw Jeff.

"Let's go," she heard Scott say.

Kenzie stood up and followed Crow across the street, moving quickly.

"Stay behind me," he whispered.

Two SWAT members held the ram at the side door. Scott skirted the side steps, pulling himself up onto the porch by the railing so as not to disturb any prints. Kenzie and Crow moved up behind him. Scott nodded and the men swung the ram. The door near the doorjamb shattered into toothpicks.

Scott kicked in the rest and moved inside the house, gun and flashlight before him. Kenzie and Crow covered him, looking left and right. Nothing in the kitchen. Nothing in the living room. Clear in the bedroom, the bathroom, and the other bedroom. They flipped on the lights room by room, checking under the beds, in the closets, under the mattresses even. And when they were convinced the house was completely empty, they holstered their guns.

"Wrong place?" Jeff asked.

"No way," said Kenzie. She had gone back into the kitchen and was walking toward them with a pile of papers she'd found on the countertop. "Look at these."

They were crayon drawings. A big man had the label "Daddy" with the initial letter *D* backward. A little girl with yellow hair had tears dripping from her eyes. Four included a big bear with huge teeth and sharp claws. The last was signed, "Zoe."

"Not wrong at all," Kenzie said softly, "just . . . just too late."

"Hey, look at this," Crow said, emerging from the bedroom. His gloved hand held a paperback book. He raised it so Scott and Kenzie could read the title, *Who Killed Catherine Jones?* Crow's eyes were bright. "You want to know why there were so many similarities with Waller's crimes? This is one of those true crime books. The kidnapper's been studying it. He's even got stuff underlined."

"Well, that explains it," Scott said.

"That fits!" said Kenzie. "Grayson Chambers has no criminal history. Instead, he studies a book to figure out how to pull off his crime."

"All right," Scott said, sharply, "I want everybody out so the evidence techs can get in here."

With all the activity and the evidence truck parked outside, the raid on the Tulip Circle house was no longer a secret and a few nearby neighbors had gathered to watch the show. FBI agents and deputies were interviewing them. Two of the techs were vacuuming the entire house, looking for hair and fiber evidence. Others were checking for prints. Someone collected a hair-brush found in the bathroom for DNA evidence. And outside, Scott crouched down next to Crow, who was pointing out some tire tracks he'd found in the mud of the road.

Crow gestured toward the tire prints. "I'm seeing three motorcycles. One's a recumbent. I can tell from the radius of the turn. The other one has very expensive tires on it. The lab will be able to tell you the exact type. But I know they're unusual." He shrugged. "We might be able to trace them to the owner if they were purchased around here."

"Good," Scott replied. He looked exhausted. "Tell one of the techs we need plaster casts of these prints, OK? I want them rushed down to the lab, to Harold Wilson. He knows everything about tire treads."

"Will do."

Scott looked at Kenzie. "We got close, very, very close."

But close wasn't good enough. She knew it and he knew it. "What's next?"

"Crow!" Scott called to the agent, who was talking to a tech. "Let's go over there and strategize." He pointed to the hill across the street.

"You want to bring in the sheriff?" Crow suggested when he arrived on the hill.

"Yes," Scott responded.

Once Sheriff Hughes had joined them, Scott opened the discussion. "All right," he said. "Where do we go from here? Who was here? Where are they now? And how do we find them?"

"Maryland issued a driver's license to Grayson Chambers six months ago. But I don't see any vehicles registered in his name," Crow said. "I thought I'd try California to see if he just never switched tags after he left there."

"Good," Scott said. "Who was the prior owner on this house?"

Crow looked at his notepad. "His mother, Edith Summers."

"Summers?"

"Second marriage, I guess."

"Any vehicles under her name?"

"I'll have someone check that," Sheriff Hughes volunteered.

"All right. We're doing a door-to-door in this neighborhood. Crow found some motorcycle tire tracks he thinks are distinctive. So we need to check all the custom motorcycle shops, the clubs, the repair places, and see if anyone has noticed anything . . . a kid who seems out of place, new purchases, that sort of thing." Scott sighed and rubbed the back of his neck. "Kenzie, you're going to have to continue to monitor the Internet. I guess that means going back to Grable's."

"Wait. You can set up in our conference room if you like," the sheriff said. "I can get you Internet access and everything."

"Great. Terrific, Sam. Thank you," Scott said.

"I'll even throw in a coffeepot."

Kenzie smiled.

"Sheriff," Scott said, "in a county this size, I'm thinking you pretty much know who the bad boys are."

"Pretty much."

"What's your thinking?"

Sam Hughes rubbed his jaw. "Thing is, we're right on the highway between Baltimore and Frederick. Every scumbag in central Maryland can pop in here easily. Our local boys, they mostly get into fights when they're drunk and deal a few drugs. Beat up a woman now and then. But I'll tell you what, we'll circulate among our regulars, if you want, and see if we can shake something out of them."

"Good," Scott said. "You got a motel around here? We're going to need some rooms."

"Sure. Come over here. Let's get on the radio."

Grayson Chambers lay bound and gagged in the trunk of his mother's car. He could feel every bump in the road, every curve, and every turn. His head hurt, his wrists ached, and fear and anger had coalesced into a potent brew in his stomach. He wanted to throw up.

The men who had abducted him were the kind of raw meat bullies he'd loathed since elementary school. They lived by brute force. They were cold-blooded, callous, stupid, ignorant animals. To beat them, he would have to use his wits.

Sandy had gotten him into this. He'd suspected from the beginning she would do him in. So stupid!

Moving around in the trunk to find a more comfortable position, Grayson began to plan, to scheme, the way he always had. How could he get the upper hand? Trouble was, he'd never been in real physical danger before. Desperately he racked his brain. What should he do?

The car stopped suddenly and the engine cut off. Grayson heard what sounded like a garage door closing. Then a car door shut, and he heard footsteps. The trunk popped open. "C'mon, you," Billy said, and he pulled Grayson out into the night.

What a relief to get out of that trunk! Still, Grayson could barely stand up. His legs ached. His head hurt. He sagged against the car.

He was in a stinky, junky garage. Billy grabbed his arm and propelled him toward an interior door and into what looked like an office. A pinup calendar hung on the wall, greasy work orders and parts catalogs lay strewn about, and a metal desk and two chairs filled the rest of the room. Billy pushed him down into one of them.

"Now look," the man said, roughly. "Ain't nobody can hear you out here, understand? Nobody. I'm going to take that gag off, and then we're gonna talk. You cooperate with us, and it'll go fine. You don't, you'll wish you never met my sister."

No problem there, Grayson thought.

"Billy, what are you going to do?" Sandy stood at the door of the office. Zoe was asleep in her arms.

"Just something to help us all out, Sis. Don't you worry about it. I'm not gonna hurt this guy."

"Well, what am I supposed to do?" Her voice sounded like a whine. Grayson hated that.

"Take the kid upstairs. Go to bed. I got to talk to him," Billy said, and he grinned as he motioned his head toward Grayson.

The four hours of sleep Kenzie got at Scott's insistence helped a little to restore her energy level. When her alarm woke her up at six a.m., she felt hungry.

Scott had rented four rooms at the motel and made a simple arrangement. The desk clerk would keep the room keys behind the counter; anyone involved in the investigation who needed to sleep would show creds and be given a key to an empty room.

Kenzie had brought her jump bag with her, so after a shower and a change of clothes, she returned her key to the clerk, found some breakfast at an all-night diner, and drove to the sheriff's office. In the conference room, an exhausted Scott sat slouched in a chair staring at a computer screen.

"Your turn. Go to bed," she said.

He shook his head. "Can't. We don't have a vehicle. We don't have an ID on the men the neighbors saw. Or the redhead people saw at the house. We have no idea who was there last night, or why, or where they've gone."

"But if we did, you'd want to follow those leads. So go to bed now."

"Can't."

"Sounds like somebody needs breakfast," Kenzie said, and she put a Styrofoam container in front of him.

His smile showed a little life. He opened the container. "Scrambled eggs, pancakes, butter, syrup—but where's the veggie sausage? The granola?"

"I decided to be easy on you. Plus, Hank's All Nighter hasn't heard of granola. Or veggie anything." Kenzie smiled. She looked around. "Where's the promised coffee?"

"Right through that door," Scott said, pointing.

Kenzie got a cup for Scott and one for herself. She put the coffee in front of Scott and sat down next to him. "No other postings from Jackson423, right?" she said.

"Right. Alicia's been on it all night."

"How about the senator?"

"So far I've convinced him to stay there. So far."

Kenzie sipped her coffee. "I'm sure he's anxious."

"We should have something from the lab on those tire treads in the next few hours, I'm hoping anyway. The techs cast some footprints, too. One may match the print we found the night you were assaulted."

Kenzie nodded. "Of course."

"The sheriff's deputies have been rousting bad boys all night, trying to get a lead. It's amazing how many unpaid speeding tickets this county has, so deputies need to inquire about them in the middle of the night."

"Is he still thinking these were out-of-towners?"

"Yes. That's his theory." Scott scraped his fork over the Styrofoam container, getting the last of the scrambled eggs. "Did you sleep?"

"More or less. Why don't you go now? Get some rest?"

Scott glanced at his watch. "I'm afraid if I did, I wouldn't wake up, even if you called me. I'm beat to shreds."

"So I'll get the clerk or a deputy to pound on your door."

He thought about it for a minute, but then shrugged. "Look, I'm just going to lie down over here."

"On the floor?"

"It's carpeted. Wake me up, OK? If anything happens?"

Five minutes later, the sound of his soft snoring told her that floor or no floor, Scott had had no problem falling asleep.

"Look," Grayson said, trying to be as non-threatening as possible. He shifted position in the chair, trying to get comfortable. "Here's the deal. Let me loose and I'll pinch Zoe's father for eight hundred thousand dollars. I'll tell him I changed my mind. I want more than I said originally. I'll split it with you, so you and your friends each get a hundred grand. That's a lot of money. You can buy a lot of motorcycles for that."

Billy snorted. "You don't know nothin' about motorcycles, do you?"

Grayson kicked himself.

Sandy's ugly brother kept playing with a handgun. Every time he twirled it, Grayson's stomach got tighter.

"Tell me again how your plan works," Billy said.

"I'm posting messages on the Internet to give the senator instructions. In fact, I've got to post again soon, or they'll get suspicious."

"Are the cops onto this Internet junk?"

Grayson lied. "No. Not yet. It's just me and the senator. So here's the deal. He's going to put money in my account, and then I'm going to release Zoe."

Billy shook his head. "No good. She's seen all of us."

"She's five years old!"

"Kids can be smart. Nope, the kid's gotta go."

"Go where?"

Billy looked at him like he was an idiot.

A cold chill swept over Grayson. This is out of control, he thought. Way out of control. He cleared his throat. "Let's get on with this. I need to give one, maybe two more instructions to Grable. Then we'll have the money, I'll cut you in, and that'll be that."

Billy stroked his chin. "I gotta think about this." He yawned and stretched. "Joe!" he called.

One of his buddies came in. He smelled like sweat and beer, and a wave of revulsion swept over Grayson. "Yeah?" Joe said.

"Watch him," Billy said, standing up and handing Joe the gun. "I gotta get some shut-eye."

28

Maybe he dozed off and maybe he didn't. For the rest of the night, Grayson sat tied up in the office chair growing stiff and cold and angry and frustrated. Stupid thugs. Stupid Sandy.

When Joe fell asleep, Grayson tried twisting against the ropes binding his wrists but he could not get loose. He nearly fell off the chair trying. By the time dawn began to break, he felt exhausted and nauseous with fear.

Around seven a.m., Billy came in the room with a plate of scrambled eggs in his hand. Seeing Joe asleep with his head on the desk, he set the plate down, eased the gun out of Joe's open hand, and kicked his chair as hard as he could.

"Wha . . . ?" Joe said, his head snapping up.

Billy grabbed him and threw him onto the floor. "You stupid son of a . . . !" he said.

Joe scrambled out of his reach. "Lay off, Billy! Come on!"

Billy walked over and kicked him, hard.

Grayson's heart pounded. *What now? What now?*

Billy reached down, pulled Joe to his feet, and shook him. "You had enough sleep? 'Cause we got work to do."

"Yeah, yeah, OK," Joe responded, pulling away from the larger man.

"All right, you," Billy said, turning to Grayson. "Here's what we're gonna do. You eat. Then we're gonna do this . . . this Internet thing." He put his beefy hand around Grayson's neck and the bound man's eyes widened. He gasped for breath. "I don't want to feed you," Billy said, "so I'm letting you loose. But I'm right here, understand, me and this gun, and you try anything I'll blow your brains out."

Grayson swallowed hard as Billy released him. He meant what he said. The jerk would kill him in a heartbeat.

Taking the plate of eggs, he shoveled them into his mouth. They were cold, but he was hungry. Billy sat at the desk, the gun in his hand, watching him. "We'll have to go somewhere to get on the Internet," Grayson said.

Billy waved toward the grimy computer. "Nah. We got it here."

Nuts. Grayson had been hoping they'd have to get out. Over the course of the long night, between cursing Sandy and trying to figure out how to escape, he'd nearly given up on getting the money Grable owed him and he'd decided his best bet would be to play the victim, to implicate Billy as the mastermind of the whole plan from beginning to end. He figured he could do that. It wouldn't be a big problem to convince a jury of his innocence, especially with his ability with words. Maybe he could even collect the twenty-five thousand dollar reward. Sure, he wouldn't get all the money Grable owed him, but neither would he spend the rest of his life in jail. What a ridiculous waste that would be!

Grayson finished the eggs and put the plate in the trash by Billy's desk. "Thank you. That was good," he lied. "Now," he said, beginning to rise, "if I can get to the keyboard . . ."

"Sit down!" Billy snarled, shoving him back in the seat. "Joe, tie him up again."

"Why?" Grayson protested. "You want me to help you or not?" he said, as Joe pulled his arms behind him. He felt the ropes being wound around his wrist again and panic rose in his chest.

Billy pressed the button on the tower to boot up the computer. "You tell me," he said, "what website to go to and what to say, and I'll do the typing."

When Sandy woke up, Zoe lay curled up next to her, sleeping with her mouth open, drooling slightly. Sandy stroked the little girl's hair. How had things gone so wrong? Why had her brother butted in? He always caused trouble.

On the other hand, maybe it was karma. She was having second thoughts about going to Jamaica with Grayson, even if he had bought her a ticket. That man had a temper! Since he'd brought Zoe into their relationship, his dark side had emerged. She wondered if he were a Taurus. Or a Cancer. That would certainly explain it. How could he be so mean, not just to Zoe, but to her?

He was certainly nothing like the suave, generous man who'd picked her up in a bar in Frederick. Nothing like the guy who had plunked seventy-five cents in a jukebox to play her favorite song—not just once, but ten times in a row. And when she'd mentioned she'd always wanted to go to a particularly expensive French restaurant, he'd taken her there.

Gently, Sandy kissed Zoe on the head. The little kid had been clinging to her like she was her mommy. How she'd missed being a mommy. For the first time, Sandy thought about Zoe's mother. The little kid constantly asked for her dad, but what about her mom? Did she miss her little girl? Was she worried about her? How did she get through each day not knowing where her Zoe was?

For the very first time since she'd met Grayson, guilt began to wind itself around Sandy's heart, like a vine strangling a tree.

When Crow walked into the conference room at 7:45 a.m., Kenzie was on the phone with someone at Grable's office, trying to glean suggestions in an attempt to identify the other actors now associated with this case. "A list of Chambers's friends would be good, or exercise partners, or bar buddies . . . even other legislative aides. Anybody he could be working with." When she hung up the phone, she exhaled with frustration.

"No luck?" Crow asked.

She shook her head. "Chambers had no friends, no hobbies, no church, nothing. The guy seems like a walking loner."

"I'm not surprised," Crow said. He looked at his watch. "I'm going to meet a deputy in a few minutes and we're going to start rousting the owners of motorcycle shops in the area."

"Not many open yet," Kenzie suggested.

"It's why we're rousting them. We have a preliminary ID on the tire tread. Somebody should remember selling a bike with those tires." Crow looked over to where Scott lay asleep on the floor. "He's out," he said, nodding toward him.

"He needed it. I'm supposed to wake him up at eight."

Crow stood up. "All right. I'm on the radio." He started to leave, then turned back to her. The expression on his face said he wanted to say something, something important, or personal, or profound. But instead, he just raised his hand, lowered it, then walked away.

As he left, Kenzie turned back to her computer screen. Minutes later, her eyes widened.

Jackson423: *The kidnappers would finalize the plan quickly. Before everybody gets there shorts in a wad. So as soon as the $$ is wired and the deposit confirmed, Joie would be let go.*

Kenzie's chair scraped as she pushed it back. "Scott, Scott!" she said, racing over to him.

"What?" he mumbled as he struggled to rouse himself.

"Scott, he posted again. Jackson's online again."

Scott pulled himself up to a sitting position, then lurched to his feet. "Let me see. Make sure IT is tracing it!"

Kenzie called the IT support staff at WRO. "OK, they're on it," she told Scott. "I've called Alicia, too, and told her we'd respond from here." She gestured toward the computer screen. "What do you make of it?" Kenzie asked, her heart drumming.

"You tell me. My head's not working yet."

"Look at the improper use of 'there.' Should be t-h-e-i-r. And he's never used dollar signs for money. Something has changed." She tapped her lip with her finger. "Either he's under duress and making stress mistakes, or someone else is doing this."

"What's your vote?" Scott asked.

Kenzie considered the options. "Someone else."

"Working alone?"

"Without Chambers?" She tilted her head while she thought. "No, maybe with him, because he didn't change the instructions for the payoff. Chambers still has to be in this somehow." She hesitated. "How should I respond?"

Scott rubbed his head. "Just a second. I need coffee so I can think."

He came back a few minutes later with two Styrofoam cups in his hands. He put one down in front of her.

"I've checked the other websites Chambers blogged on," Kenzie said. "There's nothing new from him. So do you know what I'm thinking?" She turned to look at Scott. "Based on the language he's using, I'm afraid we may be dealing with a whole new kidnapper."

"Tell me."

"I'm thinking somebody found out what Grayson was doing, and decided to get in on it."

"Who?"

"That's the problem. Could be anybody. The whole world has seen our press conferences."

Scott sat down heavily in the chair next to her. "Good grief," he said. "This has blown wide open."

The two agents were quiet for a minute as they each absorbed the implications of that. Then Kenzie spoke. "Look, we have him posting again. We know a few more things than we did before. We know where they've been for a few days. We know there were motorcycles involved with this last move. We have a description of the car Chambers has been driving, from the neighbors. We have a description of the redhead he's been with. And IT should be tracing this message."

"And we should have some fingerprints, hair and fiber evidence, those tire marks . . . we'll have some hard evidence to work with soon."

Again they were quiet. "So how do I respond?" Kenzie said, finally.

Scott ran his hand through his hair. "What are our options?"

"He's trying to hurry things along. Clearly, that's to our advantage. We need to find out when the IT guys will have the phony website functional. Then we'll tell Chambers we'll have the money deposited by that time, plus two hours. To give the IT guys some wiggle room."

Kenzie sat back. "Meanwhile, as soon as they identify the computer he's using, we can go in."

"In the meantime, anything could happen."

Kenzie looked at him. "What do you mean?"

"We don't know who's in charge now."

Kenzie's stomach sank. "You're right." She looked up at him. "This stinks."

Scott nodded. "Hold off for just a few minutes, will you? I really need some time to work this out."

By that she knew he meant "pray it out."

• • •

"So why didn't they say nothin' yet?" Billy asked.

"The senator isn't online all the time. He's a busy man." In a way, Grayson felt glad there'd been no immediate response to his post. Because any intelligent person would realize it would indicate the FBI was monitoring the message board. Of course, Billy was far from being an intelligent person. It was, in fact, Grayson's best hope. If he could get the guy to mess up, or if he, Grayson, could get to a phone, or the gun, maybe he could still make something of this.

"I have another idea," Grayson said suddenly. "Let's put up another post."

Billy looked at him as if he were sizing him up, then wiped his nose with his hand and turned toward the computer. "Shoot."

If only I could, Grayson thought. "All right," and he began to dictate a message while Billy typed with his two forefingers.

High Stakes happens fast. To keep the plot moving, I think I'd have Joie have a hidden disease. Like diabetease. She's getting sick quick. Therefore, the ones who took her are anxious . . .

"How do you spell that?" Billy said.

Good grief, Grayson thought. He wished he could see that screen! He spelled "anxious" and continued.

. . . to get there money. And anxiuos to dump

358

her. Hard enough to have a hostige without her being sick. In fact, she could die.

Grayson hesitated. Should he try something? Could he count on Billy's stupidity? He continued.

The bad guys have changed location. Now the drop off will be in Catoctin . . .

"Hey!" Billy said suddenly. "What are you doing? You're tipping this guy off . . ."

"No! No," Grayson protested, fear flashing through him. "No. I just thought you wouldn't want to drive to Fairfax."

Billy grumbled. "I'm taking that last part out. I'm stopping at 'In fact, she could die.' What else?"

Sweat dripped down Grayson's neck. "Leave it at that. I'm sure the senator will respond to that."

"Idiot," Billy said, swearing.

"Second message, Scott," Kenzie said as her partner walked back in the room. She read it to him. "Several misspellings, some bad grammar —either Grayson's trying to communicate to us he's no longer in charge or there's another person at the keyboard. Either way, we have a new unknown suspect."

"All right." Scott stretched his neck. "I called our IT guys. They'll be ready to go at noon. And they'll have those messages traced soon."

"So we tell him the money is coming in and we'll be ready at two p.m."

They discussed the options for a few moments. Kenzie made some suggestions on the wording of the next post. Scott agreed to them, and she typed.

"All right! Is this it?" Billy asked, turning the computer monitor toward Grayson.

The captive winced when he saw the misspellings in Jackson423's last post. But the response clearly came from the senator, and Grayson's heart raced with an odd mixture of anger and hope, conflict and connection as he read it.

I think CISU would have had to tap many sources for that kind of money. But the last of it would be in by two. Then everything would be in place. They would be very anxious to get Joie back.

"So, they're going to wire the money at two. That means we can confirm it and drop the kid off by, say, four p.m."

"There ain't gonna be no dropping the kid off. I told you that before."

"Well, we have to pretend, anyway, don't we? To lead them on? Otherwise, why would they give us the money?"

Billy grunted. "Give me what to say then."

So Grayson dictated the next message, setting

up a fictitious drop-off at Foxstone Park as soon as the bank confirmed the transfer. "That should do it," Grayson said, satisfied. "You'll soon be a rich man, Billy."

"All right! Crow's got a lead," Scott said, snapping off his cell phone. The sheriff and Kenzie looked up. "A dealer in Frederick remembers selling some of those tires. His records show the buyer was a guy named Joseph Mitchell."

"I'll get someone on that," Sheriff Hughes said. Within minutes, he had information. Mitchell showed up as a motorcycle enthusiast and small-time drug dealer with a couple of arrests for possession.

"We have an address?" Scott asked.

"Sure." The sheriff read it.

"Let's go." Scott slid into his vest. "I'll call Crow, and he can meet us there. Kenzie, I guess you have to watch the computer?"

"No way," she said, standing up. "I doubt he'll post again. But Sheriff, do you have a deputy who can monitor it?"

"I'll get you a clerk."

"All right." A young woman came in quickly. Kenzie instructed her. "This is your job. Watch this message board. Anything gets posted from Jackson423, you call me. Do not answer him, OK? Just call me."

"Right," she said, sitting down in Kenzie's place.

When Kenzie turned around, Scott was ending a call on his cell phone. "Let's go."

Kenzie put on her vest as they walked out of the room.

Scott inserted his key into the ignition of his Bureau SUV. He glanced in his rearview mirror. Sheriff Hughes and two deputies were right behind him in unmarked cars. Whether they'd need SWAT or not was a question. Right now, the game plan was to go to Joseph Mitchell's house and find out what they could.

"Grable's insisting on coming up here," Scott said to Kenzie.

"How'd you wave him off?"

"With blood, sweat, and tears."

Kenzie kept quiet. "I admire his commitment to his daughter," she said, after thinking about it. "He wants to do everything he can for her."

Scott nodded. "He's a good dad."

Kenzie raised her chin. "And you know what? I think Beth could be a good mom if she had half a chance. And if she got help with her own issues."

"Billy, we got to end this," Sandy said, walking into the small motorcycle shop office after a restless night's sleep. She held Zoe's hand while the little girl half-hid behind her leg. "Zoe needs to go home."

"Yeah, so she can turn us all in? You think I want to spend the rest of my life in jail?" her brother responded. He sat at the desk fingering the Glock pistol.

Instinctively, Grayson, sensing the tension, started scooting his chair away.

Sandy frowned. "Billy, come on! There's twenty-five thousand dollars in reward money sitting out there! You can have the whole thing. Honest. I don't need none of it."

"Are you kidding? This guy's got eight hundred grand coming at him." He motioned toward Grayson with the pistol.

"You listen to me, Billy!" Sandy said. She sounded exactly like a big sister chastising a little brother. "Don't be stupid. You've got no reason to believe him." She grabbed the barrel of Billy's pistol to get his attention. "He may not even give you any of it."

"Sandy, get off!" Billy tried to pull the gun away from her but as he did, his finger slipped. A huge explosion filled the room. Grayson nearly jumped off the chair. Zoe began screaming.

Sandy straightened up, an expression of shock on her face. A red stain began spreading over her pink T-shirt. "Billy," she whispered, and then she collapsed on the floor.

Zoe, crying, tried to run out of the door, but a man blocked her way. She retreated to a corner.

"Billy," Joe said breathlessly, gripping the

doorjamb of the office. His eyes dropped down to the woman on the floor. "Holy cow! What'd you do?"

"Shut up! Just shut up!" Billy said, bending over his bleeding sister.

"Billy, the Feds been at my house!" Joe yelled.

"What?" Billy said, standing up.

"The cops. They been at my house."

Billy cursed. He turned and grabbed Grayson and began shaking him. Grayson's eyes widened with fear. "I thought you told me the cops wasn't onto you! You son of a . . ."

"Billy!" Joe said. "We're all over the news."

29

"We gotta get out of here." Billy said, shoving Grayson away. His motion tipped the chair over, and Grayson lay on the floor, still bound to the chair, helplessly staring into Sandy's dead face. The lips which had been wordlessly moving just moments before were parted. A trickle of blood ran from the corner of her mouth. "What do we do with him?" he heard Joe ask.

"Bring him."

"What about the kid?"

"I dunno. Bring her, too. She's worth twenty-five grand, anyways."

Outside Joseph Mitchell's ramshackle house, Scott, Kenzie, Crow, and Sheriff Hughes stood looking over a map spread out on the hood of Scott's car. Mitchell hadn't been seen in three days. His mother worried that he was hanging out with his friends, men she didn't trust. One of them, Billy Foster, owned a motorcycle repair and parts shop in an industrial area of Frederick. What's more, the IT unit in Washington had traced the messages posted to Foster's business.

The shop stood on a dead-end street, and Scott wanted to carefully plan out their approach. If Foster had Zoe there, they had to be very, very cautious.

"We come down here," the sheriff said, pointing, "and they won't be able to get out."

"On the other hand, they might feel trapped and kill Zoe," Crow said.

"How about if I go in first," Kenzie said. "I won't appear threatening to them. Let me ask about some . . . some motorcycle thing. Maybe I can find out who's in there."

Scott frowned. "Not safe."

"I can do it," she insisted. "I'm the least cop-looking of anyone."

"How about those pants?" He nodded toward her khaki tactical pants.

Kenzie looked around. A Walmart lay down the street. "In fifteen minutes, I'll be somebody's girlfriend in shorts and sandals."

"And your gun?"

"A big purse." She put her hands on her hips and tilted up her chin. "Scott, I can do this."

Scott took a deep breath. "Sheriff?"

He shrugged. "You know her better than I do. We can get right outside the building on the blind side and probably hear her if she hollers."

"What do you think, Crow?"

The agent had his eyes fixed on Kenzie. He looked down, unwilling or unable to affirm her offer.

Scott seemed to be taking forever to make up his mind. "All right," he said, finally. "We'll give it a try."

● ● ●

Fifteen minutes later, Kenzie emerged from the store. Her sunglasses covered her eyes and her hair hung loose. She'd bought a flowered fabric hobo-style bag—it held her gun and her radio. She climbed into Scott's empty SUV. He and the sheriff were in the county car, preceding her to the industrial park. She called Scott on his cell. "I'm leaving Walmart," she said. "Tell everyone I've got on khaki shorts and a white tank top."

"Will do," he responded. "Be careful. I'm going to be right outside. Something gets hinky, you yell and I'm in there, OK?"

"OK."

The industrial park looked deserted on this weekend morning. Kenzie drove all the way to the back, took a right into the last lane, and parked in front of Billy's Cycle Shop. She spoke quietly into her radio, hidden in her purse. "I'm set." Scott acknowledged her communication. Then she walked up to the door, her heart pounding.

Oddly, it was ajar. "Hello?" she called, opening it just enough to look in. "Anybody here?" She heard no answer. The door led into a grimy, magazine-strewn waiting area. "Hello?" she called again.

She walked across the room to another door leading to the shop. She started to push it open, then jumped as she noticed a spider crawling right where her hand would have gone. She stifled a gasp. Gingerly, she reached down to the knob, swung the door open, and stepped through.

The shop bays were full of oily tools, cycle parts, and discarded coffee cups. She picked her way through the mess, to yet another door on the other side. It, too, stood several inches open, and as she got close, her heart leaped. She could see a body on the floor.

Carefully she reviewed her options: Pretend to be a customer looking for a mechanic and walk on in. Or retreat and come back with reinforcements.

At the Academy, safety ruled the day. She retreated. Outside the building, she reached into her purse and pushed the radio transmit button. "There's a body, a woman, in the interior office. I didn't see anyone around. If someone's in there, I didn't want to surprise them."

"Smart move," Scott said. "We're coming to you."

Within seconds, Scott, Crow, and Sheriff Hughes came around the sides of the building. Then she saw marked cars coming down the street at a fast clip, and deputies get out to cover the back.

"OK, stay behind me," Scott said and, guns drawn, the three retraced Kenzie's steps, through the waiting room, through the cluttered shop. When they got to the office door, Scott silently counted with his fingers held high. On three, he kicked open the door, and they burst into the room, yelling "FBI! FBI!"

But the dead no longer hear.

"So who is she?" Kenzie asked as she and Scott stood by watching the evidence team go over the cycle shop. It seemed so eerie. The redhead lay on the floor, her T-shirt bloody, her hair sprayed out in a sunburst pattern, just like the little girl they'd found earlier.

"I'm thinking this is Sandy Sheffield. She used to be a waitress at a bar not too far from here. Her brother owns this place. He has a rap sheet," the sheriff said, glancing at the papers in his hand. "Petty drug dealer, thug. Into meth." He shook his head. "I know him well. Matter of fact, he was my first arrest."

Scott looked up. "Your first arrest?"

"Yep. Just brand-new on the force. Caught him with a baggie of pot after I stopped him for running a red light. He was just seventeen years old." The sheriff took a deep breath and nodded toward the body. "From the looks of it, she got shot at close range by a good-sized gun."

"How'd they get along?" Crow asked.

"Him and his sister? She bailed him out more times than I can count. I thought they were OK."

"So what's her connection with Chambers?" Kenzie asked.

"Unknown," said the sheriff.

Scott took a deep breath. He looked at Kenzie. "She's got to be the redhead he's been seen with. He meets her in a bar, she's not bad-looking, he figures he can use her, and bingo, they're in a relationship."

"Women fall for that kind of stuff all the time," Kenzie said.

One of the evidence techs came out of the shop. He had a brown toy dog in his hand. "Found this upstairs."

Kenzie took it in her hand. She could imagine Zoe holding it. She stroked it with one finger.

"There's an upstairs?" Scott asked.

"Supposed to be storage, like an attic. But somebody had a bed up there. And I found some kid's clothes."

"Bag them," Scott said. "Run them for evidence." The tech nodded and left. Scott shook his head. "We're one step behind," he said to Kenzie and Crow, "just one step behind."

Grayson Chambers felt like he would pass out any minute. The air in the trunk was stifling, and he felt every bounce of the rough road in his joints and in his chest. He wondered if he'd even make it to wherever they were going.

Why'd they have to tape his mouth? It made it so hard to breathe. The darkness in the trunk and the thick air made him so tired. He just wanted to close his eyes and get away from the image that kept playing in his mind: Sandy, dead on the floor. Sandy, blood dripping out of her mouth. Sandy, with that huge stain on that pink shirt.

If that happened to Sandy, it could happen to him.

The thought brought him close to panic.

Finally, the car lurched to a stop. The trunk popped open, and bright sunlight blinded him. Joe and the other guy grabbed him and pulled him up and out of the car.

They were in the woods somewhere, in the mountains that edged Frederick. The Catoctin Mountains, part of the Appalachian chain. Grayson scrambled mentally to remember what he knew about them. The Appalachian Trail ran through the range and the presidential retreat, Camp David, lay hidden somewhere in them. What he wouldn't give to see a Secret Service agent right now!

Joe had him by the arm and marched him up toward a cabin. Billy walked ahead, dragging a reluctant Zoe. *The kid has spunk,* Grayson thought, and for a moment he hoped she'd give Billy the same tough time she'd given him.

The cabin looked old. It had two stories with a roofed porch on two sides. Billy stepped up on the front porch. He had picked up a shotgun and a whole bunch of ammo from somewhere; it seemed clear he intended to make a stand.

Inside the cabin, Grayson noticed immediately

the abundance of spiders. Webs were every-where. That was the trouble with being in the woods. Spiders. And snakes. He never did like the woods. He'd hated Boy Scouts.

Joe shoved him and Grayson fell down on the floor. He quickly scooted over to a wall, and tried to look inconspicuous. What were they going to do here?

Zoe cried. Billy started spanking her. "Shut up! Shut up!" he yelled and his blows grew so harsh, the little girl froze.

"Billy, stop! She's just a kid," the third thug said. Grayson thought Billy called him Fred. He didn't know where the fourth guy was.

Zoe managed to stop crying. She stared at Billy, her face full of fear. Then he threw her down on the ground near Grayson.

She took one look at him and moved as far away as she could, until she was half-hidden by a couch.

"All right," Billy said, "we come up here to think. Let the heat die down. Nobody knows about this place. We'll be safe here for a while."

"Let's just take the reward and go," Joe suggested.

"You're forgetting something," Billy sneered. "Sandy."

"That were an accident!"

"Yeah, and you think the Feds are gonna believe that? Once they see my sheet?"

Fred paced back and forth. "I think he did it," he said suddenly, pointing at Grayson. "I think HE killed your sister."

Grayson felt his face grow red with anger. He thought, *Don't try to pin that on me, you scum! Don't you even think about it.*

But Billy did think about it. "He's why she's dead, for sure," he snarled, and he walked over and kicked Grayson hard, right in the ribs. The tape over his mouth muffled Grayson's scream. "It ain't right I take the rap for something he brought on."

His ribs hurt. *He must have cracked one,* Grayson thought. *What a jerk! What right did he have . . .* He blinked away tears.

"So let's turn him and the kid in, take the twenty-five G, and cut our losses," Joe suggested. "We all stand by the same story: He kidnapped the kid and killed Sandy. We saved the kid."

Billy looked thoughtful. He had small dark eyes, like a snake, and when he got serious, his brow furrowed and his eyes got even more reptilian. "This guy is in line for eight hundred grand. You know how much that is?" he spit.

"I was just thinking." Joe backed away.

Billy walked over to Grayson, and jerked the tape off his mouth. It hurt like crazy, and he had to blink away tears again. Billy grabbed his shirt. "You better be right about this! You better be right!"

"He'll pay, I swear, he'll pay," Grayson said, trying to control his fear. This guy could kill me, he thought. He glanced toward Zoe. The kid had crawled even further behind the couch. He couldn't blame her. He'd be there, too, if he could fit.

"What do we gotta do to get the money, slug?" Billy asked him, spit flying from his mouth.

Grayson rubbed his cheek on his shoulder to get the spit off. "I told you. We've got to finalize the deal. For that, we'll need the Internet. And you need me."

"Forget you! Forget you! I can do it myself."

Panic rose in Grayson in a wave. If Billy didn't think he needed him, he'd kill him. "You most certainly do need me. You don't know the code words. You don't know where the park is. You don't even know the pass code for the bank account." Grayson shook his head. "You need me, Billy, and I need the Internet. And my laptop."

Billy looked hard into Grayson's eyes, judging his sincerity.

"Let me help you get what's coming to you, Billy. I tell you what. I'll give you two-thirds. Because of Sandy and all."

Billy's eyes flickered. He grunted and strode away toward the other side of the room. Then he turned around. "I ain't going nowhere for a while. It gets dark, we'll go to town and get on the Internet. Till then, I'm staying here." He turned to Fred. "Get me a beer."

"We don't have none."

"What?" Billy roared. "No beer?" He cursed. "How can we have no beer? You get on your bike and get some. Hear me? And make sure nobody's following you when you come back. You," he said, gesturing toward his friends, "are a bunch of sorry losers."

Scott, Kenzie, Crow, and the sheriff returned to the sheriff's conference room to regroup once workers had removed Sandy's body from her brother's motorcycle shop. The FBI evidence teams would be at the shop for hours, doing grid searches, lifting fingerprints, taking photos and video, and vacuuming for hair and fiber evidence. Scott had seen enough to believe Zoe had been there. But where was she now?

"I want every scrap of information we can get on Billy Foster, Joe Mitchell, and Sandra Sheffield," Scott said when they got back to their command post. "Sheriff, can you send some deputies out to the bars?"

He looked at his watch. "It's pretty early. But I will."

"I want to know height, weight, marital status, hobbies, where they like to eat, what they like to drink. I want photos to pass around. I want to know what they drive and what kind of tooth-paste they like. Everything."

"Understood. Mary!" the sheriff called out. "I need some digital photos printed. And some copying done."

"All right, what else?" Scott said.

"Landlords, banks, ATM withdrawals, and credit card usage," Crow suggested.

Kenzie paced the floor. "I think we ought to watch Internet cafés, the library even." She motioned toward the computer. "Chambers hasn't posted again. But we clearly put the bait out there . . . that account posting. So either he's away from Internet access or . . . or something has happened to him."

"Right. Internet cafés. We can do that."

"And ERs," Crow continued, "in case some-body else got hurt."

For the next two hours they sorted, coded, and compiled the scraps of information reported from agents and deputies working in the area. Billy had an ex-girlfriend and a little boy. He was supposed to take the kid to the park that day. The girlfriend complained about money and said she didn't trust him. He used meth. But a court order gave him visitation rights and as long as he paid, she had to comply with that.

Would he hurt a child, the interviewer asked. He'll do anything that suits him, the woman responded.

Someone else found out that Joe Mitchell had spent some time in Jessup, the notorious Maryland correctional facility. Nobody knew what he did for a living and he was three weeks late on his rent. His landlady said she intended to evict him. Pennsylvania had a warrant out for him for burglary and armed robbery.

Her former boss, the owner of a bar, called Sandra Sheffield "a sweetheart." Heart of gold. Would do anything for anybody. Just not real bright. When the agent showed him a picture of Grayson Chambers and asked if the bar owner had ever seen him, he said sure. That was Sandy's new boyfriend. They were running off together somewhere. "I'd never seen her happier," he added.

Finally, they got their break. A deputy familiar with motorcycles pulled over a guy on a rocket bike zipping through town. Sure enough, the bike was equipped with special order tires.

"He's bringing him in for questioning," the sheriff said, animated.

"Great. Crow, Kenzie, let's go," Scott replied.

30

Rocket Man, as they immediately dubbed him, was a wiry, brown-haired, brown-eyed, sun-tanned ex-con with an expired driver's license. "Hey, I just forgot to renew it, you know?" he told the agents. "That never happens to you?"

Scott and Kenzie sat across the table from him, while Crow and Sheriff Hughes monitored the conversation, watching a video feed from an adjoining room. Kenzie had recommended a game plan with Scott. Now they were putting it into action.

"What's your friend's name?" Scott said, throwing an eight-by-ten picture of Billy Foster in front of Rocket Man, whose name, at least on the expired license, was Frederick Fisher.

Fisher glanced at it. "I don't know him."

"You don't know him? You buy stuff from his shop, don't you?" Scott said, bluffing.

Fisher shrugged. "So maybe I seen him once or twice. It ain't like he's a friend of mine."

"Who's all the beer for?" Scott asked.

"So now it's illegal to buy beer?" Fisher shook his head. "Me and some guys. We're out enjoying the day, you know? Doing a little fishing. Can't do much without beer."

"So where do you fish around here?" Kenzie asked, feigning interest.

"Monocacy River. Or one of the lakes. Farm ponds sometimes."

"You have a license?"

Fisher's face darkened. "Look, not everybody does things by the book, OK? It just ain't gonna happen all the time."

"Who are these guys you're out fishing with?" Kenzie asked.

"Just some friends, all right? A guy named Bob, and a guy named Junior."

"Junior what? Is that his name, or the suffix to his name?"

"What?" Fisher seemed puzzled. He shook his head. "It don't matter. I just call him Junior. Been calling him that for years."

Scott rubbed his chin. "Fish biting today?"

"Yeah, man. We're catching a lot. Sunnies. Bluegill. That's why we needed the beer, we're having so much fun, we're going to stay longer."

Kenzie opened the folder in front of him and took out an eight-by-ten picture of Zoe. "Mr. Fisher," she said, rising to her feet and plopping the picture in front of him, "kidnapping is a federal offense. There's no parole in federal cases, did you know that? And if this child dies, it could be a capital offense. Did you hear me, Fisher? You could be charged as an accomplice in a capital case. That's the death penalty, Mr. Fisher. The Big Sleep."

"What? What are you talking about? I never seen this kid!" Fisher's face turned red. Sweat had formed on his brow.

"Mr. Fisher, it's ninety-five degrees outside," Kenzie continued, pressing him. "Fish don't bite when it's that hot, especially in midday. They go deep in the water, where it's cooler. You haven't been fishing. That beer isn't for your fictitious friends. You've been lying to us, Mr. Fisher, and we don't like it when people lie to us."

A drop of sweat ran right down the side of Fisher's face.

Scott jumped in. "Wait, wait," he said, holding up his hand to stop Kenzie. "Relax. You know what I think? Mr. Fisher's a victim, too, I think."

Kenzie pretended to be disgusted.

"It's true, isn't it, Mr. Fisher?" Scott said, looking sympathetically at the man. "Sometimes we can get roped into things, can't we? We're with some friends, we go along with the crowd, and suddenly, we're in trouble." Scott furrowed his brow. "I don't think you wanted to kidnap a little girl, did you, Fred? I don't think that was your idea at all. Am I right?"

"He's guilty, can't you see that?" Kenzie exclaimed to her partner. "We've got his motorcycle tire treads at that house where they had Zoe!"

"Wait! Stop! He's right!" Fisher yelled. "I didn't want nothing to do with no kid! Nothing!"

"Then tell me," Scott said, leaning forward. "Where is Billy Foster? And where is Zoe?"

Fisher looked up at Scott, then at Kenzie, then back to Scott.

"You tell us where we can find them," Scott said, softly. "I'll get you a deal. That's the way it works. You know that. You've seen the TV shows."

"Don't let him off the hook!" Kenzie said.

But Scott continued. "There's no reason you should go down for this, man. It wasn't your idea! This little girl's father is a powerful man in D.C., a very powerful man. I know he'd be grateful to anyone who helped get her back."

Fisher swallowed hard. His eyes darted around the room, like he was looking for a way to escape. Then he dropped his head. "There's a cabin, up in the mountains," he mumbled. "I can show you on a map."

"Where is Fisher?"

Grayson cringed at the sound of Billy's voice. The man seemed restless, looking out of the window, stepping out on the front porch. Grayson figured he was listening in vain for the sound of Fred's motorcycle making its way back up the rutted path to the cabin and growing angrier by the minute. And in the short period of time

Grayson had known him, he'd learned that an angry Billy was a man to be avoided.

Once again, he tugged at the ropes binding him. Still tight. A motion caught his eye. He looked to his right. Zoe had progressively moved farther and farther along behind the couch until she'd gotten all the way to the far end. Now, she began creeping up the stairs.

The kid was smart. She'd been quiet for so long, everybody had forgotten about her. Now, she would wait for Billy to look the other way, then she'd move up a step. Gradually, she was making her way up to the second floor.

Grayson sighed. The kid had all the luck.

Scott's eyes were bright as he checked his gun. "All right," he said. "The SWAT team is suiting up. They'll be here within the hour. Sheriff, is your emergency response team on deck?"

"Absolutely. They'll deploy when I call them."

"All right. We're going to go scope out this cabin. If it's what we think it is, we'll bring them on." He looked at Kenzie and Crow. "What do you think about asking Alicia to bring Senator Grable to Frederick? I promised him we'd bring him closer once we had a fix on Zoe's location."

Kenzie took a deep breath. "I think Fisher's description of the child and of Chambers makes it pretty clear. At least up until about ninety minutes ago, Zoe was at this cabin."

Crow nodded. "I agree."

"All right then." Scott said. "Check your weapons and your radios. Make sure SWAT is up on A-One. I'll be ready in a minute."

The twenty-minute ride up into the mountains would have been beautiful had they been going for any other reason. Kenzie's mind raced with possibilities and contingencies. Scott would call the shots, but she still wanted to think things out, to test her developing field skills, at least in her own mind.

Scott drove quickly up the curvy mountain road. He followed the sheriff, allowing the man more familiar with the terrain to take the lead.

"What did Grable say?" Kenzie asked Scott. "He seemed very excited."

Kenzie looked at the passing trees. The hardwood forest had been uncut for at least half a century; the trees were sixty to eighty feet tall and the forest was dense with underbrush and outcroppings of rock. "Isn't Camp David around here somewhere?" she asked.

"Yes. For the president, it's a short hop on a helicopter but a world away from the White House."

"You're not kidding." She looked at Scott. He stayed quiet for a while, concentrating on the road and probably praying, she figured. Suddenly, she remembered Scott giving her a piece of paper the night they'd driven up from Washington. She shoved her hand in her pocket and retrieved it. He'd written a Scripture verse on it: "When you pass through the waters, I will be with you; and through the rivers, they shall not overwhelm you; when you walk through the fire you shall not be burned, and the flame shall not consume you. Isaiah 43:2"

Scott glanced over at her. Their eyes met. "That's what I've been praying for you, Kenzie. I don't know why. He's with you, Kenz. He loves you. Don't ever forget that."

Silently, she refolded the paper and put it back in her pocket. It seemed they were nearing the top of the mountain. "So, tell me the drill," she said.

"The sheriff says that the cabin is in a small clearing in the woods. There's no real road leading to it. It's been abandoned for years. We're going to park near the paved road and hike in through the woods. Then we're going to watch the place for a while, while the SWAT team gets assembled. When I hear they're set, if I haven't seen any reason to wave them off, we'll do it."

Despite the fatigue, despite the frustrations, they could be close to ending this thing. Recovering Zoe. Beating the bad guys. "Are you going to be first in?" she said.

"After SWAT. And you can be right behind me. Well, behind Crow. I think he'll want to be in front of you." He shifted in his seat. His eyes, fixed on the road, were squinted in tension. "When you were at the Academy, did you see that training video about the Miami shootout? 'Firefight'?"

"Sure."

"Do you remember what that agent said?"

She looked at him quizzically.

" 'If you lie down to die, you *will* die.' Whatever happens, Kenz, don't lie down. Don't quit."

"Why are you saying that?" she asked, alarmed. "Do you know something I don't know?" But he wouldn't respond.

The sheriff had pulled into a fire trail, moving far enough from the paved road to hide their cars. Scott's SUV bounced over the ruts. When Sheriff Hughes parked his car behind a stand of trees, Scott pulled up next to him. "It's go time," he said, turning to Kenzie.

She nodded. Her mouth felt dry. Scott was freaking her out.

The heat seemed particularly oppressive this August day. Thunderstorms were in the forecast. Kenzie looked around. A couple of leaves on the poplar trees had already turned golden yellow, foretelling the coming of fall, but it would be another six weeks before the cool weather would arrive.

Poplars, oaks, pines, and dogwoods covered the mountainside. Half a century before, to create the Catoctin National Forest, the federal government seized land owned by families for generations. They paid them well, but some people had never gotten over the loss of the homesteads, the hunting cabins, and the mountain farms.

The cabin where they were going was a two-story rural retreat once owned by a wealthy Maryland political family. They had used it as a summer respite from the heat in Washington. The government had never bothered to tear the old place down. The locals, knowing it had been abandoned, sometimes appropriated it for themselves for short-term use. The locks were long gone.

To get to the place without detection, the agents had to walk a good twenty minutes up a steep mountain incline. The ballistic vests the four were wearing were heavy and hot, and it wasn't long before all of them were sweating. Kenzie's head ached and a couple of times as they went over some of the more precipitous rock out-croppings Crow turned around and gave her a hand up.

They were paralleling the rutted path leading up to the cabin. A couple of newly cut trees and neatly stacked wood were indications a local Boy Scout troop maintained the path as a hiking trail.

Kenzie tripped as they went down into a ravine. Crow caught her, his hand gripping her arm. They came up the other side, walked about fifty feet more, and then the sheriff motioned for them to stop. He pointed forward. There, through a thick stand of cedars, they could see the cabin.

Scott wordlessly motioned them to move to where they could see what appeared to be the front porch. The cabin, old as it was, still looked sturdy. Four steps led up to the covered porch. Another porch ran along the back. The two-story structure had windows on both levels. A car and one motorcycle sat parked out front.

"I don't see any electricity or phone lines, or any other utilities," Kenzie whispered.

"That's right," said the sheriff. "If you come up here, you've got to port your own water and use the woods as a latrine."

"That car is the same make and model as Grayson's mother's car," Crow said quietly.

"Let's move around," Scott said, motioning toward the back of the house.

The four of them crept through the woods, careful to keep a screen of vegetation between them and the cabin. Crouched back in the forest, binoculars trained on the house, they finally got their break.

"There he is," the sheriff whispered. A large man stood silhouetted in the kitchen window. "That's Billy."

Kenzie froze. All the stress and dashed expectations of the last couple of days coalesced into a charge of adrenaline so potent she trembled. They'd found them. Was Zoe alive?

When the figure moved away, Scott motioned to them to back off. Time to call for reinforcements. They moved back toward the rutted path with Scott in the lead. Kenzie was following him, and the sheriff and Crow trailed slightly behind. He was leading them back to a place they could regroup and make a plan. They'd call in the SWAT team and figure out the best way to extricate Zoe.

Kenzie's neck was slick with sweat and she felt slightly light-headed from the heat and the tension. She focused on the yellow-orange "FBI" on the back of Scott's ballistic vest. A bee buzzed around her head and she swatted it away.

Suddenly, Scott stopped. "FBI!" he yelled. He whipped his gun out of his holster and crouched into a shooting position. "Put down your gun! Put it down!"

31

An electric shock of adrenaline ran through Kenzie's body, a blue-white heat like a lightning bolt. She grabbed her gun, moved to Scott's right, and took cover behind a tree, aiming in the direction of his focus. Down the trail, a twenty-something man with scruffy brown hair and dressed in jeans and a T-shirt stood smoking a cigarette, holding a shotgun casually at his side.

"Put it down!" Scott yelled, and the man looked up. For a moment, Kenzie thought he would comply. But then, almost with a shrug, the man pulled the gun up and fired twice.

Automatically, Scott and Kenzie fired back. Bam-bam-bam-bam! A staccato burst of bullets exploded from their guns. Her ears rang, her head spun and her eyes could see nothing besides her gun and the man on the trail.

She saw the man collapse. She saw his gun fall to the ground. She saw dust fly up as his body hit the ground. She saw his body jerk twice.

Scott continued standing in the middle of the trail. Why hadn't he taken cover? Kenzie expected him to go forward, to cuff the guy. She braced herself to cover him. But he didn't take a step. He didn't move at all. She glanced at him. He was holding his gun in his right hand but his hand was shaking, hard. Something seemed wrong. Scott's mouth dropped open slightly. And then suddenly, he dropped to his knees and his head sagged forward.

"Scott! Scott!" Kenzie yelled. She ran to him, holstering her own gun. The sheriff emerged from the woods and raced past her. Glancing over her shoulder, she saw him next to the downed suspect. When she looked at Scott, she gasped.

His left arm had shattered into a mass of white bone and bloody flesh from his elbow to his wrist. Blood poured onto the ground, forming red splotches in the dirt, splotches which had already begun to trickle off in small streams.

Within seconds, Crow was next to her. "I've got him," he said, and he crouched down and began examining Scott.

Kenzie glanced over her shoulder. The sheriff had cuffed the suspect, who still lay on the ground, and was trotting back, the man's shotgun in his hand. When she looked back, Scott raised his head and looked at her with glazed eyes.

"Go get Zoe," he said, his voice fissured by pain.

"We need a Medevac," Crow said. He began pulling medical supplies from his backpack. "You're going to be all right, Scott. Just hold on." He eased Scott off his knees and into a seated position.

"What can I do?" Kenzie asked.

"Get the sheriff to call in a Medevac," Crow repeated. He pulled his GPS device from his belt. "Here's the lat and lon. Tell them to get in as close as they can." Then he snapped on gloves.

Kenzie stood up. "He's dead," the sheriff said, nodding his head toward the gunman. His eyes traveled beyond Kenzie to Scott.

"We need a Medevac," she said, her heart drumming. "I have the location on the GPS. Can you call it in?"

The sheriff nodded and began making the call as Kenzie stood by, forcing her mind to stay calm. To her right, Crow was tying a tourniquet around Scott's upper arm. She turned to Sheriff Hughes. "Get our SWAT team and your emergency response team up here, too," she said, and he nodded in response.

"Kenzie, I need you," Crow said. "Can you help me?"

"Yes." She crouched down and put on the gloves he handed her.

"Press down here."

She put her hand on Scott's arm, just below the elbow, as Crow took his hand away. She fought nausea at the sight of the blood and the protruding bones and the sound of Scott's labored breathing. She looked into his eyes, saw the pain, and looked quickly away. She began praying silently. *God save him. God don't let him die. God help him.*

Crow pulled out more supplies from his backpack. "I've got to stabilize this arm," he said to Kenzie. "Come over on this side," he motioned his head toward the left, "and hang on to him. This is going to be more than a sting."

She moved around, jerked her gloves off, and grabbed Scott's right hand. His face looked white. He turned toward her, sweat glistening on his upper lip. "Go get Zoe," he whispered. "Go get her . . ."

"We're going to help you. Then we'll go."

"Hang on!" Crow said.

She turned Scott's head so he was looking at her. She kept her hand on his jaw, to keep him from seeing what Crow was about to do.

To her right, Crow probed the wounded arm with both hands, feeling for the shattered bones. "You hold on to me, Scott Hansbrough," she said. "You hold as tight as you want. We're going to get you through this, OK? You just hold on."

If you lie down to die, you will die. Had he had a premonition?

"Look at me, Scott," she said out loud. "You're going to be OK."

"Here goes," Crow said, and suddenly Scott arched his back and threw his head back. He grimaced and stifled his screams, but his grip on Kenzie's hand remained hard.

"Oh, God!" he said, gasping for breath, his eyes watery.

"Hold on, Scott. Hold on!" She grabbed his shirt with her other hand to keep him upright. He looked like he would pass out.

"How long until your ERT gets here, Sheriff?" Crow demanded.

"They're on the way. Twenty minutes. Maybe a bit more."

"And the Medevac?"

"Fifteen. They'll find a landing spot as close as they can. An ambulance is on the way, too."

"Stay with us, Scott," Crow said. He glanced at Kenzie. "What's Billy going to do? He had to have heard those shots."

"I don't know."

Crow continued dressing Scott's arm.

"He's gonna run," Scott said, his voice breathy. "He's going to grab Zoe and run."

Kenzie looked at the sheriff. "Go watch the house, will you?"

"Sure."

Crow had pulled a windbreaker out of his pack. "I'm going to use this as a sling. I may try to walk him out to meet the ambulance."

"OK," Kenzie said.

"Go," Scott whispered. His teeth were chattering.

The sheriff came back, breathless. "Zoe is on the porch roof! She must have climbed out of the second-floor window. I think she's trying to get away. I could hear Billy yelling, cursing. He knows she's gone."

"Go! For God's sake, go!" Scott said. He struggled as if he were going to get up.

Crow held him down. "Stay still, man!" He glanced at Kenzie. "I'll stabilize him and start fluids and then go get Zoe. You stay here with him until the medics get here. All you need to do is . . ."

"No. You stay!" she responded. "You're the medic."

"No!"

"Both of you go," Scott grabbed Crow's shirt. "Go!" but as he said it, he grimaced in pain and his eyes began rolling back in his head.

"Scott! Scott!" Crow said something in Navajo that sounded to Kenzie like a curse. He patted Scott's cheeks to try to rouse him. Sweat glistened on Crow's face.

"I'm going! I'll be all right." Kenzie rose, touched his shoulder, and started toward the cabin.

"Take the high ground. Watch first. And be sure your radio is on A-One!" Crow yelled.

Kenzie and the sheriff approached the cabin, staying slightly uphill, and using the mountain laurel and wild hollies to shield them from view. She could see Zoe up on the rear porch roof. The little girl, dressed in blue denim shorts and a red shirt, was barefoot.

The clouds were starting to move in, dimming the bright sunshine. Kenzie thought she heard a chopper, then realized it was just thunder, off in the distance. "I can climb up there," Kenzie whispered to the sheriff, sweat running off her face. The cabin had been constructed of logs that crossed at the corners, like old Lincoln Logs, forming Xs she figured she could scale.

"Wait," he said, touching her arm. The back door of the cabin opened and Billy walked out onto the porch. He held a shotgun.

"We can't confront him, not with her there," Kenzie whispered. "If she slides off, she'll be right in the line of fire."

Sheriff Hughes nodded.

Billy cursed loudly and went inside, slamming the back door.

Kenzie would need to run down the wooded hill, cross a thirty-foot clearing, get up on the porch railing, then climb up on the roof to get to Zoe.

The sheriff said, "I'll create a diversion out front. Then you go. I'll meet you back here when you have her."

Kenzie nodded. "That'll work."

"Give me three minutes."

She looked at her watch. Sheriff Hughes began skirting around the edge of the forest. Zoe crouched on the roof, right next to the house, obviously trying to figure out what to do next. Thunder rumbled in the distance. The storm announced its approach.

Three minutes. Kenzie heard a noise in the front of the cabin, like a small tree falling. Then another. Then she heard the sheriff shouting. She made her move. She ran across the clearing, and quietly pulled herself up to the porch railing, biting her lip as pain streaked down the back of her skull and into her neck. Then she used the cross-laid logs at the corner of the cabin to climb up to the porch roof. Within seconds, she and Zoe were eye to eye. As soon as she was within reach, Zoe grabbed onto her. "I've got you now, Zoe," she whispered. "You're safe now."

But then she heard the back door open and footsteps on the porch below. Kenzie froze, the prospect of a firefight with Zoe in her arms an unthinkable option. The only place to hide was back inside. She grabbed the window ledge and, holding tightly to Zoe, quietly stepped back into the house.

She heard Billy yell, "Where the . . ."

The little girl looked up at her, her eyes full of fear.

Kenzie silently kissed her forehead. "Be quiet," she whispered. She looked around. The bedroom looked small, dark, and totally empty. Her eyes adjusted. Off to one side, under the eaves, was a small door. Outside, thunder rolled again.

"Billy! Billy!" She heard the sheriff's voice, coming from in front of the house. He must have seen Billy go to the back and was trying to draw him off of her location.

"Billy! Come on out. It's Sheriff Hughes. Let's talk, Billy."

She heard Billy's muffled voice. Then more shouting. And cursing. Someone was bashing something around. She didn't dare go out of the window again, but she wasn't feeling secure in the room, either.

Kenzie moved to the eave and opened the small door. She pulled a small flashlight off her belt and shined it into the storage area. The space had a good floor, and it was empty. Except for spider webs.

Lots of spider webs.

If she tried crawling out of the window, she chanced Billy coming back to the porch again and the strong possibility she'd get into a gun battle with him. But she could wait in the crawl space until the SWAT team came. She just had to deal with the spiders. And the close quarters. Could she do it? "Oh, God, please help me," she whispered.

Just as she was trying to figure out her next move, she heard footsteps on the stairs.

Her heart jumping, Kenzie clicked off her light

and crawled inside the small space, clutching Zoe tightly. As she quietly shut the door, she heard two shots, two huge explosions. Had to be a shotgun, she thought, followed by a series of retorts from a handgun. Who was shooting? Where was the sheriff? Her heart pounded.

Kenzie sat in total darkness with her back braced against a roof truss. She held her gun in her right hand, ready to blow away anyone who tried to get in. Zoe lay curled up in her lap, sucking her thumb. "I'm a friend of your daddy's," Kenzie whispered. "I'm going to get you out of here. But we have to be very quiet." Within seconds, Kenzie felt the little girl relax in her arms. She kissed the top of her head. She touched her hair. Suddenly, the memories came flooding back. Her angry mother. The small closet. The dark. Spiders.

She forced herself to stay calm. I am not a child, she thought, I can do this. But a wave of fear began sweeping over her. She saw images of Scott, bleeding, his arm mangled, images of her mother, her face twisted in rage, her father, lying on the floor.

Kenzie tried to focus on something else, tried counting and recalling the lyrics of a song but the fear seemed predatory, creeping over her like a malignancy. She thought she felt something on her hand, and shook it off. Then she imagined something crawling up her pants leg.

She flicked her light on momentarily. Nothing.

Kenzie shivered. She could hear muffled voices downstairs, angry voices, scared voices, and heavy footsteps. Then she heard something breaking, furniture maybe, and screams. She trembled. Her mouth was like cotton. She held on to Zoe.

Where was Sheriff Hughes? Where was Crow? Panic began to swirl around inside her. For a moment, she wanted to jump up and run. But what did that verse say? The one Scott gave her? "When you pass through the waters, I will be with you." *Are you with me now, God?* she thought.

What had Scott said? God was omnipresent. He was everywhere. God was here. Nothing could touch her without his permission. That's what Scott said. God is sovereign. And Crow had said Navajos believe every effect has a cause. And his grandfather said, God is the first cause, sovereign over everything. Everything. Even this. Even now.

Kenzie stroked Zoe's arm. The little girl snuggled against her chest. Her hair smelled like baby shampoo. *God,* she breathed, *I wish I had Scott's faith. All I have is a little tiny bit of Sunday school-type faith, from a long time ago. He's right: I've been holding out on you. I'm scared of giving up control to you. But I know now I've got to. Because I'm in over my head. I need you. Please, God, help me save Zoe. Keep me calm. Help me!*

A song came into her head: "Jesus Loves Me." She hadn't heard it in twenty years. Hadn't thought about it for decades. *Jesus loves me.* She began singing it in her head to calm herself down. *Little ones to Him belong . . .*

She heard more crashing. More screaming. And another noise, a rhythmic beating, a chopper overhead. Not thunder. Definitely a chopper. Billy began yelling and then she heard three loud booms. Was he shooting at the chopper?

Once more, she considered making a run for it. But she just couldn't tell where he was and what he was going to do. All the gunfire told her he was behaving very erratically.

The minutes ticked by. Kenzie tried adjusting her position. She put her gun down momentarily and flexed her hand, trying to keep it from cramping up. It felt so hot. She pulled out her water bottle and took a drink. Zoe opened her eyes, looked up at Kenzie, and reached for the bottle. Kenzie gave it to her, and she drained it. "Do you know how to pray?" Kenzie whispered.

The little girl nodded.

"OK, let's ask God to help us."

Obediently, Zoe folded her hands and bowed her head. Someone had taught her something about God. Kenzie wondered if it was her nanny. "Dear God," Kenzie whispered, "please help us get out of here. Keep us safe. We ask in Jesus' name."

"Amen," Zoe added.

Kenzie opened her eyes and picked up her gun again.

Finally, she heard what she'd been waiting for: A bullhorn. SWAT had arrived. Or the sheriff's ERT. Either way, help had come. She couldn't quite make out the words but she could imagine what they were saying. *Billy Foster. Come out with your hands up. Let's talk, Billy. Let's end this thing now.*

His response was gunfire, two more rounds from a shotgun.

Her earbud came alive. "Kenzie, where are you?" Crow! Her heart jumped. *Thank you, God.*

"We're in a crawl space off the back bedroom," she whispered into her radio. "Second floor. The window above the porch roof, on the left. Get the shooter to the front and keep him there. I'll bring Zoe out."

"I'm coming to you."

But even as the bullhorn called to Billy, she heard footsteps coming up the inside stairs again. Adrenaline poured through her. She squeezed Zoe and whispered, "Shh . . . shh."

Kenzie focused on the small access door. She could hear someone enter the room. Then she heard a strange sound, a liquid splashing rhythmically, like the person was intentionally spreading something. And then she smelled it. Gasoline.

32

He's going to torch the place, Kenzie thought. Create a diversion as a way of escaping. And burn them alive.

No, he isn't. Kenzie put her gun down, flicked on her small flashlight, and lifted Zoe off her lap, putting her back in a corner of the eaves. She held her finger to her lips to tell her to be quiet, and Zoe nodded, her eyes big. Then Kenzie pocketed her flashlight and gripped her gun.

The door to the crawl space swung outward. Counting to three, she kicked it open. She crouched in the opening. Billy stood six feet away in the doorway of the room, a lighted rag in his hand. Behind him sat a gas can.

"FBI, move back!" Kenzie yelled as she stood up. The smell of gasoline almost overpowered her. She held her gun in both hands, her arms extended, and she focused on her gun sights. Her stomach clenched. She stayed focused. "Move back!" she said again. And then Billy smiled a slow, deranged smile, and threw the burning rag at her.

She got off four shots, bang-bang-bang-bang, before the room exploded in a ring of fire. Zoe screamed. Billy clutched his chest, stumbled backward, and slid down the wall, leaving a trail of blood.

Kenzie holstered her gun. "Zoe, come here!" The room, ablaze with yellow and orange fire, quickly became an inferno. The smoke attacked Kenzie's lungs and tears filled her eyes. She reached into the crawl space and grabbed the terrified little girl. Within seconds, the heat had become unbearable as the fire caught the dry wood of the old cabin. Flames licked at her legs. Thick, gray smoke filled her lungs. Clutching Zoe to her chest, trying to shield her from the flames, Kenzie moved toward the window, crouching down to get closer to the floor. Her eyes were stinging. Zoe choked, unable to breathe. Kenzie reached out. Her hand touched the wall and she moved to the right. The window—where was it?

Then she felt it. With the fire roaring in her ears, she pushed Zoe through the opening into the fresh air. The flames tore at her back. Her legs were stinging from the heat. She looked down. Her pant leg had caught on fire! She kicked her leg against the wall, trying to snuff it out, and stepped out onto the sloping roof, still holding Zoe. Her foot slipped. She lost her balance, fell, and began sliding. "Zoe!" she yelled, gripping the girl with one hand and grasping for a hold with the other.

"I've got her! I've got her!"

Crow!

He grabbed Zoe's arm with one hand and

Kenzie with the other. "Let go! I've got Zoe!" he said.

Through tearing eyes, Kenzie saw Crow swing Zoe down off the roof into the waiting arms of a SWAT team member. By then, Kenzie lay half off the roof herself, her legs extending out into mid-air, her pants still smoking. She gripped the edge and her eyes met Crow's. "Hold on, girl," he said softly, "hold on!"

Then other hands grabbed her legs. "Watch her!" she heard Crow say, and she let go of the roof, and let herself fall into the arms of two SWAT team members. She was out. She was safe. And so was Zoe.

Thank you, Jesus.

The downpour began as she sat in the back of a four-wheel drive Sheriff's Office vehicle. Zoe sat buckled in next to her. The little girl had plastered herself as close as she could get to Kenzie, who stroked her head and talked softly to her between coughing spasms. They both smelled like smoke. A sheriff's deputy would drive them down off the mountain, to a helicopter waiting to whisk Zoe away to a nearby hospital.

Kenzie glanced back and saw that the entire second floor of the cabin was engulfed in flames. The falling rain vaporized as it hit the hot roof, adding rising steam to the billowing smoke, creating an otherworldly atmosphere as lightning flashed and thunder rumbled. Her head hurt, her legs hurt, but she had little Zoe Grable sitting safely next to her.

Crow climbed into the passenger seat on the other side, and Zoe pressed herself tighter to Kenzie's side.

"Hey, sport," Crow said, patting her knee, "you are one brave little girl."

Zoe looked up at Kenzie. "He's a good guy," Kenzie assured her, and she coughed again.

"Take us down, Mack," Crow said, patting the back of the driver's seat.

The SUV began bumping down the dirt road. Tears of gratitude sprang to Kenzie's eyes. *They were safe. They had Zoe. Thank God, thank God!* "What about Scott?" she asked Crow.

"He'll make it." Crow sat turned in the seat, facing the little girl, and he had his medical kit next to him. "Zoe," he said in a soft voice, "I've got to check now to see if I can remember how to count. Will you help me?" She looked at him skeptically, but he gently took her wrist and found her pulse and began counting out loud. "One, three, two . . ." he said, and Zoe solemnly corrected him. "Oh, OK," he said, "one, two, three. Is that better?"

Zoe nodded.

"OK, now let's see if I can hear." He pulled out his stethoscope and placed it on her chest.

"Thump, thump . . . thump, thump." Zoe smiled a little.

"I don't think she is burned at all," Crow commented. He glanced up at Kenzie. "You protected her well."

Thank God.

By the time Crow got to the finger prick so he could take Zoe's blood-sugar reading, he had built up her trust. Zoe only whimpered once. He quickly comforted her. Crow's eyes met Kenzie's. They were deep pools of emotion. "Her blood sugar is two hundred. High, but not too bad. Everything else is good, too." He shook his head. "Wow."

"Are you an Indian?" Zoe asked in a tiny voice.

"Yep."

"Are you a medicine man?"

"Sort of," he responded. "Want to hear me speak Indian?" Zoe nodded, and Crow began saying something in Navajo. As he did, he looked at Kenzie, full in the face.

"What did you say?" Kenzie asked.

He winked at her. "Tell you later."

A warm rush filled her and she pressed her lips together as tears flooded her eyes. Yes, something had changed. *Thank you, God.*

Twenty-five minutes later Kenzie stepped out of the SUV onto a steaming asphalt road. Zoe, completely charmed by Crow, wanted him to hold her until she saw her father. Senator Grable emerged from a black Bureau car and raced to his daughter, tears streaming down his face.

"Daddy!" Zoe cried, and he swept her into his arms.

"Oh, Zoe . . . thank God, thank God!" the senator cried.

The storm had moved east. The bright, setting sun had peeked out from under the clouds and was bathing the hill in a golden light. Rain dripped from nearby trees and the drainage ditch that ran next to the road and down the mountain churned with runoff. All around them, police cars and FBI vehicles sat, lights flashing, parked in hurried disarray, their drivers scattered like chessmen over the field, watching.

Then Kenzie's jaw dropped as Beth stepped out of the car. The fashionable former sorority girl had close-cropped her beautiful blonde hair, so she looked just like Zoe.

"Mommy!" Zoe cried. Senator Grable handed the little girl to Beth, and soon the two were laughing and rubbing each other's head.

As she watched, teary herself, a collection of images, like flashing scenes from a hyped-up movie trailer, played over and over in Kenzie's mind. Zoe on the roof, the tiny closet, the smell of gasoline, the fire erupting from the end of her gun as she shot Billy, the sound of it firing, her hands jerking, blood splashing, and then . . . the inferno.

The last image was Crow . . . Crow, on the porch railing of the cabin grabbing onto her to keep her from falling. He was walking up to her now, a water bottle in his hand, his face broadened by a smile, his black hair glistening in the sunlight. "Here," he said, handing the bottle to her.

Behind him, the EMTs were ushering Zoe and Beth Grable to the waiting helicopter. Kenzie thought it sweet the senator had encouraged Beth to go in the chopper with Zoe. Maybe some good could come from all this. Maybe they could work things out.

She thanked Crow, unscrewed the cap, and took a drink. He insisted she have her lungs and the burns on her legs checked at the hospital, but she refused to go in an ambulance. Finally, he said he'd take her himself, and she was being a pain, but he was grinning at the time, and she knew he didn't mind at all.

"I asked them about Scott," Crow said, motioning toward the crew of the Medevac helicopter. "He stayed fully conscious all the way to the shock/trauma unit in Baltimore. They had him on fluids and morphine, and the docs at the hospital were preparing for surgery. They're bringing in an arm specialist from Johns Hopkins."

"Can we go see him?"

"After you're cleared."

Alicia had already driven off with the senator in a Bureau SUV, lights flashing, taking him to the hospital where they were transporting Zoe. Scattered around the landing area, other agents and cops stood watching the bird lift off. Crow took a long, slow look around, as if to make sure no one else was close to them. He crossed his arms and shifted his weight, until his bicep was touching her upper arm. She felt it and didn't move away. The throbbing of the chopper blades intensified.

The bird lifted up, heading south. Crow, watching, said, "Seeing you come out of that smoky cabin with Zoe in your arms was beautiful. A miracle! When I saw you, something shifted within me. All I could say was 'thank you God, thank you, God.' "

Kenzie looked at him. "I felt so grateful you were there."

Below them, rescue workers began packing up their gear, and cops and agents were getting in their cars.

Kenzie shifted her weight and asked the question that had been running through her mind. "Could he have known? Scott? He seemed to have had a premonition." She pulled the paper out of her pocket, the one with the Scripture verse on it, and showed it to Crow . . . *when you walk through the fire you shall not be burned, and the flame shall not consume you.*

"He gave it to me on the drive up from Washington. Could he have known?" she asked again.

Crow shook his head. "I don't know." He laughed softly. "There's a lot I don't know." He looked at her, his black eyes shining. "You are an amazing woman, a strong and beautiful woman, a *naataanii,* a leader, and I'm proud of you. And I'd like to get to know you better. I'd like to take you hiking on Old Rag Mountain and canoeing on the Rappahannock. And I'd like to show you my home, the Reservation. I'm glad we worked on this together, Kenzie. Maybe more people than Zoe were rescued."

Tears began streaming down her face.

Epilogue

Kenzie trotted up the steps to her mother's house. She hadn't called first. For some reason, she'd wanted to spend the hour and a half trip from Baltimore to D.C. in silence, just thinking, processing the events of the last few days, reveling in the successes, mourning the failures. She didn't want a conversation with her mother to interrupt that.

While her burns were checked at the local hospital, Scott had undergone three hours' worth of surgery in Baltimore to pin his arm back together. He'd spent a day or so in intensive care, but the doctors expected him to fully recover. His family was with him. In fact, Kenzie had a great picture of him in bed with his daughter, Cara, curled up next to him, their matching pink casts brightening up the room.

John Crowfeather was filling the director in on the resolution of the case. Grayson Chambers was dead in the burned-out cabin. The ME prelim said he'd died of smoke inhalation. Billy was dead, too. His body had dropped down when the second floor of the cabin collapsed but it was clear that three of Kenzie's four bullets had found their mark. The fourth suspect had fled the burning structure, but not soon enough: Agents and police had easily captured him in the woods.

Zoe would be fine. She was in Children's Hospital in D.C., her parents at her side, undergoing treatment from one of the foremost pediatric diabetes specialists in the nation.

The only unhappy law enforcement official was the assistant U.S. attorney charged with prosecuting the influence-peddling case against Senator Grable. He was furious the director had ignored his warning that assigning Kenzie to the Zoe kidnapping case would mess up his case against Grable.

Ah, well, Kenzie thought.

She knocked on the dark oak door of her mother's home. She inhaled the scent of the boxwoods on either side of the porch, the smell of her childhood. Seconds later, the door swung open.

"Well! You certainly picked an inconvenient time to show up," her mother said. She was dressed in a beige silk suit, high heels, and her hair was swept up in a French knot. "My bridge club is here!"

"I'm sorry, Mom," Kenzie said, stepping in. "I just came to get Jack."

"He's in the backyard. I had no idea how much hair dogs left around."

"I'm sorry."

"Mackenzie, whatever did you do to your eyebrows? Gracious!"

Kenzie walked from the front door straight down the hallway to the kitchen, being careful not to interrupt the conversation going on in the dining room. The bridge ladies took their game seriously. She opened the back door and looked around. There, lying in the cool earth under a hydrangea bush, lay her dog. He looked asleep.

"Jack!" she called. The black-and-white spaniel's head flew up. "Where's your ball?" He leaped to his feet. He threw himself at her, jumping on her and licking her. He turned in circles at her feet as she petted him. "You missed me, didn't you?" Kenzie thrust her hands into Jack's soft coat, relishing the feel of his fur. "I missed you, too," she said, and she thumped his side. "I really, really missed you." She knelt down and he kissed her on the chin. She wrestled with him in the grass, pushing him, tackling him, and grabbing his muzzle, and he wiggled with delight.

Then she lay down, and looked up into the bright blue sky. He snuggled next to her, and she stroked him. She felt his soft fur, smelled the hydrangeas, and relished the warm sun. She felt very aware of the burns on her legs, burns that would take time to heal, burns that reminded her of her walk through the fire.

"Oh, God," she said out loud, "thank you. Thank you so much!"

And she squeezed Jack a little harder, and he licked her face, and she laughed. "There's this guy," she began, "named Crow, and you'll like him . . ."

Discussion Questions

1. Kenzie had a difficult childhood, marred by her father's death and her mother's emotional abuse. How did she compensate? What are some other ways people cope with childhood loss or pain?

2. Kenzie recalled watching the Perseid meteor showers with her father. What's a favorite childhood memory of yours?

3. Scott was quite open and unabashed about his faith. Have you ever known someone like that? How did you feel around him or her?

4. What problems do you have openly living your faith in your day-to-day life? How do you decide what's appropriate and what's not?

5. Crow had suffered the loss of his beloved fiancée in Iraq. How did he react? Would you consider that healthy? Why or why not?

6. If you had a friend who had suffered a loss like that, what would your advice be?

7. Crow and Kenzie were opposites in many ways. Were you ever in a relationship (friendship or romantic) with someone who was really different? What were the benefits? The

challenges? How do we cross cultural barriers in friendships?

8. Both Kenzie and Crow were reserved in their relationships to God, skeptical even. But Crow admitted, "If what Scott and my grandfather say about God is true, then it isn't just true for them, and it isn't a matter of it 'working' for them. It's a matter of reality." How certain are you about your faith? What do you know for sure? And what do you have questions about?

9. If you are a believer, what one incident in your life propelled you toward faith in Christ?

10. Kenzie had a strong fear of spiders. What are you most afraid of? And how do you cope with that?

11. Who was your favorite character in this book? Why?

12. Do you think there's hope for the Grables's marriage? Why or why not? What would your advice be to them?

Be sure to visit Linda online!

http://www.lindajwhite.com

Center Point Large Print
600 Brooks Road / PO Box 1
Thorndike, ME 04986-0001 USA

(207) 568-3717

US & Canada:
1 800 929-9108
www.centerpointlargeprint.com